the Twelve Months of Christmas

the Twelve Months of Christmas

SHEILA ROBERTS

mira

ISBN-13: 978-0-7783-0531-6

The Twelve Months of Christmas

Mira
22 Adelaide St. West, 41st Floor
Toronto, Ontario M5H 4E3, Canada
BookClubbish.com

Printed in U.S.A.

In memory of Jill Spiese, 1948–2014

HOW IT BEGAN

1

Sunny Hollowell had planned a perfect day for her first Christmas as a wife and stepmom and it was a fail. Who was it that said something about the best-laid plans getting screwed up? Whoever it was, her mom liked to quote him a lot.

"The best-laid plans of mice and men," her mom had begun when Sunny told her about the latest development as she and Dad walked in the door, presents in tow.

"And women," Sunny had added before Mom could finish. Women who were trying their best to be a good wife and mother, women who only wanted to bring two families together for a memorable day.

The day was memorable all right, but not in the way Sunny had intended.

It all began at eight in the morning. Sunny had found a recipe online for a crescent roll breakfast pastry with a cherry filling shaped like a candy cane and, to her surprise and glee, it had actually turned out like the picture, ready for the kids to be dropped off by their mom at nine o'clock. She was laying it out on the family room coffee table for everyone to enjoy while they opened presents when the Weed called Travis to let him know that she wasn't going to bring the kids over for the big day.

"What do you mean you're still stuck in Spokane?" Travis had growled into his cell phone.

Sunny had watched the anger roll over his features like a breaking storm. *Scratch two kids from the guest list. Tansy strikes again.*

"You did this on purpose," he'd accused.

Of course, Tansy would deny it. That was how she rolled. Mess with the ex and his new wife as much as possible but never let it look like you meant to. Was Tansy's mother psychic when she named her daughter after a noxious weed?

"Well, thanks a lot," Travis had growled. "Way to screw up Christmas for the kids."

"Okay, what happened?" Sunny had asked after he ended the call and dumped his phone on the coffee table.

"She did it again, managed to screw us over," he'd said, and slumped on the sofa. "She and Jared accidentally—" he held up exaggerated air quotes "—missed their flight home last night and are stuck at his parents' place."

"Can't they get another flight out? There has to be something going out today." Of course, by the time they got to Bremerton, Washington, breakfast and Christmas dinner would long be over.

"Not until tomorrow."

Sunny had made a superhuman effort to blink back tears. Poor Travis was already upset about not getting to be with his kids. She didn't need to make things worse by having a holiday meltdown. But darn, she'd sure wanted to. It seemed particularly cruel that Tansy had waited twelve hours after their missed flight to tell them the kids wouldn't make it.

"I'm sorry, babe," he'd said, and he'd looked like he wanted to cry.

"It's okay. We'll have a nice day and do a belated Christmas with the kids later."

But it wasn't a nice day. Here she sat in her PJ bottoms and red sweater and her Santa hat, watching as her husband of eight months fumed his way through the morning. Her father wasn't beaming, either. Dad wasn't a fan of Travis.

According to Dad, Travis wasn't good enough for her. Divorced and with kids and a problematic ex—he had baggage, and the theatrics today weren't doing much to prove otherwise.

Sunny was thirty. Everyone she knew had baggage. And it wasn't Travis's fault his ex was a weed. Besides, she loved him. Which meant helping him carry his baggage.

"Anyone want more coffee?" she asked, trying to sound cheerful.

"Yeah," Travis said sourly, handing her his mug. "Lace it with whiskey." This made her dad frown, and, seeing it, Travis added, "I'm going to be Irish for the day."

"How about you, Dad?" asked Sunny.

"I'll have some more. Plain. I'm not Irish," he said, looking at Travis like a school principal ready to put a problem student on suspension. Since Dad had been a school principal, it was an expression that came easily to him.

"I could use a refill," her mother said, and followed Sunny to the kitchen.

"This is so not what I imagined today would be like," Sunny said in a low voice as she set the cups on the counter. She looked to where the two men sat, the bad boy and the disapproving principal.

Her mother laid a comforting hand on her arm. "I know. Try to remember that it's only one day."

"It's an important day. Christmas is supposed to be fun and filled with love," Sunny said.

She'd hoped this would be a chance to connect with her stepkids, and maybe impress her mother-in-law just a little bit. Self-pity got busy in the tear factory, producing a couple of nice fat ones to trickle down her cheek.

"There's still love here," her mother said. "And your turkey is already smelling delicious."

Sunny harrumphed. "Not that there's many of us here to eat it. I still can't believe Rae chose Will's family over us. We've always all been together at Christmas, and we really should have been this year with Gram gone."

"Your sister has another family to consider now," Mom pointed out.

"They're not married yet. She could consider her new family next year," Sunny argued. Okay, she was sounding like a brat. She knew it. She poured coffee into the mugs, ignoring Travis's whiskey request. No Irish coffee for him on Christmas Day. Why should he get to numb his pain when she didn't? "It's wrong that Travis doesn't get to see his kids," she said in defense of his foul mood.

"You're right," said her mother.

"I had so many cool things planned for our first Christmas with them," Sunny continued. So far, they hadn't had any stellar firsts, but Christmas was different. Christmas mended all kinds of broken fences. At least that was what she'd always believed.

"Dylan would have loved the Santa treasure hunt," Mom said.

"So would Bella," Sunny said.

Her mother didn't say anything, but her sympathetic smile made it clear she didn't think so.

"She would," Sunny insisted.

Okay, she was deluding herself. Her thirteen-year-old stepdaughter probably would have deemed a hunt for her Christmas presents beneath her and then glowered her way through the rest of day. It seemed like everything Sunny tried to do with or for her was met with derision.

"She's at a difficult age," Mom said in Bella's defense.

"You'd think she'd see the benefit of getting a bonus mom," Sunny said. "Double the Christmas presents."

"It's not that simple," Mom said. "Her parents turned her

life upside down when they split and now both Tansy and Travis have added new parent figures into her life. That has to be upsetting."

"But I'm nice," Sunny protested. She wasn't an evil person. She tried to be kind, gave money to good causes, was always buying little gifts for the kids. And she never yelled at them. What more did they want?

"You are nice," Mom said. "So don't worry. Dylan's adjusting and Bella will come around eventually. Give it time."

"And what about Jeanette?" Would Travis's mom ever come around? How much time did she need?

Sunny's father-in-law, Harry, had called not long after Tansy dropped her holiday bomb to say that he and Jeanette wouldn't be coming over for Christmas dinner. Jeanette wasn't feeling well and he had to stay home to take care of her.

"That was such a pitiful excuse for bailing on us," Sunny groused to her mom.

"Maybe she really isn't feeling well," Mom said, being irritatingly reasonable.

"I'd bet a stocking full of gold coins she's feeling fine now." This was so not right. "What have I ever done to these people? Why do they hate me?"

"It's not you they hate. It's seeing everything changed."

"Well, they knew it was going to change." Sunny could feel her voice rising. She lowered it and continued, "Travis and Tansy were already over when I met him. Tansy's moving on, so how come he doesn't get to? How come the welcome mat got yanked out from under my feet?"

She already knew the answer. Tansy had pulled the proverbial wool over Jeannette's eyes early on, convincing her she was a sweet, lost soul, and they'd bonded. Jeanette had nursed hopes that Travis and Tansy would get back together. Sunny's arrival on the scene killed those hopes.

"Come on, the coffee's getting cold. Let's finish opening our presents," Mom said and led the way back to the family room.

A family room with barely any family in it. Happy holidays.

Christmas wasn't going any better for Arianna White—once upon a delusion, Arianna Jorgenson. Thirty-five had not been a good year for her. She'd gotten divorced, said goodbye to her house and moved in with her mother.

She'd loved that house. They'd bought it five years earlier and she'd envisioned them growing their family in it and then growing old. But after they divorced, it felt like a house of horrors, mocking her with memories, reminding her that Wyatt was no longer there to leave his dirty clothes on the floor or sneak up behind her and lay a sloppy kiss on her neck.

They'd survived COVID but their marriage hadn't. She'd worked her tail off at the hospital, coming home and going through the motions like a zombie. Zombies, it turned out, didn't make good wives. At least according to Wyatt.

One night when their daughter, Sophie, was in bed and Arianna was collapsed on the couch watching *The Gray Man* on Netflix with Wyatt, he'd suddenly aimed the remote at the TV, killing the show and then killing her by announcing, "Ari, this isn't working for me anymore."

"What? The show?"

"No. Us."

She'd gaped at him, wondering if her lack of sleep had finally started causing delusions.

How had that happened? Why hadn't she realized it wasn't working? More to the point, what kind of man had she married? She figured that out soon enough—when the going got tough, he got going...in search of someone who wasn't a zombie.

At six years old, Sophie was perfectly fine living with Grammy. She loved Grammy, and she loved sleeping in the bed that had once been Arianna's. She still didn't understand why

Daddy hadn't come with them but was happy enough to visit him. On weekends when he could fit her into his busy born-again bachelor schedule. They'd worked out a plan for splitting time with Sophie but Wyatt rarely bothered to stick to it.

Except for today. Arianna had kept Sophie for Christmas Eve and the morning, so that she could open her presents and see what Santa brought—an art activity book featuring unicorns and a Got2Glow Fairy Finder, which she'd been thrilled with. But there'd barely been time for pancakes and presents, it seemed, before her father was calling to say he was on the way to get her.

"You've had her long enough," he'd informed Arianna when she'd protested him coming so early. "I get her Christmas Day and it's Christmas Day so deal with it."

Deal with it. It seemed to her that she'd already had enough to deal with, thanks to him. He had never acted like this when they were married, and she was still reeling from the day-to-night change in the man she'd thought she'd spend her life with.

She wasn't dealing with any of it very well. She'd picked up her old childhood habit of biting her nails and now they were ragged and ugly—rather like her life. But, hey, she'd picked up new habits, too, like spending nights in her mother's guest room eating ice cream in bed—such a cliché—and streaming reality shows.

And crying. There had been lots of crying. On her way to work. On her way home from work. After she'd tucked Sophie into the bed that once was hers. On her mother's shoulder.

With the holidays she'd made an effort to dry the tears. She couldn't sit around and feel sorry for herself for the rest of her life. At least that was what her mother, Mia, told her. Mia had cajoled her into baking cookies together and she had enjoyed shopping for Sophie, enjoyed Christmas Eve. And, up until only a little while ago, enjoyed Christmas morning.

Sophie had taken her Fairy Finder with her when she left. She'd also taken her mother's Christmas spirit.

"I hate him," Arianna said to Mia as she watched Wyatt's Mustang disappear down the street. She executed the nail on her index finger and sent it flying.

"I'm sorry," Mia said, coming to stand with her at the window. "Try to think of all the fun you had yesterday. Sophie loved making cookies for Santa and watching *Rudolph the Red-Nosed Reindeer.*"

"And she loved having your chocolate chip pancakes for breakfast," Arianna said, smiling as she remembered her daughter's happy face.

"The same ones I always made for you every year."

Arianna hugged her mother. "Thanks for letting us move in with you. It's been great for Sophie, and it's been a lifesaver for me."

She'd been busy working on her health-centered website, which she was hoping to monetize. Plus, even though she was still only working part-time, she had long shifts and there were days, especially when there was no school, that she appreciated having her mother's help. It sure beat day care.

"I promise we won't stay forever," she added. It wasn't fair to her mom. She'd stay just until she could figure out her next step. Hopefully it wouldn't be off a cliff.

"Don't be in a hurry. I like having you girls here," said Mia.

"You've got a life."

"And you're the most important part of it."

"I'm sucking you dry." She was an emotional vampire, and she knew it.

"No, you're not. How about some eggnog?"

"That sounds good," said Arianna.

They didn't have much planned for their holiday dinner. With Sophie gone, Arianna hadn't seen the point and Mia had said she didn't care one way or the other and was happy enough with the leftover French zucchini soup she'd made for their Christmas Eve supper.

"And eggnog," she'd added. "You have to have eggnog on Christmas Day."

There were a lot of things you should have on Christmas Day, like a Daddy at home to watch while your little girl opened her presents. Arianna scowled. Wyatt was such a shit. A needy, immature shit.

"While you get the eggnog, I'm going to put on some Christmas music and make a fire," she said. There was still some snow on the ground. That called for a cheery fire in the fireplace.

She had the perfect fire starter—the last bunch of pictures she'd found of her and Wyatt. She'd scrubbed her phone and laptop clean of them, but some still remained in a box that had been waiting for when she got around to scrapbooking. Now she was glad she hadn't had time for scrapbooking. What a waste that would have been.

Out came the shoebox, half-full of memory triggers.

She plucked out one of him and her at the beach on their honeymoon in Hawaii. She was in a string bikini, showing off a body she'd never get back. Maybe she'd cut him out and keep it. It would be nice to have proof someday if her daughter ever asked, "Mommy, were you ever skinny?"

"I'm not fat now," she told herself. "I'm curvy." There was nothing wrong with curves. Every woman should celebrate her body, no matter what its shape.

Whose body was Wyatt helping celebrate this holiday season? She knew he'd broken up with Office Barbie because he'd come crawling back in the summer, hoping Arianna would be willing to hit restart. In his dreams. He'd probably gotten a new girlfriend for Christmas. She fetched scissors and cut him out of the picture with one clean snip.

There were so many pictures, so many memories that should have been happy but were now painful. Them on his motorcycle *Hit the road, Wyatt.* Them out to dinner for their anniversary. *Barf!* She'd lost the man but kept that dress. Maybe she should burn it, too. Then there was one of them after they'd brought Sophie home from the hospital. She had Sophie in her arms and he was sitting next to her, looking on and grinning like a proper family man. Looks were deceiving. She ground her teeth and crushed it.

She crumpled a bunch of newspapers, then scattered the pictures on top. Next came a tent of kindling, lots of it, and more pictures, and a couple of small pieces of wood, enough to get a good flame going but not enough to smother the fire. Once that all caught, she'd add a nice fat log.

Her mother returned with the eggnog. "The New Year will be better," she said.

"Yeah, because there'll be no man in it," replied Arianna. "I should roast marshmallows over these."

Mia handed her daughter a glass. "Sorry, we don't have any. And roasting them over burning photos would probably make them toxic, anyway."

"Oh, well. Eggnog is better." Arianna took a sip. It had a satisfying amount of rum in it.

"Just the way your dad liked it," Mia said.

Her dad. Now there was a good man. He'd adored her mother and claimed there was no sense in looking at another woman since none could compare with his wife. They'd had twenty-five years together before he died, far too young.

We loved more in twenty-five years than some people do in fifty, Mia liked to say.

Twenty-five years. Arianna and Wyatt hadn't even made it to ten.

"You'll find someone," her mother said softly.

"Not holding my breath," said Arianna. She turned on the TV and started streaming Christmas songs. On came the Jackson 5 singing, "Santa Claus Is Coming To Town."

"Oh, that's a fun one," said her mother.

Yes, it was. Arianna turned up the volume. Then she grabbed

a long match from the can where Mia kept them and struck it against the hearth. It came to life with a hiss and she smiled as she touched it to the papers under those pictures. They burst into flame, curling the pictures to black swirls, chewing on the wood and producing smoke. One failed relationship up in smoke.

Good thing Santa had already come. This would have toasted his toes. Ha ha.

The pictures vanished as the flames grew and produced more smoke.

More smoke, and it was coming out of the fireplace instead of going up the chimney. Oh, no. The damper!

"The damper, hon," her mom said, her voice almost calm.

"I can't remember where it is," Arianna cried. "What side is it on?"

"On the right," said Mia as Arianna felt around for it. Chimneys weren't that big. How hard was it to find a damper? She stuck her head into the smoky cloud and tried to see up the chimney but all she saw was inky smoke. She came out coughing, her eyes burning.

She squeezed them tight and reached in again, feeling around for the stupid thing. Where was it? Ow! It was hot in there.

Meanwhile, the smoke was wafting out into the living room, like a gray ghost, and the heat was trying to melt off her hand. There was only one thing to do. "Let's get out of here!"

2

Arianna opened the living room window in the hopes the smoke would scram once the fire ran out of fuel, grabbed coats for them from the coat closet, then raced her mother and herself out the front door.

"I'm sorry about this, Mom," she said as they stood on the front walk, pulling on their coats, "It'll die down, then we can go back in."

Her mother shook her head and smiled. "This will be an interesting deposit for the memory bank."

Arianna looked for the humor and didn't see it. What a way to end Christmas Day.

Alden Brightman had worked the night shift at Saint Michael's Hospital. He'd fallen into bed at eight in the morning after setting his alarm for 1:00 p.m. That was how it went at Christmas. Even though he'd done the big Christmas Eve gathering with his extended family before going to work, his parents still expected him to come over to open presents at two o'clock followed by Christmas dinner. Before he started working night shift as a nurse, it had been presents and brunch. His family had moved their gathering time back in an effort to accommodate him and he appreciated it. He didn't do well on less than eight hours, but for Christmas he could suck it up and function fine on five.

He'd hoped to get five this morning, but it had taken him a while to get to sleep. It had been a crazy night in the emergency room—one man who'd celebrated too much had managed to fall off his deck and break his arm. Another guy came in needing help with an artificial bladder that was malfunctioning. That had been a new one for the books. A middle-aged woman had stripped off all her clothes and gone streaking through the emergency room (it had taken Alden and two orderlies to catch her), and another woman who needed to be hooked up to an EKG but wasn't a fan of male nurses had screamed at him to get out. No wonder he always needed a full eight hours of sleep. His job could really take it out of him.

He was dreaming when the sounds of The Jackson 5 singing "Santa Claus Is Coming To Town" drifted in through the bedroom window he kept cracked open for fresh air, pulling him awake. It was probably just as well. Dreaming about trying to hook up with the Sugar Plum Fairy was sick and wrong. His subconscious was obviously still whacked out from having broken up with his girlfriend earlier in the year.

Except Cynthia was no Sugar Plum Fairy. She'd been a drama queen who could sit through the saddest movie dry-eyed but cry over a ruined dress. He'd stood by through six months of constant selfies, constant compliment-fishing and constant complaints over everything from where he took her to dinner to what he wore when he took her and what he said or didn't say when they were eating.

"Are you really serious with that girl?" his mother had asked when Cynthia threw a fit after one of his nephews accidentally ran into her with his hot dog at a family Fourth of July barbecue and got mustard on her top. "She does not like children."

Of course, he'd had to defend her. "No, she doesn't like getting smeared with mustard."

Deep down he'd known Mom was right, and it had finally begun to sink in that his dream girl had a nightmare side to her. In the end he'd realized Cynthia didn't like anyone as much as she liked herself. As for him, he was just a placeholder, someone to use while she waited for a better model to come along.

Well, life went on. He hiked, he mountain biked, he worked. He hung out with his friends and he played with his dog. And once in a while checked his dating app. Then shrugged and repeated the whole cycle again, filling in the spaces in between with as much sleep as he could manage. Which he sure wasn't managing at the moment.

In addition to the Christmas serenade pushing its way in through his window, he realized he smelled smoke. He sat up and rubbed his eyes, which put Buster, his Boston terrier on alert. He got out of bed, making Buster bark with excitement and join him as he looked out his window. It gave him a good view of the house next door.

He saw his neighbor and the woman he assumed was her daughter bundled in coats and standing on their snow-speckled front walk. The mother was tall, with light brown hair highlighted with silver. Her daughter was shorter and curvier. She'd probably come up to about his shoulder. Her hair, also a light brown, was long but she had it up in that kind of messy-bun thing women often did to their hair. She wore pajama bottoms and slippers under her coat. It had obviously been a quick exit. Smoke was wafting out the open front door of their house. What the heck?

Not your problem, he told himself. The older woman, Mia White, was nice. She'd brought him cookies when he first moved in. But the daughter was a shrew. He'd seen her standing on the front porch and heard her screaming into her phone on more than one occasion. She was good-looking—nice legs and a pretty, round face with full lips and a delicate nose. But he'd seen that pretty face contort into a scary mask when she was on the phone. (From a distance, thank God.) Yeah, there was a turn-on. If you were a masochist. Now what was she doing, trying to burn down her mom's house?

Mia was rubbing her arms and stamping her feet, trying to keep warm. Chivalry demanded he go over there and see if he could help. Who bothered with chivalry these days, anyway? The shrew was bouncing up and down in an obvious effort to keep warm.

Well, shit.

"We shouldn't be awake," he informed Buster as he pulled a sweatshirt over his bare chest, glancing at the alarm clock that wouldn't go off for another hour.

Buster didn't agree. He barked and raced for the bedroom door.

If there was a fire, the women had probably already called 911. He slipped his boots on over his pajama bottoms, then informed Buster that there was nothing for him to do out there, shutting him inside the house. Probably nothing for Alden to do, either. But he'd be a rotten neighbor not to offer to help.

"Are you ladies okay?" he asked as he approached them.

"Oh, yeah, it's a great day to stand around in the cold," the younger woman said in a snotty voice. Hazel. Her eyes were hazel-colored.

Who cared? He'd left his nice warm bed for this? He ignored her and spoke to her mother, who appeared to be a rational human being. "Is there anything I can do to help?"

Miss Snotball spoke for her. "No, we're fine. We just had a little accident with the fireplace."

"We forgot to open the damper," her mom explained.

He nodded. "I assume it's open now."

"No, it's not, I can't find it," snapped Miss Snotball.

Okay, well, that was an easy fix. He started for the house.

"The fire's going out," the snotball called after him.

"Getting the damper pulled out will help with the smoke,"

he called back. Who started a fire in their fireplace and didn't pull out the damper? Someone who wasn't the brightest bulb in the string of Christmas lights.

He took a deep breath, then entered the house. The living room was filled with smoke and stank. They'd be leaving the door and windows open for a long time. He found the kitchen, grabbed a towel from where it hung on the stove handle, and wrapped it around his hand. Then he opened the kitchen window, took another breath and went back into the living room. A small fire was still burning and the smoke was still floating out of the hearth. He felt around for the damper, found it and pulled, and the smoke reversed direction and began swirling up the chimney.

Okay, good deed done for the day. His bed was calling. He dumped the towel on the coffee table and went back outside and joined the women.

"Got your damper pulled. You're probably going to have to air out your house the rest of the day," he said.

"Thank you," said Mrs. White, and smiled at him.

"Thank you," said her daughter. No smile on those pretty, pouty lips. It was almost as if she resented having to be polite. Who had knocked down her holiday snowman?

"No problem," he said. And now, to bed. "When you go back in, could you turn down the music?"

The snotball smiled now. It was a snarky one. "No Christmas spirit?"

"I've got plenty when I've had enough sleep," he snapped then. Before she could say anything else to irritate him, he marched back to his house. If ever there was a candidate for receiving a lump of coal, she was it.

"Not your finest moment," Mia scolded her daughter as they walked back to the house.

Arianna rubbed her aching forehead. "You're right."

Not the best way to meet the neighbor she'd only had glimpses of since she'd moved in.

According to Mia, he'd moved into the neighborhood shortly before Arianna came back. His grandma had owned the house but she was gone. "I think he might work nights so I don't see much of him," Mia had said. "He seems nice."

"He didn't have to come help us," Mia said, continuing her motherly reprimand.

Arianna sighed. "I know, and I was a stinker. I'll take over some cookies tomorrow and apologize. We have plenty left."

"Hopefully they don't smell like smoke," said Mia.

"Okay, I'll buy some."

They opened every window, then cranked up the heat and shut themselves in Mia's room and found a movie to stream on Arianna's laptop—*It's a Wonderful Life*, Mia's all-time favorite movie.

"Some Christmas," Arianna muttered as she started the movie.

"It could be worse. We could have burned down the house," Mia said.

There was that.

"And at least you got rid of the last of your unwanted pictures," her mother continued.

If only she could as easily get rid of the taunting memories. She sighed deeply and prepared to watch George Bailey learn that he'd had a wonderful life.

Bah humbug.

Christmas morning was long gone by the time Molly Fielding got to her daughter's house. But it was still Christmas Day, and it was never too late to enjoy cinnamon rolls. Or so she'd told herself when she picked some up at the Safeway bakery department. And they were Ava's favorite.

Ava wasn't smiling when she opened the door to her condo,

and the sight of the cinnamon rolls didn't change that. "Finally," she said.

"I'm sorry I didn't make it over last night," Molly said.

The plan had been for her to come over for Christmas Eve and spend the night so she'd be on hand for the early morning festivities. She'd done it in the past and she wasn't above sharing a bed with her daughter, but Ava tended to thrash around and talk in her sleep, and all Molly had wanted from Santa was a good night's rest.

"You missed seeing Paisley open her present from Santa," Ava said. It made Molly feel like a criminal in the witness stand with the lawyer for the prosecution trying to destroy her.

Guilty as charged. "Did she like it?" Molly asked.

"What's not to like about a new iPad?" Ava retorted, swinging the door wide. She was dressed in jeans and a black top that showed off a perfect figure. To match her perfectly done hair and makeup. Not that Ava needed makeup.

Sometimes Molly wondered how she'd wound up with such a beautiful daughter. And smart, too. She, herself, was so...average.

And yet, here was Ava, still single in spite of her beauty and intelligence. It seemed she did everything right in her life except relationships.

"Good. I'm glad she liked it," Molly said.

She'd chipped in for that present and was supposed to have been on hand to see her granddaughter's reaction when she discovered it under the tree. Santa was going to put Molly on his naughty list for bugging out and claiming she was sick.

No lie, really. She was sick of the holiday stress that came with being a postal clerk. And as head clerk of the Bremerton office, she had more than her share of it. Cranky customers, cranky workers. Hours on those poor feet of hers.

People thought the job ended when the windows closed. Not so. There was always more to be done. Then, after her shift, trying to fit in housework, errands, shopping and grandparenting. It was hard to show enthusiasm for those holiday extras. It seemed like she had ever-dwindling energy and enthusiasm for those holiday extras. Working the post office was like doing hard time.

She'd dutifully attended Paisley's winter program at school and then dozed off and missed seeing her granddaughter's appearance as part of the singing snowflake choir. She'd also promised to make Christmas bonbons with Paisley but hadn't, and Ava had been disappointed over that, too. She and Ava had made them together every year when Ava was growing up and this was the year she was supposed to begin the tradition with Paisley. She was striking out all over the place. Maybe she needed vitamins. Or her own personal team of helper elves. Or a better attitude. How did Santa keep managing to ho, ho, ho year in, year out?

Oh, yeah, he only flew once a year. Delivering toys to good little girls and boys? Piece of cake. She'd like to see him do her job. If only she could run away...to Hawaii, Costa Rica. The North Pole. She'd rather supervise the work up there than where she was.

Ava took the cinnamon rolls. "I've got coffee," she said, leading the way to the living room where her small tree sat, decorated with the princess and animal ornaments Molly had given her every year of her childhood, along with the newer more grown-up ones she was still giving Ava now that she was an adult. There were also the handful Molly had bought for Paisley sprinkled throughout, along with several handcrafted ornaments Paisley had made as school projects.

The presents had been opened and were displayed under the tree, the wrapping paper already disposed of. Ava was a single mom. She worked as a receptionist in a law office and was taking an online course to become a paralegal. Busy as she was, she still managed to keep her place neat, work out at the gym and spend quality time with Paisley. Molly herself had been a single mom, but she'd never been as pulled together as Ava.

It was too late for any pulling together now. At fifty-five Molly was who she was. And tired of it.

Paisley was seated at the little dining table, still in her pajamas and working on the mosaic kit Molly had given her. Her black curls were, of course, perfectly coiled, and Molly was sure Ava had made her brush her teeth before opening her presents. She was a beautiful child, with the same warm tawny skin as Ava, and big brown eyes. She could have been doing ads for The Gap.

"Look who's here," said Ava.

Paisley's eyes lit up at the sight of Molly. "Grandma!" she cried, pushing away from the table. She ran to Molly and almost knocked her over as she wrapped her arms around Molly's waist.

"Hello, my little elf," Molly said, hugging her back.

This child was as sweet as she was pretty and Molly adored her. She mentally kicked herself for not getting over the night before like she'd promised.

"Come see what Santa brought me," Ava said, and towed Molly over to the tree.

There sat the prized iPad. Molly was surprised she wasn't playing on it.

"We loaded stuff on it but Mommy said I had to wait for you to come over before I can play on it," said Paisley. "I'm glad you're finally here. Mommy said you'd probably been kidnapped by Santa."

Funny Mommy. That had most likely been delivered with a load of snark.

"Well, I'm here now, so let's have some fun."

Paisley led the way to the couch. "I have *Despicable Me: Minion Rush*. Want to play it with me?"

"Of course," said Molly.

She wasn't big on video games, but she was big on sitting on the couch with her granddaughter propped against her. At least Paisley wasn't mad at her for not being up with them at the crack of dawn.

Ava returned with their cinnamon rolls on a plate and a cup of coffee for Molly. Then she fetched her own cup and settled into a chair.

"One game," she said, "then we're going to watch Grandma open her presents."

Paisley was entirely too engrossed in her game to reply.

Molly helped herself to a cinnamon roll. She used to say that calories didn't count at Christmas. Now she didn't care if they counted or not. Cookies and cinnamon rolls were one of life's greatest pleasures.

"There's no hurry. We have all day," she said. "And it's nice to have the whole day to relax." She needed it.

"I guess yesterday was awful," Ava said above Paisley's squeals and running commentary. A daughterly peace offering.

"It was." The post office closed early on Christmas Eve, but that didn't mean the employees got to rush home right away. As head clerk, Molly had to wait for all the carriers to come in and then she had to deliver the mail to the truck that would take it to the distribution center. There'd been a lot. Everyone had last-minute cards and packages to send off.

Before that there'd been the usual seasoning of angry postal patrons all morning, wanting to know why their packages hadn't been delivered. Molly relayed her run in with one of her non-favorites.

Mrs. Bigman, a woman whose small stature did not match her name, had brought in her receipt with the tracking numbers on it, insisting her son's Christmas cookies hadn't gotten to him. Molly had double-checked for her and assured her that the package had been delivered to the address she'd printed on her package.

"Is it possible a neighbor picked it up?" Molly had suggested.

"Who would do that?" Mrs. Bigman had demanded.

Who knew?

"You are so…careless. And unconcerned!" Mrs. Bigman had ranted.

"I tried to reassure her that I was concerned, but I couldn't follow the package all the way to Antelope, California," Molly finished. "Maybe next time I'll suggest she stick me in a big old box, ship me to her son's house and let me wait on the porch to catch the cookie thief."

Ava snickered and took a sip of her coffee. "Don't do it. She might take you up on it."

"I don't have to worry about that. Next year she's going to use FedEx."

"I guess she never saw *Cast Away*," Ava said, and they both snickered.

"I understand people's frustration," Molly said. "I'd be unhappy, too, if a present I sent someone didn't reach them." Still, being held responsible for every hiccup and mishap was frustrating and exhausting.

Which was probably why, when the pressure was off, she had a tendency to nod off. After opening the present from her granddaughter—another T-shirt that extolled her grandmotherly virtues—and a jar of her favorite body butter from her daughter, and settling in to watch *The Polar Express*, she felt her eyelids getting heavy.

"Grandma, you're missing it!" Her granddaughter gave her a nudge that had her waking up with a snort.

Molly shot a guilty glance in her daughter's direction to see if Ava had noticed. Of course, she had. But this time she wasn't frowning in disapproval. She looked worried.

"Maybe you need a different job, Mom," she said.

"Oh, honey, it's too late for that. I'm too many years in."

Trapped in a job she'd burned out on. There was a depressing thought. *Just a few more years to retirement*, she reminded herself. Maybe, if she could find a way to lose the grumpy Grinch vibes that invaded her postal kingdom every year, it wouldn't feel like a life sentence.

She struggled to keep her eyes open for the rest of the movie, and after some hot chocolate, woke up enough to play a game of Sorry! with the girls. Then it was time to go home, take a hot bath and hope she didn't fall asleep in the tub and drown.

"Merry Christmas," Ava said, giving her a hug and a kiss, her earlier irritation forgotten. "Love you, Mom."

"Love you more," Molly replied, then repeated the same routine with Paisley.

She smiled as she drove back to her little house in Manette, one of Bremerton's favorite neighborhoods. The holiday season had a way of grinding her down, but all those little pieces of her that were left sure enjoyed spending the time with her girls.

She did feel badly about not getting around to making the bonbons with Paisley. They'd been such a mother-daughter tradition when Ava was growing up.

But darn it all, Ava could start that tradition with her daughter herself. Ava was busy, but Ava was still young. Molly was… worn out.

She managed to stay awake for her soak in the tub, then crawled into bed, her cat Marlow jumping up to snuggle at her feet. Ah, warm covers and a purring cat—the perfect ending to a perfect day.

And tomorrow she had to go back to work.

Her smile dropped away. Why on earth had she allowed that thought to come into her mind?

"The holiday rush is over," she reminded herself.

But the Grinches and Scrooges would still be around, waiting to find a way to make her New Year miserable.

Don't even think it.

Too late. She had, and she paid for it in her dreams.

There she was, back at work, dressed in red onesie pajamas

and a Santa hat. The look was not a flattering one. It showed every roll and fat bubble.

Behind her, Ebenezer Scrooge looked over her shoulder. "You've messed up Mrs. Bigman's order. Her son is never going to get his cookies."

"I did not," Molly insisted.

Suddenly there stood Mrs. Bigman, shaking a finger at her. "The cookies didn't arrive! Where's your boss? I'm going to get you fired."

"I'm her boss," said Ebenezer. "And she'll pay for this."

Suddenly there stood all the carriers, and Helen, one of the mail clerks, pointing fingers and chanting, "She'll pay for this!"

"What can I do? I'm only human," Molly wailed.

"Make her pay!" cried Mrs. Bigman.

"Oh, she will," said Mr. Boss Scrooge.

Suddenly he was ten feet tall. He grabbed her by the neck of her red onesie, lifted her up and carried her over to a giant carton filled with packing peanuts and dropped her in.

"What are you doing?" she cried.

He slammed the lid of the box down and she could hear tape being stretched over the top.

She banged on it. "Let me out! I'm claustrophobic!"

"Too bad," snarled Scrooge. "Ship her to the North Pole. Let Santa deal with her."

The Santa in her dreams would hardly have been a candidate for the Macy's Thanksgiving Day Parade and he certainly wouldn't have been hired by any mall. Over his red suit he wore a black Dracula cape and when he smiled, he had fangs.

He grabbed her by the shoulders and held her up in front of him so she could see his glare close up. "So, you have a problem with the holidays, do you?"

"No, I don't!" she insisted, struggling to get free. "I don't!"

She awoke to find herself tangled in her covers and her cat long gone, and she sighed. Merry Christmas.

★ ★ ★

Arianna stopped by the post office on her way home from work to mail the thank-you notes Sophie had written to her two aunties—Arianna's best friends from college, who lived far away but never failed to send Sophie a little something for Christmas. The trip to the post office gave her a chance to see her neighbor Molly, who she and her mother had known for years. Molly had been the one to host the bridal shower for Arianna when she got married. Molly had also sent her flowers the day her divorce was final, along with a card that said, *I'll throw another bridal shower when the right one comes along.* Molly was favorite aunt, big sister and best friend all rolled into one.

Even though she lived only a few houses down the street, it seemed like lately the only times Arianna saw her was when she had to mail something. Of course, it was the season to be busy.

It wasn't so busy on this day, though. After the preholiday mailing rush the post office didn't have many customers, something for which Molly was probably grateful.

Except the one customer she was with, a skinny woman in leggings and UGGs and an oversized parka, who looked like she was going to do her best to cancel that gratitude. "You can't close my PO box!" the woman snapped.

"I'm sorry," Molly said. "You had forty-five days to pay. That's all we can allow. Other people are waiting to get post office boxes and we can't hold ones that haven't been paid for indefinitely."

"What about my mail?" the woman demanded.

Molly looked almost guilty, as if it were somehow her fault this woman hadn't paid for her post office box. "It's returned to the sender."

"My aunt's sending me a check!" the woman screeched. "What is wrong with you people? Don't you know it's Christmas?"

"Look, you can apply for another box," Molly said.

The woman had some very uncomfortable suggestions for what Molly could do with another post office box. She whirled around and marched off toward the stairs, swearing under her breath and nearly knocking Arianna over as she passed.

"Looks like she's going to have a happy New Year," Arianna observed as she stepped up to the window.

Molly shook her head. "I hate my job."

Poor Molly. She sure didn't deserve the grief so many of her postal customers gave her.

Molly had a big heart and a big smile, and Arianna often marveled that she was able to keep that smile in place when dealing with a cranky postal patron.

"I hope at least your Christmas was good," she said.

"The parts I didn't sleep through. Honestly, this job drains me sometimes. Why can't people be nice?"

"I don't know. I think some people are put here just to mess up our lives." Gee, who was she thinking of when she said that?

"Uh-oh," Molly said. "What's Wyatt done this time?"

"Actually, he's been a good dad for once, so I guess I can't complain."

"Sure you can," Molly assured her.

Arianna smiled at that. Molly always knew what to say.

"I should be glad he actually came and took her for the day yesterday, especially after being so hit-and-miss. Every time he gets a new girlfriend, he slacks off."

"Well, that's not necessarily a bad thing. You don't want Sophie witnessing a parade of ho-bags."

"True," Arianna laughed. "But it's so hard to let her go. I'm sure the only reason he took her yesterday was so his parents could see her."

"And I'm sure they appreciated that. Grandparents shouldn't be deprived of seeing their grandkids."

"You're right," Arianna said. "I need a book of stamps, by the way."

"I still have some angels left."

"Angels will be perfect," Arianna said.

"Was the day good before that?" Molly asked.

"Oh, yeah. But it was all downhill after she left. I tried to smoke us out," Arianna said, and shared her fireplace mishap.

Molly chuckled. "At least you didn't burn the house down. Things can always be worse."

"They were already bad enough. Worst of all, I let Wyatt get to me and ruin my day and turn me into a walking lump of coal. I wish I could have a do-over."

"Oh, no. No do-overs. That would mean I'd have to suffer through another preholiday season of crankiness. I'm glad Christmas only comes once a year. I don't think I could take it if it was more."

"I love Christmas," Arianna said. "At least I used to. This year I just smeared ugly over the good parts. I was too angry."

"I was too tired."

Arianna took the stamps and put away her wallet. "It's supposed to be a time for love and good cheer and kindness." She sure blew that. She'd been unloving and grumpy and rude.

"Better luck next year," Molly said.

"Yeah, right," Arianna said cynically. Who knew what the next year held? She was afraid to look.

She thought about her conversation as she stepped outside of the post office. More snow was predicted for later that night—not a lot but enough to coat the world white again. She loved the way the air smelled when it snowed—so fresh and pure. Snow buried all the dirty roads and messy lawns. It said, *There, now. The past is gone. I've put it to sleep. Soon it will be spring, and you can replant and begin again.*

Beginning again sounded wonderful. She'd have liked nothing better than to begin again, starting with Christmas. It was too bad she'd have to wait a whole year to do that.

3

"Grammy and me are making gingerbread people," Sophie informed Arianna when she came home. "We made snowballs, too."

"In case you wanted to follow through on your resolution and take some cookies next door," Mia added. "These won't smell of smoke."

"But Grammy says we get to keep some for us," Sophie put in, making sure all the gingerbread people wouldn't run away.

"We should definitely keep some for ourselves," Arianna said, and picked up one of the ones her mother had decorated. It was a gingerbread girl and Mia had piped a perfect trim on the skirt and bodice of her dress. Once a baker, always a baker.

The cookie was buttery, spicy and delicious. A few of those coupled with the little cookie balls dusted with powdered sugar would, hopefully, make a good holiday peace offering for their neighbor. Peace on earth, goodwill toward men next door. Still, she had no desire to go tromping over there. She had no desire to do anything, actually. She needed to recover from her Christmas stress.

"Can I take them over?" Sophie asked eagerly.

Their neighbor would probably be more inclined to take something from her cute little six-year-old with her freckled nose, flour-dusted chin and chestnut curls. The curls were done up in pigtails, using the tie-dyed scrunchies her father had given her for Christmas. She was wearing a red top with a snowman appliqued on it and white leggings with Santas on them that her other grandma had given her. (Wyatt's mom gave Sophie a lot of presents. Too bad she couldn't have given Sophie a dad who understood the meaning of commitment.)

"Let's let your mommy deliver the cookies," Mia said. "She and the nice man need to talk about some things."

Ugh. Yes, they did. Arianna abandoned the cookie in favor of chewing off a thumbnail.

"Like what?" Sophie asked.

"Just boring grown-up stuff," Mia said. "Do you want to put cinnamon candies on your man's toes?"

It was enough to distract Sophie, which was fine with Arianna. She didn't want to have to explain to her daughter that the grown-up stuff involved her mother apologizing for acting like a child.

"Maybe I'll wait until later," she ventured. "He's probably not home." Even though the lights were on next door.

"Never put off till tomorrow..." Mia said.

"What you can put off till the day after tomorrow," Arianna said, earning a motherly frown.

It didn't matter what age you were. Motherly frowns never lost their power. Arianna sighed and got busy assembling a plate of cookies, then covered them with plastic wrap and tied red curling ribbon around the plate, prettying it up with plenty of curls. She donned her coat and a smile and made her way next door.

The smile faltered a little when he opened his door and gave her a wary look, so she got right to it and held out the plate. "Peace offering. I was channeling the Grinch yesterday. I'm sorry."

"We all have Grinch days," he said, his wariness seeming to melt away as he smiled. His smile was the kind of smile that could make a girl want to climb up on his lap and tell him everything she wanted for Christmas. Arianna tamped that urge down stat.

"I was dealing with my ex. I guess that's really no excuse, though."

"Exes happen," he said.

She bent to pet the little black Boston terrier, jumping on her leg. "I'm Arianna White. My daughter, Sophie, and I are living with my mom for a while."

"Alden Brightman," he said. "And Buster," he added.

"Hello, Buster. You are so cute." *Like your master.*

Alden Brightman was a head taller than her, with sandy hair and brown eyes edged with the beginnings of laugh crinkles. He had gorgeous big shoulders and thick pecs and a movie star mouth—the kind of mouth that made a woman want to feel it moving down her neck.

"Don't swell his head," said Alden. Then, "Did you get the smoke out of your living room?"

"Finally."

"Good. Well, thanks for these," he said, saluting her with the plate.

That signaled the end of the conversation, which was just as well. She was inclined to stand around and talk to Alden Brightman for a long time, and a long conversation with a hot man... with any man, was not something she needed to be considering right now.

"And thanks for helping us," she said. "Happy New Year."

"You, too," he said.

She turned and walked down his front steps. He shut the door. That was that.

Still, that smile wouldn't get out of her mind, and she couldn't help wondering about him. What kind of work did he do? What did he do when he wasn't working? Did he have a girlfriend?

He was obviously a nice guy, so of course he had a girlfriend. All the best ones were taken.

You're not interested, she reminded herself. But at least they were on good neighborly terms now. She'd take her clear conscience back home and enjoy her evening. And after dinner she'd grab another gingerbread boy, pretend he was Wyatt and bite off his head. The thought made her smile. And that was an improvement over the day before.

"How was your Christmas?" Sunny asked the next day as Arianna ushered her into the kitchen where they were going to be filming a reel for *To Your Health*, Arianna's YouTube channel and website, which Sunny had created for her.

"I've had better." Arianna took a mug from the cupboard and fixed her friend a cup of peppermint tea.

"Yeah, me, too," Sunny said. "What a fail."

"Uh-oh," Arianna said.

"You can say that again. The kids didn't come."

"Weren't you supposed to have them on Christmas Day?"

"Yes, but the Weed conveniently didn't get back from Spokane in time."

The Weed. Arianna appreciated the cleverness of Sunny's nickname for her husband's ex, but it did give her pause. Would Wyatt someday have a new wife making up a crummy nickname for her? Ugh.

"I know you had a special day planned," she said. She didn't know a lot about Travis's ex, though from what Sunny had shared, she sounded incredibly selfish and immature.

"I did." Sunny frowned at her mug. "It was so disappointing. Of course, Travis was ticked. My dad was ticked because Travis was ticked and being grumpy. It sucked." She sighed. "How was yours?"

"I tried to smoke us out. Forgot to open the fireplace damper."

"That had to be interesting," said Sunny.

"It was. Our neighbor came over to help and I turned into a Christmas bat. Had to take over cookies last night and apologize. All in all, it was a crappy Christmas. I wish I could have a do-over."

"Same here. Christmas in January."

Arianna smiled at the thought. "Christmas all year long. At the rate I'm going, it would take twelve months of practice to get it right for next year."

"It'd take twelve months of presents to make my stepdaughter like me. If I'm lucky."

"Oh, well. You've got to move on," Arianna said. Maybe that should be her mantra for the coming year. Sunny didn't appear to be listening. "Sunny?"

"Huh? Oh, sorry. I was just thinking about the idea of Christmas in January. Why not? It's kind of a blah month, anyway. And think of all the sales you can take advantage of."

There was no reason you couldn't keep the Christmas spirit going. Or, in Arianna's case, resurrect it. She could do a repeat and in this version not have to worry about her ex stealing away her daughter before the day had even begun.

"It could be fun," Sunny continued. Sunny was all about fun, which had a lot to do with why she and Arianna had gone from provider and client to friends in the year they'd worked together. "We could start a whole new trend, like the Christmas-in-July thing."

"That's just about watching movies."

"Pretty half-hearted. If you're going to do Christmas in July you should do it right, with carols and Christmas cookies and presents."

"And sweaters?" Arianna teased.

"Okay, maybe not the sweaters, but at least Santa hats."

"Go for it."

"I just might."

Arianna chuckled. "Right. Good luck bringing Santa out of hiding. You ready to start?"

"I am if you are. Got your talking points ready?"

"I do. And my show-and-tell," Arianna added, pointing to the fruits and veggies lined up on her counter. "Mom made the granola for the recipe. Feel free to take the jar home with you if you want."

"I won't say no to that. Thanks. Where is your mom, by the way? And Sophie?"

"Sophie had a play date and Mom's off at the senior center, line dancing."

"Your mom's so pretty. I think you should feature her at some point, do a health-for-seniors feature and use her as an example of how to stay healthy."

"Good idea. Maybe I will. She's done a lot over the years to get healthy—quitting smoking, losing thirty pounds."

"Not easy to do when you're a baker," Sunny observed.

"She even switched from milk chocolate to dark."

"Ick," was all Sunny had to say to that.

"Hey, it's good stuff."

"So are Cadbury Easter eggs," Sunny retorted, making Arianna laugh.

They got to work, fine-tuning Arianna's display and adjusting the light ring. Arianna went over her notes again, and then Sunny pulled out her cell phone.

"Let's do this," she said.

They did, and got the video done in two takes.

"I'll get this up for you and lift some content out for your Insta account," Sunny said.

"Great. Thanks."

"And now I have to go home and start thinking about what I'm going to do for Christmas in January."

"You're serious?"

"Why not? I bet I can bring Santa back for an encore," said Sunny.

A Christmas refresh, unspoiled by ex-husband complications. It sure sounded tempting.

"Maybe I'll join you," Arianna said.

"Yeah?"

"Yeah. Why not? Heaven knows I could use a do over."

"That would be awesome. We could throw some kind of party together."

"I like that idea. You know who else might want to party with us? My neighbor Molly."

"Mail Lady Molly?"

"Yep. She had a hard time finding her Christmas spirit this year. Maybe something like this will help her."

"Let's do dinner tonight and talk about it," Sunny suggested. "Can you get away?"

"Let me check my busy social calendar," Arianna joked. "Yeah, I can."

"Horse and Cow?"

"Sounds good. I'll pick you up."

Molly was pooped and her feet hurt. The last thing she wanted was to go out. But when Arianna had called she was insistent that Molly go out to dinner with her and her new friend Sunny.

"You can rest your feet at Horse and Cow," she'd said.

So here they were, in the popular pub that had been part of downtown Bremerton for seventy years. It was small and noisy but offered plenty of atmosphere, displaying all kinds of submarine memorabilia as a tribute to the city's naval history. And it served the best burgers in town.

With her blond hair and happy smile, Sunny was well named. Molly was instantly charmed.

And felt old next to these two, especially when Sunny talked about doing a repeat of Christmas with a party in January. "It could be so much fun," she enthused.

"And so much work," Molly said. This all sounded like a pain in the posterior.

"Not necessarily. If we all pitched in," Sunny argued.

"Or if we went somewhere," said Arianna. "Like up to the mountains."

A whole day driving up to the mountains, wandering around in the cold. "You two have fun. I don't ski."

"Me, neither," said Sunny, "but I like to go inner tubing."

"I'd probably fall off," Molly said and Arianna frowned in disapproval over her lack of enthusiasm. "Plus, it would take hours just getting there."

"But your granddaughter would love it," said Arianna.

"She'd love going to a movie, too. And I can sit through that." Their hamburgers arrived and Molly dug into hers.

"What if we went somewhere nearby?" Sunny said. She snapped her fingers. "Ice-skating!"

"There's no rink here," said Arianna.

"There is in Edmonds. We catch the Kingston Ferry and it's only a quick ride away. I bet Sophie would love it."

"So would Paisley," said Arianna, looking at Molly.

"I wouldn't have to skate, would I?" Molly asked.

"You can take pictures," Arianna told her.

"I could do that," Molly said.

And, after her holiday slacking, her daughter would be thrilled to see her doing more activities with Paisley. Maybe Ava would come, too.

"It would be a great Christmas do-over," Sunny said, and chomped on a French fry.

"I'm all about trying again," said Arianna. "I need some holiday happiness. I have a whole year worth of misery to make up for."

"This could be a good start," Sunny said.

"Maybe it will be enough to hold me through February," Arianna said, and frowned. "That's going to be a fun month, with Valentine's Day to look forward to."

Sunny turned thoughtful. "What if you had something else to look forward to?"

"Christmas in February?" Molly joked. Oh, no. She could tell by their expressions that the other two were taking her seriously.

"Oh, yes!" Sunny enthused. "Let's leave our trees up and decorate them for V-Day."

"Heck, let's leave them up in March and decorate them with shamrocks," said Arianna.

"Let's hire leprechauns to come clean our houses and bring us energy drinks," Molly said. These two were getting out of control.

"What if you could do Christmas all year?" Arianna mused. She turned to Molly. "I know how people treat you at the post office during the holidays. Wouldn't it be nice to enjoy that holiday cheer without the stress of the Christmas rush?"

Actually, it would. But she didn't need twelve months of it, did she?

"Christmas all year long—my step-kids would love it!" Sunny exclaimed. "What if we did something different around the twenty-fifth of every month to celebrate Christmas?"

It sounded like work to Molly.

"I'm so in," Arianna said. "This last year has been miserable and I've had enough of that. I want to make my life worth living again."

"A new one is waiting," said Sunny, who was obviously an optimist, "and I'm determined to spread the love to my in-laws."

"I could stand to rediscover my joy," Molly admitted. "But all year long?"

"Why not? It would give us something to look forward to every month," said Sunny.

"A new year of new beginnings," Arianna added with a smile.

"I'm all about that," Sunny said. "No matter what life throws at us we can keep our stockings hung and fill our lives with good stuff."

"Keep up our trees and our spirits," chimed in Arianna. She looked expectantly at Molly.

It all sounded great but Molly still hesitated. "Umm."

"No grumpy postal patrons involved. Good times with your granddaughter," Arianna said. Then she added the kicker. "You can make up for falling asleep during her winter program."

"Okay, I'm in," Molly relented. Maybe, if she had a whole year, she could even find time to make those bonbons with Paisley.

"All right! Here's to twelve months of Christmas," Sunny said, raising her glass of beer.

Arianna raised her glass also. "Twelve months of Christmas. Better attitudes, better times, cookies, presents…"

"And a partridge in a pear tree," Molly finished and raised her glass of Pepsi as well. She had to be out of her mind to let these two talk her into this.

But maybe she needed something fun to look forward to every month. Maybe she could rediscover the enthusiasm she'd once felt for the holidays. For life. She'd fallen in a rut. It was way past time to crawl out. She only hoped she'd have the energy.

After Arianna dropped her off, she texted Mia.

Molly: You will not believe what your daughter has just suckered me into.

Mia: Neighborhood block party?

Molly: Worse! Christmas all year long.

Mia: Sounds charming. Ho, ho, ho.

Molly: I ho, ho, hope I survive it!

This was going to be an interesting year.

Arianna returned home feeling like a new woman. The past was gone, the New Year lay ahead. Christmas lights were on sale. She'd pick up some and string them along her mom's porch— better late than never—then maybe she'd take Sophie shopping, buy her something fun. She'd buy herself something fun, too. Jewelry was always on sale in January. She'd get herself a new ring to replace the wedding set she'd stuffed in her jewelry box. Maybe a garnet. Or a small ruby. Something Christmassy. No diamonds, that was for sure. Diamonds were not forever.

Mia was ensconced in front of the TV, crocheting and watching a family holiday movie on the GAC channel, Sophie curled up by her side.

"How was dinner?" she asked.

"Great!" Arianna plopped on the couch and pulled her daughter over to her, giving her a little tickle and making Sophie giggle.

"It looks like it," Mia observed, cocking an eyebrow.

"We made plans. And guess what?" Arianna said to Sophie. "We are going to celebrate Christmas all year long."

"Yay!" cried Sophie. "Is Santa going to come?" she asked, wiggling with excitement.

"I don't know. You'll have to wait and see," said Arianna.

"Molly just texted me about that. It sounds cute, but what does it actually involve?" Mia asked.

"Every month around the twenty-fifth we are going to do something fun to keep the Christmas spirit going. Want to join us?"

"As an observer," Mia said. "All that planning sounds like work."

"But fun work."

Her mother smiled at her. "It's been a long time since I've seen you so happy."

"There's always something to be happy about at Christmas," Arianna said. "Even when it comes in January."

Travis was watching football when Sunny returned. "Did you have fun, babe?" he asked casually, his gaze glued to the TV.

"I did," she said. "Arianna and her friend Molly and I have come up with a plan."

That got his attention. He aimed the remote at the TV and shut off the sound. "Okay, what are you up to?"

She snuggled up against him on the couch. How she loved cuddling up to Travis. He was a big chunk of man, solidly built. He'd played football in high school and, although he was in his forties, his work at the shipyard kept him as fit as any twenty-year-old. She loved how solid he was. In so many ways. Tansy was a fool to have let him go.

"We are going to celebrate Christmas in January," she announced.

His eyebrows shot up. "Huh?"

"To make up for December."

"Okaaay. So I guess the tree's not coming down."

"Nope, it's not. In fact, it's staying up all year."

"All year," he repeated, trying to keep up.

"Yes! Because we're not only going to celebrate Christmas in January. We're going to celebrate it in February and March and April and every other month clear through next December."

"What did you have to drink at Horse and Cow?"

"I drank the Christmas spirit Kool-Aid," she joked. "It'll be fun and the kids will love it."

He smiled. "Have I told you recently what an awesome stepmom you are?"

"Yes, but feel free to tell me again."

Someone needed to tell her. It sure wouldn't be her resentful thirteen-year-old stepdaughter. The belated Christmas dinner with the kids had been anything but jolly, and, as Sunny's mother had predicted, her stepdaughter had declared her holiday treasure hunt lame and refused to participate. Until Sunny hinted at the special gift card she'd find. Still, the hunting had been done grudgingly and the thank-you said without an ounce of gratitude.

"You are an awesome stepmom. Not a bad wife, either," Travis joked, and kissed her.

It was such a good kiss, he came back for seconds and then thirds. And then he grabbed the remote and turned the TV off. "We should start celebrating your twelve months of Christmas right now," he said.

"Good idea," she murmured.

Later that night she lay in bed, as excited as a kid on Christmas Eve. She was brimming with good ideas. There were so many ways they could make the coming year special for their families and she could hardly wait to start. It was going to be a great year.

4

The afternoon of January first the women met at Mia's house to plan their Christmas-in-January celebration.

"It's bound to be more exciting than my New Year's Eve was," Sunny said.

"I thought the kids were coming over," said Arianna.

Sunny frowned at her half-finished mug of coffee. "They were supposed to but only Dylan made it. He and Travis spent the night gaming and I ate all the rest of the Andes Mints chocolate cookies." Her frown upgraded to a scowl. "I think I have a chocolate hangover," she announced, and took a gulp of her coffee.

"So, what happened to Bella?" Arianna asked.

"Sleepover at a friend's."

"That is hard to compete with," said Mia as she poured more coffee for everyone.

"I'd thought I could at least lure her out for afternoon mani-pedis," Sunny said.

"Teen girls, they're all inhabited by aliens," Molly said in an obvious effort to make Sunny feel better.

"Barely teen. And I'm the wicked stepmother," Sunny explained.

"Ah." Molly nodded knowingly. "The unwanted replacement mom."

"That sums it up," Sunny said, and helped herself to one of the puff pastries Mia had baked for everyone. "She did lower herself enough to go out for burgers at Red Robin before we dropped her off."

"Well, there you go," said Arianna.

"Yeah, that was fun. *Not*," Sunny said.

"It'll get better," Molly assured her. "All girls go through a bratty stage."

"Not me," joked Arianna.

"Of course not," Mia said from the kitchen where she was kneading bread, and winked at her.

"How long does it last?" Sunny wanted to know.

"Till they become moms," said Molly, making Sunny groan.

"At least you have Dylan," Arianna pointed out.

"Who sees me more as his servant," Sunny grumbled.

"That's what moms are," Molly said. "And at least something was happening at your house. At my house it was me and Maisey Yates."

"Who's that?" asked Arianna.

"The new romance writer I'm reading. But I finished with Maisey by nine and was asleep by nine fifteen. My life is one big thrill after another."

"It's going to be this year," predicted Arianna.

"For all of us," said Sunny. "Let's get planning."

"Good idea," approved Arianna.

"You all have fun," said Mia, wiping her hands on a towel. "I'm going to rescue Sophie from the TV and work on that puzzle with her."

"Thanks, Mom," Arianna said.

"It's so great you all are living together," Molly said as Mia moved from the kitchen into the living room where Sophie was parked in front of the TV, watching a kids' show.

"I don't know what I'd have done without Mom. Although I kind of feel like a mooch," Arianna admitted.

"You're not mooching, you're regrouping. And besides, your mom loves it, and it's great for Sophie. Anyway, we all have to hit restart once in a while," Molly said.

"It's been harder to hit than I thought it would be," Arianna confessed. "I'm still so mad at Wyatt. I honestly think I hate him for what he's done. And yet, sometimes I wish I could go back to what we had. It felt so…secure. Even though it wasn't," she hurried to add.

"If there's one thing I've learned, it's that you can't depend on others for security," Molly said. "You have to stake your own tent."

"That's profound," Sunny said in awe.

Molly chuckled. "Yeah, that's me. Profound."

"Someone has to be," Sunny said. "Heaven knows, I need all the help I can get."

"Oh, I'm very good at managing other people's lives," Molly joked.

"Speaking of managing," said Arianna. "What day do we want to do our Christmas-in-January party?"

Sunny brought out her phone and checked the calendar. "The twenty-fifth is on a weekday and that might be a pain getting over to the skating rink. How about we do it the Saturday before?"

"I can do that," said Arianna. She looked to Molly, who shrugged and nodded.

They worked out the details, and then Sunny announced that she needed to get going. "But first," she said, digging in her purse, "I have something for you, Molly." She produced a bobblehead Santa. "For you to take to work. I figure he'll help you keep your Christmas spirit this year, and he might even inspire some of your customers."

Molly chuckled. "Thanks. Maybe he'll serve as a reminder that Santa's watching them."

"Here's to Santa, then," Sunny said. She held up her mug and finished her coffee.

"And to keeping Christmas all year long," Arianna added. What did they have to lose?

The first Saturday of the New Year found Arianna on the porch, hanging the Christmas lights she'd gotten—on sale, 50 percent off, thank you!—her daughter "helping" by holding the tail of the string while Arianna worked.

Both of them were wearing their new bling. She'd found a cute necklace for Sophie with a unicorn pendant and a pretty ring for herself. The stone wasn't a real ruby but it sure looked like it, and the price had been right. She was wearing it on her right hand, and every time she looked at it, sparkling there, it made her smile. *Somebody loves you: you!*

She'd finished with the railing and was about to climb the stepladder and start on the roofline when she caught sight of her neighbor, who had let his dog out. She immediately lost her helper, who ran next door to greet the dog.

"Happy New Year," she called, and waved. Like a good neighbor.

He gave her a wave and called back, "Happy New Year to you, too." He cocked his head. "It looks like you're...putting those up?"

"I am," she said with a lift of her chin. "I'm having a holiday redo—Christmas in January."

He nodded. Slowly, politely. The way you would to someone whose mental health was of grave concern.

"It wasn't the best Christmas ever. Or the best year, so I'm starting the new one off on a positive note," she explained.

"Interesting," he said.

Interesting. That was the polite word for *weird*. Was this whole idea silly?

No, she told herself. Lots of people left their lights up all year long. And she was not only redoing this year's Christmas. She was also getting a jump start on next year's.

He motioned to the string of lights in her hand. "Need some help?"

"No." That sounded abrupt and ungrateful. Shades of Christmas Day. "Sophie's helping me, but thanks for asking. I'm sure you've got things to do."

He shrugged. "I'm about to head over to my folks to help take down the tree and the lights and watch the game."

He wore jeans and boots and a jacket that showed off those beautifully broad shoulders. Stringing lights together sounded so idyllic, like something you did when you had a Hallmark-happy relationship. Except Wyatt had convinced her that there was no such thing.

"Go Hawks," she said.

"You a football fan?"

"Actually, I hate football," she confessed, "but I like Super Bowl parties." Crud in the mud. Did she sound like she was fishing for an invite to a Super Bowl party. "I used to host one when I was with my husband. My ex." As if she needed to remind him she had an ex. It looked like more fishing. Not fishing here. Not even going near the pond!

He nodded. "Can't beat nachos and beer."

"And those meatballs in the special sauce," she added. This was a ridiculous conversation. She clamped her lips shut.

"Well, if you're sure you don't want help."

"I don't," she said. "But thanks for asking," she added, to make sure he knew she really was a nice person and not the lump-of-coal finalist she'd looked like on Christmas Day. Not that she was interested, but she didn't want anyone thinking she was the woman she'd behaved like then.

He nodded, saluted her, told Sophie she was doing a great job helping her mom and then he and his dog went back into his house where life was probably normal and drama-free.

"I like his dog," Sophie informed Arianna when she returned to the porch.

"He's very cute." So was his owner.

A few moments later Alden's truck backed out of the garage and he zipped off down the street. He was probably on his way to pick up a girlfriend to take to his parents' house. He had to have a girlfriend. Of course, he had a girlfriend. And she wasn't interested, anyway.

Christmas in January, huh? Alden thought as he tooled his Chevy off down the street, Buster harnessed in next to him and riding shotgun. Different. Actually, a little nuts, if you asked him. Not that she had.

And that was just as well. It was hard to be diplomatic when you thought someone was nuttier than a payday candy bar. Better to stay away. She'd seemed nice enough when she brought him those cookies, but he kept reminding himself he'd seen how irrationally angry she could get on those porch-front calls, and the last thing he needed was to infuse his life with fresh girlfriend drama. Or even neighbor drama.

He got to his parents' place on Kitsap Lake in plenty of time to help his dad take down the Christmas lights and cut up the tree. His older brother, David, managed to be just late enough to miss out on the chores. His parents made the Griswolds of the old *National Lampoon's Christmas Vacation* movie look like slackers.

"About time you got here," he called to David as he and his five-year-old son, Davie, came up the walk.

"Meg wouldn't let me go until I took down our lights," said David.

Alden shook his head and muttered, "Whipped."

"No, happy," corrected his brother. "Happy wife, happy life."

David did have a happy life. He had his son and a new baby

girl, a wife who laughed at all his dumb jokes and a thirty-year mortgage on a two-story fixer-upper not far from their parents that he revered like a work of art. Lucky dog.

David stopped long enough to help their father roll up and stow away the last of the lights in their red plastic bins and stack them in the garage, sending Alden and Davie in ahead of him. Davie hugged his grandma, then got involved in a serious game of tug-of-war with Buster over a blue chew toy shaped like a bone.

Alden went on into the kitchen to wash his hands and snag a bottle of beer. "The lights are now down for the year," he informed his mom, who was busy pulling together enough food to last them through the game and into the next millennium. His mom loved to cook and since she was always on a diet of some sort, trying to take off those twenty pounds that were probably there to stay, contented herself with stuffing her family instead of herself.

"Thank you, darling. I know it's a big job."

"No bigger than putting them up," said Alden. Although it was more satisfying putting up holiday lights than it was taking them down. "Funny," he mused. "You're taking your lights down and my neighbor's putting hers up."

"Really?" prompted Mom.

"It's crazy. She says she's having a Christmas redo."

"Is this the woman you were telling us about who started the fire and didn't pull out the damper?"

"Yep." That had made for some entertaining talk at the dinner table on Christmas.

"Didn't you say she's single?"

"Divorced," he corrected his mother. "With a kid."

"She probably had a rough year," Mom said.

"I would guess so, from all the times I heard her out on the front porch this summer."

"It's not easy suffering through a breakup," said Mom.

Didn't he know it?

"Your poor Aunt Jen had a terrible time."

He still remembered his aunt sitting at their kitchen table, crying, his mom patting her on the shoulder and telling her she was well rid of Uncle Alan. He'd seen enough of Aunt Jen's nagging and put-downs over the years to wonder if it wasn't Uncle Alan who was well rid of her.

Funny how after Alden had broken up with Cynthia his mom sang a different tune. "I never liked that girl," she said when he showed up at a family gathering alone. "She didn't deserve you."

Alden knew there were two sides to every story. Was his neighbor's ex's mother saying the same thing to him or was he the undisputed villain in the breakup?

"Tell me more about this neighbor," said Mom. Great. Her matchmaking radar was now activated.

"There's not much to tell. She's got a kid and she's living with her mom." *And that image of her standing on her porch with the string of lights is now stuck in my mind.*

It was the leggings. She'd looked great in them.

"Wouldn't Gram have loved it if the house she left you turned out to be right next to the perfect woman?" Mom said with a smile.

"I don't know if I'm going to keep it." *And I wouldn't exactly call my neighbor perfect, no matter how good she looks in leggings.*

"Not keep it?" Mom looked shocked. "I thought you were going to fix it up."

"I am, but it seems kind of stupid to keep the place when I don't have a family."

"You will," Mom predicted.

"Yeah? What do you know that I don't know?" he teased.

"I know plenty," she said. "The Lord works in mysterious ways."

His dad was in the kitchen now, wondering how the cheese dip and wings were coming.

"Everything's ready," she said.

"Good, I'm starving," said Dad.

"I know," she said, patting his cheek. "You're wasting away to a shadow."

"A pretty big shadow," Alden teased, patting the old man's beer belly.

"Hey, that's muscle," Dad said, trying to tighten up his gut.

David came into the kitchen just in time to hear that and let out a guffaw.

"Don't you be making fun of your father," Mom scolded. "He's perfect just as he is."

"Yeah, right," scoffed David.

Alden didn't say anything, but he couldn't help thinking, *I hope I find someone as cool as my mom.*

Molly had gotten a sudden burst of energy after meeting with her Christmas compadres and went out the very next day and bought a Dremel and some red and green paint. She found the perfect block of wood at Hobby Lobby and took everything home and got busy. Two days later her bobblehead Santa was ensconced on her desk atop a holiday brick that proclaimed she was *Keeping Christmas All Year Here.*

"What's that supposed to mean?" demanded Mrs. Bigman as she set her package on the counter.

"It means I want to keep the Christmas cheer going," Molly replied. "Nobody likes a Grinch." *Hint, hint.*

Mrs. Bigman's response to that was a harrumph. "Nobody likes it when the post office Grinch loses their cookies, either."

Mrs. Bigman was not getting the message. Big surprise.

"I'm sorry about the cookies," Molly said. "I checked and verified that they'd been delivered."

"Well, my son never got them, so somebody messed up," Mrs. Bigman insisted. She tapped on the package wrapped in brown paper. "These had better make it."

"I'm sure they will," Molly said. Especially now that the new policy was in place. Molly typed the address in her computer. "I need you to check the screen and verify that this is the correct address."

"I know my son's address. You're the one who needs to be checking."

Molly decided it was best to ignore this comment. "If it is, please hit yes." She pointed to the small screen facing Mrs. Bigman.

"Yes, it is. New procedure," the woman muttered. "It better work this time."

"I'm sure it will," Molly said, even though she knew beyond a shadow of a doubt that the first package had reached its destination.

The package was properly processed, and Mrs. Bigman went on her way and Molly breathed a sigh of relief. And here came her reward from putting up with Mrs. Bigman—Reggie Washington, one of her favorite customers.

Reggie was a big man with a big smile and he reminded her of the husband she'd lost so many years ago. His hair was white and from his regular daytime visits, she figured he was retired. He bought a lot of stamps and sent a lot of cards—mostly, he claimed, to far-flung friends. "Everybody likes to get a card in the mail once in a while," he once told her. The closest living relative he had was a cousin in North Carolina. "Shoulda got married," he said once, "but never found the right woman."

Too bad, she often thought. Reggie sure seemed like a nice man.

Every once in a while the thought flitted through her mind that she wouldn't mind having a nice man in her life to watch a movie with or enjoy a morning coffee with. It would feel good to be hugged by a big man with a big smile.

He gave her bobblehead Santa a pat on the head. "You got a new helper here?"

"Something like that," she said.

"Keeping Christmas all year, huh?"

"I'm going to try." It was either that or run away to the North Pole.

Reggie smiled that big smile of his. "Good idea. The world needs more cheer and not just during the holidays."

"That's what I think. What kind of stamps do you want today?"

"Got any flags? If not, I'll take whatever you have," he said as he pulled out his credit card.

"Oh, Reggie, I wish all my customers were like you."

He chuckled. "Someone should clone me."

"Yes, someone should," she agreed, and pulled out a sheet of stamps for him. "You always make my day when you come in."

"Funny you should say that. It makes my day when I come in and get your window."

Molly felt her cheeks warming. "You are a flatterer."

"Not really. I never learned the art."

"I guess it comes naturally to you, then," she said.

He chuckled again. "It's easy to say nice things to a nice woman."

The woman in line behind him cleared her throat impatiently.

He got the message and paid for his stamps. "Thanks for the stamps. You and Santa have a good day," he said.

Their conversation set the tone and the rest of her day was good. It was easy to smile at people when you were happy.

After work she stopped by the Safeway deli and picked up a chicken breast and some potato salad. Then she went home, slipped off her shoes and kicked back on the couch to watch a rom-com. It turned out to be a tale of second chances and she went to bed wishing she'd looked a little harder for a second chance when she was younger.

Too late now. Love was a thing of the past for her. That sleigh had left the hangar.

Still, it sure would be nice to have someone to pal around with, maybe even cuddle up next to and watch TV. Was it too late to look for that?

CHRISTMAS
IN JANUARY

5

"Christmas in January?" Ava repeated after Molly had called to invite her to the skating party. "What's that about?"

"A chance to get out and do more," Molly said. "With both of you. I'm turning into a lump."

"Of coal?" Ava teased.

"You are cute," Molly said, unimpressed.

"That's what you always told me."

"So, are you up for it?"

"Of course. And it will be fun for Paisley. She's never ice-skated."

"Neither have you," pointed out Molly. "Why didn't I take you ice-skating?"

"Maybe because you were busy working so you could pay the bills?" Ava suggested. "Anyway, you took me and my friends to Skateland for roller-skating and that was just as good."

She hadn't even done that very much. The old skating rink was no more so she'd never be able to take Paisley. She had more money now, though. She needed to start planning more adventures for her granddaughter to make up for what she hadn't been able to give her daughter.

"I never did get you to Disneyland," she said. One of her parenting failures.

"I went with the marching band so it was okay."

"I always wanted to take you myself."

"Is it my imagination or are you feeling guilty again?"

"I should have done more of those big things," Molly said.

"You did the important things. I loved that you were never too busy to spend time with me or listen to my problems."

It had been just the two of them after Booker died, and Molly had made spending time together her top priority. She hadn't had a ton of money to spend on fancy outings but she'd managed visits to Dairy Queen and had mother-daughter baking binges and craft nights and hosted her fair share of slumber parties.

"And you were always there for me when I screwed up," Ava added, and they both knew to what she was referring.

Ava's big love had been a big disappointment, but they'd gotten Paisley out of the deal. Ava had ditched the loser and come away a winner.

"I'm glad you're my mom," Ava added, making Molly tear up. "And I'm glad you're making time to do more stuff."

"If not now, when? Right?"

"Right," Ava said.

They said their goodbyes and I love yous and Molly ended the call feeling excited about both their January excursion and the upcoming year. Sunny had been inspired and they were all going to benefit from it.

The following day Reggie was back in the post office, mailing a card, and stopped by her window to say hi. "You're looking happy," he observed.

"I am happy. I have a Christmas-in-January party coming up. Some of us are taking our families to the rink over in Lynwood to go ice-skating."

"A good activity for January," he said. "Do you like to skate?"

"I haven't skated since I was a kid. No way I'm getting on the ice. I'll break my tailbone," she said.

"You could bring along a pillow," he teased.

"I don't think so. Some things you just shouldn't try."

He cocked his head. "Really? I think you should try everything that comes your way. Otherwise, you might miss out."

Another customer had come in so he moved on, his parting words, "Never say never."

"I'll remember that," Molly joked.

Later, as she was on her way home, she did remember his words. She'd had a good life so far, of course, but she'd also missed out on a lot of things over the years. Widowed young, she'd told herself she'd never fall in love again, so she hadn't bothered to see if she could. She'd told herself she could never afford to take Ava to Disneyland so she'd never made it a goal and saved for it. She'd never taken dancing lessons because, well, she wasn't going to fall in love again so what was the point? Hmm. Maybe it was time for a new pattern. They were all going skating. Why did she want to sit on the sidelines? She'd take along a pillow for her bottom and break that pattern…and, hopefully, not a hip.

The day of the party, Travis and Sunny loaded up the kids and headed for the rink. Dylan was excited. Bella was apathetic and spent the entire car and ferry ride texting her friends. *At least she's here*, Sunny told herself. It was a beginning.

The rink already had several skaters on it. Some were gliding along the ice effortlessly; others were stumbling along. One or two pros were at the center of the rink, practicing the kind of fancy moves Sunny loved to watch on TV when there was any kind of skating competition. She'd always wanted to learn to ice-skate. Now she had the chance. And to do it with…well, one of the kids.

But lo and behold, what was this? Bella had gotten skates and was actually lacing up. Would wonders never cease? Travis already had his skates on.

"Come on, babe, let's go for it," he said.

She finished lacing up and then handed her phone to Molly, who was waiting to get out on the ice until she'd taken pictures for everyone. "Get a video of all of us if you can, okay?"

"Sure thing," Molly said.

"Then I'll take one of you when I'm done."

"Take your time," Molly said.

Sunny pointed to the sofa pillow Molly had brought. "No backing out, not when you came prepared."

"No backing out," Molly promised.

Arianna and Sophie were already on the ice, Sophie holding Arianna's hand and Arianna holding the rail at the edge of the rink. They were both laughing. It was too bad Mia hadn't felt well. She'd have loved seeing her daughter and granddaughter out there. Ah, well, that was the beauty of technology. Molly shot a short video and texted it to her.

Sunny took Travis's hand and they hobbled their way to the ice. Whoa, that was one thin blade she was supposed to balance on. She was barely on the ice before she went down.

"This is harder than it looks on TV," she said with a laugh.

Jock that he was, Travis was almost balanced. "You can do it." He held out a hand and she took it.

"Glide into it," Molly called. "Push your foot forward."

Glide into it. Sunny took a glide and then a slide. Ow! Ice was not very forgiving.

"Don't give up," called Molly.

"Not me," Sunny called back. This had been her idea. She was going to skate before the day was over.

Travis helped her up and they began to wobble their way

around the rink. Hey, she was still upright. She hoped Molly was recording this. Sunny was going to show it to her sister and brag.

Dylan was in front of them, beginning to smooth out of his own wobbles. Where was Bella? Sunny didn't see her ahead of them but she didn't dare look behind her. If she looked over her shoulder, she knew she'd go down. They made it around once with only one spill, Sunny losing her balance and taking Travis down with her. Ow again!

She didn't care. Travis was a good spot, and she was still having a great time. Everyone else seemed to be enjoying themselves as well. From her position sitting on the ice, Sunny caught sight of Bella on the other side of the rink, looking surprisingly good. Dylan had caught up to her and he was making serious progress.

"Look at your kids," she said to Travis, "they're naturals, just like you."

He laughed as he helped her up. "Some natural. I don't think I'll be playing ice hockey for the Kraken any time soon."

A little girl's cry drifted over to them and Sunny saw that Sophie had fallen and was sitting on the ice, Arianna leaning over her. "Oh, crap," she muttered. "This was supposed to be fun."

"She's probably fine. I'll go check on them," Travis said, and skated off to help Sophie and Arianna.

He glided off and Sunny started making her own way around the rink, still wobbly, but less than before.

She was finally getting the hang of it when the human equivalent of a Zamboni crashed into her left shoulder, sending her flying. She let out a screech and put out her hands to stop her fall and her left hand touched down hard. And, oh, pain. Pain, pain. Not simple ow-pain but shoot-me-and-put-me-out-of-my-misery pain. Tears raced to her eyes and she took a couple of deep breaths.

"You okay?" asked Dylan, leaning over her.

"She should watch where she's going," Bella said as Sunny tried to scramble up.

Travis arrived a moment later, and helped her. "What happened?" he demanded, lowering his brows at both his children.

"Bella ran into her," tattled Dylan.

"It was an accident," Bella said. She posed with one hand on the railing, her feet scissoring back and forth. How quickly she'd found her footing on those thin blades.

"Just get me off the ice," Sunny said between gritted teeth.

Travis took ahold of her arm and another skater stopped to help. Between the two of them, they got her back to where Molly was guarding the coats.

"I hope you didn't get that on video," Sunny said as Travis undid her skates.

Molly said nothing, but she was frowning.

Sunny took her phone back from Molly with her one remaining good hand.

Travis took her skates off, then started on his own. "I'm going to get some ice for your wrist."

"Just let me lie down and wake me when I'm better," Sunny cracked. She pulled off her glove and winced.

Molly looked at her swelling wrist. "I think you sprained it."

Sunny groaned. "I can't believe this."

"I'm sorry," Molly said. She hesitated a moment. "The whole thing is on your phone, but I'm not sure you're going to want to watch it."

"Grandma, when are you going to come skate with me?" called Paisley from the ice.

"Now," Sunny called on her behalf. "I'm not going anywhere. I'll watch the coats," she said to Mollly.

"No, I'll keep you company," said Molly. "I'm too old for a fall like that."

"Travis will keep me company. Don't let my clumsiness keep you from having fun with your family. You won't fall if you hold on to the railing. Go."

"I'll wait till Travis comes back," Molly said. She dug around in her purse and produced a pill bottle. "Ibuprofen. I think you're going to need it."

"I think so, too," Sunny agreed as she watched the video Molly had taken.

Travis did return with ice and some hot chocolate, and Molly made sure she took a pain pill before leaving Sunny to Travis's ministrations.

"Any idea what really happened?" he asked.

Yes. She'd deleted the video immediately after watching it. Travis didn't need to know everything.

"We're all out there sliding around on ice," she said, trying not to whimper as he applied the ice pack to her wrist. It felt a lot better on her wrist than it had on her butt.

"Talk about rotten luck."

"I guess I should have quit while I was ahead." She took a sip of the hot chocolate. Homemade was so much better. She wished she were home at that very moment, sitting on the couch, drinking some.

"You poor kid," he said. He put an arm around her shoulder and snugged her up against him. "Here you organized this whole thing and now you're the one who's sidelined."

"At least everyone else is having fun," she said. "And it could have been worse. I could have broken my head."

He kissed the side of that head. "You're a trooper."

She didn't have much choice. She wasn't about to end the party for Arianna and Sophie, who'd ridden with them. Or for anyone else.

"I'll be fine," she said.

"Once we get back, I'm taking you to the emergency room to have that x-rayed. We need to make sure it's not broken."

Sunny didn't know about her wrist, but her heart was. Molly had gotten some great pictures on her phone. There were some funny ones of her splayed on the ice in various embarrassing positions. But then had come the video. There she was, klutzing her way along, and then there came Bella, aiming for her like a cruise missile.

The little beast. Ooh, she'd like nothing better than to…

She stopped her thoughts before they could turn rancid. Bella was a kid—a resentful, foolish kid—but a kid all the same. Sunny was the adult here.

But she should tell Travis. Bella needed to be punished. Kids needed to suffer the consequences of their actions. They needed to be disciplined. They needed to feel badly when they did something wrong.

Sunny took a long deep breath. If she told Travis, it would be one more black mark in her and Bella's relationship. Maybe sometimes what kids needed more than punishment was a gentle poke to the conscience. Maybe if she let it go and forgave Bella, it would help activate that conscience that Sunny knew was still alive somewhere under all the snottiness. And show Bella that they didn't have to be enemies.

The skaters were returning to the bleachers and both kids and adults were taking off their skates.

"That was fun," said Paisley.

"Yes, it was," said Ava. "And Mom, you didn't even have to use your pillow."

Molly chuckled. "I surprised myself."

Sunny realized she was supposed to have taken pictures. Between her pain and her mental anguish, she'd fallen down on the job.

"I'm sorry. I blew it. I should have taken a video of you," she said to Molly.

"Don't worry, I got some pictures on my phone," Ava told her.

"Good," Molly said. "Send 'em to me. I want proof that I braved the ice." Her kindly smile turned cold as she looked at Bella and said, "I got a lot of pictures of you kids, too. Some of them were real interesting."

Bella paled and looked at Sunny like a deer in the headlights.

Sunny cocked an eyebrow at her, and her face turned as red as Santa's suit. She dropped her phone in her purse. "You got so many. I probably won't keep all of them. I don't think I should. Do you, Bella?"

Bella bit her lower lip and got busy putting on her sneakers.

The ferry ride home was filled with excited chatter, fueled by a sugar buzz thanks to the candy Sunny had brought for everyone. Bella never fessed up or apologized, but she did say a subdued thank-you when Sunny and Travis dropped her and Dylan off at their mom's before proceeding on to the emergency room.

Did that count as progress? Sunny hoped so. Too late to do anything if it didn't. She'd already deleted the evidence.

Sophie bounded into the house, excited to share all about her ice-skating adventure with her Grammy. Mia was on the couch, crocheting a granny square blanket she'd recently started in shades of pink and lavender—Sophie's current favorite colors.

"I only fell three times," she announced, plopping on the couch next to Mia.

"Good for you," Mia said, setting down her work.

Arianna settled on Mia's other side, producing her phone and bringing up pictures of Sophie, rosy-cheeked and smiling, wearing the pink-crocheted hat Mia had made for her for Christmas. In spite of having her life turned upside down, Sophie was a happy child. With their worst year behind them, Arianna was determined to keep the happy vibes going.

"Look at you," said Mia. "You're a natural."

"It hurt when I fell down," Sophie confessed.

"Falling can be painful, but each time you get up, you do better," Mia told her, and smiled at Arianna.

That was Mom, always looking for a chance to slip in a bit of wisdom and encouragement.

"You look like you're feeling better," Arianna said.

"I am. Are you hungry? I made soup," said Mia.

"Chicken noodle?" Sophie asked eagerly and her grandmother nodded. "Yay!" she said and hopped off the couch.

"Hang up your coat and wash your hands first," said Arianna. "You going to join us?" she asked Mia.

Mia shook her head. "I'm not very hungry. You go ahead."

"Okay. Do I need to check the mail?"

"Yes, please. I ordered a book. It should be here."

"I'll run and check," Arianna said.

She got a text as she was going out the door.

Sunny: No broken bones. Just a bad sprain. Looks like I'll be typing with one hand for a while.

Arianna: At least it's not broken. Sucks that you got hurt when you were the one who planned this.

Sunny: Oh, well. Now I know I'll never qualify for the Winter Olympics.

That was Sunny, always shrugging off the bad, always looking for the humor in a situation. Arianna sent her a laughing emoji to end the conversation.

She stuck her phone in her back pocket and went to the mailbox, half wanting to skip. Except for Sunny's mishap, it had been a great day. Sophie had had a wonderful time and Arianna was feeling like this whole Christmas–restart thing was exactly what she needed.

Alden Brightman's truck pulled into his driveway and Arianna suddenly found herself stalling at the mailbox, looking through each piece of junk mail as if it contained vital information. The garage door on the house next door went up. The truck pulled in. A moment later she heard a door shut, heard a dog barking, and little Buster was racing out onto the front lawn. He found a bush at the edge of the lawn, marked it and trotted over to the flower bed in front of the house to sniff his way along its border.

And there came Alden. It would be rude not to say hello.

"Hi," she called.

He waved and called a hello back, then sauntered over her way. "How's it going?"

"Great," she said. "My daughter and I just got back from our Christmas-in-January skating party."

"No broken bones?"

"Nope. Maybe some wounded pride. I went down a lot more than I thought I would. But it was fun to get out and try."

"You gotta try things," he agreed.

Her daughter was waiting for soup, her mother was waiting for her book, which Arianna had snagged. Arianna was waiting for inspiration as to what to say next.

"Looks like you've been out and about," she said. *Oh, brother.*

"Took my nephew and nieces to a movie."

Being a good uncle. "Lucky them," she said. Did that sound like some kind of double entendre? "To have such a nice uncle," she added.

Would he date a woman with a kid? Not that it mattered. The last thing she needed was to jump into another relationship when she was still limping along emotionally.

Her cell phone chimed with an old Linda Ronstadt song, "You're No Good." Wyatt's ring tone. *Oh, go away.*

"Looks like you got a call coming in," Alden said.

She frowned. "My ex."

"Guess you need to take that."

What did Wyatt want now? She'd as soon ignore him but there was Alden, being all polite, expecting her to be polite. "Yeah, I guess so."

"I'll see you later," he said. Calling to Buster, he started across the lawn back to his house.

Of all the crummy timing. Arianna took the call with a sharp, "What?"

"Yeah, nice to talk to you, too," Wyatt said.

"I don't know why you're calling. You don't have Sophie till next week." Of course, that was why. "Don't tell me, let me guess, you're not going to be able to see her."

"No, of course I can see her. But I'm gonna be late with the child support."

"What?"

"Hey, lighten up. Stuff happens."

Stuff happened a lot with Wyatt. "You shit!" Okay, the whole neighborhood had to have heard that. She lowered her voice. "Why?"

"Like I just said, some stuff came up."

"What kind of stuff?" she asked suspiciously. Blonde or brunette?

"Just stuff. Shit, Ari, give me a break."

"I'd like to," she muttered. Right around his kneecap.

"I won't be that late with it. I just wanted to give you a heads-up."

She heaved a sigh. They'd be okay. She had some money left in savings and, although she'd insisted on giving her mom something every month, it wasn't like she was going to get evicted if she came up short.

"Okay. Thanks for letting me know." There, how was that for mature and polite? "But you can't make a habit of this," she added. "You don't owe me anything, but you do owe your daughter."

"You don't need to lecture me. I know."

She didn't want to lecture him, but it appeared someone needed to. She took a calming breath.

"Do you want to talk to Sophie? We went ice-skating and I know she'll want to tell you all about it."

"I'll pick her up next Saturday. She can tell me then."

"I thought you'd be getting her on Friday."

"Can't. I've got a date."

Wyatt was turning out to be as subpar a father as he'd been a husband. How could someone who had seemed so charming and fun to be with have turned out to be everything she never wanted? She'd been captivated by his sense of humor and his easygoing attitude. That attitude had turned out to be more irresponsible than easygoing, and it had covered over a thick vein of selfishness. She'd thought he was so wonderful when they first got together, had been so sure when he said, "I do," To those vows that he'd meant it as much as she had. He'd fooled her for seven years.

But it was what it was, and he was who he was, and she was going to have to resign herself to dealing with it. "Okay," she said. "I'll have her ready Saturday."

"I won't get over until late morning," he warned.

Which meant his date was going to be more than a date.

"Fine," she said, and ended the call without bothering to say goodbye.

She was fuming when she walked back in the house.

"Oh, good, my book came," said her mom.

"Can we have our soup now?" asked her daughter.

"Yes, we can," Arianna said, handing the envelope to Mia.

Her mother had a new book, which she would, of course, share. They had homemade chicken noodle soup to enjoy. Arianna may have been divorced, but she'd landed in a safe place. And she'd just celebrated Christmas in January. It had been a great day and Sophie was happy. Was she going to let her ex ruin it? Not even in a parallel universe!

Arianna White's angry "You shit!" reached all the way to Alden's front porch. Like a river diverted, it turned the direction of his thoughts. Only a moment ago he'd been admiring her willingness to try something new, even when the attempt wasn't perfect. But that temper... It reminded him of Cynthia.

Except who could blame someone for being pissed at their ex? Most people were, especially when the breakup had yet to move into the distant past. Still, Arianna's outburst made him leery, especially since it wasn't the first one he'd overheard. Why was the ex the ex? Weren't there always two sides to a story? What was his?

For that matter, what was Arianna White's? Alden didn't know. Did he want to know? It was a good thing he'd be working the next few days. Less chance of encountering his neighbor. With other things to focus on, she'd hardly enter his thoughts at all.

What was her story?

CHRISTMAS
IN FEBRUARY

6

Molly was not having a good Valentine's Day, and her Santa bobblehead and the elf one she'd added to keep him company were not doing their part to lift her spirits. It started with a customer whose card was declined. "It's always worked," he said, glaring at the offending card.

"Try again," Molly suggested. Again didn't work any better than the first time. He glared at her.

"Do you have another card?" she asked.

The second card didn't work any better than the first.

"Cash?" she suggested.

"Cash? Who the hell carries cash anymore?" he demanded.

People whose credit cards weren't working. "I'm sorry," she said. "How about a debit card?"

"I don't have one." He sounded surly.

And he didn't seem inclined to leave. People in line behind him were starting to fidget.

"I wish I could help you," Molly said.

"Well, you can't," snapped Mrs. Bigman, who was back like a bad smell you couldn't get rid of. "Move on, mister."

He turned his angry face at her and snarled. "Mind your own business, lady."

The man may have been twice her size, but he didn't intimidate Mrs. Bigman. She pointed a skinny finger at him. "You are holding up the whole line with your fouled-up finances."

"There is nothing wrong with my credit cards," the man informed Molly. "It's your machine." Yes, it was always the fault of the post office, never the customer.

Okay, enough already. "There's a cash machine at the bank across the street. We're open till five. I'll be happy to help you if you come back with cash," Molly said.

He lifted his chin, gathering his tattered pride around him with a sniff and said, "I won't be coming back here." He turned and walked past the line of customers, calling Mrs. Bigman a name under his breath that made her blink in surprise.

"Well, I never," she huffed as she stepped up to the window.

No package in her hands, only a receipt. Molly knew what was coming.

Sure enough. "Something is very wrong with your system," she informed Molly. "My son has not gotten his cookies. And I overnighted them. Remember? Do you know how expensive that is?"

It was all Molly could do not to say, "No, I have no idea. Do tell me." She held out her hand for the receipt. "Let me check."

Of course, checking only confirmed what she knew she'd find. The package had been delivered. "And you had delivery confirmation," she told Mrs. Bigman, showing her the receipt.

"I know that, but it lied. My son didn't get his cookies!"

"Does your son, by any chance, have some sort of video surveillance? Someone might be stealing his packages off his porch."

"Who would do such a thing?" Mrs. Bigman demanded.

"It happens," Molly said.

"Well, I'm going to talk to my son tonight and get to the bottom of this."

"I hope you can," Molly said, and she meant it. She'd had enough of dealing with Mrs. Bigman's cookie crisis.

In fact she'd had enough. Period. She'd loaded almost every PO box with card-shaped envelopes. Valentines for all! Why it had left her feeling grumpy, she wasn't sure. She'd hadn't received a valentine card in years so there was no reason to expect one this year.

Except…

She turned her mind away from except. Just because a nice man had been coming into the post office the last few months, smiling at her and chatting with her, it didn't mean a valentine card would come floating through her post office window.

But suddenly there was the nice man, wearing a red-checked shirt under his well-worn jacket, carrying a single chocolate rose. "Thought you might like a treat," Reggie said, handing it over.

Her heart fluttered and she suddenly felt twenty again. "How did you guess?"

He shrugged. "All women like roses, and they all like chocolate. Don't they?"

"I don't know about all women, but I do. Thanks, Reggie. That was really sweet of you. You made my day."

"Then my job here is done," he said with a smile. "I suppose you got a date tonight."

Was he just making conversation, or did he really want to know? "With my granddaughter. She and I are going to make bonbons while my daughter goes on a date."

"Bonbons, huh?"

Interested. At least in candy. "I might have some to give out tomorrow if you're in the neighborhood," she said, bringing out a flirty smile she hadn't used in years.

"Then I might be in the neighborhood," he said.

She watched him walk away. He was a big lumbering man, the kind of man who probably loved puttering around the house. Would he like to putter around hers?

★ ★ ★

Arianna's work at the hospital was about more than physical healing. Emotional health was the rule of the day, with patients receiving valentine cards, flowers and visitors to cheer them up. She was happy to see so many of her patients in good spirits as she made her rounds to check blood pressure, give sponge baths and carry out the other varied duties of a nurse. Laurel Peterson, one of her favorites, was recovering from a hysterectomy after having been diagnosed with uterine cancer. Dr. Dimatrova was delighted that the cancer had not spread, and Laurel would be going home that day. But first she had to have a lesson in giving herself a blood-thinning injection. It would be part of her regimen for the next month. She'd been up and walking earlier in the morning but then didn't feel so good. Arianna suspected it had a lot to do with worrying about the upcoming shot lesson.

Now she was feeling better and it was time.

"I hate shots," Laurel fretted. "I can't do this."

"Trust me, you can," Arianna said. "You're stronger than you think."

Laurel saw the needle and whimpered.

"Don't worry. Just a pinch of skin and poke," Arianna said. "You don't have to try and find a vein. You're going to use your abdomen."

"My abdomen," Laurel repeated weakly. "I'm going to look like a pin cushion."

"Don't worry. You'll find plenty of places," Arianna assured her. "This is going to be easier than you think."

Laurel took a deep breath. "Okay."

Arianna showed her the needle and the container she'd dispose of it in when done. She explained how to use it, then she handed it over, saying, "I'm right here so don't worry."

"What if I do it wrong?" Laurel fretted.

"You won't. This is nearly impossible to mess up. Honest."

Another deep breath, then Laurel pinched a section of skin,

poked the needle in and pushed the little plunger. The whole thing was done in a second.

Laurel looked up at Arianna in surprise. "That was pretty easy, actually."

"Yep," Arianna confirmed. "I knew you could do it."

Laurel's husband arrived in time to hear Arianna praising her and came to the bedside to give her a kiss and a box of valentine candy. "Good for you, hon. Happy Valentine's Day," he said.

Amy's Decadent Chocolates, best chocolates in all of Kitsap County. Oh, yeah, those would make any woman happy. Arianna felt a pang of jealousy and had to treat it by reminding herself of all Laurel Peterson had just been through. She'd earned her candy.

"Funny how I let that shot loom so big in my mind," said Laurel.

"Often those challenges of life do, but once we face them and wade in, we find we can make it to the other side," Arianna said.

As she headed for the nurses' station, she couldn't help thinking how true that was proving in her own life. When Wyatt moved out, she'd thought she'd curl up in a ball and die. Yet here she was, still breathing. And more than that, moving forward. Happy with her life. Well, except on days like this.

Normally work was a great antidote for self-pity. Even though she was working part-time, those days she was at the hospital were long—twelve hours. Twelve busy hours of changing faces and needs as she cared for post-op patients. Twelve busy hours of routine sprinkled with gossip and giggles shared with the other nurses. But today was a stumble day. It was hard seeing the flowers that had been delivered to her coworkers.

Ginny Banks, one of the other nurses, was happily sharing the plans she and her husband had for a late dinner. "Brad's grilling steak, and he bought my favorite cookies at Heart."

"I love that bakery," said their supervisor, Karen Hall.

"He's even making Caesar salad. From a bag," Ginny said with a laugh, "but that counts." She caught sight of Arianna's jealous frown and the corners of her mouth fell. "I'm sorry, Arianna. I shouldn't be bragging"

Arianna White, Valentine's wet blanket. "Don't be," Arianna hurried to say. "You should brag, and you should have a great night tonight. Don't pay any attention to me. I need an attitude adjustment."

"Just remember, you're well rid of him," said Ginny.

"I think you should show yourself some love," said Karen. "By tomorrow all this stuff will be fifty-percent off. You can stock up. That way you can give yourself a dose of chocolate whenever you're feeling down."

"Good idea," said Arianna. Chocolate healed a lot of wounds.

When she checked on the last patient of her day and found the woman's husband sitting by her bedside, reading poetry, it made her wistful. That was how love should be. Where were the men like that?

Burnt offering, it's what's for dinner, Sunny thought miserably, looking at the beef Wellington she'd turned into black leather.

Darn it all, she'd been determined to make sure she and Travis had a perfect Valentine's Day dinner. He'd wanted to take her out, but she'd insisted on cooking even though cooking wasn't exactly her greatest skill. But with the internet you didn't need to be an expert. You downloaded the recipe, bought the ingredients, waved your magic chef's wand and said abracadabra and there was dinner.

She'd gotten champagne, a deli salad and a cheesecake to go with it, set the table with the fine china that her grandma had given her as a wedding present and the crystal his-and-hers goblets, also a wedding present, along with candles and a pretty floral centerpiece she'd gotten at Paul's Flowers. She'd assembled her beef Wellington, popped it in the oven and then shut herself in her home office and gotten busy working on a website for a new client.

And lost track of time. She'd been so absorbed she hadn't heard the oven timer go off. Even her nose had fallen down on the job...until the smell of Beef à la Crematorium drifted upstairs to her.

"Shit," she muttered, echoing what had come out of her mouth as she'd raced down the stairs. "Shit, shit, shit!"

Yep, that about summed it up.

"Hey, babe, I'm home," Travis called.

"Shiiiiiiit."

"Where are you?"

"Out here," she called back miserably.

He entered the kitchen smiling and carrying a ginormous box of chocolates. The smile faltered on seeing the look on her face.

Then he took in the mess sitting on the stove. "Uh-oh."

"It was supposed to be beef Wellington," she said miserably, and twin tears slid down her cheeks.

Travis set down the chocolates and hugged her. "Hey, it's okay. It's the thought that counts."

"I have champagne and cheesecake," she began.

"What more do we need?" he said.

"Meat!"

"We don't need no stinkin' meat," he said. "We got each other."

"Oh, you're full of it," she said irritably, refusing to be comforted.

"No, I'm not. I mean it."

"I wanted this to be special."

"It is. We're together," he said, and kissed her.

It was a light kiss...at first. But then it got more intense, like milk chocolate shifting to dark. Oooh, she loved dark chocolate.

"You know what men really want for Valentine's Day, right?" he murmured, kissing her neck.

"Chocolate?" she joked. His lips were moving farther down

her neck and his hands, which had started out at her waist, were moving upward.

"Chocolate-covered wife," he said, and she snickered.

And here she'd thought her big Valentine's Day celebration was going to be a failure. Silly her. Travis was happy. She was happy. And since the kids were both with their mother, there was no resentful stepdaughter around to witness the kitchen fail. Yep, happy V-Day.

Arianna came home to the aroma of chicken casserole left warming in the oven for her. Her mother and daughter were cozy in the living room, Mia working on her blanket and Sophie camped in front of the coffee table, sorting through the valentine cards she'd gotten from her classmates.

"Mommy!" she cried happily, and jumped up to race to Arianna.

Ah, yes, Valentine's Day was more than romance. It was about love. Hugging her daughter and seeing her mother's welcoming smile, she was reminded that she wasn't love-starved. Sex-starved, but not love-starved.

"Did you have a great day?" Arianna asked her daughter.

Sophie nodded eagerly and towed Arianna over to the coffee table. "We cut out hearts and wrote nice things on them. Mrs. Johnson is going to take them to her grandma's nursing home to give out. And we all got valentine bubbles. And I got lots of valentines at our party."

"I can see that." Arianna shrugged off her coat, hugged her mom and sat down on the floor next to her daughter.

"This one's from Carlos," Sophie said, holding up a colorful card with a cartoon dog on it that told her she was pawsome. "He wants to marry me but I told him I have to stay with you and Grammy so I can't."

Mia chuckled. "Once she's sixteen, we'll barely be able to get her to spend an evening with us."

"That's very considerate of you," Arianna said to Sophie.

"I might marry him someday, though, for a little while, like you and Daddy did."

Guilt gave Arianna a painful poke. Was this the message she and Wyatt had sent to their daughter? Marriage was just for a little while? She looked at her mother, hoping Mia might have some pearl of wisdom to drop into the conversation.

"Someday, when it's your turn, you probably will want to be married for a long time, like your grandpa and I were," Mia said.

Sophie shrugged. "I wish Mommy and Daddy were still married."

More guilt. Arianna pulled her daughter's hair back from her face and kissed her cheek. "Daddy and I…" What? How did you explain a marriage fail to a child? "Made a mistake. We were kind of like Carlos, in too big a hurry to get married and we should have waited until we were…better friends. But there's one thing that wasn't a mistake, and that's you," she hurried to add. "We both love you so much."

"I know," Sophie said, and moved on to pick up a handmade card. How quickly children moved on. "This is for you," she said, handing over the card. It was a folded piece of pink construction paper and had a small heart cut out from red paper sloppily glued on the front.

Heart happy overflow! "For me?" Arianna took it and opened it. *My mommy is the best mommy*, it read. *I love you.* "This is the best valentine ever," she told Sophie and hugged her.

"Grammy taught me how to cut out hearts."

"But she made the card all on her own with no help," said Mia.

"I'll keep it forever," Arianna said to her daughter.

"Grammy and me made cookies this afternoon, too. We saved some for Aunt Molly and Mr. Alden."

Arianna shot a look at her mother and frowned. "Did you?"

"We thought it would be nice. I don't think he has anyone

to make him cookies," Mia said innocently, working her crochet hook.

"They're good. Grammy let me have two," said Sophie. "And
I made a card. Want to see?"

"Of course," Arianna said.

Sophie ran to fetch her card from the kitchen counter and
Arianna said, "Mom, really?"

"I thought you wouldn't mind delivering them."

"There's only one light on in Alden's house. I don't think
he's home."

"He might be."

"Cookies as man bait. It's so obvious," Arianna said in disgust.

"No, it's neighborly."

"No, it's fishing. I hate fishing. Besides, he's had plenty of
time to ask for my number."

"Time maybe, but not opportunity," Mia argued.

Sophie was back with her card—another piece of pink construction paper folded in half. This one had a flower drawn on
the outside. Arianna opened it up and read, *Happy Valentin day
from Sophie and Mommy.* "Very nice," she said, "but you didn't
sign Grammy's name."

"Grammy said not to."

Another look at Mia who was still very absorbed with her
crocheting. "Really, Mom?" Probably the last thing the man
wanted in his life was a snappish woman who came with a kid.

"Can we take the cookies over now?" Sophie asked.

"That's an excellent idea," said Mia.

"Sure," said Arianna, resigned to her fate. "Let's put your
card in with them."

The card was dutifully set on top of the cookies inside a plastic
container. "We're not going to make a habit of this," she warned
her mother as Sophie ran to the coat closet.

"It doesn't hurt to be kind to the neighbors. You never know when you might need their help," Mia said. "We made a package for Molly, too."

"Subterfuge," Arianna said. "You're not fooling me."

Mia just smiled.

"You and Sophie could have delivered these."

"I got tired."

Too tired to deliver cookies—a likely story.

So embarrassing, Arianna thought as she followed her daughter out the door. If Alden answered, she was going to tell him they were from her mother.

"Let's go to Aunt Molly's first," Sophie said, and started off down the street at a run.

Arianna followed with a sigh. After being on her feet for twelve hours, the last thing she wanted was a walk around the neighborhood.

"Whoa, what's this I spy with my hungry eye?" Molly greeted them.

"Cookies!" crowed Sophie as Arianna handed over the plastic container.

"Mom's been baking," said Arianna.

"God bless her. I could use a sugar fix," Molly said. "Come on in."

"We can't. We still have another delivery to make."

"Covering the whole hood, huh?" Molly guessed.

"Only you and the new neighbor. He's single and Mom thinks cookies are the way to his heart."

"It's one way, for sure," Molly said. "I've seen him a couple of times. Nice eye candy."

"Candy isn't good for you," said Arianna.

Molly chuckled. "Tell that to the Easter Bunny."

"I love the Easter Bunny," put in Sophie, jumping up and down.

"You know, it's been long enough. You could give someone new a chance," Molly said to Arianna.

"Oh, look who's talking," Arianna retorted.

"So maybe I'm not above looking."

Arianna leaned against the doorpost. "Yeah? Is there something you're not telling us? Maybe I should come in."

"Get out of here and go finish your deliveries," said Molly.

Hmm. Interesting. Was Molly playing post office with someone? Arianna smiled. She hoped so.

Okay, on to the next delivery.

She dutifully rang Alden's doorbell, just in case he was home and his truck was in the garage and he was saving on electricity by only having one light on.

He didn't answer. The only one home was his dog, who barked up a doggy frenzy in the hope that someone would break in and play with him.

"We'll leave them here on the porch for him," Arianna said. "Set them right down there."

"What if someone steals them?" Sophie worried.

"No one will." *We should be so lucky.*

This was the last goody delivery she was making here, she vowed. She was not desperate and she was not interested.

Where was Alden Brightman? Did he have a date?

7

Alden hadn't gotten what every man wants for Valentine's Day, but his mom had stopped by earlier in the day with a giant cupcake—banana cake with buttercream frosting, his favorite—and a dog treat for Buster, and that would have to do. Meanwhile, he had plenty to occupy his mind.

An emergency room was always busy, even on Valentine's night. There was the woman who hadn't discovered her engagement ring in her chocolate mousse and had swallowed it. Both she and the boyfriend had been worried that they'd seen the last of the ring.

"This too shall pass," Dr. Swan had joked to Alden.

Alden didn't think the woman would see the humor in that smart-ass remark. Fortunately Swan had been diplomatic, assuring the pair that the ring would show up in the toilet in a few days. Pretty gross, and Alden vowed never to hide a ring in any kind of food, especially chocolate mousse.

Then there was the couple who had been enjoying a candlelight dinner until she leaned forward to enjoy a bite of cheesecake that he was feeding her and managed to catch a lock of her freshly hair-sprayed hair in the flame of the candle. The burns weren't bad, but the boyfriend felt terrible, and Alden felt sorry for him. And all the other patients who came in with their day sliding sideways.

Of course, an evening sliding sideways beat a whole relationship sliding sideways. He remembered his last Valentine's Day. What a disaster. The restaurant wasn't the one Cynthia had hoped he'd take her to. Really? This was the best he could do for Valentine's Day? He'd only sent her roses and brought chocolates. No ring hidden anywhere. *Very disappointing*, she'd informed him.

About as disappointing as their relationship had become. There'd been no ring because the warning voice at the back of his head had been getting louder. *Think about this, dude. Once you buy the ring that's it.*

V-night was when he finally admitted the voice was right. When Cynthia was happy, everything was great. The problem was Cynthia was unhappy a lot. How did you please a woman who couldn't be pleased? The evening had ended in a heated conversation in his truck instead of a heated session in his bed. She'd told him he'd better get it together or she was leaving. He'd informed her what he had was as together as he was going to get so maybe it was time for her to leave.

If she'd cried, said she wasn't giving up on them, done anything, it would have drowned out the voice. She hadn't.

"I can do so much better than you!" she'd spat. "You're not even a doctor."

Ow. He was perfectly happy doing what he did, being what he was. He didn't need to be anybody's status symbol.

"Good for you that she's gone," his sister had said. "She was like a hurricane in your life, always tearing it up."

She'd been right. Work, with all its drama and chaos, was nothing compared to the stress Cynthia had brought into his life. He was well rid of her.

Even so, it wasn't so easy recovering from the damage she'd

inflicted. Even though she'd made him crazy, he'd still been crazy about her. Her final words coupled with how easily she'd vacated his life had left a wound. He'd spent the last year trying to put those words out of his mind. They remained lodged there, a bullet too close to the heart to remove.

"Love overlooks faults," his mom liked to say, but even she had been relieved when things had ended. "I'm sure there's someone better waiting in the wings," she'd said.

Or next door?

No. Arianna White made his pulse jump, but not always in a good way. She was wounded, too, and wound too tight. He wanted someone mellow, easygoing, with no issues.

Did such a person even exist?

He got home a little after seven thirty in the morning to find a plastic container sitting on his front porch. He picked it up and saw cookies on the other side of the opaque plastic. The neighbors, of course.

Buster was barking on the other side of the door and Alden opened it and let him outside to race off his energy and pee on his favorite bush. They'd have to do a walk before Alden went to bed. Maybe he needed energy for that walk. He opened the container and found heart-shaped cookies with pink icing. On top of them sat a folded kid-made card. He opened it, read the misspelled message and smiled. Little Sophie next door was one cute kid, just the kind of little girl he hoped he'd have someday.

Her mom was cute, too, and for a moment he indulged in a vision of her in a little black dress. All those curves—she would really fill it out. And if she got rid of the dress.... Black bra and panties underneath. And if she got rid of those?

He pulled his wandering thoughts back in line and set aside the cookies. Then he got Buster's leash and started them down the street. Buster was ready to go next door, but Alden directed him the other way.

"No, dude," he said. "We're not getting any friendlier with those guys."

But when he got home, he couldn't resist sampling a cookie. Man, it was good. Had Arianna made them? It didn't matter. He was not interested. Not. Interested.

How had she celebrated Valentine's Day?

On Arianna's lunch break the day after Cupid's big day she made the rounds of the two main drugstores in Silverdale, where the hospital was located, as well as the dollar store. Her mother blinked in surprise when, after Sophie went to bed, Arianna hauled in three bags filled with everything from candy kisses, peanut butter hearts and large valentine hearts filled with chocolates to small cheap heart-shaped boxes.

"Were you planning on reselling those?" Mia asked. "If so, it's too late."

"I'll put them to good use." Arianna plopped on the couch and dug out a large box of mixed chocolates.

"And put yourself in a sugar coma."

"Have one."

"I'll pass," said Mia.

"Your will power is disgusting," Arianna teased.

She bit into a dark chocolate square and the chocolate danced on her tongue. Oh, yes. The day after Valentine's Day was even better than the day itself.

"Seriously, what are you going to do with all this?" Mia asked.

"We need treats for Christmas in February." And wasn't that the beauty of keeping this whole Christmas spirit thing going? You didn't need Cupid, you didn't need a man, you simply needed a joyful heart and a happy attitude.

Arianna showed off her haul with Molly and Sunny when they met at Noah's Ark, a local favorite burger joint.

"All that chocolate would sure make me happy," said Sunny, eyeing it.

"I figure we can use it for our Christmas-in-February party," Arianna said.

"Great idea," Sunny approved. "We can stuff mini-stockings with a bunch of these."

"Let's have it at my house," Arianna offered. "I want to fill it with love and joy."

"Fine by me," Molly said. "I'm too pooped to clean, and I think the dust bunnies ate my Christmas spirit."

"Your bobbleheads aren't helping?" Sunny asked.

Molly shrugged. "They are, and not everyone is a jerk. It's just that I had some real winners in today. I guess it's put me in a sour mood."

Arianna handed over one of the big boxes. "Take this. You can pass out candy and sweeten everyone up."

Molly smiled and took it. "I don't know about everyone, but it will sweeten me up."

"So, what can we do for this party?" Sunny asked, returning them to the reason they were meeting.

"Eat," Molly said.

"Besides eating," Sunny clarified.

They all fell silent.

At last Sunny spoke. "How about making a rom-com?"

"A rom-com," Molly repeated.

"Yeah, our own Valentine's Day movie. We can make something up about…"

"Someone who hates chocolate and learns to love it," Arianna said, holding up the bag.

Molly snickered. "Why not?"

"I think Santa should be in the movie," said Sunny. "After all, it is Christmas in February. Travis can be Santa. You have that great roofline over your front porch. We can get him to stand up there and wave at everyone as they arrive."

"Oh, I like that," said Arianna.

"And then he can come in and make a guest appearance in the movie."

"Who's gonna write this movie?" Molly asked. "I don't even like writing emails."

"The kids. We can help them," Sunny said.

Arianna tried to imagine Sunny's stinker of a stepdaughter on board with that and failed. But the other kids could get a kick out of it. Molly's granddaughter was a ham. So was Sophie. They'd get into it.

"I think that sounds like a great idea," she said.

"I think the chocolate sounds like a great idea," said Molly with a smile. She picked up her shake. "Here's to Christmas in February."

"Yes," echoed the other two.

But there was that old saying about the best laid plans of mice and men again. What mice had to do with anything Arianna was never able to figure out. But she sure understood the underlying principle. Sunny called the morning of the party to report that they'd lost Santa.

"Where'd he go?" asked Arianna.

"To bed. He's got a nasty cold. I've dosed him with meds and he's now snoring away."

"Well, darn," Arianna said. "I was looking forward to having Santa on my roof."

"Too bad we don't have another man to sucker into playing Santa."

Wait a minute. "Who says we need a man?" Arianna dropped her voice and offered a "Ho, ho, ho."

"You?"

"Why not? Get over here before the party and pad me into the suit. I've got a ladder. I can climb up on my roof."

"You couldn't get me on a roof if you offered me a million bucks and a lifetime supply of Godiva," said Sunny.

"Nothing to it," said Arianna.

Sunny dutifully came over early to drop off the Santa suit and pillow padding before heading back home for the kids. "Maybe we should bag the Santa thing. It's supposed to rain again later and that'll make everything slick. You could fall off your roof."

"We have to have Santa," Arianna said.

"No, we don't."

She waved away her friend's concern. "Yes, we do, and I'll be fine."

"I hope so. I don't want it on my conscience if you fall and break your neck."

"I won't."

"You are sooo brave."

Arianna laughed and said, "That's me."

Hardly, she thought when she was donning the Santa costume. She'd felt anything but brave after Wyatt moved out, then after her divorce became final and that double-income budget dropped down to one. Every night she'd lain awake, worry keeping her tossing and turning. What if the house didn't sell? How would she make the mortgage? What if Sophie blamed her for Daddy moving out? Her mother kept things stable for Sophie, while Arianna wobbled on a tightrope above despair, not bothering to get out of her pajamas on her days off and watching reality TV shows. That beat her own reality hands down.

But this was a new year. She wasn't staying down. She had her health website up and running. It was getting a lot of hits, and, hopefully, she'd soon have advertisers. She was coping with Wyatt's deadbeat-dad phase (please let it be a phase). She was creating good memories for her daughter, getting a life. And climbing up on a roof dressed as Santa.

So maybe she was becoming brave. Maybe she wasn't letting silly things like fear of rejection and fear of failure influence her decisions anymore. Just because her marriage hadn't worked out, it didn't mean she couldn't make the rest of her life work.

She let up the garage door, grabbed the ladder, walked around to the side of the house and got busy climbing. Nothing to it.

Oops. Except as she got off she managed to kick the ladder sideways and it fell. Great.

But no problem. She'd have the last grown-up guest stay out and put it back up for her.

She was in place well before the others arrived. She suddenly felt excited and giggly. This was going to be fun.

A fat raindrop landed on her nose. Then another. The morning rain was back. Too bad Santa didn't have a raincoat. Oh, well. The rain wouldn't last long.

Molly, Ava and Paisley were the first to arrive a little before four. Paisley got out of the car, holding a cupcake holder filled with the red velvet cupcakes Molly had made. At the sight of Arianna on the roof she dropped it and ran across the front yard, calling, "Santa! Santa!"

"Ho, ho, ho," Arianna hollered down.

"Santa, it's not Christmas," Paisley called up to her.

"I know, but I found some gifts that the elves forgot to pack in the sleigh," Arianna replied, thinking fast. "I was in the neighborhood and thought I'd stop by and drop them off. They're inside under the Valentine's Day Christmas tree." Which Sophie had enthusiastically helped decorate, cutting out paper hearts for them to hang on it, along with lighted pink tinsel Arianna had purchased online at Kris Kringl, her favorite Christmas shop.

"Yay!" Paisley whooped and raced for the front door.

Molly picked up the discarded cupcake carrier—luckily it had only dropped a few inches from Paisley's hands, so the contents were probably safe and sound inside—and gave Arianna a thumbs-up as they went in, calling, "Good job, Santa. I hope you don't drown up there."

Arianna gave her two thumbs-up in return. "Santa's tough." But Santa sure hated being cold and wet.

Sunny arrived shortly after. Dylan was first out of her SUV.

He merely pointed to where Arianna stood and laughed, then raced on ahead to the house. Bella was next, taking her time going up the walk.

"Ho, ho, ho," Arianna called down.

Bella looked up, stared right through her and continued on inside.

If ever there was a kid who deserved a lump of coal... No, make that a whole truckload.

"What's with her?" Arianna called down as Sunny straggled up the walk.

"When she found out Travis was sick, she didn't want to come. I made her anyway."

"The wicked stepmother," Arianna teased. "Santa will have to bring you a medal for courage under fire."

Sunny just shook her head and started in.

Poor Sunny. Arianna had to admire her friend's determination. Even the new improved her would have given up if she were in her friend's shoes.

Oh, well, hopefully everyone else would have fun. It sounded like they already were. Happy voices and music were drifting up to her as the door opened. Sophie had volunteered to DJ, and had cranked the stereo up to levels not heard since the great smoke debacle of Christmas Day.

Good. And now, to get off the roof, get out of the rain, which was as cold as the Grinch's fingers, and get out of this getup.

Wait! The ladder.

"Sunny," Arianna called. She couldn't have gone in already. "Sunny! Sunnnny!"

Shit.

8

Alden was in his kitchen, cooking up hot dogs for Buster and himself while pulling together his contribution to the gaming party at his buddy's house later that evening—his mom's dip that involved nothing more than onion soup mix and sour cream, which he would elegantly pair with a bag of potato chips—when the faint sound of someone hollering crept through the window over the kitchen sink. What the heck? He looked out the window at the house next door and saw... Santa?

Santa standing on the Whites' roof at the end of February. In the rain. Sure.

He grabbed a jacket and went outside to investigate, leaving Buster inside, protesting furiously.

"Sunny!" cried Santa. "Somebody!"

Santa had a high voice. Santa was... Arianna White. Why wasn't he surprised?

He moved to the corner of the house where she was standing, rubbing her arms, trying to stay warm. The woman had a gift for getting stuck outside in the cold.

"Got a problem?" he called up.

She frowned. "Yeah, my sleigh was hijacked."

"Seems like your sleigh should be at the North Pole and so should you."

"It's Christmas in February," she informed him. "We're having a party and Santa had to greet everyone as they arrived."

In the rain. He nodded. "Of course."

"I knocked over the ladder getting up here, and the last guest went in before I could ask her to put it back up. Someone will come out any minute," she added.

"Someone is out. Which side of the house is it on?" he asked.

"The one nearest yours."

He nodded and made his way to the side of the house where the ladder lay. The grass was sparse on this neglected side where trash and recycle bins resided and the rain, added to what had already fallen, had turned the ground muddy and slick.

He picked up the ladder and leaned it against the roof, then held it for her as she got on. And admired the view of a cute round butt in oversized Santa pants as she started down.

"Isn't it about time to give Santa a break?" he suggested.

"No. I'm not done making up for my sucky Christmas," she said emphatically, and stomped down on the next rung as though stomping out Scrooge's cigar.

"There's gotta be an easier way."

She looked over her shoulder and gave him a scolding frown. "This *is* easy. I'm going to find my Christmas joy even if it kills me."

Just then her booted foot slipped on the rung and she lost her grip on the ladder. Fortunately she was almost all the way down. Unfortunately she finished her descent by landing on him, and toppling them both onto the wet muddy grass. The ladder hit the ground with a soft plop. They both landed with an "Oomph."

And suddenly, there he was, lying beneath his cute curvy clumsy neighbor as she tried to wiggle off him, and some crazed gremlin at the back of his mind rejoiced.

"Aack," she cried, a frantic hand pushing his belly button into his backbone.

Never mind, said the gremlin.

She'd tried to get up too quickly and she came back down on top of him again, this time face-to-face, her cheeks pink with embarrassment and those big hazel eyes even bigger. He could smell her perfume. It would be so easy to wrap his arms around her...

"Sorry," she muttered and made another effort to get up.

This time her foot slipped, sending her knee into jockstrap central, making him see stars.

Get us out of here, begged the gremlin.

"Aaaaah," groaned Alden.

"Oh, my gosh, I'm so sorry."

She leaned over him in concern. A curl popped out from under her sodden Santa hat. A raindrop fell off her nose and landed on him. "Are you all right?"

"Yeah," he managed. *Breathe*, he told himself.

Let's get out of here even if we have to crawl, the gremlin implored.

"Ice?" she suggested.

He gulped down the pain, nodded. His instincts had been right all along. This woman was dangerous.

"Let me help you up," she said.

He didn't want to get up. He just wanted to lie there curled in a fetal ball and hope he'd still be able to father children.

He raised a hand to ward her off. "No. Please. Don't help me."

"I'm so sorry," she said again.

"It's okay." He made it to his knees, took a deep breath and managed to get to his feet. He'd have felt like a fool if all his attention hadn't been concentrated on trying to shake off the pain.

At that moment a woman, obviously one of her party guests, came around the corner. "There you are. We were wondering what happened to you." She took in the sight of the two of them. "Are you okay?"

"I'm fine," Arianna said. "The ladder fell and I was stuck on the roof." She pointed to Alden. "This is my neighbor, Alden. He put it back up for me."

The woman gave him an assessing look. Oh, great, the beginning of the notorious girlfriend inspection. He was in no shape for one of those.

"Nice to meet you," he said. He gestured toward his house. "I'm just gonna go inside and…" *Die.*

"Thanks again. I hope you feel better," said the human nutcracker.

"No problem," he said, and started back to his house, his walk probably looking like a cross between Frankenstein and that old cowboy actor, John Wayne. *Ah, yup, little lady. Glad to be of service.* He *really* needed to stay away from Arianna White. She was hazardous to his health.

"What on earth happened?" Sunny asked as she and Arianna hurried to the garage. The scene of Arianna bending over a wet and muddy man struggling to get up had been movie-worthy.

"Just what I said, the ladder fell when I was getting up on the roof. I was up there hollering like a fool and he either saw me or heard me and came out to help."

"So why were you guys mud wrestling?"

"I lost my footing on one of the last rungs. These stupid boots have no traction."

"You could have lost your footing on the roof," Sunny said, horrified.

"I think I'd have rather done that. I fell on him."

"You fell on him?" Sunny began to giggle.

"Twice."

The giggle grew into a laugh. "Oh, my gosh, that's priceless."

"Oh, yeah. Priceless. I think I damaged his manhood."

"Or his pride," Sunny said and laughed some more. "They're basically one in the same."

"I'm glad you can laugh."

"You guys will laugh about it someday. Is he single?"

"Yes, but I don't think he's looking. And he's sure not going to be looking at me, not after the encounters we've had."

"There've been more?" Sunny asked as they entered the garage.

Arianna started stripping off her wet Santa suit and told her friend about their exchange on Christmas Day. "I brought him cookies and apologized but then he heard me yelling at Wyatt. I'm sure he thinks I'm a bitch. Now, I'm dangerous, too."

"Which makes you intriguing."

"Yeah, right. That's why my marriage blew up, because I was so intriguing. Anyway, I'm not looking."

"That's when you find your soulmate." *With the daughter who'd like to roast your soul over an open fire.* "Does he have kids?"

"Just a dog."

"That makes him perfect. Dogs love everybody."

"Bella will come around," Arianna assured her.

"I keep trying," Sunny said as they walked through the door. Sunny's wrist had finally healed, but Bella still hadn't admitted to what she'd done at the ice rink. Now Sunny was beginning to wonder whether the girl had any conscience to poke, after all.

The party was in full swing now, the gang playing pin the wings on Cupid. Of course, the only one not playing was Bella, who was rooted to a chair in the corner, ignoring everyone for her phone.

Paisley scored a Cupid bull's-eye and crowed, "I won!"

Sunny came over and checked it out. Sure enough. A perfect landing.

She pulled the gift card envelope out of her pocket. "There you go. Winner, winner, chicken dinner."

Paisley took it with an enthusiastic thank-you, and to make sure no one felt like they'd missed out, Sunny suggested they check out the presents under the Valentine's Day tree. All the kids made a dash for it. Even Bella left her chair, but she walked over at slug speed to show Sunny that she really couldn't care less and was only being a good sport. Sunny imagined herself pinning some Cupid wings right on the girl's butt.

Dylan had already found his present and opened it to discover a video game. "Awesome!"

The two girls were tearing into theirs, rejoicing over the crafting kits they got—fairy potions for Sophie and string art for Paisley. Bella opened the small box Sunny had slipped under the tree for her. It was a set of boho stackable rings, fabulous if you asked Sunny. Obviously not so fabulous if you asked Bella. She shut the box without trying on a single ring.

Sunny sighed and went in search of punch. Molly joined her at the punch bowl. "She won't be a brat forever," Molly said.

"Really? You sure?"

"Actually, no. I just wanted to make you feel better."

"Very funny," Sunny muttered. "If we weren't drinking from it, I'd dunk her head in the punch bowl."

"We could lure her into the bathroom and give her a swirly," Molly suggested with a wink as she helped herself to an iced heart-shaped cookie.

The toilet—that was where Sunny's plans to win her stepdaughter's love kept landing. Hurt, anger and frustration all warred in her for predominance.

"Just ignore her," Molly advised. "She's trying to get to you."

"She's succeeding."

"She's enjoying making you chase her. Don't do it. It's only feeding the monster."

"I have to…"

Molly held up a hand. "I know exactly what you think you have to do. You have to be the perfect stepmother. But you already are. You've been nothing but kind. You don't need to grovel. She wants that power over you. Don't give it to her. It won't do either of you any good."

Sunny could remember a few times when she'd stomped off

to her room and shut herself in, assuming her family would be so sorry that they'd been deprived of her presence that they'd come begging her to return and bless them with her presence. It hadn't worked because no one had gone into mourning over her absence. Molly was right, of course.

"Come on, we have a rom-com to write and film," Molly said.

It was a short film, with Paisley claiming the starring role and Dylan agreeing to act opposite her only with the promise of a gaming gift card. The kids came up with a simple plot, which involved Dylan and Paisley fighting over the last piece of chocolate and Sophie, wearing the much-used Cupid wings, stepping in and instructing them to share. It was all so adorable Sunny momentarily forgot about the pouter and enjoyed filming the whole thing for posterity. Dylan's mortified expression at the end when Paisley ad-libbed, saying, "I'll always share with you," and kissing him on the cheek was priceless.

"They're so cute together," Molly said, standing at her elbow. "Who knows? Maybe someday he'll want her to kiss him."

The laughter and applause for the actors didn't lure Bella from her self-imposed separation and, with a suppressed sigh, Sunny moved them on to the final activity she'd planned for the day.

"Okay, everyone, we're going to play *Forgot My Deodorant*," she announced.

"Eew," said Paisley, wrinkling her nose.

"Don't worry, nobody's going to really stink," Sunny assured her. "Everyone move over to the dining table."

The game was really the vintage one of *Old Maid*, but she wasn't about to cast aspersions at any single ladies out there. She liked her game title better, anyway. After all, nobody wanted to pair up with someone who forgot to de-stink the old pits.

Everyone gathered around the table as she dealt out cards she'd already sorted into pairs. Except, of course, the party pooper, who disappeared off down the hall. A moment later Sunny heard Arianna's bathroom door shutting.

The game went quickly, and then the kids helped themselves to more punch and cookies, while Sunny went to see if she could lure the girl out. Not groveling, just…groveling. The door to the guest bathroom was still closed. Maybe Bella had climbed out the window and was now out looking for another party to poop on.

Sunny hovered by the door. Should she knock and ask if Bella was okay? No. Molly was right. She didn't need to feed the monster.

She was turning to leave when the monster spoke, the vitriol seeping out from under the bathroom floor. "I hate her."

Big news flash, Sunny thought bitterly. Still, it was a knife to the heart.

But what came next was even worse.

9

"She stole my dad. If it wasn't for her, Mom and Dad would still be together."

Sunny blinked in shock. Now she wasn't just the evil step-mother, she was also a home-wrecker? Where did Bella get that idea?

Not hard to figure out. Tansy, of course. The Weed struck again. More than anything Sunny wanted to bang on the door, demand Bella open it and listen to the truth. But the girl wouldn't. Truth was whatever her mother told her.

"We're leaving," Molly called to Sunny. "See you later."

Sunny swallowed hard, nodded and moved down the hall to where Molly's crew were donning coats.

"Remember what I told you," Molly whispered as she hugged Sunny.

Molly's advice was great for simple teen misbehavior, but this... How to deal with this?

It explained so much, even her mother-in-law's attitude. Tansy must have poured her lies into Travis's mom, Jeanette's ears as well.

"We need to leave, too," she said to Arianna. What she needed was to slap sense into Tansy. Of course, there was one need that would go unmet.

Anger propelled her back down the hall—anger not directed at her stepdaughter but at the woman who had dumped this misery on them simply out of spite.

"We're leaving," she said tersely and banged on the bathroom door. Great. Listen to her. She did sound like the wicked stepmother. It looked like bitchiness was contagious.

Bella opened the door and glared at her.

"Maybe someday somebody will tell you the truth, but it won't be your mom," Sunny said, trying to keep the anger from bleeding into her voice. "Get your coat. I'm taking you home." Something Sunny was starting to accept her house would never be.

The ride back to Tansy's house was a tense and silent one with Sunny at the wheel as chauffeur and the two kids in the back. Dylan sat with a stocking full of chocolate hearts and gift cards, happily clueless. Bella was scowling and Sunny was fuming. Good thing Travis had gotten sick and asked her to take the kids back to Tansy's a day early. She didn't think she could have coped with trying to create a happy family breakfast the next morning.

They pulled up to the house and Dylan got out, said a careless, "Bye," and started up the front walk.

"I hate you," Bella spat, and hurled her present at Sunny's head before getting out of the car.

The box connecting with the back of her skull was nothing compared to the knowledge of why her stepdaughter hated her. She had no idea how to correct that mistaken impression. And she shouldn't have said anything. She'd only made matters worse.

She held it together till the car door slammed shut and Bella stalked off after her brother, held it together until she was at the end of the block, then she set the tears loose and howled all the way home.

She was still crying when she walked in and found Travis right where she'd left him, on the couch under a blanket with a box of tissues and a half-consumed glass of orange juice on the coffee table in front of him.

At the sight of her, the sleepy smile left his face and he said, "Oh, no. What happened?"

"Tansy, that's what," Sunny said. She grabbed a tissue and fell into the chair opposite him. "You have got to talk to your ex."

He closed his eyes and sighed. "Babe, I'm too sick to deal with Tansy."

"Well, as soon as you're well, you need to."

He coughed, grabbed a tissue and blew his nose. "What's she done now? Didn't she let the kids come to the party?"

"Oh, yeah. Maybe she's figured out it's the best way to make me miserable. Let me see how much Bella hates me as often as possible."

"She doesn't hate you," Travis said wearily, and pinched the bridge of his nose.

"Oh, yes, she does. She just told me. And you know why? Because your wicked witch ex has told her that I broke up your marriage."

He stopped pinching and gawked at her. "What?"

"I overhead Bella telling a friend. Who else could have planted that idea in her mind but Tansy?"

His eyes narrowed. "I can't believe she would stoop that low."

"She's made a lie sound like the truth."

He groaned and rolled onto his back, covering his face with his arm. "What did I ever see in that woman?"

Good question, but beside the point. "What are we going to do?"

"I'll talk to Bella."

"She won't believe you."

"I'll talk to Tansy."

"She'll stick to her story with the kids."

"We'll figure out something." He sat up, looked at Sunny earnestly. "I'm sorry you have to put up with this shit. Do you wish you'd never met me?"

"No." She settled next to him and he wrapped his arm around her waist and leaned his head against hers.

"Don't give up on us, please. You're the best thing that's ever happened to me and I don't want to lose you."

"Never," she said. But Bella was another story.

Sunny was still upset later that week when she went to Arianna's house to do a photo shoot and video. This one was going to deal with helping people work more anti-inflammatory foods into their diet. Arianna was ready to roll, dressed in her nurse's uniform. She had most of her recommended anti-inflammatory foods already laid out on the counter—organic kale, spinach, bags of walnuts and almonds, oranges and blueberries, as well as canned tuna and sardines.

Arianna hadn't been excited at first to do videos. She felt self-conscious in front of a camera, but Sunny had argued that people wanted that one-on-one feeling, especially with someone in health care. "You need more than a website," she'd argued. "You need wide exposure and a channel on YouTube. You're a health-care expert. People want to feel like you're in their living room, talking to them."

Along with each advice post or video, they put up all the usual legal language and reminders that people should consult their health-care provider when making any diet or exercise changes, and Arianna had been scrupulous about citing her sources. But people were beginning to see her as their own personal Dr. Oz and her following was growing, and Sunny was thrilled to be a part of it.

"Want coffee?" Arianna offered and Sunny nodded and plopped down on a stool at the kitchen counter, where Arianna had her show-and-tell ready. "I meant to call you after

Saturday," Arianna said as she got busy with the Keurig. "I'm sorry Bella was such a pill."

"I found out why. She blames me for breaking up her dad's marriage."

Arianna set down the coffee mug she'd just taken from the cupboard, turned and frowned. "Really?"

"That marriage was doomed almost from the beginning," Sunny said. "But it's easier to make me the bad guy."

"Wasn't Travis divorced when you guys met?" Arianna wanted to know.

"No…"

Sunny saw a look of betrayal settle over her friend's face. She didn't even get to finish her sentence before Arianna lit into her. "Sunny, if they weren't divorced, then you did break up her dad's marriage, didn't you?"

"Wait. No."

Arianna's eyes narrowed. Sunny had never seen this side of her friend and she found herself backing away from the counter.

"I can't believe you've been playing the victim all this time. No wonder Bella hates your guts and I don't blame her. You have no idea how it feels to be the wife of a cheater, and you can make all the excuses you want for what you did, but dating a man who's still married—that's cheating."

Sunny stared at her friend. Arianna hadn't even let her finish explaining, had no desire to hear her side of the story.

"I don't believe what I'm hearing," she said.

"Neither do I. I thought you were better than that."

"Now you're judging me? Seriously? I thought we were friends."

Arianna said nothing to that. She dropped her gaze, shook her head.

"I don't need this shit," Sunny growled. "You can find someone else to manage your website and social. I'm sure you won't have any problem finding someone as perfect as you." She marched out of the kitchen, grabbed her purse and coat, and left.

"Fine with me," Arianna muttered as the door closed on her friendship and all her anger from the last year bubbled back up.

She didn't need Sunny and her ridiculous Christmas-all-year-long parties. She pretended to be so sweet but she was pond scum. Arianna had been consoling her, telling her she wasn't the bad guy, and her stepdaughter would realize that eventually. *What a joke.* Sunny was a bitch, a home-wrecking, man-stealing bitch.

Mia entered the kitchen. "Where's Sunny? I thought I heard you two talking."

"She's gone," Arianna said shortly, and began to make herself a coffee. "Can you help me film this?"

"I'm not good at that sort of thing," Mia protested.

"All you have to do is aim the phone," Arianna said. So there wouldn't be any fancy bells and whistles. So what? She could make her own stinkin' videos. She could manage her website and YouTube channel.

What was the password?

"Arianna," Mom said firmly. "What's going on?"

"I'm not using Sunny anymore."

"What on earth happened? You two are friends."

"Not now. You know why her stepdaughter hates her? It's because Sunny wrecked her husband's first marriage, that's why. I can't be friends with someone who doesn't respect someone else's marriage."

"So, she told you that?" Mia sounded doubtful.

"Yes, she did."

"Are you sure there isn't more to the story?"

"Other than excuses? I don't have time for those, Mom. You know I've been on the other end of that kind of thing. You've seen how much it hurts." Just remembering how abandoned and unloved she'd felt when she learned Wyatt was moving on without her, moving on with someone else, a woman…more upbeat and fun, drove the tears to Arianna's eyes. "I can't be friends with someone like that."

Mia hurried to her side and hugged her. "I'm sorry, darling."

"Women like her, they swoop in and make us feel so…inferior."

"It's the men who do that," Mia said.

"The women help!"

"Darling, no one knows what goes on in someone else's marriage. You don't know what was going on in Travis's."

"Nothing would justify him being with another woman while he was still married. Nothing justified Wyatt being with another woman," Arianna finished tearfully. "I did nothing wrong. Nothing!"

Nothing other than come home from the hospital, from her long hours, so exhausted that the only thing she could think to use their bed for was sleep. It was hardly any wonder. All health-care workers had been physically pushed to the limit, including Arianna. And Wyatt had done little enough around the house to help her regain her energy.

Was a phase of mental, emotional and physical exhaustion reason enough to leave a woman you'd promised to keep in sickness and in health? To abandon the family you'd built together? Evidently, if someone sexy and fun came skipping along, someone with energy to burn in bed and no leftover baby fat, someone who wasn't carrying the weight of the world on her shoulders…someone like Sunny.

"Darling, you are well rid of him," Mia reminded her, probably for the thousandth time since the divorce. "You know that."

She was, she knew it. But there were times when that old wound opened. Sunny Hollowell had pulled it wide and poured salt in it.

"I still think you might have jumped to conclusions with Sunny," Mia said.

"You weren't down here, Mom. You didn't hear what I heard." And Arianna knew what she'd heard.

A little elf kept whispering in her ear that her mother might have been right, but she wasn't about to listen to either her mom or the elf.

Sunny had come home, cleaned the bathrooms, the kitchen counters, the windows, removed every speck of dust from every knickknack and piece of furniture in the house. All the scouring and scowling hadn't left her feeling any better. She was still steaming when Travis came home from work. Over beers she told him about her severed friendship with Arianna.

"That's nuts," he said. "My divorce was almost final when we met, there was zero chance Tansy and I were getting back together and you wouldn't even give me your phone number until it was."

She'd been waiting tables at McCloud's Grill House, a popular down homestyle pub that offered pool tables and a wood dance floor. She'd been working there several nights a week to pay the bills while by day she worked getting her web design business off the ground.

She'd fallen for Travis the minute she saw that hard body and easy smile, enjoyed flirting with him, imagined kissing him, been ready to say yes the second he asked her out. Which he finally did. Still, she'd picked herself right back up when she learned he wasn't divorced. Separated didn't cut it. She knew that. And she couldn't believe that Arianna would think so little of her.

"I don't care how rotten your wife was, she's still your wife till you can prove she's not," she'd told him. But she'd told him to check back when he was officially a free man.

The day his divorce was final he was at McCloud's. He'd laid the divorce papers on the table and asked for her phone number. And she'd given it to him.

On their first date, he took her to the Boatshed, a popular waterfront restaurant in Bremerton, making sure they had a window seat and champagne to drink. "I'm a free man," he said. "Consider yourself taken."

She had and she'd never regretted it. They'd waited six months before he introduced her to the kids. It had seemed long enough at the time. Clearly it hadn't been. They'd waited a year to get engaged. That had been too soon, too. Although they could have waited five years and it would have been too soon.

"How about I go over there and fill Arianna in?" he suggested.

Sunny shook her head. "No. If she's going to be that quick to judge me, I don't want her for my friend."

She said as much to Molly the next week when she stopped in at the post office for a stamp for the birthday card she was mailing her aunt in Idaho.

"This is nuts," Molly said after Sunny had explained what happened and why she needed to bow out of their monthly Christmas celebrations.

"It is what it is," Sunny said with a philosophical shrug. "I'm sorry. I was really liking hanging out with you."

"What, you're dumping me because Arianna dumped you?" Molly demanded. "I'm Switzerland. I'm neutral."

"You know there's no such thing when it comes to friendships, and you two knew each other long before I came along."

"I happen to like you both," Molly said. "So this ain't happening, girl."

That afternoon Arianna got a text from Molly. More like a command.

Dinner at Horse and Cow at 6. Be there.

She showed it to her mother.

"I guess you'd better be there," said Mia. "I'll entertain Sophie. She's been wanting to learn to crochet. Tonight will be a good night to start."

So Arianna obeyed the summons. It felt strange walking into the restaurant, knowing it would only be Molly and her, that Sunny would be missing from the table. She shoved away the wistful moment with a reminder of what kind of woman Sunny was. She wouldn't be missed.

Molly had already ordered wings for them, and two glasses of iced tea sat on the table. "We need to talk," she said firmly as Arianna slid into her seat.

"About what?" Arianna asked, suddenly wary.

"About friendship."

Arianna knew what was coming next and her gut clenched. "Who've you been talking to?"

"Our friend," said Molly.

"She's not my friend. Not anymore."

"Then you're a fool."

Oh, nice. Sunny had gotten to Molly and prejudiced her. "What did she say to you?" Arianna demanded.

"What she was trying to say to you. That girl didn't break up a home."

"Oh, yes, she did. She said—"

"That she met Travis when he was still married. I know. He was separated, waiting for his divorce decree. She refused to go out with him until he had it."

"She didn't say that to me," Arianna said defensively.

"You didn't give her a chance."

Arianna stared at the plate of wings in front of her. She'd lost her appetite. In fact she felt sick.

"You know, it's easy to jump to conclusions about people," Molly said, softening her voice. "But in the end, you lose out on a lot. Ask me how I know this."

"Personal experience?" guessed Arianna.

"Yeah, with my mom. She so didn't approve of the man I

chose. Prejudiced woman that she was, she judged him by the neighborhood he came from. In the end, she made me choose between her and him. She was wrong so I chose him. I don't for a minute regret my choice, but my mother made it a bad deal for everyone and in the end we all lost out."

"I never knew," Arianna said.

"I never shared," Molly replied. "It was all ancient history by the time I met you guys. And Booker was long dead."

"He died?" Molly had never talked about Ava's father. Arianna had always assumed she was divorced.

"When Ava was a toddler. He was something else—smart and good-looking, with a smile that could melt me faster than butter on the griddle. But he was stubborn. He loved roaring around on that stupid motorcycle of his. Who rides a bike in LA? I begged him to get rid of it. He didn't. He thought he was invincible. A part of me died right along with him."

"Did you ever patch things up with your mom?" Arianna asked. "I mean, she had a granddaughter."

Molly shook her head. "No. She wanted nothing to do with a biracial grandchild. She missed out."

"Gosh, that's so awful. I'm sorry."

Molly shrugged, took a drink of her iced tea. "I made the right choice. Booker was a good man, a hard worker who loved his family, and he rocked my little world, for sure. Anyway, that's enough about me. What about you? What are you going to do?"

Arianna took a deep breath. "Call Sunny and hope she hasn't blocked me."

"In person is always better," Molly said, and nodded to the door where Sunny was walking in. She got halfway to the table, saw Arianna and turned to head back out.

Arianna pushed away from the table and hurried after her. Sunny was on the sidewalk and almost to her car when Arianna caught up with her.

"Wait," she said. "Don't leave. Please."

Sunny stopped and glared at her.

She deserved that glare. "I'm sorry. I'm so, so sorry. I jumped to conclusions."

"Yeah, you did." Sunny's voice was as frosty as the night air.

"I'm awful."

"You're a bitch. Say it."

"I'm a bitch. I just..." Arianna heaved a sigh.

"Thought the worst of me."

"Yeah."

"Didn't even let me finish my sentence."

"True."

They stood in silence a moment, looking at each other, one still with a hard stare, the other holding her breath.

Arianna broke the silence. "That whole other-woman thing, it left me..."

"Scarred," Sunny supplied. "I get that. I really do. But I don't want to be dumped in the same category as the other woman in your marriage. I had no part in ending Travis's. That was all between him and the Weed. I was never so desperate that I had to go around taking what belonged to someone else."

"I just..." Arianna stopped. How to finish that sentence? Her heart hurt and her thoughts were a jumbled mess. "I was wrong."

"Yeah, you were. We were friends, and you were ready to throw me away like trash. No one should be that quick to judge someone else. There's always more to the book than the cover."

Sunny was right, of course.

"And when it comes to your husband...isn't it just as well someone did take him away? If things were falling apart."

"I didn't realize they were falling apart. How clueless was I?" Arianna said, then burst into tears.

Sunny pulled her into a hug. "I'm sorry you didn't see it coming. Nobody notices a small tear in a relationship until it becomes a big rip."

"He broke my heart," Arianna sobbed.

"You're mending it. You'll be okay. You've got friends."

Arianna let out a small sob. "Including you?"

"Including me." Sunny dug a tissue out of her coat pocket and handed it over. "And because I'm such a good friend, I'll let you pay for my dinner."

Arianna gave her nose a final blow and managed a smile. "Deal. We'd better get inside. Molly's waiting. I guess she texted you, too," she added as they turned back toward the pub.

"Yep, told me something important was happening and I needed to be here."

"Something important was. A big life lesson for me," Arianna said.

"Okay. Dry your eyes, friend. Now, we have another important thing to take care of—our next Christmas party," Sunny said and smiled.

10

"Those Christmas-in-February pictures you posted were so cute," said Ginny Banks the next morning as Arianna got ready to double check the meds she was about to distribute. "Are you going to do Christmas in March, too?"

"We're going to do it all year long."

"It's such a fun idea. And it's nice to see you smiling again and meaning it," Ginny added.

"It's nice to be able to smile and mean it," said Arianna.

The rough waters she'd been riding for so long were smoothing out and she was beginning to feel positive about her future thanks to the people in her life—her friends, her daughter, of course, and especially her mom, who had given her so much more than a place to stay. Without her mother's encouragement she wasn't sure she'd have made it through all the trauma and drama of divorcing and putting back together the broken pieces of her life.

The month wasn't even over before the waters got rough again. On her day off Arianna cleaned the house and made pork chops and baked potatoes for dinner, along with broccoli fritters, a recipe she'd gotten from one of her favorite Instagrammers.

Sophie gobbled up everything, but Mia left her pork chop untouched and chose only to scoop out the inside of her potato and pick at it.

"Mom, you don't want the pork chop?" Arianna asked. Her mother loved pork chops.

"I'm having a little trouble swallowing," Mia confessed.

Trouble swallowing. When had that started?

"How long has this been going on?" Arianna cast back in her mind, trying to remember what and when her mother had been eating. They'd had a lot of soup lately, but it was winter. She hadn't thought anything of it.

"I don't know," Mia said evasively. "It's probably my acid reflux acting up."

That would be a nice, easy answer, but Arianna wasn't so sure. "I think we should get this checked out."

"It's nothing," said Mia.

"Nothing can turn into something. Better safe than sorry. I'm sure Doctor Rogers can fit you in."

"I don't want to make a big deal out of this," Mia said.

"Getting checked isn't a big deal," Arianna said.

First thing the next morning she called scheduling and got an appointment for the following week for Mia. *Mom's right. It's nothing*, she told herself. *Don't go looking for the worst.*

Still, she had trouble sleeping over the next few days, and any fingernail daring to grow was immediately bitten off. What if it was something?

When she sat in the exam room with Mia and Doctor Rogers said, "I think we should do a bronchoscopy," she knew she hadn't been worrying for nothing.

"Do we really need to?" asked Mia.

"I think we should," said Doctor Rogers.

The bronchoscopy was done at the hospital and Arianna was on hand to hover and worry as her mother had a camera fed down her throat and into her airways, looking for something she hoped they wouldn't find.

"It'll be okay," Mia assured her as Arianna drove her home afterward.

Please God, let her be right.

She wasn't. It was three long days after the procedure before the doctor gave them the bad news. "I'm afraid it's cancer," she said to them when they returned to her office. "I'm going to refer you to a specialist."

"Cancer," Mia repeated.

Arianna didn't say anything. Fear had jammed up her vocal cords. Her tear ducts were working fine, though.

Doctor Rogers put a hand on her shoulder. "Yao is really good."

Arianna nodded. She knew the doctor. She was, indeed, good. But this was cancer. Could they beat it?

"I'm sorry," Mia said once they were in the car. Tears were streaking down her cheeks, mirroring what was happening with Arianna.

"Oh, Mom," Arianna said, and reached across to hug her.

The car was cold and the windows began to fog up, but still they sat there, crying and holding on to each other. The whole while Arianna kept asking herself, *How long will I be able to hold her like this? Can we beat this?*

Mia began to shiver, so Arianna pulled away and started the car, got the heater and defroster going. "We'll get through this, Mom."

"Of course, we will. I'm just so sorry to pull you into this mess after everything you've been through in the last year and a half."

"This isn't your fault. Stuff happens," Arianna said.

Still, it didn't seem fair that this kind of stuff had landed on them. Her mom was so kind, so sweet, so full of life.

Full of life. A fresh batch of tears sprouted, this one filled with bitterness.

"We have to be strong for Sophie," Mia said.

Sophie. "How am I going to tell her?"

Mia sighed. "Let's keep it simple. Right now she only needs to know I'm sick."

"Good idea," Arianna agreed. They could beat this. They would beat this.

They stopped at the grocery store on the way home. Arianna ran in and picked up some soup from the deli and chocolate ice cream, her mother's favorite. She wasn't sure Mia would even be able to enjoy it, but maybe it would be some small comfort.

Sophie came home from school, happy and bouncy as usual, and delighted with the idea of soup for dinner. Arianna made her daughter a grilled cheese sandwich to go with it. None for her. She didn't even want the soup. She had no appetite, and the idea of enjoying any kind of food under the circumstances felt heartless.

"You have to eat," Mia said.

"So do you," said Arianna, and they both dipped their spoons into the bowls and forced down a swallow.

"How about some ice cream for dessert?" Arianna said after Sophie had wolfed down her dinner.

"Yes! Strawberry?" Sophie asked.

"No, we're having chocolate. It's Grammy's favorite."

"I like chocolate, too," Sophie said, easily adapting to the change.

"Just a small bowl for me," said Mia.

Arianna dished up bowls for her mother and daughter and passed on the ice cream herself. She wasn't sure she'd ever want ice cream again.

After dinner she helped Sophie with her spelling of words and then the moment couldn't be delayed any longer. Mia had already gone to bed, exhausted, and it was just the two of them.

"Sweetie, I took Grammy to the doctor today and we got some sad news. Grammy is sick."

"Is that why she went to bed? Does she have a fever?" Sophie asked.

"No, it's a different kind of sick. This sickness is probably going to last a long time."

"Does she need cough drops?"

If only. "No, she needs something a little more than that. For the next few months she's going to feel bad and have some icky things done to her. We'll have to do our best to take care of her and make her happy. Can you help me do that?"

Sophie nodded eagerly. "I'll make her a card."

"That's an excellent idea. Why don't you do that before your bath?"

"Okay!" And with that, Sophie was off to the drawer where they kept her craft supplies.

It was one hurdle out of the way, Arianna thought as she watched her daughter get to work.

She held it together until she had Sophie tucked in for the night, then she donned her coat and went out onto the front porch, where she collapsed on the stairs and indulged in a really good noisy cry.

It was Alden's day off. He'd finished a game of half-court basketball with his buddies and had come home and showered, then taken Buster for a walk. They were returning to watch the latest installment on the *Reacher* series when he heard sobbing coming from next door. There, on her front porch steps, sat his neighbor, all bundled up in a down coat, crying as if her heart was breaking.

Oh, no. More drama, probably with the ex. He should go inside, pretend he hadn't seen her.

But he had, and he couldn't ignore a crying woman. "Come on, Buster," he said, giving Buster's leash a gentle tug. "Let's go see Arianna."

He may have seen her, but she hadn't seen him and jumped when he said, "Hey, there."

His ex had always managed to keep every speck of makeup in place when she cried but Arianna White was a wreck. Her eyes and nose were red and her skin was blotchy. She had no makeup on and he wondered if she'd cried it all off. It was all he could do not to take her in his arms.

He sat down next to her. "What's wrong?"

"My..." She let out a fresh sob.

"Your kid?"

She shook her head violently, trying to rein in another sob.

"Has your ex done something?" Probably not. He'd seen her talking to the ex on the phone enough and that would have left her mad and breathing fire.

"My...mom has cancer."

"Shit. Man, I'm sorry. Breast?"

"No. Esophageal. I just, I can't... She's all I have."

"No one else?"

Arianna shook her head. "I lost my father, I lost my marriage. I can't lose my mother. Oh, dear God." She buried her face in her hands and howled.

That was when he knew he had to follow his instinct and take her in his arms. He pulled her to him, "It'll be okay," he said, rubbing her back. "You'll get through this."

"I can't," she whimpered. "I can't."

"Yes, you can. You've got a daughter. She needs you."

"*I* need someone," she wailed, oblivious to Buster, putting his front paws on her knees.

"You got friends," Alden reminded her. "And neighbors. And I happen to be a nurse, so I can help with anything you need."

"A nurse?" She pulled away and looked at him in surprise blinking and wiping at her streaming eyes.

"I work third shift at Saint Michael's. Emergency room."

"I work at Saint Michael's. Post-surgery."

"Small world." He half smiled. But big hospital. It was hardly surprising that they'd never met.

She sniffed, wiped at her nose with a shredded tissue, petted Buster, who began to lick her tear-salted hand.

"Between the two of us I'd say we're qualified to take care of your mom," Alden said.

"I'm qualified," she said, "but it's so different when it's some-one you know. I don't know how I'll cope."

"You will," he assured her. "And I've got your back."

"You hardly know me, and after growling at you and, uh, squishing you," she added, her cheeks turning red, "the last thing you're going to want is my back."

True, he could think of other parts he wanted more. "Hey, I owe you. Those cookies you brought me were awesome."

She managed a half smile. "That was my mom. She used to be a baker and she's the cookie queen." The smile vanished and her lower lip started to wobble.

He gave her a one-armed hug. "Hey, it'll be okay. And I meant what I said. I can help." How could he not, seeing her so miserable and knowing what she was up against? Only the most hard-hearted bastard would walk away, especially when a woman was looking up at him like this one was, her eyes filled with misery.

"That's really kind of you," she said. She took a deep breath. "But we'll be okay."

"Okay. Just know if you need me, I'm right next door," he said, and left it at that.

"Thanks. And thanks for listening." She bit her lip and low-ered her gaze. "You caught me at a bad moment again."

"We all have 'em," he said.

"I've had a lot. I'm really not... I mean." She heaved a huge sigh. "I'm not an awful person."

"Who said you were?"

"Anybody who's seen me lately would." Her cheeks turned pink and she looked away. "I'd better get back inside."

He got the message and stood up.

She stood, too, and gave Buster one final pat. "I may have to bake your human more cookies to thank him for being so nice," she said to the dog. She gave Alden a quick look, managed another small smile.

"Hang in there. One day at a time and all that," he said. *One shitty day at a time. Poor her.*

She nodded and ducked back inside her house.

Arianna White wasn't what he'd thought she was, he decided, and as he walked back to his own house, he found himself wanting to get to know her more, be there for her.

His mom would probably say this was Cupid at work, putting him there right when Arianna needed a shoulder to cry on. His mom had probably sicced Cupid on him. He still remembered her words to him on Valentine's Day. *Quit hiding your head in a paper bag and start looking. I want more grandkids.*

And he wanted kids. He liked kids. But he wanted to make sure he had them with the right woman. Was Arianna that woman? Like she'd said, he barely knew her. But he could at least pull off the paper bag and take a closer look.

Arianna texted Sunny who texted Molly who texted Ava, and the next evening they gathered at Mia's house to console mother and daughter with chocolate and chicken soup and bread that Sunny had picked up at WinCo. While Sophie and Paisley colored, Ava heated soup and popped the bread in the oven.

Sunny had a "Chemo is hard" care package for Mia made up of scarves, body lotion, peppermint tea and antacids for in case the chemo made her sick. Arianna knew the doctor would prescribe meds to ward off the upset stomach, but she appreciated the thought.

So did Mia. "You're all so kind."

"I don't know if it's so much about being kind as it is about sticking together," Sunny mused. "Strength in numbers, right?"

"Right," Mia said, and smiled.

Arianna didn't feel strong, but she did feel comforted having her friends there with them.

Still, friends couldn't be with you 24/7, and it was only her and Mia and Sophie when the next tidal wave of terror hit a few nights later. They were having soup and rolls, and Mia had just taken a bite of her roll when she put a hand to her throat. Her eyes closed and her brows drew together.

"Mom, what's wrong?"

Mia shook her head, choked, coughed up the bite of roll onto her plate. "I...can't swallow."

11

Panic flooded Arianna. "You can't swallow? At all?"

Mia's expression of guilt broke her heart. "Saliva," she said with a weak smile.

"Okay, we're going to the emergency room," Arianna said, forcing herself to sound calm. "Sophie, get your coat. You're going to hang out with Aunt Molly for a while so the doctor can take a look at Grammy's throat. Okay?"

"What's wrong with Grammy's throat? Why can't she swallow?" Sophie asked, worry on her face.

"We're going to find out," Arianna said. A minute later they were all in the car, racing down the street to Molly's house.

"Out you go," she said to Sophie.

"Why can't I go with you?"

"'Cause you'll have more fun with Aunt Molly."

"I want to go with you and Grammy," Sophie protested.

"Not this time," Arianna said firmly. "Say bye to Grammy."

"Bye, Grammy," Sophie said miserably. She got out of the car and slouched her way up Molly's front walk, Arianna rushing past her.

"No problem," Molly said when Arianna hastily explained.

"Come on in, darling. You can watch *Wheel of Fortune* with me," she said to Sophie, and ushered her in.

"I don't know how long I'll be," Arianna said in a low voice.

"Don't worry about it. I still have a spare key to your house. If we have to fetch jammies for an overnight, we will. I'll let the others know."

Arianna shot her a grateful look, then kissed her daughter and raced back to the car.

At the emergency room Arianna explained to the admitting nurse what was going on and everyone went into hyperdrive. Before you could say help, Mia was checked into a room and hooked up to fluids. Arianna had hoped to see Alden, thought maybe he'd turn out to be one of the nurses helping her mom, but then realized his shift hadn't started. It added to her devastation. She'd worked in this hospital for years, but Emergency wasn't her area, and she longed to see a familiar face. His familiar face.

She was thankful that a bed had been found so quickly for her mom, but it was the only thing she could think to be thankful for. "Oh, Mom," she whispered as she held Mia's hand.

Mia squeezed hers. "It will be okay."

If she lost her mother, nothing would ever be okay again.

It looked like it was going to be a long night, and since Molly had to work in the morning, Sunny volunteered to take Sophie home to Mia's house and stay with her there.

"When's Mommy coming home?" Sophie asked.

"It might be a while, sweetie," Sunny said to her. "Your Grammy needs some extra help and your mommy wants to stay with her."

"Grammy's sick," Sophie said.

"Yes, she is."

"When will she get better?" Sophie wanted to know.

With cancer, it wasn't a question of when but if. How to answer this question? Would Arianna want her to lie?

She opted for vague. "I don't know. But your mommy's working real hard to help her."

It was the right answer. Sophie nodded. "Mommy's a nurse. She's good at taking care of people."

"Yes, she is," Sunny agreed. "So, missy, I bet it's getting close to bedtime. Does your mom have you take a bath before bed?"

"Yes. And then we read a story."

"How about I read with you tonight?" Sunny offered.

Sophie frowned, but then said a resigned, "Okay."

Later, as they sat side by side, reading one of Suzanne Selfors's latest children's books, Sunny couldn't help wishing they were doing it under happier circumstances. Arianna hadn't checked in with anyone yet, and in this case Sunny worried that no news didn't mean good news. It put her own problems in perspective. What was a bratty teen compared to a life-threatening illness? Hopefully Bella would eventually grow up and come around to seeing Sunny as a friend and not an invader. But Arianna's story didn't look as hopeful. If Mia died...

The story ended and it was time for bedtime prayers. "And God bless Grammy and make her all better," Sophie finished. "Now Grammy will be just fine," she told Sunny as Sunny tucked her in.

"You sleep well now," was all Sunny could think to say to that.

She'd just come downstairs when Arianna texted her. On my way home.

Fifteen minutes later she was walking through the door. She didn't bother to take off her coat, simply fell onto the nearest chair.

"So, I guess they're keeping her," Sunny said, stating the obvious.

Arianna nodded, pinched the bridge of her nose. "They have her sedated and are giving her vital fluids."

"What happens now?"

"I'll go back first thing in the morning and find out. I wanted to stay but…" Her words trailed off.

"You could have. I'd have spent the night."

"I know, and thank you," Arianna said. "I thought about it, but if Sophie woke up and I still wasn't here, I didn't want her to panic."

"So far, she's doing great," Sunny said. "She did ask me when Mia was going to get better."

"What did you say?"

"I told her the truth, that I didn't know."

Arianna nodded. "Good answer." She fell silent a moment, staring off at something, most likely the scary future.

Sunny tried to find some profoundly comforting words to fill the silence, but none came to mind. The best she could do was, "I'm sorry."

Arianna nodded. "I really appreciate you hanging here. I…" She bit her lip and her eyes filled with tears. "I'm sorry I was so awful to you."

Sunny waved away the apology. "We already settled that."

Arianna leaned her elbows on her knees and dragged her fingers through her hair. "I don't know what I'll do if I lose Mom."

"Let's not go there."

Arianna sighed, nodded.

"You got any OTC sleep meds here?" Sunny asked.

Arianna looked up, almost unseeing. "Sleep?"

"Yeah, that thing you need if you're going to cope with difficult circumstances."

Arianna shook her head. "I'll be okay."

"I'll be back," Sunny said. She grabbed her purse and coat and left, drove to the nearby Walgreens and bought a couple different kinds of sleep aids. Hopefully one of them would work. Fifteen minutes later she was back at Arianna's house, showing her the two different packages. "Choose one."

Arianna frowned, shook her head.

"You're going to have a lot to deal with tomorrow. You need sleep."

Arianna sighed, took one of the boxes and Sunny went for a glass of water. "Drop Sophie off whenever you're ready tomorrow morning and I'll get her to school. I can pick her up after for you and she can spend the night at my house if you need her to."

"I can't let you do that," Arianna protested.

"Sure you can. That's what friends are for."

Arianna smiled up at her, tears in her eyes. "Thank you."

"It'll be fun having a kid at the house who actually likes being with me," Sunny said. "Anyway, you'd do the same for me."

"I would. Thank you for being my friend."

"Of course. Molly and Ava are here for you, too, so whatever you need, don't be afraid to ask. Okay?"

Arianna nodded.

"Take your pill and call me in the morning," Sunny said.

She stayed long enough to make sure Arianna took the pill, then she left.

She had a lot to think about on her drive home. Yes, she had her problems, but her mom was alive and well and she had a husband who loved her. She had a lot for which to be grateful. Having so much made her rich, and with a rich life came the responsibility to help those in need.

She thought about the twelve months of Christmas they'd committed to celebrating. Giving was such a big part of the holiday. It looked like over the next few months she and the other members of their little holiday band were going to be giving in ways they hadn't anticipated.

The pill helped for a while, but then, in the wee hours Arianna was awake, staring into the darkness, tears sliding down the sides of her face. How could this be happening? Why was it happening? Hadn't it been enough that she'd had to cope with a falling apart marriage and a divorce? This wasn't right.

Life doesn't always go the way you want, her mother had told her often enough, *but it's still good.*

How could she see the good when the bad was looming right in front of her face, blocking her view of anything else?

At five o'clock she dragged herself out of bed and made coffee. At five thirty she showered. At six o'clock she got Sophie up and told her to get dressed. At six fifteen she called Sunny, who answered with a mumbled, "Hello."

"I'm sorry to wake you," she said.

"I'm awake," Sunny lied. "Bring her on over. I'll make pancakes."

"Great. She loves pancakes," Arianna said.

She went to Sophie's room to get her and found her in her underwear and T-shirt, sitting on the floor, using one of her socks as a puppet and talking to it. "And then the princess turned the mean boy into a toad."

Lack of sleep combined with worry were a recipe for impatience. "Sophie, what are you doing? You were supposed to be getting dressed," Arianna snapped. She bent and yanked the sock off her daughter's hand. "Honey, we don't have time for this."

"Mommy, don't," Sophie protested.

Arianna ignored it and slipped the defunct sock puppet on her daughter's foot. "We have to get going and I find you in here playing."

"I wasn't playing. I was turning Timmy Timmons into a toad," Sophie protested, and began to cry.

There was no time to find out what Timmy had done to deserve a life sentence as a toad. "You can't turn people into toads. It's not nice." Arianna pulled a pair of pink leggings from the dresser drawer.

"I don't want to wear those!"

"Okay, you pick," Arianna said, trying desperately to stay patient.

Sophie went to her dresser and stood, regarding the choices in the drawer.

"Now." Arianna's voice came out harsh. Total patience fail. She'd probably be the next one to get turned into a toad.

Sophie sat down on the floor and began to cry. "You're being mean."

"And you're being naughty," Arianna said, in no mood to admit her own guilt. "Now, come on, stand up."

Sophie stood, still crying, and stepped into the pink leggings. "I'm gonna tell Grammy you're being mean."

She was, and she suddenly wanted to cry, too. "I'm sorry, baby. I am. But please, we have to get going. I need to get to the hospital."

"To see Grammy? I want to come."

"You have to go to school."

"I don't want to go to school," Sophie said with a pout.

"And I don't want to go to work," Arianna said. "But we both have to. Now, go brush your teeth."

"But I haven't had breakfast."

"I know. You're going to Sunny's and she's going to make you pancakes."

"But I always brush my teeth after breakfast."

"We have extra toothbrushes in the bathroom drawer. You can take one of those with you and brush your teeth at Sunny's after breakfast. Okay? Now, come on, let's hurry."

Sophie didn't know the meaning of the word, and Arianna had ground down her molars by the time they finally got out the door. It was a hasty drop-off and a heartfelt thank-you at Sunny's house, then she was racing to the hospital, hoping to squeeze in a few moments with her mom before her shift started. It would be a very few.

Her mother was awake and looking haggard when Arianna

popped into her room. "I'm sorry I wasn't there to help with Sophie," she said.

"It's okay. She's at Sunny's house, eating pancakes. They won't be as good as yours, though," Arianna added.

Mia managed a weak smile. "Mine are nothing special."

"Yes, they are." Everything Mia did was special.

Great. Here came the tears again. "Oh, Mom."

"Don't cry. You'll depress your patients," said Mia.

Arianna gave her a watery smile and kissed her forehead. "I'll be back on my break."

She was just leaving when Alden showed up. "I saw your mom was admitted last night. Didn't get a chance to see her. How's she doing?"

"Not good. She couldn't swallow her food. I'll know more when I talk to the doctor."

He gave her arm a comforting rub. "Hang in there. You know she's in good hands here."

All Mia could do was nod.

"I'm done with my shift. I'll stay with your mom for a while," he said.

Probably all he wanted to do was go home and get some sleep, but she wasn't about to turn down his offer. "Thanks."

She hated to leave her mother, but at least Mia had someone to keep her company. Arianna left reluctantly.

"Oh, my gosh, Arianna, what are you doing here?" said her coworker Ginny when Arianna told her about Mia. "We can cover for you. Go sit with your mom. You don't want to miss the doctor."

She thanked Ginny, finished her rounds, then went to check on her mother. Alden had left but the doctor had arrived. Dr. Yao was one of her favorites. A petite woman with long thick hair, she was a powerhouse when it came to medicine and Arianna knew they couldn't have been in better hands.

Still, it wasn't a comforting conversation.

"I wish I had better news for you," the doctor finished. "The tumor has taken hold and spread up the esophagus, creating nodules, and they're too well-defined for surgery or radiation. But we can do chemo. We'll be putting in the feeding tube today. Then the next step will be the port for chemo."

A feeding tube. Chemo. They had a fight on their hands, a fight against both cancer and time. Arianna nodded, shoved away the panic coming at her.

But it kept coming, rushing toward her in waves as she stayed with her mother while they got her prepped for surgery. "We'll get through this," Arianna told herself as they wheeled Mia away. She only wished she could believe what she was saying.

The empty bed felt...ominous. She went in search of her supervisor.

"I need to take sick leave," she finished. She had three weeks' worth. It wasn't much considering what they were facing, but it was better than nothing.

"Of course, you do," said Karen.

"I'm sorry. I know we're short-staffed," Arianna said.

"You'd be sorrier if you weren't there for your mom. We'll work it out," Karen assured her.

"I'll finish out today," Arianna promised.

Mia came through her surgery fine and was maintaining a positive attitude when Arianna came to sit with her. Arianna not so much. She'd dealt with feeding tubes, but it was different seeing one in her own mother.

"It'll be okay," Mia said, patting her hand.

"What if it's not?" *Oh, great. Way to comfort your mother.*

"Darling, you are jumping ahead to bridges we don't have to cross for a long time."

"I know. I just... Oh, Mom. You have to fight this and win."

"I'm going to do my best."

Dr. Yao stopped by to see how the patient was doing. "She's a champ," Arianna said.

"Yes, you are," Dr. Yao said to Mia. "We should give you a medal for bravery."

Arianna knew she wouldn't be getting one. She got the doctor aside and raised the guilty concern that had been burning at the back of her mind. "I'm a nurse. I should have seen this."

"Don't beat yourself up," said the doctor. "Once this takes hold, it moves fast."

"Mom never said anything."

"She probably didn't want to worry you."

"She thought it was acid reflux."

The doctor nodded. "People often misdiagnose themselves. Sadly, they either don't want to bother their loved ones or they don't want to go to their doctor and look foolish so they wait to do something. Try not to worry. We're going to treat this as aggressively as we can."

It was the best the doctor could promise. Arianna wished she could promise more.

Sophie was in good hands, so Arianna spent the night in her mother's room on a little foldout sofa. Alden came up on his break, appearing like a guardian angel in scrubs, bringing her a vending machine candy bar and a bag of chips.

"I figured you wouldn't leave. This is good for when you're in the trenches," he said, which was exactly where she felt she was. "Hang in there. You'll get through this," were his parting words as he went back to the emergency room.

She wasn't so sure. Every little moan her mother made woke her up and had her standing by the beside, checking monitors. Every nurse's visit she was awake and watching. By seven the next morning she felt like she had sand in her eyes and her head ached.

She brought Mia home later that day, along with the flowers Molly had sent to the hospital. Before bringing her mother home, Arianna talked to Sophie on the phone and did her best to prepare her.

"You can kiss Grammy but don't hug her. The doctors had to fix her and she's sore," Arianna cautioned when Sophie rushed toward Mia.

"I'm sorry you're sick, Grammy," Sophie said, stopping short of falling onto Mia, who was in bed. She handed her the folded construction paper card she'd made. "This is for you."

"This is lovely," Mia said. "Thank you, sweetie."

"Want me to read you a story?" Sophie offered.

Mia looked like what she really wanted was to sleep, but she nodded and said, "That would be nice," and Sophie ran to get one of her beginning reader books.

"One story only," Arianna called after her. "Grammy needs to rest."

So did Mommy but that wasn't going to happen. She was too wound up, anyway.

She tried to find a time when she could discreetly deliver the needed nourishment to her mother without Sophie underfoot, but no matter how many times she sent Sophie to another part of the house on some made-up errand, she boomeranged back faster than a fighter jet.

Now she was back again, gawking. "What is that?" she asked, pointing to the apparatus.

"This is a special way of feeding Grammy that we have to do right now," Arianna said.

"Does it hurt?" Sophie wanted to know.

"No," said Mia. "Only my pride," she added sadly.

Arianna had barely gotten her mom taken care of when Sunny called to tell her not to worry about making dinner. "We've got it covered."

"Thank you," Arianna said. What would she have done without her friends?

Ava showed up at six o'clock with a Costco lasagna, French bread and a salad. "I figured if you have leftovers, you can freeze them," she said to Arianna.

"It's only Sophie and me eating, so I'm sure we will," Arianna told her. "Thank you."

They did, indeed, have leftovers, and Molly added to the food pile by bringing over mac and cheese and a salad the next day. "This and what Ava brought yesterday will probably last us for a while," she said to Molly.

"Are we smothering you in food?" Molly asked.

"A little."

"Okay, I'll tell Sunny. She's taken over as Food General. You look awful, by the way. I don't suppose you're sleeping."

"Sleep's overrated."

"Yes, until you collapse. Use those pills Sunny bought you," Molly instructed.

"I will," Arianna lied.

The next day Sunny brought over a baby monitor. "This way you can sleep and you won't have to worry about not hearing Mia if she needs something."

Arianna thanked her. "I don't know why I didn't think of that."

"Probably because your brain is fried."

"My everything is fried," Arianna said.

Molly and Sunny weren't their only visitors. Alden came over later the next evening after Sophie was in bed and was happy to eat some of the leftover lasagna. He'd also brought his computer, loaded with a selection of rom-coms for Arianna and Mia to choose from.

"Thought you might need some distraction," he said.

"Thanks. That was really nice of you," Arianna said.

He shrugged off her compliment with a joke. "That's me, Mr. Nice Guy."

"You are," said Arianna. *How is it you're still single?* She wanted to come right out and ask but didn't let herself. She wasn't looking and he wasn't interested, just being kind.

With his arrival, Mia insisted she was ready to go to bed. "You're a good neighbor," she said to Alden before leaving them.

"Not really. I just got bored over there by myself," he told her. As if he had no life.

"And you lie beautifully," Mia said, before starting up the stairs.

His only response to that was a chuckle.

"I bet you haven't been sleeping much," he said to Arianna as he connected his computer to her TV.

"What was your first clue?" she cracked.

"The raccoon eyes."

She gave a bitter snort. "Raccoons are cute."

"Even raccoons need to sleep."

"I know," she said. "I'm pooped when I lie down but then I can't turn my mind off."

"Sometimes you need to give your mind a vacation. So, how about it? What should we watch?"

You. He was very watchable. "I don't care," she said. "You pick."

"Rom-com."

"Really?"

"Hey, I like rom-coms."

So there they sat on the couch, him slouching with his legs stretched out, her curled around a sofa pillow, watching characters move about on the screen, him making silly comments to amuse her. Then, of course, there was the big kiss scene, which could have felt a little awkward, but he lightened it up by wondering how often actors had to use mouthwash before filming scenes like that.

Her eyelids began to feel like they were being dragged down with lead weights, and she realized she'd dozed off and missed the ending scene when she felt his hand on her shoulder. He'd already packed up his computer.

"Time to go to bed," he said.

"With you?" she mumbled. Then realized what she'd said. Her whole face caught fire and her eyes popped open so wide that it was a wonder her eyeballs weren't falling out. "Sorry, I was dreaming." Okay, that didn't sound much better. The flame on her face turned into a three-alarm fire.

He smiled and picked up her phone, put his contact info in it. "Call me if you need anything."

She needed everything. She needed her mother to get well. She needed a good night's sleep. She probably needed a shower. She wouldn't have minded him joining her in the shower. *Don't say that out loud!*

"I don't know how to thank you." Well, she could think of a way. *Don't say that out loud, either!*

"Hey, what are neighbors for?"

Of course, it was a rhetorical question, so she didn't make any suggestions. Tumbling into bed to try to find sleep again, she realized she wanted something more than sex. She wanted someone to hold her until she fell asleep, wanted someone spooning next to her who could sweep her hair out of her face, kiss her softly and say, "I'm right here."

She shot up a prayer shaped like a whimper. "How am I supposed to get through this?"

She could have sworn she heard her mother whisper, "Have faith. You will."

She supposed, in the end, she had no choice.

Alden took Buster for a walk, all the while thoughts of Arianna White walking along with him. He came back home and played some late-night *Call of Duty* but tired of it quickly. It was hard to concentrate when all he could think about was Arianna and what she and her mom were facing. Arianna White, he'd come to see, was not the drama queen he'd first thought she was. She was simply a woman trying the best she could to rebuild her life after a broken marriage, and now she'd been dealt a new rotten hand. It was a hand no one should have to play alone. He was going to make sure she didn't.

He pulled out his phone, went online and ordered flowers to be delivered to her house the next day. For the card he typed, *I've got your back.*

Early that afternoon he got a text from her. The flowers are amazing. I could kiss you.

Arianna White kissing him, there was a vision to hang on to. He didn't dare put the moves on her, though. Not when she was coping with so much with her mom.

Anyway, it wouldn't be fair to her, because he still felt twitchy about throwing the dice on a new relationship. But he sure wanted to.

Bad fingers! Why had she texted that to Alden? She had to be out of her mind. He was a neighbor who was being nice to her, nothing more. She couldn't go romanticizing a new friendship into a blooming romance. That way lay heartbreak and she already had enough on her emotional plate.

"I hate that you're having to do this," Mia said as Arianna put the formula in her feeding tube.

"You took care of me. I owe you," Arianna joked.

Mia sighed.

"Anyway, I'm a nurse, remember? I do this kind of thing all the time."

"Not to your own mother. Next I'll be in diapers and you'll be changing those."

"Hey, let's not rush things," Arianna said.

Mia smiled at her. It was a grateful smile but trimmed with sadness and embarrassment. "I don't know what I did to deserve such a wonderful daughter."

"How about being a wonderful mother?"

A mother she didn't want to lose. *Oh, no. Don't think that.*

"No tears," Mia said sternly.

"No tears," Arianna repeated, and blinked them back.

"Who were the flowers from?"

Here was a much more pleasant subject. "Our neighbor."

"Alden?"

Arianna nodded.

"What a sweet man."

"Yes, he is," Arianna agreed.

"I think he's interested in you."

"No, he's not. He's simply trying to make us feel better."

"Us? Was that *us* he was on the couch with last night?"

"Only because you went to bed. It didn't mean anything," Arianna insisted.

"It could. You never know. Just be open, darling."

Just be open. Did she dare?

CHRISTMAS
IN MARCH

12

February celebrating was over and it was time to fill a new month with Christmas spirit.

"What are you planning for Christmas in March?" Mia asked as Arianna inserted the formula into her feeding tube.

"I'm not planning anything," Arianna replied. "We've got too much going on."

"Too much going on to take time to enjoy life?" Mia cocked an eyebrow.

"Yes, as a matter of fact." As if Arianna could enjoy anything at this point.

Mia laid a hand on her arm. "Darling. Please. Don't do this."

"What?"

"Don't let your entire life revolve around my sickness."

It was impossible not to. That was how it was when someone was battling a serious disease. It never affected only the person who was sick. The whole family got sucked into the tornado. And, as far as Arianna was concerned, that was how it should be. No one should have to suffer alone, especially not her mother, who was the sweetest woman she knew.

"How much of your life revolved around me when I was growing up?" she argued.

"That was different."

"Different but the same. You've always been there for me. Why wouldn't I want to be there for you?"

"I don't want this to consume you," Mia said.

"Right now, getting you well is the most important thing in my life."

"But it can't be the only thing. You have a daughter, you have friends…"

"Who understand and who also want to be there for you."

"And make me happy?"

"Of course," said Arianna.

"It would make me very happy if you'd keep doing your monthly Christmas celebrations."

Arianna shook her head at her mother. "Very sneaky."

"I mean it. I want to see you keep doing this, and I want to be part of it whenever I'm feeling up for it. I think by the end of the month I'll be ready for a little fun."

"You think so?"

"Yes," Mia said emphatically. "Life isn't all storms and thunder. Let's enjoy the moments of sunshine as well. They're good for the soul."

Moments of sunshine, of course. She'd been so focused on her mother's physical health she'd completely forgotten about her emotional health.

"Okay, we'll do something in March."

"Actually, I want to do a couple of things in March."

"Name it," said Arianna. Whatever her mother wanted, she'd make it happen.

"I want to shave my head."

Arianna's hand stilled. "You do?"

"I've heard enough about what chemo does and I don't want to stand in the shower and watch my hair fall out in clumps. I want to attack this thing that's attacking me."

"Oh, Mom," Arianna said tearfully. Her mother's hair was thick, mostly still brown, with only a few gray hairs. She was such a pretty woman. It was hard to imagine her with no hair. It would happen, though. Arianna had seen it enough times to know that some hair loss and chemo often went hand in hand, and she had to admire her mother's determination not to let that loss get her down.

"I have those scarves Sunny gave me, and I think I'll buy a wig. Maybe blond. I always wanted to be a blond."

"Okay, I'll call Michael."

Michael Lowenstein at Ross Michael Salon had been doing her mother's hair and hers for years. He could give a great haircut in his sleep and was a genius when it came to hair color. He'd become a family friend, and Arianna was sure he'd be the right person to shave Mia's head.

"I think you should take a video of it," Mia added.

Filming her mother in a vulnerable, horrible moment. She recoiled at the thought. "Oh, I don't know."

"I do," Mia said firmly. "It's hard for a lot of women to deal with the indignity of losing their hair on top of the pain and fear that cancer brings. I want to show them that they can beat all the nasty emotional bites this disease takes out of them, starting with this one. And let's do an introductory video first, let your followers know that we're going to take them all the way to the end with us."

All the way to the end. Arianna cringed. "Let's not put it that way."

"Yes, let's. They can go with us to the end of the story, however it turns out."

Arianna took a deep breath. "Okay, I'll make an appointment with Michael, and I'll call Sunny."

Sunny was enthusiastic when Arianna told her what Mia wanted to do. "This is going to be fabulous," she said. "And it's so brave of your mom. It will resonate with a lot of women. When do you want to do it?"

"The sooner, the better. For everything," Mia said when Arianna checked with her.

Michael booked out weeks ahead, but on hearing what was going on and what Mia wanted to do, he promised to juggle his schedule and set aside time for her the very next day.

"I'll get Mel to come in and do her makeup so she can rock the new look," he said. His wife, Melody, was heavily involved in the business and was a gorgeous woman. Arianna knew having her help would give her mother an emotional boost.

The following day, before Mia's appointment, Sunny positioned Mia and Arianna on the living room couch, two mugs of coffee on the coffee table in front of them, along with a small floral arrangement. Mia looked beautiful in a teal-colored blouse and jeans. Arianna was also in jeans and a pale blue blouse. Both outfits had been vetted by Sunny, as well as their makeup, which was understated. For Arianna that meant concealer, blush, eyeliner, mascara and lipstick. Mia had never been big on makeup and wore only some lipstick.

"I didn't see much point in putting on more," she said to Sunny, "not when Michael's wife is going to do that later."

"You look fine," Sunny assured her. "You both know what you want to say?"

Mia nodded.

"Okay, let's see if we can do this on the first take," said Sunny. "Be sure to hold your smiles for a sec before you start talking. On three."

Smile? No way.

She counted them down. Arianna forced a half smile. It was the best she could do.

"Hi there. I'm Arianna, your host of *To Your Health* and this is my mom, Mia. We're going to be doing a series of videos together, and this will be for all of you who are facing big health challenges like we are right now. Mom, you want to tell them what's going on?"

Mia nodded. Cleared her throat. "I have esophageal cancer."

And they were supposed to keep talking casually about this, like it was no big deal. Arianna bit her lip, swiped at a corner of her eye.

Mia didn't miss a beat. "As you can see, this is hard on my daughter. But we're going to fight it together."

Her mom was a trooper. Arianna sucked it up and kept going, talking about the symptoms, confessing how guilty she felt for not noticing. Mia fessed up about not wanting to face what was happening and postponing telling her daughter.

"At first I didn't think it was anything serious, and I didn't want to worry her," she said. "But really, I shouldn't have waited. And I would encourage you to not wait when you feel something is off with your body. Deal with it right away and don't let it get away from you."

"Speaking of dealing with things right away, we are off to our favorite hair salon where Mom is going to cut off her hair," Arianna chimed in.

"Before I have to watch chemo strip it off for me," Mia added.

"You are welcome to join us for that at Ross Michael Salon, and you're welcome to join us as we battle this thing. Mom is determined to show you how to be your best even when you're not at your best. Wish us luck."

That was it. She took her mom's hand, tried her best to smile for whomever would be watching and held the pose.

"Wow, one take. You two were great," Sunny raved.

Arianna took in a deep breath. "I feel like I've been dragged into a dark alley and beat up."

Mia, however, was beaming. "I feel like I just summited Mount Rainier."

"You're my hero," said Sunny.

"Mine, too," Arianna said, and hugged her.

"Don't be swelling my head," Mia said. "I'm just trying to get through this."

"You're getting through it beautifully," Sunny assured her.

"Early days," said Mia.

She was right. They had a long road ahead of them.

They took some pictures of Mia and Arianna—one of them hugging, one of them toasting each other with their coffee mugs, and another only of Mia. Then mother and daughter relaxed while Sunny worked on getting the video up on YouTube and the website as well as all the other necessary social media. She also posted their pictures everywhere, with thoughtful captions and tags.

"You two are going to become celebrities," Sunny predicted.

"I don't want to be a celebrity," said Mia.

"Me, either," said Arianna. She'd never been interested in looking for the proverbial spotlight.

"Well, you are going to get a lot of followers, so be ready," Sunny told them.

"I do want followers," Arianna admitted. "It doesn't do any good to put out information if nobody sees it."

"They'll see it. And they'll go back and check out all the other information you've been sharing."

Still, this wasn't exactly the way Arianna wanted to get more exposure.

"I don't want to take advantage of what Mom's going through," she said to Sunny when Mia was in the bathroom. "I don't want to pimp her out."

"You're not pimping your mom out," Sunny said. "You're giving her a chance to feel useful instead of like a burden."

"Okay, good point. I see that. Still, let's make sure we do some other posts and segments that don't have anything to do with Mom's cancer."

"Of course," said Sunny.

At that point Mia joined them and it was time to head to the salon.

"Hello, you two," Michael greeted them. "Mia, you're lookin' good."

"Not for long," Mia said.

The words revealed so much. She'd kept a brave face and was getting out in front of the chemo, but it didn't mean she was looking forward to losing her hair. Arianna wanted to cry but her mother didn't need that.

"You'll still be lookin' good when we're done," Michael assured Mia.

Sunny got busy filming as he went to work. Arianna stayed out of the frame, surreptitiously wiping at tears and watching as her mother's hair fell to the floor.

"I'm going to save a lot of money on haircuts and products," Mia joked.

"I'm gonna go out of business," Michael joked back. "I still expect you to come in and see me, you know."

He finished trimming Mia's shoulder-length hair to less than an inch, then got out his shaver. When he'd finished, Arianna had to remind herself that this woman she'd never seen before was her mother.

"Lucky you. You've got a great shaped head," Michael said.

"Lucky me," Mia repeated, her sarcasm showing what she really felt about her luck.

After filming Mel doing Mia's makeup, Sunny sped the video up in editing, showing Mel transforming Mia's face. By the time she was done, Mia looked like a glamorous mannequin come to life.

Sunny slowed down the video at the end to focus on Mia's delighted reaction. "I feel pretty."

"Oh, so pretty," sang Michael, and everyone laughed. "You're a good example of how to make the most of what you have," he said, then added, "You're beautiful even without the makeup, Mia."

It was so true.

That afternoon Sunny got the videos up, and come evening she was calling Arianna. "Have you seen how many views you've got so far?"

"No, I've been busy with Sophie and Mom."

Sophie. There had been a challenge. They hadn't warned her what they were going to do and she'd been horrified at her grandma's new look.

"Grammy, where's your hair?" she'd wanted to know.

"We cut it off," Mia said.

This had led to an honest but difficult discussion about the medicine Grammy was taking. "We want her to get better so we have to deal with some of these side effects," Arianna had explained. "Grammy was going to lose her hair and she wanted to get a head start on looking pretty without it."

"Would you like to help me try on one of my scarves?" Mia asked.

Sophie had been all over the fashion thing and happy to help Mia try on the scarf that Sunny had given her. "It's pretty," she'd said. "But I like your hair better, Grammy."

"It will grow back," Mia had said.

We'll get through this, Arianna had told herself for the hundredth time that day.

Seeing the number of views on everything from YouTube to TikTok was an exciting shock. They'd gone viral on Instagram.

Mia was on the couch, crocheting. Arianna joined her and turned her phone so Mia could see one of the sites. "That many views?" she said in surprise.

"And look at the comments. 'You are my hero,'" Arianna read.

"Desperate for a hero," muttered Mia.

"And this one. *I was just diagnosed with breast cancer. I'll be doing the journey with you. Thanks for the encouragement.* And this one, *I can do this, too. Thanks!*" Arianna read some of the other posts on other sites. They were all positive, with women either sharing their own survival testimony or asking questions. "You're a hit, Mom."

"Lemons out of lemonade," Mia murmured.

If you had to have the lemons, it was good to at least make the lemonade.

★ ★ ★

Sunny stopped off at the post office to find Molly chatting with a handsome white-haired black man. He was broad-shouldered with a movie-star smile and wore faded jeans, boots and a Seahawks sweatshirt under a faded windbreaker. The way Molly was smiling at him suggested he was a favorite. Sunny wondered if, with that great smile and deep voice, he was a little more than a favorite customer.

Molly caught sight of her and called hello and Sunny strolled up and introduced herself.

"I'm Reggie Washington," he said.

"My best and nicest customer," said Molly.

His smile widened. "Is that so?"

Molly blushed. "You know you are."

"I don't know about being your best customer but I'm your biggest fan," he said. He gave the counter a tap. "I'd better get moving. Nice to meet you, Sunny. Happy holidays."

"Right back atcha," said Sunny. "Oh, he is cute," she said to Molly as he went down the stairs.

"He is a sweet man."

"A sweet man?"

"Just a friend."

"Looks like he wants to be more. What if he came and camped out under your Christmas tree. Would you bring him eggnog and cookies?"

"Well, I couldn't let someone camp under my Christmas tree and not feed him, right?"

"Of course not. You can also invite him to one of our parties, you know." From his parting remark, it was obvious he knew what they were doing.

"We'll see," Molly said, not committing one way or the other.

"Speaking of parties, have you got time to get together and plan our next one? I'm thinking we should take care of all the details so all Arianna has to do is come."

"Good idea," Molly agreed. "Come on over to my place tonight."

"I'll bring that quart of eggnog I stuffed in the freezer," said Sunny. "You can keep whatever we don't drink in case a certain holiday camper shows up under your tree. You do still have it up, right?"

"Of course, I do," Molly said. "I'm ready for whatever Santa wants to bring me this year."

"Good on ya," said Sunny. All she wanted that year was for Santa to bring her a new and improved Bella, but she wasn't holding her breath. Travis had tried talking to his daughter, but it hadn't helped. The Weed sure wasn't doing her part to make things better.

Later that evening they sat at Molly's little kitchen table, enjoying their eggnog and the view of Dyes Inlet from her window. She'd had her corner lot house in Mannette, a charming Bremerton suburb, for years, bought it long before real estate prices shot sky-high. Mia's house down the street had a peekaboo view of the water but Molly's view was a sweeping one, and she never got tired of enjoying it while she had her morning coffee, either inside or, in nice weather, out on her deck. She'd already offered her house for their Fourth of July celebration because between the deck and the good-sized backyard, it was a perfect party spot and would give them a great view of fireworks on the water.

"I think we need to incorporate leprechauns since it's Christmas in March," she said to Sunny.

"They double as Santa's helpers?" Sunny suggested.

"Yes."

"Maybe we should bake cookies for them on the night before on the twenty-fourth. It's a Friday night."

Molly groaned. "I'll be tired."

"Okay, you sit and supervise and the rest of us will bake."

"That works for me."

"We can do the party at my house but what do you think about baking at Arianna's? That way Mia can be part of it if she has the energy. We can shoot a video and put that up on Arianna's website."

"Are they going to be up for that?" asked Molly.

"I think so. Did Arianna tell you how many views the last two videos got?"

"No."

Sunny brought up the one of Mia getting her head shaved and turned it so Molly could see. "It's only been up a few days."

"Holy moly, that is amazing."

"They're facing this like Spartans. Except I know Arianna's worried about money."

"She isn't making any yet on her website?"

"I think she's getting close. Meanwhile, though, once her paid vacation time runs out, it could get scary. So I've got an idea."

13

"What do you think?" Sunny asked after she'd shared her idea.

"I think Santa would be proud. I'll be the first contributor," Molly said.

"Actually, you'll have to settle for second," Sunny said with a grin. "I already got it going."

"Second works fine. I'm sure Ava will want to be your third."

"She'd better hurry. This thing is up and running."

Molly smiled. "You're a good friend."

"Just like you. We're the Three Musketeers."

"All for one and one for all," said Molly.

"Unless it's Frango mints. Then it's all for me and none for you guys," Sunny joked.

"Some Christmas spirit," Molly joked back.

"Okay, maybe one for you. Now, what do we want to do on the twenty-fifth? And where do we want to do it?"

"We can use my house. And how about looking for four-leaf clovers?" Sunny suggested.

"Good luck with that, especially if it rains."

"Then we'll cut 'em out of green plastic garbage bags. And

if it's too cold we can hide them inside the house. The person who finds the most gets a pot of gold coins."

"I like it," Molly approved. "And we could watch an Irish movie."

"Not *Darby O'Gill and the Little People*," Sunny said. "My grandma showed me that when I was a kid and the banshee scared the snot out of me."

"Okay, not that. You pick."

"I will. And we can have green beer for the grown-ups and green Kool-Aid for the kids. And some of the shamrock cookies we're making for the leprechauns."

"I've got a salad you make with green Jell-O, crushed pineapple and cottage cheese and whipped topping," Molly offered.

"And corned beef and cabbage for the main course?"

"Sure."

"Okay, that does it," Sunny said. "We are ready to party."

It turned out Tansy wasn't ready for them to party when Sunny called a couple days beforehand to make arrangements to pick up the kids for the weekend.

"I promised my grandma we'd go see her for the weekend," Tansy said. "She's all the way down at Ocean Shores so we can't exactly be running back and forth."

"You can't be running at all," Sunny informed her. "It's Travis's weekend to have the kids."

"But it's Grandma Nolan's birthday."

"We'll bring them back Saturday night. Go see Grandma on Sunday."

"Sorry, we can't do that," Tansy said, not sounding even the tiniest bit sorry.

"You know, you don't get to keep pulling this stuff," Sunny snapped. "Travis has rights."

"He also wants to do what's right. He wouldn't want the kids not to see their great-grandma on her birthday."

"Sunday is a great day for a ride to the beach," Sunny said, determined to win this battle.

"It's too hard on the kids with school the next day. You guys can have them next weekend."

"This weekend is our Christmas-in-March celebration."

"Big deal," sneered Tansy. "Bella thinks these parties are silly, anyway. Look, I gotta go." And with that, she was gone, leaving Sunny glaring at her phone and swearing.

She was still steaming when Travis came home from work. "She's done it to us again."

He heaved a long-suffering sigh. "Now what?"

Sunny told him what was what. "I knew you should have been the one to call her."

"Sorry. I thought we'd reached the point where we were being civilized."

"You can't civilize weeds. Anyway, you should be the one talking to your ex about this stuff, not me. I bet her grandma doesn't even have a birthday this weekend," Sunny fumed later as they cut up veggies for salad.

"I really don't remember," Travis said. "If she does, I don't want to be the villain who ruined Grandma's birthday celebration. Do you?"

Sunny made a face. "I guess not. But this is such a bunch of rotten eggs she's feeding us."

He set down his knife and wrapped his arms around her waist. "She'll eat her own share of rotten eggs one day. You know what they say. What goes around comes around."

"It can't come around for her soon enough," Sunny muttered.

"I got an idea," he said. "Let's go over there right now and take the kids out for burgers."

Here was a great idea. "Yeah?"

"Yeah. Why not? Stick the chicken in the fridge for tomorrow."

"I'll get my jacket," said Sunny.

Moments later they were in his vintage Mustang, driving over to the house he'd once shared with Tansy.

Her look of dismay and surprise when she opened the door of the two-story Victorian and found them standing on the porch did Sunny's heart good.

Not so much good, though, when Travis announced they were there to take the kids out for dinner and Tansy informed them that Bella was at a friend's house. Then it was all Sunny could do not to resort to violence and wipe that satisfied smirk off the woman's face.

The smirk disappeared when Dylan showed up behind her, saying, "Hi, Dad."

"Hey, dude. Want to go to Noah's Ark for a burger and shake?"

"Yeah!" Dylan said, and was out the door faster than a lightning bolt.

"He can't stay out all night," Tansy said sourly. "He has school in the morning."

"Don't worry. We'll have him back in plenty of time," Sunny said airily, and followed Dylan off down the stairs.

He was happy to tell them about how his basketball team was doing and when his next game was, and Sunny promised they'd be there to watch it. Amazing how pleasant a meal could be when a certain angry girl wasn't present.

"That went well," Travis said after they'd dropped Dylan back home.

"It did," she agreed.

"He likes you."

"Well, at least he tolerates me."

"It's progress."

Yes, it was. *Baby steps*, she reminded herself. And baby steps were better than no steps.

Mia's next adventure was getting her port put in. "I hate it," she said, looking down at the lump under the skin on her chest. "It looks like an alien implant."

"Lots of women get implants," Arianna joked.

Her mother frowned.

"This will be so much better than trying to find a vein every time," Arianna said.

Mia sighed. "I guess this ruins my chances of being Mrs. America," she said in an attempt to assert her own sense of humor.

"You can compete next year," Arianna said.

"I'm dreading chemo," Mia confessed.

Who wouldn't? Arianna was thankful Dr. Yao had prescribed both something for nausea and anxiousness.

When it came time, Mia was happy to take both.

Her first chemo treatment almost was a nonevent. Her appointment was for late morning, and once she arrived at the hospital, she was set up in a comfortable recliner with a drip bag. She and Arianna played cards while the medicine did its work.

Sunny joined them to film a video.

"I'm here with Mom, keeping her company while she's getting her first chemo treatment," Arianna said to her viewers. "How is it, Mom?"

"So far, so good," Mia reported.

"As you can see, we've found a way to pass the time," Arianna said, pointing to their cards laid out on the chair's tray. "She's beating me, by the way."

"Just like I'm going to do my best to beat this cancer," Mia said. "Meanwhile, I'm savoring time with my daughter. Even when life is bad, it can be good."

Sunny stopped it right there. "That was a perfect ending."

"Was it? I only shared how I feel," Mia said.

"It was an inspiring share," Sunny told her, and she smiled.

"You sailed through that," Arianna said later as they left the hospital.

"I don't know what I was so afraid of," Mia said.

The unknown. That was always scary. And there was a lot of it ahead of them. But they'd face it one day at a time.

Mia felt fine the rest of the day, and the next, but by the third day she ached all over and was too weak to do anything but lie on the couch under a blanket and watch TV. She wasn't a lie-on-the-couch kind of woman, and it was hard to see her like that.

"We all have our bad days," Mia said, "whether it's cancer or something else."

"Mom, don't minimize this. It's a big deal."

"It is. But I'm not going to let it get so big it crushes me, and I don't want it to crush you, either. I'm sure I'll be much better tomorrow."

"We should cancel having the baking party here," Arianna said.

"No, don't do that. You don't want to miss out on the fun."

How was she supposed to have fun when she was so worried?

"That was part of why you girls decided to celebrate Christmas all year, wasn't it?" Mia continued. "To find your Christmas spirit, make up for your earlier disappointments?"

"Yes, but this is different."

"There will always be something sneaking up on you and trying to steal your joy. You can't let it, and the only way to combat it is to keep bringing in good things and focusing on your blessings. Anyway, I'm craving some smiles and laughter. Don't deprive me."

Happily Mia didn't get deprived. She was feeling well enough to sit on a barstool and visit while the friends baked and frosted their cookies and even to be at the party the next day to observe the fun.

The party was a success. Everyone had a good time. Paisley and Sophie especially enjoyed the hunt for the four-leaf clovers, and the grown-ups especially enjoyed the green beer. The best part was later, when the friends were cleaning up in the kitchen and Sunny gave Arianna the envelope with money in it.

"What's this?" she asked.

"It's your no-worries insurance," Molly said. "Sunny started a GoFundMe account for you and we've all contributed."

"We're going to make sure you don't have to worry while

you're getting your business off the ground," Sunny added. That sounded a lot better than mentioning the fact that Arianna was dealing with her mother's health crisis.

For a moment Arianna could only stare at them through the tears in her eyes. Finally she managed to say, "You all are amazing."

"No," Sunny said, "amazing is what you and Mia are doing."

"We're with you all the way," Molly said.

With you all the way. After the party Arianna pulled out her laptop and wrote a blog post for the website. *When you're at your weakest your friends will be at their strongest,* she concluded. How true!

In some ways it had been nice not to have the two-legged black cloud that was Bella at the Christmas-in-March party, but Sunny still regretted both her absence and Dylan's. Part of the point was to try to break down the barriers between them.

Afterward she put some of the cookies in a plastic container and she and Travis drove to Tansy's house to leave them on the porch. It was a shock to see the living room lights on and the TV screen flickering.

"What's this?" she wondered.

"We're gonna find out," said Travis. He looked ready to punch something. Or someone. Not good. He got out of the car and began marching up the walk with Sunny hurrying behind.

Not only was the TV on, but there were also bodies on couch and in chairs. Including two kid-shaped bodies.

Travis gave the doorbell an angry push.

Tansy quickly covered her surprised look when she opened the door and saw them. She narrowed her eyes at her husband. "What are you doing here?"

"I guess you didn't go to Grandma's," Travis observed.

Tansy's chin lifted a notch. "She got sick."

A likely story. If she did, it was the thought of seeing Tansy that had made her sick.

"What do you want?" Tansy demanded.

"How about to see my kids when I'm supposed to, you lying bitch," snarled Travis.

Sunny stepped in before things could get ugly. She held out the container. "Things happen. We really just came to drop off some cookies from the party for the kids."

Tansy took it from her. "I'm cutting down on their sugar intake."

Travis was going to explode. Sunny took his arm. "Well, maybe they can have one."

"We'll see," said Tansy, and tossed the container on the hall table. Then, before either of them could speak, she shut the door.

Travis began banging on it.

"Travis, stop," Sunny begged. "Let's deal with this when you're calmer."

He scowled, gave the door an angry slap and then stalked back to the car.

"Now I know how a door-to-door salesman feels," Sunny muttered as she followed him. If there even was such a thing anymore. If there wasn't, she could figure out why. Having a door slammed in your face sucked.

"Grandma got sick, my ass," he growled as he started the car.

"I don't blame her. Tansy makes me sick, too," said Sunny. "I'm so tired of playing these games. She needs to grow up."

"Yes, she does," he agreed. "And I'm done letting her get away with this BS."

It took him a while to calm down, but once he did, they settled in the living room for Round Two. He put the phone on speaker so Sunny could hear also. And she didn't like what she heard.

"All right, so I might have told a little white lie," Tansy admitted after he confronted her.

Little? More like a big fat whopper.

"But I was just covering for Bella. She hates going over there and she hates these stupid parties your dipsy wife keeps thinking up."

Dipsy! Sunny was sure the steam coming out her ears was going to scald her husband.

"Okay, you are now way over the line," Travis snapped. "Sunny is not dipsy. She's trying hard with the kids, and she doesn't need you sabotaging her."

"I'm not!" Tansy protested.

"Oh, yes, you are. And you're messing with me, too. This was my weekend to have the kids and you deliberately screwed it up. Unless you want to end up back in court, you need to cut this shit out."

Tansy's only response to that was to end the call.

Sunny heaved a sigh. "She won't do anything different."

He clawed a hand through his hair. "She'll never forgive me for finally having enough of her crap and getting out. And she'll sure never forgive me for ending up with someone as great as you. You show her up and she doesn't like that."

"I don't care about what she likes. It's the kids."

"They'll come around, I promise," he said.

Don't make promises you can't keep, Sunny thought.

Travis wrapped his arms around her. "I'm sorry, babe. I really am. You know why she's doing this. She wants to get to us, wreck what we have."

"Well, she's not going to," Sunny vowed.

"Don't give up on us."

She studied his face, saw the worry in his eyes. "I'm not. We're in this together. I meant those vows I took. For better or worse." She only hoped the situation wouldn't get too much worse.

Alden was home so Arianna took over some cookies. Delivering cookies didn't count as fishing anymore, she decided, not when he'd come forward as a friend to help them. This was simply one friend taking cookies to another friend.

"Whoa, what's this?" he greeted her.

"The cookie express," she said, and bent to pet Buster who was jumping up, madly vying for attention.

"Want to come in?" he offered, swinging the door wide.

Mia was ensconced on the couch, crocheting, and Sophie had gone to Ava's house for a sleepover with Paisley.

"Just for a minute," Arianna said. "Mom could probably use some alone time."

"How's she doing?" he asked as he led the way into his living room.

Like hers and many of the houses in Manette, his was an older home. It had a modest-sized living room with hardwood floors. He'd modernized the fireplace surround and a flat-screen TV hung over the mantel. An M.C. Escher print hung on the wall opposite a leather couch, two matching leather chairs under it. A dog bed occupied prime real estate next to the couch and several dog toys lay scattered around. The coffee table held a half-empty glass of pop, along with the TV remote and a half-read book, lying face down. The room looked masculine and lived in.

"I love what you've done with the fireplace," she said. "Ours could use some updating down the road. Who'd you use?"

"Myself."

"Wow," she said. Hunky and a handyman. "Impressive."

"Not really. You watch enough stuff on YouTube and you can do anything."

And humble. She liked a man who wasn't all full of himself. Like a certain ex-husband.

"I want to do some upgrades, then I'm gonna sell."

"So, you bought this house to flip?" Somehow that seemed sad. With its front porch and gables, it had a lot of character.

"I inherited it. My gram thought I needed stability," he said with a shrug. "Places like this need kids, though."

"And dogs. You've got that part going." Buster had dropped

a looped dog toy at her feet. She went to pick it up and he grabbed it.

"He doesn't do fetch," Alden explained. "He's waiting to play tug-of-war."

Tug-of-war. It seemed like the whole last year she'd been entrenched in her own tug-of-war—herself versus discouragement and fear. Just when she'd figured she was winning, fate had stepped in and started a new round.

"Aah." She grabbed an end of the toy and pulled. Buster hung on with a growl.

"He always wins," said Alden.

"Somebody has to win." And she *would* win her tug-of-war.

"Want something to drink? Beer? Pop? I've got Pepsi in the fridge."

She loved the idea of flopping on Alden's couch and hanging out. Talking. Maybe even doing more than talking. Remembering the comforting feel of his arms around her when she sat crying on her porch made her thirsty for more than pop. But...

"I'd better get back to the house," she said.

"Everything going okay over there?"

Nothing was okay, but she knew what he meant. "We're good."

"You'll get through this."

She sighed. "We will." Anyway, there was no other way but through.

Buster was ready to follow Arianna right out the door, but Alden picked him up before he could. "No, you don't. You live here, dude."

Buster whined.

"You're way too easy," Alden informed him.

Buster was happy being easy. He barked and struggled to get down. Then, the minute he was, positioned himself at the door and barked.

"You don't need to whiz," Alden informed him. "We already went out." His dog was a sucker for attention.

Maybe he was, too. He watched from his window as Arianna walked back to her house and found himself wishing she'd stayed. That brave face, that determination, that smile—she was getting to him. He wished he could swoop into her life like some movie hero and fight all her battles for her. Protect her, keep her safe. And darn but he was thinking more and more how it would feel to kiss her, to let his hands wander those tempting curves. What would his house be like with her living in it? What would it be like to step into a ready-made family?

"Probably not a good idea," he said to Buster.

Buster had bonded with Arianna. He cocked his head and studied Alden. *What are you, crazy?*

Alden didn't know.

Molly had kept some of the cookies from the party to take to work and share with her customers. On Monday she set them out on a green plate.

"Leprechaun Christmas cookies," she said to everyone. "Merry Christmas in March."

"Such a cute idea," said one woman. "Molly, you know how to make the most out of life."

"I'm working on it," Molly told her.

"It wasn't leprechauns who stole my check," snarled a forty-something woman wearing a faux fur jacket, ripped jeans and UGGs. "It should have been in my box and it's not."

"I'm sorry," Molly said, using her diplomatic postal-worker voice. "We put out all the mail for today so it must be delayed."

"Delayed into somebody's pocket. Who puts the mail in the boxes?"

"I do, along with my coworkers," Molly said.

She could feel her temper rising. As if she or any of the other employees had time to look through envelopes in search of something that might contain money. Mail had to be in all the post office boxes by 9:00 a.m. and it could be a rush to get that done and then be at the window to serve people.

"Somebody stole my check!"

"I can assure you, nobody took your check," said Molly.

"Yeah? I want to talk to your supervisor."

"I *am* the supervisor."

"Well, then whoever's in charge of you," the woman snapped.

"If you have a complaint, you can go to the post office on National," Molly said. She could think of another place to tell this woman where to go but that wouldn't be professional.

For a moment she envisioned herself instantly growing another ten feet, leaning out the window and baring big fangs at the woman, pointing a bony finger with a foot long fingernail dripping blood at her and asking, "You got a problem with me, bitch?" Envisioned the woman shrinking to the size of a mushroom, saying in a tiny little bug voice, "No, I'm really sorry. You're wonderful and I love your cookies."

"Don't think I won't," the woman said, and marched toward the stairs. She was starting down them just as Reggie was coming up. "Don't give these people any business. They're all crooks," the woman snapped as she tromped past him.

"Whoa," Reggie said as he walked up to Molly's window. "Have you been raiding people's envelopes again?"

She frowned and shook her head. "It's not funny. Accusing me of stealing her check! As if I know who gets checks from whom. As if I have time to go looking!" She grabbed one of her cookies and stuffed half of it in her mouth. Sugar, her drug of choice. "And why would anyone steal a check they couldn't cash, anyway?"

"People always need someone to blame when life's not going right." He pointed to the plate of cookies. "What are you giving us today? They sure look good."

Reggie had such a way of blowing away gray clouds with only a simple sentence or two. Molly felt her scowl dissolving.

"Christmas cookies for the leprechauns. We had leftovers so I brought them here to share."

"I like sharing," Reggie said, and helped himself to one. He took a bite, chewed, swallowed. Smiled. "This is good stuff. The icing—what did you put in it? Not vanilla."

"Reggie, how would you know about what to put in cookie icing?" she teased.

"Hey, I've done a little baking over the years. So, what's the secret ingredient?"

"Rose water."

"Rose water. I never would have guessed. It's good," he said, and took a second bite. Savored that one, too. "You sure know how to bake, Molly."

It had been so long since a man had raved over her cooking. It felt good.

"Anytime you want help in the kitchen, I'm your man," he said. He pulled out his wallet and removed a business card—simple, with only his name and phone number. "It might be against postal regulations for you to take people's phone numbers, so I'll just forget this and leave it behind...for someone to find," he finished with a smile.

What would her mother have thought of Reggie Washington? He was older than her and probably not so well-off, if that scruffy old jacket was anything to judge by. But her mother had never been a good judge of character. And that was what was important when deciding what people to let into your life. As for the age difference, people could be friends at any age. She, Arianna, Mia and Sunny and Ava were all proof of that.

She picked up the card. "Someone might just find it," she said, smiling back.

Oh, yes, someone might get an urge to bake and need a little help.

Reggie was the first customer in the door the next day, bringing a reindeer bobblehead. "I got to thinking. You might have found a certain card with a phone number but not known what to do with it. I think we should go out to dinner and talk about that."

Her heart rolled over. Out to dinner with Reggie.

"I think we should," she said.

He grinned. "Friday night?"

"Friday night sounds great." A date! After all these years she had a date!

"All right, then," he said.

"Give me your phone," she said. He did, and she added her number to his list of contacts.

"I'll call you," he said, then left.

It was the first time he'd ever come in and not bought so much as a stamp. No more excuses needed to see her. She smiled.

She wasn't smiling, though, when she remembered she was supposed to be going to Chuck E. Cheese for pizza with Ava and Paisley that night. Hopefully Reggie would be up for rescheduling.

"No problem," he said when she called him. "But I have a better idea. How about I take you all out for pizza?"

"Oh, Reggie, I couldn't make you do that."

"Nobody's making me do anything. I'd like to. And I'd like to meet your daughter. If we're going to be spending time together—and I hope we are—I think it would be good to know your family."

That felt a little soon, but she went ahead and agreed.

"We have an extra body joining us," she said when Ava checked in.

"Sunny?" Ava guessed.

"No. It's none of the Christmas gang."

"Who then?"

"One of my post office friends. Well, customers."

"Oh."

"You don't mind, do you?"

"No, that's fine," Ava assured her.

"Good," Molly said, relieved. "We'll meet you there at six."

"Great," Reggie said when she talked to him. "I'll pick you up at twenty till."

When he did, it was clear that Reggie, indeed, lived on a tight budget. His car was not old enough to be classic or even vintage. It was simply…old, with a dent in one fender and a crack in the windshield. She wondered how long that had been there.

"What hit you?" she couldn't help asking.

"The windshield? A rock from a gravel truck. Don't worry, the window won't break. I'm not bothering to repair it cuz old Martha's going to get replaced pretty soon."

"Martha?"

"Martha Washington," he said with a grin. "She's been a good old car, but it's time for a hybrid. Guess I'll have to get that fender fixed, though, if I'm gonna sell her."

Who would want her?

"She still runs like a champ."

Was he really going to get a new car or was he just making that up to save face? "Maybe it is time for a replacement," she ventured.

"I've never been one for doing things just to impress people." He slid a glance her direction. "Although I've been rethinking that since meeting you."

"You don't need to impress me," Molly said. He already had with his kind words and ready smile.

But Ava hadn't been exposed to those yet. She pulled her three-year-old SUV into the restaurant parking lot at the same time as Molly and Reggie. Paisley caught sight of them and waved excitedly, but the expression on Ava's face wasn't quite so smiley. Had this been a mistake?

14

"Grandma!" Paisley squealed and raced to give Molly a hug.

Ava approached at a slower pace, her smile tentative. "Hi, Mom," she said, and traded kisses with Molly. Then she turned to Reggie and the smile was barely there. She looked like a woman about to shake hands with a con artist.

"This is my daughter, Ava," Molly said.

Reggie held out a big hand. "I'm happy to meet you, Ava."

Ava didn't echo back his words, but she did shake his hand.

"And this is Paisley," Molly said.

"Hi," Paisley said. She had no problem greeting Reggie with a smile. Any friend of Grandma's.

"That's a nice name," Reggie said to her.

"My mommy gave it to me."

"Your mommy has good taste," he said.

Molly could almost hear her daughter thinking, *And that's more than I can say for my mommy.*

"Shall we go in?" he suggested.

"Yes!" hooted Paisley, and ran off toward the entrance.

"Watch for cars!" her mother called after her.

The place was, as usual, kid mayhem, with at least two birthday parties in progress. Once they'd gotten game tickets, it was the last they saw of Paisley for half an hour. It gave the adults time to talk. Or at least try to over the noise level.

"So, you're one of my mom's customers?" Ava started.

"Yep, been coming into the post office for the last year to buy stamps. At least twice a week."

"That's a lot of stamps," Ava observed.

"I write a lot of letters to my representative," he said with a chuckle. "And I never buy a whole book. Otherwise, I wouldn't have an excuse to see your mother's smiling face."

"It's your face that's always shining," Molly told him. "There've been a lot of times when you were the one bright spot in my day."

"Do you live around here?" Ava asked. He cupped an ear in an effort to hear over the din, and she repeated her question.

"In Bremerton," he said. "Been here for years. I started out working at the shipyard back when I was a young buck."

Ava nodded thoughtfully. "Have you got any family here?"

This was starting to feel like an inquisition. Molly began to squirm.

He shook his head. "Sadly, no. Never had a family. Both my folks are gone, and I lost my baby sister to breast cancer last year. Only got a cousin left, and he's in North Carolina."

"Gosh, that's hard," Molly said.

Ava said nothing.

"That's life," he said with a shrug.

After an hour of grilling by Ava, interspersed with encouraging comments from Molly, it was time to eat. Paisley was on a kid-gamer high, devouring her slice of pizza and ready for more excitement, but Ava said, "No, we need to get going."

That brought on a pout, until Reggie distracted her. "Paisley, there's something behind your ear." He reached over and magically produced a dollar bill.

"Wow," Paisley breathed.

"I remember when people did that trick with a quarter," Molly said.

"Inflation," he replied as he handed it to Paisley. "Ava, thanks for letting me crash the party."

"Thanks for the pizza," Ava said, minding her manners. Finally.

"Thanks for joining us," Molly said to Reggie. "It probably hasn't been very restful."

"It's been fun," he said. Between the chaos and the daughterly grilling, that was stretching it.

"You are an awful good sport," Molly said once they were in his car. "I'm sorry about my daughter giving you the third degree."

"I didn't mind," he said. "She loves you and wants to know who you're hanging out with. I had a good time and I hope we can do something again. I'd like to hear more about your life."

"Not much to tell," she said.

"You've got a lovely daughter and granddaughter. I'd say you've done some living."

"More lately than I've done in a long time," she said, thinking of how the Christmas-all-year gang had pulled her out of the doldrums. She went on to tell him about her friends and how much happier she was now that she was expending some extra energy. "It's funny, I was so tired before this, but I think I just needed a good shot in the emotional arm. I've been in a slump for a long time and not realizing how big a slump it was."

"We all get in slumps," he said. "I did after my sister died."

She could identify with that. "I lost my husband when Ava was just a toddler. I wanted to fall into a slump back then, but I didn't have time. I had a girl to raise."

"Looks like you did a good job with her," he said.

It didn't seem to Molly like Ava had been on her best behavior. "She's normally more friendly."

"She was fine. And I'm sorry about your husband."

"It was a long time ago." But sometimes it felt like only yesterday. "There are still times when I miss him."

"It's no fun being alone," Reggie said. They pulled up in front of her house and he put the car in Park, smiled at her. "Thanks for including me tonight. Want to go out to eat again? Not the pizza place," he hurried to add, "but somewhere?"

"I'd like that," she said.

He nodded, smiled. "Good. Stay right there. I'll get the door for you."

Men still did that? She stayed put, let him open her door and walk her to her porch. She'd gotten out her key and was pondering whether or not to ask him in when her cell phone rang. Ava, of course.

"Go ahead and take that. I'll see you later," he said, backing away. Then with a final wave, he was off down the walk, moving toward his car.

"Is Reggie still with you?" Ava asked.

"No, he just dropped me off." Molly opened the door, then settled onto the nearest chair.

"Mom, you can't really like this guy," Ava said.

"Why not?" Molly demanded and began shrugging out of her coat.

"Oh, come on. It's obvious he doesn't have any money. He's probably planning to mooch off you."

"Just because he doesn't drive a new car, which, by the way, he's replacing."

Ava gave a disdainful snort. "So he says. And that coat he was wearing, I mean he's not exactly dressing for success."

"He's obviously retired and doesn't have to."

"Yeah, retired. How old is this guy? He's got to be at least ten years older than you. Maybe more."

"Oh, for heaven's sake, Ava, you're being ridiculous. So what if he's a little older?"

"A little? Mom, I had no idea you were that lonely but don't do anything...desperate."

Molly scowled at her phone. "I'm not desperate and I'm not lonely." She wasn't. She was...wistful.

"Just don't rush into anything, okay?"

"Strappin' on my saddle and off to the races," Molly muttered. Honestly, how foolish did her daughter think she was?

"I'd better go," Ava said.

Yes, you'd better.

"I love you," she added.

Which, of course, was why she worried. And Molly got it. Ava had had some rocky relationships. Paisley's dad had been irresponsible and into drugs and had eventually—thank God— wandered out of their lives. The two others that followed hadn't been much better, and one of them, Ava quickly figured out, had considered her Miss Booty Call of Bremerton. Love losers. It was no wonder Ava had a suspicious mind.

But Molly was sure Reggie wasn't a love loser. Granted, he did look a little money-starved, but she wasn't looking for a wallet. And so what if he was older? She wasn't exactly a baby herself. Anyway, they weren't talking about running off to Vegas in search of a wedding chapel. They were just friends.

So far.

"I love you, too," she said to her daughter, and ended the call. *And I really like Reggie Washington.*

It was time to make another video for the YouTube channel. The topic this time was living life to the fullest. Mia had dressed in her favorite black leggings, a black top and turquoise sweater. She was wearing one of her new turbans and had accented it with dangly rhinestone earrings. She'd worn full makeup as well, and looking at her, no one would think she was undergoing chemo. Except for the turban, which was a giveaway.

"Mom and I want to keep sharing in the hopes that what we're doing will encourage someone else who's going through this. It's hard, emotionally," Arianna said. "For the both the patient and the family. No matter what the health issue, you can't take your emotions out of the equation because our health, whether it's good or bad, affects our emotions."

"And our emotional state can either make it easier or harder to deal with health problems," put in Mia. "Which is why I think it's important to do things to keep your spirits up."

Her mother was a champ at that.

"Of course, it all depends on what your loved one is battling and how much energy that person has," said Arianna. "What medications are being taken. You also have to consider safety issues."

"But we believe there is always something you can do," Mia put in.

That was the cue to start running down their list of suggestions. They ranged from afternoon tea parties with a teapot and scones set up next to the bed to looking at old family pictures to video chatting. Mia showed off the manicure Arianna had recently given her and talked about the stack of books her daughter had brought her from the library.

"Sometimes, the best gift you can give someone is a few hours of escape," she said.

Sadly the escape wasn't permanent, but Arianna didn't mention the obvious.

"There's one other thing we're doing," Mia said, going off-script, and Arianna looked at her in surprise. "My daughter and her friends have decided to celebrate Christmas all year long, so every month, as close to the twenty-fifth as they can get, they do something to celebrate. We recently celebrated a St. Patty's Day Christmas, and I enjoyed watching while the girls made Christmas cookies for the leprechauns."

"Who we made honorary Santa's helpers," Arianna said, going with the flow.

"What's on for April?" Mia asked, putting her daughter on the spot.

"You'll have to wait and see," Arianna said. Then turned back to the camera. "Stay tuned."

They held their smiles for a minute, until Sunny said, "That was great. I didn't know you were going to talk about our twelve months of Christmas."

"Neither did I," Arianna said.

Mia shrugged. "I think it's a cute idea. I'm enjoying what you girls are doing, and I want to grab as much Christmas as I can while I can."

"There will be plenty more Christmases to come," Sunny assured her.

Darn straight there will be, Arianna vowed.

CHRISTMAS
IN APRIL

15

April twenty-fifth fell on a Monday. When the gang met at one of the many Starbucks branches, they had a decision to make. Weekday or weekend?

"Let's do the weekend. We're supposed to have the kids. If the Weed doesn't sneak them off somewhere," said Sunny.

Ava, who had been invited to join them, took another sip of her latte. "You shouldn't let her pull that crap."

"Travis is too soft on her," Sunny said glumly. "She pays about as much attention to the custody schedule as we all do to speed limits."

"I pay attention to speed limits," Arianna said.

Of course, she did. Arianna did everything right and to the T and expected everyone else to do the same. "That's not the point," Sunny said, irritated. "The point is that she always finds a way to mess with us."

"Can't Travis have a talk with her?" asked Molly.

"He did. He's had it with her. He even threatened to take her back to court, but I don't think it did any good," Sunny said, irritation bleeding into her voice. "He was so mad after the stunt she pulled last month I was afraid he was going to throttle her.

But in the end, he won't push the issue. He doesn't like to rock the boat for the kids' sake."

"Rock it, already," said Molly in disgust.

And let the Weed fall out and drown. But... "He thinks if we make a big deal out of the schedule, she'll just find some other passive-aggressive way to stick it to us. She already did a good job of messing up Travis's plans to do something with Bella on her birthday."

"At least she liked his present," Arianna reminded her.

"A collection of gift cards for everything from Etsy to Regal Cinema. Who wouldn't? Anyway, it's the gift that counts," Sunny cracked, trying to make light of their latest disappointment.

"I'm sorry you have to deal with this," Ava said. "Makes me glad Paisley's dad is history. I don't have to share her."

Arianna frowned at her to-go cup. "I hate sharing. Wyatt has Sophie this weekend and I miss her."

"Sharing is caring," Sunny quipped. "And I'd love to share with Tansy. Maybe some hot pepper on her thong. She already thinks she's got a hot ass."

Ava gave a snort. "I've seen those pranks on YouTube. That's awful."

"And it wouldn't happen to a more deserving person."

"I should have put some in Wyatt's tighty-whities," said Arianna.

"Okay, ladies, we are straying far from the subject," Molly said. "Is everyone okay with the weekend? I am."

Everyone was.

"We can do it at my place," Ava offered. "Although my condo is pretty small."

"I don't mind hosting," Sunny said, and that settled it. "And don't worry, guys, I'll take care of organizing everything. I just need someone to bring hard-boiled eggs and food coloring and someone to bring bunny grass and jelly beans."

"I can bring the candy," Molly offered. "It will all be on sale after Easter."

"I'll bring eggs and the coloring," said Ava.

"What should I bring?" Arianna asked.

"Yourself, and your girl," Sunny told her. "And your mom if she's feeling well." Arianna needed the fun, but she didn't need the work.

"I want to call it a Very Bunny Christmas," Sunny said when she was at Arianna's doing a photo shoot of recommended supplements.

Arianna looked doubtingly at her and nodded. "Okay."

"It will be great. You'll see."

All her plans were great, if Sunny did say so herself the day of the party. The family room was festive with pastel balloons hung all around it. The artificial Christmas tree in the corner was sporting foam eggs and carrots she'd ordered online alongside red and green ribbons. In the background she was playing a selection of songs ranging from "Here Comes Peter Cottontail" and "The Bunny Hop" (which, of course, she had taught everyone) to the "Hallelujah Chorus" from Handel's "Messiah" sung by the Royal Choral Society at Albert Hall, no less. Her mom had informed her that it was always sung at Christmas, but she didn't care. She thought it worked just fine for Easter, too.

She was thrilled that her parents and her sister, Rae, had shown up, bringing along Will, her fiancé. He'd jumped right into the fun pool and scored points for insisting he liked the cupcakes Sunny had proudly baked from scratch, even when it was discovered that she'd neglected to add the sugar.

Molly had brought a friend as well, an older man with broad shoulders and a big smile. Only his white hair hinted that he might be older than Molly. He wasn't a clotheshorse, that was for sure. His pants and shirt looked like they'd been around for a decade. The Santa hat he was sporting looked new, though.

"What's the story with Reggie?" Sunny asked Ava.

Ava frowned and shook her head. "Don't ask."

"He seems nice." Molly obviously thought so. She was looking at him like he was the last piece of chocolate on earth.

"He is, but he's not right for her."

People had said that about Travis, too, but even with the challenges they had with the kids and the Weed, there was no one Sunny would rather be with. She looked to where he stood, talking with Will and Rae and eating one of her cupcake fails and felt her heart flip over. A man who'd watch holiday rom-coms with you, ate whatever kitchen disaster you made with gusto and had absolute magic hands was the stuff soulmates were made of.

"What's next on the program?" Ava asked, closing the subject.

They'd already colored eggs, done a hunt for nests of jelly beans hidden around the house—everyone had participated but Bella—and eaten the lasagna Sunny had bought at Costco. Now it was time for pictures.

"Okay, everyone, it's time to get your pictures taken with Santa Bunny," she called. "Come on, Mom, you and Dad go first," she said, summoning her mother. "Tell Bunny what you want for Christmas."

Her parents obediently joined the giant stuffed plush rabbit wearing a Santa hat that Sunny had set up on the couch.

"I want someone else to cook Christmas dinner, Santa Bunny," said her mom.

"Uh-oh. Did you hear that, Rae? That means Dad's cooking. We're in trouble," Sunny said.

"We're in trouble if we have to eat what you cook," Rae teased.

Paisley sang to Santa Bunny and Sophie hugged him and asked him to make her Grammy well, which had the grown-ups all tearing up. Travis put them back in a happier mood by sitting on the bunny's lap and posing with a "hang ten" gesture. Like

Reggie, he was wearing a Santa hat, but he'd gone the extra mile and glued on paper bunny ears.

Another thing to love about her husband. He was so supportive of her and got into the spirit of everything.

Bella was the only one who refused to have her picture taken with "the stupid rabbit," and pronounced the whole party stupid.

Travis's easy smile fell away. "Bella, come with me," he said, escorting off into the kitchen.

Everyone chatted determinedly, trying to ignore the low-voiced scolding taking place in there. But it got harder to ignore as Bella's voice began to rise. Right along with the crescendo of the "Hallelujah Chorus," which was playing again.

"I hate her!" Bella cried and the Royal Choral Society sang, "Hallelujah, hallelujah!"

Sunny's face flamed as everyone sat in stunned silence. *Yes, people, the Grinch had a love child and here she is.*

She was well aware of how Bella felt. Hearing those words again shouldn't have come as a shock. But they did.

She looked toward the kitchen, trying to breathe normally, trying not to cry, half-wishing she could run out there and scream, "Right now I'm not too fond of you, either, you little shit!"

She saw Travis glare at his daughter, take her arm and give it a shake. "You will apologize to Sunny."

"I will not!" Bella shouted, and stuck out her chin.

Okay, this was getting out of hand. Somebody had to do something. Something smart, and maybe laying into the kid wasn't the smartest thing at the moment.

Sunny hurried into the kitchen and jumped into the fray. "You know what? You're entitled to your feelings." It was an epiphany moment. The girl was a mess, and she was making Sunny the scapegoat for her unhappiness, but how could Sunny blame her for that? Her mother had offered up Sunny from the very beginning. Still... "I'm entitled to my feelings, too," she continued, "and right now they're hurt. I'm sorry you hate me. I've tried to be kind to you, and I'll continue to."

Because that was what mature people did. Being mature sucked.

A red flush spread across Bella's face and she dropped her gaze, but not before Sunny saw tears in her eyes. "I want to go home," she muttered.

Travis looked ready to dropkick her there. "Get your coat," he growled, and she raced through the living room, not looking at anyone.

Sunny caught his arm as he started to stalk off after his daughter. "Don't say anything more. She already feels bad." Sunny remembered those stormy young years. Those humiliating moments after you'd been a brat and made a fool of yourself in public were the worst.

Travis shook his head. Considering the fact that his eyes were narrowed and his jaw was clenched that head shake probably didn't mean, "No, I won't."

Dylan wasn't in trouble, but he, too, got his coat. Sibling solidarity, she supposed.

Bella was already out the door, leaving it wide open. He followed her out. Travis marched after both of them and shut the door behind him. End of Act I.

Arianna came to stand beside Sunny and put an arm on her shoulder. "I'm sorry."

So was Sunny. She wanted to have a good relationship with Travis's kids. There was hope for Dylan, but Bella was another matter. It seemed like the harder Sunny tried, the worse Bella's attitude became. Every time the girl came over, she brought poison into their marriage. How many times could you drink poison and survive? Sunny didn't want to think about it.

"It'll get better," she said, as much to herself as Arianna. She wished she could believe it.

Sunny's mother had joined them now. "They don't stay this age forever."

Molly and Ava and Rae all chimed in on the kitchen counseling session as well. "You're doing the right thing taking the high road," Molly assured her. "But don't let her get to you."

"Too late," Sunny said miserably. "I'm a mess."

She was, indeed. One moment she couldn't stand the child, the next she was willing to crawl over glass to win her love.

"It was a great party, anyway," put in Ava.

"The party's not over yet," said Rae. "Let's have some more sugar-free cupcakes."

Her proposal was met with smiles and uneasy laughter, and everyone closed in to cover the ugly moment.

But it stayed fresh in Sunny's mind and was still there after they'd all left. What was the magic formula for winning over a resentful thirteen-year-old girl?

Sunny was sure having her father yell at her all the way back to her mom's house wouldn't help. More logs on the hate fire.

Later that evening, after their guests had left and he'd returned, Sunny asked Travis how the ride home had gone.

He frowned and shrugged. Not a good sign.

"So, not good?"

"We're both on her shit list."

Sunny reached out and gave his arm a rub. "I'm sorry."

"None of what happened is your fault. Good grief, you deserve a medal for how hard you're trying"

She did, darn it all. There was never a weekend visit when she didn't make sure to have the kids' favorite foods on hand. She tried outings to the mall, movie matinees, had even orchestrated a day trip to the historic town of Port Townsend, making sure the family visited the '50s-style soda fountain there. Where was the formula for success, anyway?

"I'm ready to give up," she confessed.

He pulled her into a hug. "Don't. We'll get past this."

Maybe. Some kids never stopped hating their stepparents.

She didn't want to make Travis feel worse, though, so she kept the thought to herself and kissed him.

She also kept to herself the ugly discovery she made the next morning when she went to make coffee. In the canister she found a piece of paper with a note scrawled on it that was hardly a love note. *I hate you and so does Dylan,* Bella had written. When had she found the time to do that with no one seeing her? The child was a criminal mastermind.

"Be glad it's not poison," Sunny told herself.

Except, really, it was. Vitriol from a poisoned pen.

Alden was off on Sunday. He'd gone to his parents' house to help his dad work on his classic '50s Dodge Wayfarer, then swung by Safeway and picked up some chips and beer for later in the evening when he had some pals coming over. Once home, it was time to take Buster for a walk.

They were just coming back down the street from Buster's constitutional when he saw Arianna and Sophie approaching, bearing a foil-covered plate.

"Hi, Alden!" Sophie called and started skipping toward him. "Hi, Buster!"

"Hi," Alden called in return and thought, *Hello, Nurse,* channeling Yakko and Wakko from *Animaniacs*. Arianna was wearing a pink top and matching sweater and a skirt that showed off that fine pair of legs. Her lipstick matched that sweater.

"We made deviled eggs," Sophie told him before bending to pet Buster. "Grammy said we should give you some."

He half wished it had been Arianna who'd suggested that. "I like deviled eggs."

"We have way too many," Arianna said.

"We colored eggs at our party," Sophie informed him.

"A lot of eggs," Arianna added with an eye roll.

"Come on in," he offered.

"Just for a minute," she said.

"We had a party, and we took pictures with Santa Bunny," Sophie informed him as they followed him into the house.

"Santa Bunny?" He raised his eyebrows at Arianna.

"Christmas in April," she explained.

He unleashed Buster, who immediately ran to grab his favorite tug-of-war toy. Sophie followed and they were instantly happily going at it.

"Still maintaining momentum," he observed. "Except you already had Easter."

"Yeah, but that's a whole 'nother holiday. We have to keep the Christmas spirit alive and well."

"I guess," he said dubiously.

"Anyway, we're milking every good moment we can out of this year," she said, and he saw the dark cloud pass over her features. He also saw the shadows under her eyes.

"How's your mom doing?"

"Good," she said.

"And how are you doing?"

"I'm good."

"Yeah, I can see that. You look like you're ready to lead the zombie apocalypse."

She looked to where her daughter was happily playing with the dog and lowered her voice. "I guess I'm not sleeping very well. I worry."

"What you need is some R and R."

"I'll book that flight to Hawaii right now."

"There you go," he said, pretending to take her seriously.

"I don't want to leave Mom."

"I bet she'd be fine without you for a few hours."

Arianna shook her head. "But I wouldn't be fine."

"I bet you would be if someone was with her."

"With her feeding tube, I wouldn't trust anyone."

"Not even a nurse? I am one, remember? A lot of ER experience, and before that I was a navy corpsman."

"You were?"

She looked impressed. He liked that. "I was. I'm off on Thursday, got nothing planned. You go out and do something fun, and I'll come over and hang with your mom and Sophie."

In spite of his qualifications, she hesitated to say yes.

"I can handle it. And besides, you need to charge your batteries. You won't be any help to your mom or your kid if you collapse from exhaustion."

"I'm not exhausted," she insisted. "Well, not totally."

"Close enough to count. Hey, Sophie," he said, "how about Buster and I come over later this week and hang with you and your grandma? We can play Sorry!"

"What's that?" Sophie asked.

"A great board game," he replied.

"Yes!" she said.

Arianna frowned at him. "That was..."

"A great idea," he supplied. "It's okay to admit it. I'll be over at noon. Need me to pick up Sophie at school?"

"No, she rides the bus. She's home by three thirty. You just have to pick her up at the bus stop."

"Okay, then, we're set."

She thanked him and smiled at him. Gratefully. Yeah, he was the man.

Come Thursday he was right on time to shoo Arianna off. It was no hardship hanging with her mom. He enjoyed visiting with Mia, hearing about her life as a baker, of all the small trips she and her husband had taken in an old camper before they got pregnant, of the babies she'd lost before Arianna finally came. Of the time she baked a wedding cake for the mayor's daughter. Alden also enjoyed teaching Sophie how to play Sorry!, the same game he and his siblings had played when they were kids. Mostly, he loved seeing how refreshed and happy Arianna looked when she came back in the door, bearing a take-out bag from Emperor's Palace.

"Food!" cried Sophie, as if Alden had starved her.

"There's enough for three," Arianna offered. She looked sadly at her mom.

"You all go ahead," Mia said. "It does smell good, though. I can hardly wait until I can have Chinese again."

"Once that tube is out, that's the first thing we'll do," Arianna promised. "Sophie, go wash your hands."

Arianna chatted with her mother and then set her up with an episode of *Friends*, one of Mia's favorite old TV series. She and Alden ate at the kitchen table, out of Mia's sight line, and Alden observed that Arianna wasn't at the table for too long before she was back in the living room, checking on her mother.

"I feel guilty that I can eat," Arianna confided once Sophie was back with her Grammy and she and Alden were in the kitchen, putting away leftovers.

"It's almost as hard for the one who's not sick," he said.

"I feel so helpless sometimes."

"You're not. You're doing great."

She bit her lip, nodded. Then she managed a smile for him. "Thank you for today. It was really kind of you."

"I hope you enjoyed it," he said.

"I did."

"What did you do?"

"Things I used to take for granted. Window-shopped. Had lunch at The Habit. Onion rings," she added happily.

"Oh, yeah. Can't go wrong with onion rings."

"I even took advantage of the sun and walked part of Clear Creek Trail. You were right. I needed a break."

"I was right? I'm gonna bask in that for a moment," he said with a grin. Then sobered. "I enjoyed time with your mom and kid," he said. And he had.

Sophie was a great kid, and Mia was the kind of woman he'd want for a mother-in-law.

Spending evenings with the three of them, he could so picture it. Yep, he was falling for this woman. Falling? He already had.

No, no, no! No falling. He needed to grab his common sense and hold on tight. There was no hurry here. They were fine just being neighbors. Good neighbors, good neighbors who helped each other. Good neighbors who hung out.

Good neighbors who hung out naked?

He cleared his throat, made the supreme effort to clear his brain, and said, "I'd better get going. Got some things I should do."

Like take a cold shower.

16

Sunny dropped off a rotisserie chicken at Arianna's place late Friday afternoon. Sophie and Mia were on the couch together and Sophie was reading her favorite book to Mia, so the two friends wandered off to the kitchen for a mug of tea.

"How's it going with Bella?" Arianna asked.

Sunny shook her head. "Would it be awful to confess that I wish she'd get kidnapped by aliens? That's where I am right now. It changes daily."

"I'm sorry. You don't deserve this," Arianna said.

"You don't deserve what Wyatt did to you. Your mom doesn't deserve what's happening to her. I guess trouble never heard of the merit system."

"Guess not," Arianna said, staring into her mug. She roused herself and returned to Sunny's problem. "You still not going to tell Travis about the note?"

"What's the point? It's just more of the same. I can't control how Bella feels and him harping on her will only make it worse."

Bella's including Dylan in her note had added a new hurt. Dylan had seemed more ambivalent right from the start, and he'd been showing signs of starting to like her. If what Bella had written was true about him as well as her, Sunny was getting nowhere. If it wasn't, his sister was positively Machiavellian.

"You're trying so hard. It's just sad."

"No, it's just Tansy. I know she's the one who started this."

"She's got a boyfriend, though, so why keep it up?"

Sunny sighed. "Because she hates that Travis had the nerve to find someone and be happy after they split."

"You'd think she'd be too busy being happy to waste time trying to make you guys miserable," Arianna said.

"That's not how she operates. She's a narcissist. She can't settle for her side of the bed being warm. She has to make sure the person on the other side is freezing."

"What did he ever see in her?"

"A facade. When she first met Travis, she pretended to be so… I don't know, everything. But when he began to see through her and started pulling away, she conveniently had an 'oops, I'm pregnant' moment. Travis loves kids and he wanted a family, so he ignored the warning bells in his head and married her."

"I take it the baby never came."

"No, then it was oops, I miscalculated. Who does that? Anyone can manage a home pregnancy test. Within months he was ready to end things, but then she really did get pregnant and begged him to stay. He thought he could make it work, but in the end, she was just too selfish. After Dylan she got bored with the whole mommy thing. The final straw came when she started making regular *runs to the store* or *visits to his mom* and then wound up going out with her girlfriends. She doesn't really love those kids. All she loves is herself."

"Sounds like Wyatt. He wanted to spend the rest of his life with me. Until he didn't. Why do people say they want a committed relationship when they don't?" Arianna mused. Wyatt had claimed he was ready for one.

"Because that's what everyone is supposed to want. Until they realize how much work it is. And now that she has to share the kids, she wants them all the time and wants them to love her and only her. I could have ended things when I began to see what I was getting into but darn it all, I loved Travis like crazy. I still do."

"It all seems so unfair," said Arianna.

"Yeah, well you know the saying that goes with that."

"I do," said Arianna, and they both quoted, "'Who said life was fair?'" then exchanged sour smiles. "Still, I'm sorry she's using the kids as a weapon," Arianna finished.

"Same here. Travis is convinced that things will work out eventually because we're the good guys, and the good guys always win."

"You are, and I hope you do."

"I'm not holding my breath. Arsenic never stops being deadly," Sunny said.

It was a crappy thought.

Ava had made plans to take Molly to the Bloedel Reserve, a 150-acre forest garden on Bainbridge Island, and a draw for flower and nature lovers all over the county. It had been meant to be a surprise, but Molly found out after telling Ava that Reggie wanted to take them all out to eat for Mother's Day.

"No," Ava said firmly. "And no, he's not invited to go to Bloedel with us. He's not part of the family and he doesn't get to horn in on Mother's Day."

"Horn in?" Molly repeated. Honestly her daughter's unwelcoming attitude was getting old.

"He's already coming to our monthly Christmas parties. He doesn't get to be part of this. It's called Mother's Day and it's for kids and their mothers."

"Okay, fine," Molly said, backing down.

"And you're rushing things with him," Ava added sternly.

"I'm not rushing. We're just spending time together."

"Well, he can go spend time with somebody else this Sunday," Ava snapped, and that was the end of that.

Molly saw her daughter's point. Mother's Day had always been special for them. It had been only the two of them when Ava was growing up, taking on life together. Then they'd added Paisley and Mother's Day celebrations expanded to accommodate the three of them.

Would that rule hold true if Ava found someone? Molly decided not to raise the issue.

"I understand," Reggie said when she told him. "I didn't think when I offered."

"It was a sweet gesture," Molly assured him.

"Your daughter doesn't like me, does she?"

Molly wasn't prepared for such an honest conversation. "She's very protective of me," she hedged.

"I know I don't look like much. Never been much of a dresser."

He didn't exactly show off well, she had to admit.

"Will you go shopping with me?" he asked.

"Oh, Reggie, you don't need to buy new clothes on my account," she protested.

"It's time I upgraded my wardrobe. Anyway, you know what they say. Clothes make the man."

"No, they don't. They're just window dressing," she said. "Don't you go turning yourself inside out for my daughter."

"She's your family, and I'd turn myself inside out and upside down for you, Molly," he said.

His words covered her in sweetness. This man was a keeper. She didn't care how he dressed.

You're rushing things with him.

She frowned. She was not. Rushing would be running off to Vegas, finding that chapel of love, then getting Reggie completely out of those out-of-style clothes. And keeping him out of them for a nice long time. She smiled at the thought. It was one she would not be sharing with her daughter, that was for sure.

Mother's Day was hard for Arianna, although it started out perfectly. Sophie brought her breakfast-in-bed—a bowl of cereal, carefully clasped in both hands. She'd made a card also, of course, using her favorite colored paper. It showed a picture of her and Arianna, block figures holding hands, walking under a sky filled with hearts.

"This is lovely," Arianna said.

"I made one for Grammy, too," Sophie said. Her smile clouded over. "I wish I could bring her breakfast-in-bed."

"You'll be able to later, after her tube is out," Arianna promised, and hoped it wasn't a false promise.

Mia was feeling good that day so they decided to visit the Bremerton City Nursery. It had always been a favorite place of Mia's. The azaleas in the front flower beds and the roses in back, as well as the ornamental thyme along the front walk were all from the nursery. Mia had already been out playing in the yard on her good days and was determined to keep doing so.

"It brings me joy," she liked to say.

So did walking around the nursery, where they picked out three baskets filled with petunias to hang outside along the front porch.

"I do love flowers," Mia said as they drove home.

"Me, too, Grammy," said Sophie, who was holding the pot of stargazer lilies that she'd picked out for her "present" to Mia in her lap.

"We are going to have the prettiest house on the block," Mia said to her.

"Yes, we are!" Sophie agreed.

Arianna smiled. Then her smile faded as she wondered if they'd be doing this come the next Mother's Day, if her mother was still with them. She ran away from the ugly thought. The idea of having to face life on her own without tapping into her mother's strength and wisdom was more than she could bear.

They'd beat this thing. Lots of people beat cancer.

Still, even though the sun was out, she couldn't shake the feeling that they were driving along under a huge black cloud.

Sunny and her sister and mom all went to see a movie—a rom-com, it always had to be a rom-com, that was the tradition.

Sitting in the dark theater, diving into her bucket of popcorn, she could almost forget that the only Mother's Day card she'd gotten had been from Travis, thanking her for working so hard to be a good stepmom. She hadn't expected anything, knew she'd get nothing, but even though she'd braced for the hurt, it had still stung. She'd always wanted to be a mom, had loved the idea of having children of her own to play with and encourage. She was running on a relationship treadmill with the kids, getting nowhere. Maybe she wasn't meant to be a mother.

"Be patient," Mom had said. "One day you'll get that Mother's Day card. Meanwhile, you don't want to get something that isn't heartfelt."

"Maybe I do," Sunny had muttered.

Maybe I do!

That night she dreamed she got a Mother's Day card, but it was sitting inside a human-sized mousetrap. She scurried over to it on little mouse feet. Mouse feet! She looked over her shoulder. What was that long thing protruding from her ass?

Never mind that. Get the card. She leaned her head up close to read the card. Something went snap and she found she was spread out flat, her neck pinned down under some kind of giant metal bar. In the background she could hear someone laughing. It sounded a lot like Bella.

"I think my neck's broken," she squeaked.

The voice was nearer. "Too bad."

"Why am I here?"

"Hey, you wanted a card."

A giant hand reached out. It picked her up by her tail—her tail!—and carried her to a garbage can the size of a car and dumped her in, trap and all. "Hope you have a great Mother's Day. Not!"

There she sat at the bottom of the can, on her tail. Her tail! The lid was off and light was shining in and she saw two faces looking down at her. The faces belonged to Bella and Tansy and they had cat ears and whiskers.

"You'll always be nothing more than an insignificant mouse," Tansy taunted her, and they both laughed.

Their faces disappeared and next thing she knew someone was dumping a plastic bag of garbage on top of her. It was followed by another, and another. She was suffocating.

She awoke to find her blanket over her head, her hair damp with sweat. What would Freud make of that?

"You know what it means," Molly said when the women sat at their usual table at Horse and Cow to fine tune the details of their next Christmas party. "That you feel like you're in a losing battle and you feel like garbage."

"But what about the mousetrap and the card?" asked Sunny.

"You feel like you're in a cat-and-mouse game," Arianna offered.

A losing one. "What am I supposed to do?" Sunny demanded irritably.

"Buy some catnip?" Arianna suggested.

"Cute," Sunny said with a frown.

"You have to keep trying. That's all you can do," Arianna said, turning serious. "But don't let Bella's resentment get you down. You've always known Tansy's behind all of this."

Sunny pushed a French fry around her plate. "I'm so tired of it. I'm stuck in a remake of *Groundhog Day*, reliving Christmas every month, only with different trimmings. Trying to fix a fail that can't be fixed. My mother-in-law is never going to come to one of our parties and my stepdaughter is going to hate me forever. Why keep trying?"

Arianna sighed. "Because you'll feel rotten if you stop. And I'll feel rotten if you stop. I need these, Sunny. I really do. Even with the drama Bella brings, our Christmas parties are still special. Sophie looks forward to them and so does Mom. And they're helping me stay sane."

"Ava and Paisley have been enjoying them, too," put in Molly. "It was an inspired idea, and it's helping me at work. Do you know I had three customers ask me what we did for Christmas in April? And they loved the picture of Santa Bunny and me."

Sunny had to smile, hearing that.

"You're inspiring us," Arianna added.

"Glad I'm inspiring someone."

"You're really inspiring my mom. She called the *Kitsap Sun* and told them about the Twelve Months of Christmas," Arianna said.

Sunny stared at her. "Your mom called the newspaper?"

"Yep. They want to send out a reporter and photographer to cover our Christmas-in-May party. So, no pressure, but we need to make it good," Arianna said.

Sunny managed a weak smile. "Great." For the first time since her Christmas fail, she found herself hoping that Tansy would mess up Travis's weekend to have the kids and take them somewhere far, far away.

CHRISTMAS
IN MAY

17

Because the twenty-fifth of May was part of Memorial Day weekend, the Christmas-in-May party got bumped up. Sunny wasn't in much of a holiday mood after her Mother's Day snub the previous weekend, but she told herself to get over it and get on with it. Getting on with it would mean more rejection and rudeness from her stepdaughter, but Bella wasn't the only one coming. Others were looking forward to this. *Find that holiday spirit!* she cheered herself. *Goooo, team!*

Holiday spirit. Wasn't that why they were doing this in the first place? Yes, it was.

"You can do this," she told her reflection in the bathroom mirror the morning of the party. Yes, she could. She put on her lipstick, then donned her Santa hat and went downstairs, ready to face the day. And the step-kids.

Her tree was decorated with silk flowers in honor of spring, and once the kids arrived, she succeeded in drafting Dylan to help her make a dirt cake—layers of cookie crumbs, chocolate pudding and gummi worms. He, at least, appeared to have recovered from his "hatred" and was perfectly happy scraping the pudding bowl before the gang arrived for their monthly Christmas celebration. Sunny had made up goody packages of "worms" for everyone and, as usual, Bella was sneering.

"Those are for kids."

Travis, serving as the antidote to his daughter's perpetual Grinch germs, popped one in his mouth. "And for kids at heart. And you used to love these." She was about to open her mouth and barf out some snottiness, but before she could, he held up a hand and said, "I don't want to hear it. And if you don't like the candy, you don't have to eat it. More for the rest of us." He took another one, gave it to Dylan, who was happy to gobble it down. Then he smiled at Sunny. "Great idea, babe."

Bella flounced off into the living room.

"Every party has a pooper. That's why we invited you," Travis sung under his breath.

Sunny shook her head at him, signaling for him to zip it. Mocking the girl would only make her feel all the more justified in her resentment.

Dessert was ready and the grill was fired up for burgers and "White Christmas" was playing when the rest of the holiday celebrants arrived, bearing all manner of green goodies. Molly had made her Jell-O salad with green Jell-O, cottage cheese and pineapple; Ava brought makings for punch—7-Up and lime sherbet; and Arianna arrived with Sophie and a tired-looking Mia. Their contribution was a salad with strawberries, pretzels and yes, more Jell-O. Red so that the partiers would have both red and green foods.

The reporter, Josh Farley, arrived just as the kids (minus the pill in the corner with her cell phone) were putting seed packets in red net gift bags for all their neighbors. He took in the tree, the Christmas-in-May gifts and the food laid out on the counter, and smiled appreciatively.

"This is impressive," he said to Sunny.

"We're having fun," Sunny told him. *Most of us, anyway.* She led him over to the table where everyone was assembling their bags and introduced him. "And that's my stepdaughter, Bella, over there," she said, motioning to where the pouter sat.

Bella kept her gaze riveted on her phone, refusing to look up and acknowledge their guest. It was all Sunny could do not to say, "I lied. I have no idea who that kid is. She wandered in off the street."

But Bella was a part of her family now. They were tied together by marriage. She was a gift.

The booby prize.

No, no, no. Someday, somehow, some way, they would have a good relationship.

"How did you ladies come up with this idea?" Josh asked.

"It was Sunny's idea," Arianna said. "We'd all had kind of crummy Christmases."

For Arianna, it had been a lot worse than crummy. And now she was dealing with more crummy. Looking at what her friend was going through always put things in perspective for Sunny. It seemed like no matter what you were dealing with, there was always someone struggling with something worse.

"So we decided to do a restart," Sunny explained.

"And that first restart was so much fun we decided to keep it going," added Molly.

"What was that?" Josh asked.

"We went ice-skating in January," Molly said.

"What else have you done?" he wanted to know.

The women filled him in on their other adventures. "Christmas comes and goes so fast. I thought it would be a good idea to celebrate the season all year long," Sunny finished.

"There's a quotable line," Josh said as he made notes on his tablet.

"What do you guys think of this?" he asked the kids, who were nearby, happily switching from filling bags to filling up on chips and dip.

"It's awesome," gushed Paisley.

Sophie agreed enthusiastically. "I liked Santa Bunny," she added.

"Santa Bunny?" Josh repeated, and looked questioningly at Sunny.

"Christmas-in-April party," she clarified.

He nodded. "Of course. What do you like best?" he asked Dylan.

"I like getting presents every month," Dylan said, making the adults chuckle.

"I'll bet," said Josh. "I'd like that, too."

Bella had wandered over, sneaking to the edge of the group. It made Sunny think of a feral cat her family had once adopted. The animal had been fearful and suspicious yet longing for the food the humans left out. What was Bella longing for?

Josh smiled at her and asked, "What do you think of your mother's idea?"

Bella was quick to correct him. "She's not my mother."

True, of course, but the way she'd said it, the sullen expression—no matter how much Sunny braced for those snubs, they still cut deeply.

A stern look from her father inspired Bella to add her assessment of the monthly celebrations. "It's okay." Damning with faint praise.

Everyone was quick to jump in and cover the moment with lots of positivity. Josh got them to pose in front of the tree and Sunny noticed Bella joined them—standing as far from Sunny as possible, but at least she was there.

One of these days, Sunny vowed, *she'll be willing to stand next to me.*

"It was a lovely party," Mia said with a tired sigh as Arianna drove them home.

"Yeah, except for the resident downer girl," Arianna said, shaking her head.

"These kinds of adjustments aren't easy for kids," Mia said.

Arianna stole a look in her rearview mirror at her daughter.

Sophie had music playing on the iPad her other grandma had given her for her birthday and was bobbing her head in time to her favorite kid sing-along. She seemed happy enough, getting shuttled back and forth between her parents. How would she adjust if she wound up with a stepmother? How would Arianna adjust to Sophie having a stepmother? Or a stepfather, if Arianna ever was ready to trust a man again after Wyatt?

"Still, they have to," Mia continued. "It's too bad that Bella doesn't realize what a good deal she got with Sunny. And she doesn't even have to live with her full-time."

"Like you did yours," put in Arianna.

"Poor Myrtle. She wasn't all that bad, but I couldn't forgive her for having the nerve to step in and take my mother's place. I'd always thought my father would mourn my mother forever and his falling for Myrtle was such an insult to Mama's memory. Of course, I couldn't wait to leave home." Mia shook her head. "I regret that I realized too late what a stinker I'd been. I regret my resentment and unwelcoming attitude."

They'd had this conversation more than once. The broken relationship left unmended had been one of Mia's few regrets in life. Her stepmother had died of an aneurysm a few years after she left home. Seeing her father widowed again and mourning so deeply had made Mia realize how unfair she'd been to want to hold him back from having a companion to love.

"Life is short, but sadly, the young don't realize that," Mia said.

Life is short. Those three painful words reminded Arianna how precious the time with her mother was. As they walked into the house, she told herself to be thankful that Mia was still with her and that they were getting to enjoy so many fun activities together.

"That kid is a beast," Molly muttered as Ava drove her and Reggie back to her house. "If I was Travis, I'd take away her phone."

"It's probably glued to her hand," Reggie said.

"Well, they should unglue it," Molly retorted. "I don't know why every child in America needs a cell phone these days. When I was raising you, we got along just fine without one."

"These are different times," Ava said. "Once Paisley's a little older, I'm getting her one. That way we can always reach each other if there's an emergency."

"Good point," said Reggie, probably sucking up.

"I guess," Molly said, "but if that girl was mine, she'd be in the corner all right, with her nose to the wall."

Ava chuckled. "I remember a few close encounters with the wall."

"Better than what I remember," Reggie said. "I remember a couple of close encounters with my daddy's belt."

"Ugh," Ava said with a shudder.

"Yeah, it was no fun. Let me tell you, I learned real quick not to mouth off to him and I learned to do what I was told."

"Out of fear," Ava argued.

"There was that, but it was complicated. He was being a father the only way he knew how at the time. My old man also never went a night without kissing me good-night when I was small. He took me fishing, and when I got old enough, financed my first car—an old beater—and helped me work on it. He got me my first job working at his pal's service station, and he taught me the value of a dollar. And he never worried about whether or not I liked him. Told him I hated him once and he said, *I'm not here for you to like, boy. I'm here to turn you into a decent human being.*"

Molly smiled at him and took his hand. "I'd say he did."

"I try," Reggie said humbly. "And you know what, I loved that man like crazy. It about killed me the day he died."

"But you told him you hated him," put in Paisley, who'd been on her iPad, but obviously listening.

"You're right, Paisley, I did say that. But I don't think I ever meant it. Sometimes you can have so many feelings inside you at once it's hard to know what they all are."

"I love my mommy," Paisley told him.

"And so you should. Your mommy works hard to give you a good life," he said.

That had to earn him some brownie points with Ava.

"It's too bad Bella can't see how hard Sunny's working to make her life good," Molly said.

"Some things you don't see till you're older," Reggie said. "Anyway, you can't force people to like you."

"I like you, Reggie," Paisley said.

That big smile of his took over his face. "I like you, too, Paisley."

"Want to come in for a while?" Molly asked Ava as they pulled into her driveway.

"Better not. We have some errands to run."

"How about you?" Molly asked Reggie.

"Sure. I got no place to be," he said.

Molly didn't have to look to know her daughter was rolling her eyes. Ava was still convinced that Reggie was too old and too broke to qualify as good boyfriend material.

Ava was wrong. There was something special about Reggie, and being with him made Molly happy.

"I don't think I've won your daughter over yet," he said as they settled on her back deck with mugs of coffee to enjoy the view of Sinclair Inlet.

"It takes Ava a while to warm up to people," Molly said.

It was no lie. Her daughter tended to be suspicious of men. Hardly surprising considering her experience with men.

"I'll keep stacking the kindling," he joked.

"She'll come around," Molly said, then mentally added, *She'd better*. Because Molly liked Reggie just fine.

Later he sent out for Chinese, and they ate at her patio table and watched the sunset. Finally he said, "I'd better get going."

She almost said, "Do you have to?" The evening had gone down smooth as her favorite rum raisin ice cream.

Instead she nodded and walked with him back through the house to the front door.

"What do you think about lunch tomorrow?" he asked. "Or am I rushing things too much?"

"Not at all. In fact, you could rush a little more," Molly said, and moved closer.

Reggie was a smart man. He picked up on body language really well.

He slipped one of those lovely big arms around her waist and snugged her up against him, setting off firecrackers in her chest. "You think so?"

"I know so."

Those lips of his, they were magic. And his arms around her made her feel like she was inside a fortress. She could taste the sweet-and-sour sauce from the chicken they'd eaten, she could smell his woodsy aftershave mingled with the musky scent of man. She was getting drunk on him.

He took his time with that kiss, and when it ended, he touched his forehead to hers. "Molly Fielding, you are some kind of wonderful."

"I'm thinkin' the same thing about you," she said.

"So, lunch tomorrow?"

"Oh, yes." And the next day and the next.

He kissed her once more and that one was as good as the first. She was a woman who'd been in the desert way too long and had finally found an oasis. She didn't want to leave, and she wrapped her arms around his neck and took a good long drink.

He was grinning when they were done. "Woman, I can't get enough of you."

"Plenty more where that came," she said.

"All right, then. Don't forget where we left off," he said with his big Reggie smile.

"I won't."

Indeed, it would be all she'd be thinking of for the rest of the night. Ava could say what she wanted about Reggie Washington, but he sure looked like the right man for Molly.

CHRISTMAS
IN JUNE

18

"How could you run out of flower stamps?" Mrs. Mason demanded, glaring at Molly.

Mrs. Mason was one of Molly's regulars, and though she couldn't hold a candle to Mrs. Bigman, she was doing her best at the moment. She liked flower stamps, no flags, thank you. As far as Mrs. Mason was concerned that meant politics and she didn't like politics. She was loyal to flower stamps, except for Christmas and then she expected either angels or the Madonna and child. Molly always tried to have what Mrs. Mason wanted, but when she didn't, Mrs. Mason was usually a good sport.

There was no good sportsmanship happening today. "I can't believe you don't have flowers," Mrs. Mason grumbled.

"I'm sorry, Mrs. Mason, but we had a run on flower stamps," Molly said. "I do have some lovely bird ones. You know, flowers and birds go together."

"They do not," snapped Mrs. Mason, and gave her left hip a scrub.

Hmm. "Mrs. Mason, are you feeling all right?"

"No, I'm not. My bursitis is killing me."

That explained it. It was hard to keep your sweet disposition when you were in pain.

"I get that sometimes," Molly said. "You know what helps?"

Mrs. Mason lost some of her anger. "What?"

"A cold compress, and I stretch at night before I go to bed, then massage the area really well, get those burses bumped around. Then I put on a pain patch."

Molly grabbed her phone and showed Mrs. Mason her favorite brand online. "These work wonders."

"Thank you, Molly," Mrs. Mason said, over her flower frustration.

"I'm happy to help," Molly said.

"I guess I'll take birds," said Mrs. Mason. "But you are going to get in more flowers, aren't you?"

"Yes, we are," Molly assured her.

"Good. Be sure to save some for me."

"I'll do my best."

Three customers down the line stood Reggie, giving Molly a thumbs-up. It made her day.

The line moved up and Molly helped another customer. At the window next to her, Helen called, "I can help whoever is next," and he let the man in front of him go ahead.

"That was very chivalrous of you," Molly teased when he stepped up to her window.

"I am a chivalrous man. You handled that situation with Mrs. Mason very well," he said.

"I guess I'm in touch with my inner Santa," she replied. "For once. You know, when you deal with so many people, it's easy to turn them into a parade of irritations. But they're just people, all trying to get through the day the best they can."

"I think you helped her," he said. He laid down the paper he'd been carrying. "You made the news today. I'm surprised nobody's said anything."

"My best customers haven't come in yet. Well, until now," she added, smiling at him.

"It's a great write-up. Oh, and I have one more thing for you." He dug in his coat pocket and produced a bobblehead figure shaped like a round Mrs. Claus. "I thought your mister needed a missus," he said. "Most misters do."

"She's darling." Molly took the figure and placed it on the windowsill next to her others. "I'm getting quite the collection."

"You can never have enough bobbleheads," he said.

"Or kind friends who come in to make your day." And friends who were becoming much more than simply friends.

"Hey, are you done talking?" demanded a man in a business suit.

Reggie turned to him. "Did you know this woman's a celebrity? There's an article about her in the paper."

"That's nice," the man said. He held up a long business envelope. "I need to overnight this."

So much for being a celebrity. "Of course," Molly said.

Reggie stepped aside and let her wait on the man, who said a brisk thank-you and then went on his way.

"Christmas spirit," Reggie said as the man left. "It's on sale today." He lowered his voice. "I guess he wasn't buying."

"Well, then, his loss," she said.

"Want to go see a movie tonight?"

"Sure," she said. Dinner, lunch and now a movie. Things were moving right along.

"We can sit in the back and neck," he said in a low voice and gave her a wink.

"I might want to watch the movie," she teased.

"Then during the coming attractions," he said. "We can grab something to eat before, if you want."

She wanted.

He gave the counter a tap. "See you later, then."

She could hardly wait.

But by later she was not quite as cheery as she'd been. Her resolution to remember that her customers were just ordinary people trying to get through the day had completely vanished by the time she saw the mail on its way for the day. Some of her regulars had seen the article in the paper and gushed over her, which had filled her holiday-happiness cup. But as many other people had done their best to drain it with complaints.

"You look exhausted," Reggie said when he came to pick her up.

"I am. I kept the Christmas spirit going as long as I could, but eventually the Grinch got to me." She let out a sigh and laid her head back on the car's headrest. "This job takes it out of me."

"You ever think of quitting?"

"Only every other day."

"Then why don't you?"

"Retirement. I can retire at sixty, but I've got five more years to go. That's not so bad."

"A few years can feel like a hundred when you're miserable," he pointed out.

"I'm not that miserable. I'm just whining," she said. "Tired of working, but I'll have a nice retirement when I'm done."

"You don't want to wait to retire to start living."

"Who says I'm not living now?" she retorted. "I'm living it up with you right now."

He chuckled. "That you are."

"I hope you're hungry for Mexican. It's Taco Tuesday," he said as he pulled into a Taco Bell parking lot.

Here was another reason Molly was determined to stick it out at her job. She didn't want to wind up pinching pennies and eating tacos on Tuesdays. She wasn't all that fond of tacos.

He must have seen the resigned expression on her face. "You don't like tacos?"

"Not particularly." She felt somehow guilty for admitting it. Who didn't love tacos?

"No problem," he said and started pulling back out. "What do you like? Fish?"

"Sure."

"Okay, fish it is," he said, and ten minutes later they were at Anthony's Home Port on the Bremerton waterfront. Not exactly Taco Tuesday prices.

"I didn't mean we had to go somewhere expensive."

"This isn't expensive," he scoffed, and went to open the car door.

"No, really, Reggie," she said before getting out.

"I can afford it," he said.

That was when she realized he was wearing new slacks. And not his usual tennis shoes. He had on expensive-looking loafers.

"You got some new clothes," she observed as they crossed the underground parking to the elevator.

"I decided my wardrobe needed some updating," he said. "Got a smart young pup in the men's department to help me out. What do you think?"

"I think you look great. But then I've always thought you look great," she added.

"That's one of the things I like about you," he said. "You look beneath the surface."

"I need to do that more with my customers," Molly admitted.

"Only if you stay."

"Which I'm going to."

"One of these days you may decide you don't need to," he said, and pressed the elevator button. The doors opened and he stepped in after her. "Going up."

Arianna hated seeing her mother so miserable. It was two days after Mia's latest chemo treatment, and that was when the body aches and exhaustion hit. Arianna gave her a back rub and tucked a blanket around her.

"I wish I could do more," she said. If only she could make some of her mother's favorite foods or…something.

"You're doing plenty," Mia said. "I feel terrible that you had to quit work to take care of me."

"I didn't quit. It is just a leave of absence." Her supervisor had been so understanding. Everyone had. "And we're doing fine. The GoFundMe money has helped a lot."

Mia made a face.

"This is temporary," Arianna assured her. "I'm getting more followers on my social media, so pretty soon we'll have more money coming in from that. I just got contacted by a health drink company, who want to pay me a nice sum for promoting their product. It won't be long before I won't need help."

"You wouldn't have had to take it if you still had your job," Mia said, and Arianna could hear the motherly guilt in her voice.

"My job will still be waiting when we're past this. Meanwhile, we'll be fine without it," Arianna said. "I'm happy with how the website is doing. I feel like I'm, I don't know, getting somewhere in life. Getting…bolder."

Before the divorce she'd been perfectly happy living small. No big dreams. There'd been no need to dream big. After all, she'd had Wyatt and Sophie, a good job. Wyatt had been the big dreamer, the man with the plan. He was going to make their fortune investing in cryptocurrency. No, real estate. No, Tesla. (He'd bought high and sold low each time.) He was going to make something happen.

Funny, he hadn't made anything happen. He was still at his same old office job, selling heating systems. He was still looking for someone better than Arianna. He was probably still talking about taking the world by storm. Whatever.

"I'm proud of you, darling," Mia said.

Arianna wasn't taking the world by storm, but she was doing something purposeful with her life. She was moving on, and she felt good about it.

"You know what, Mom? I'm proud of me, too."

Sunny was enjoying basking in her fifteen minutes of fame thanks to the article in the *Kitsap Sun*.

"It's lovely to see your genius appreciated," her mother had said.

Her, a genius. Who'd have guessed it?

"Pretty cool that your stepdaughter was finally impressed with something you did," Molly said to her as they dug into their meals at Horse and Cow.

"Yes, Tansy actually admitted to Travis that Bella's been walking around school puffed up like a toad. All her friends think I am rad."

"If enough of her friends say it, she might start to believe it," said Arianna.

"Here's hoping." Although Sunny wasn't holding her breath.

"I'm glad," Molly told her. "You've been waiting long enough."

"Now, instead of the wicked stepmother, maybe she'll see you as a fairy godmother," said Arianna.

Maybe she was going to be more than a fairy godmother or stepmother. She'd stopped at the drugstore on her way to buy a home pregnancy test.

"We need to toast to our success," Arianna said. She frowned at the sight of Sunny's glass of water. "You going to order something to toast with?"

"This will work," Sunny said.

"Only water." Molly studied her. "Is there a reason for this?"

"Maybe."

"Oh, my gosh, are you pregnant?" Arianna asked eagerly.

"I'm not sure, but I bought a pregnancy test so I'll know tomorrow morning."

"Why wait? Take it tonight," Molly urged.

"I read that it's best to do it in the morning with your first pee."

"I don't know how you'll sleep tonight," Arianna said. "I wouldn't be able to."

It turned out, Sunny did, indeed, have a hard time falling asleep. A baby! Travis would be over the moon. So would she.

She was ready, and the idea of having a child who would actually love her—after what she'd been going through with Bella, it would be heaven on earth.

She was up early the next morning, peeing on the magical strip, and when that line appeared, she squealed so loudly she woke Travis. He rushed into the bathroom, his hair standing in all directions.

"Babe, what's wrong?" The words were barely out of his mouth before he saw the home pregnancy kit and the strip, took in the grin on her face. "Oh, man. Really?"

She nodded.

He let out a whoop, picked her up and swung her around, nearly banging her foot on the toilet. "This is the best news!" He kissed her so hard he about pushed her mouth to the back of her head. "I love you, babe. I love...this."

"I love you, too," she said.

"Get dressed. We're going out to celebrate."

"You have to work," she pointed out.

"Not today. I'm taking the day off. We're going out to breakfast."

Sunny hurried into the shower. She was going to bubble over with excitement.

And she almost did. Until the thought occurred to her that maybe Travis's kids wouldn't be that excited about having a half brother or sister. *No, no, no! Do not borrow trouble.* Too late. She was already at the worry bank.

Arianna answered the knock on her door late Friday afternoon to find Alden standing there with a copy of the *Kitsap Sun*. "Thought you might want an extra copy," he said, handing it over. "Congrats on being a celebrity."

"Thanks," she said. "Want to come in?"

He nodded and stepped over the threshold, said hello to Mia, who was on the couch, busy crocheting.

"Nice to see you," Mia said, and Arianna could read the thought behind the words. *Here visiting my daughter, hopefully falling for her.*

As if in real life neighbors fell crazy in love and lived happily-ever-after. Darn it all, why couldn't real life work that way? For a moment Arianna envisioned herself saying, "How about you pretend you're Santa and let me sit on your lap, play with your beard, loosen a couple of buttons on your suit." What would happen if she did that?

He would race back to his house as if Krampus was on his heels and about to beat the tar out of him. Still, the idea of showing Santa Alden what she'd like for Christmas in June made her smile.

"Where's Sophie?" he asked, looking around.

Arianna's smile vamoosed. "With her dad." Someone who deserved to have Krampus go after him.

"Ah." Alden nodded.

The mention of Wyatt produced an awkward silence. *Say something!* she commanded herself.

"It was nice of you to bring over the paper." Now there was a brilliant something.

"It looks like your idea of celebrating Christmas all year long isn't such a bad one," he said. "In fact, that party sounded kind of fun."

"Wishing you'd been there?" she teased.

"Gotta admit, maybe a little."

Mia inserted herself into the conversation, obviously not trusting her daughter to ride this wave of opportunity all the way to shore. "You could come to our Christmas-in-June party."

He raised an eyebrow at Arianna. "Are outsiders allowed?"

She laughed. "Anyone who wants to get into the spirit of Christmas is welcome," she said. *Especially you.*

"I may just have to check it out."

"I think you should," she said.

"I've got to admit, after reading the article, the whole thing doesn't seem quite so, uh…"

"Out there?" she supplied.

"Yeah. Still, you've got to admit, it might be too much for your average person."

"I don't want to be average," she said, and realized how very much she meant it.

"Trust me, you're not," he said. Ooh, that smile. It was as warm and yummy as hot chocolate.

"You're not gonna get up on the roof, are you?" he teased.

"Not planning on it. I promise I won't fall on you." *But do I have to promise not to climb all over you?*

He nodded. "When is it?"

"The…"

"Twenty-fifth," he finished with her. "Of course."

"Ho, ho, ho," she said.

"Count me in. I really do want to check this out."

"All right," she said. "Once you see how much fun it is, you'll become a holiday-party addict like the rest of us."

"Here's to holiday-party addiction," he quipped. Then he said goodbye to Mia and strolled off across the lawn.

Never mind the parties, she thought as she watched him walk back to his house. *Just get addicted to me.*

"I think that man's getting addicted to something, but it's not holiday parties," said Mia.

"Right," Arianna said. "He's only being nice."

"No, he's interested."

"Maybe," Arianna said, but she wasn't ready to get her hopes up too much yet.

She dropped the paper on the coffee table and plopped onto a chair.

"Darling, you are a lovely woman. Why wouldn't a man be interested in you?"

"I don't know. After what happened with Wyatt…"

"Wyatt is a twit, and a narcissist. This man actually has some common sense and knows when he sees a good thing. And trust me, you are."

"You might be slightly prejudiced," Arianna said. "I'm not that special."

"You certainly are. You're starting your own business, becoming an influencer, helping create these fun holiday celebrations."

"That's mostly Sunny," Arianna said, waving away her mother's praise. "She's the creative one."

"You are, too," said Mia. "And, even more important, you are noble and kind. That is a winning combination. So don't give up on yourself, and don't give up on love."

"Well, I'm not going to give up on myself," Arianna vowed. Love, however, was a different matter.

Still, it would sure be nice to get extra neighborly with Alden Brightman.

Molly was almost too tired to go out with Reggie for burgers. Almost. But she rallied.

Still, she looked tired enough for him to say, "Molly, I'd sure like to save you from working so hard," he said as they settled at their table in Noah's Ark. Three days in a row they'd spent time together. It felt so comfortable they could have been together for a lifetime.

"Work is a good thing, and I don't need saving," she said. "Although I do wish that people would appreciate me just a little bit more. Not only me, all their postal workers."

"Everyone takes the mail person for granted," Reggie said.

She sighed. "I know. And I guess we don't deserve any special rewards, considering the fact that we're only doing our job."

"But you go above and beyond. Molly, if you didn't have to think about money or retirement, would you still be working?"

"It's a moot point. I do have to think about money and retirement."

"I'd like you to think about something new," he said.

She looked at him, puzzled.

"About a different kind of future."

Now she was suspicious. "Don't tell me, you have a business opportunity for me."

He chuckled. "No. But I do have a proposition. Marry me."

"Marry you?"

"I know we haven't been dating all that long."

"We sure haven't," she said. Even if it felt like they'd been together for years, even though she'd fantasized about running off together, she was realistic enough to know that it was way too soon for this kind of talk.

"But we knew each other long before we started dating, and we've spent a lot of time together. I know you care for me, and I am head over heels in love with you. And I want to take care of you."

"Reggie, I can take care of myself."

"Okay, then, I want to spoil you. Marry me and you can quit tomorrow."

She laughed. "And we'd live on love."

"No, we'd live on my money."

"Your money," she repeated. She'd seen how he was living on his money. She was sure if she looked up *penny-pincher* on Wikipedia, she'd see a picture of Reggie and his ancient car.

"I know, I don't exactly look like a millionaire."

"Money isn't everything," she said, not wanting him to think she was some kind of materialistic gold digger. Anyway, if she were, she'd be digging around someone other than Reggie.

"No, but it does make life easier, and I'd sure like to do that for you. I am, by the way."

"You are…what?"

"A millionaire. Although these days a million dollars doesn't go nearly as far as it used to."

She began to laugh.

"No, really. I'm not kidding. I know I don't dress like it. Or at least I didn't until I wanted to impress you. I guess that has a lot to do with the clothes upgrade and new car I'm getting. I've come to realize it's time to start living a little, and I want to do that living with you, girl," he finished with a smile.

She stared at him. "You're not kidding."

"I'm not. I was never one to run around showing off. But I do have a boat. And a place in Playa del Carmen. I rent it out most of the year, but I like to go down and fish, usually in November."

"How come this is the first I've heard of this?" she demanded, still sure he wasn't making all this up.

"I wanted us to get to know each other, wanted to make sure you could love me for me."

"That's not hard to do, but this is a little hard to take in," she said.

"I know. Believe it or not, there are a lot of men like me—men who worked hard, were careful with their money and made some smart investments. Ever read a book called *The Millionaire Next Door*?"

She shook her head.

"Well, it's about guys like me. I'm an average Joe who worked a blue-collar job. But I took some night classes, read some books, started with a small money snowball and kept it rolling until it turned into something big. Granted, I'm no Bill Gates, but I've made some smart investments over the years, and I've got enough dough to last us both a lifetime."

"I thought you were…living on Social Security."

"Don't need it, but I take it since I paid into it all those years. Most of that gets given to my church."

"So now you're just…"

"Keeping busy doing some odds and ends. Got a rental here in town, and I'm living in a nice condo over by the ferries."

He made that sound like nothing. She sat staring at him, too busy trying to digest everything he was telling her to pay attention to her burger.

"I'm a simple man, don't spend money on showy things. But that doesn't mean I won't treat you well or give you anything you want. You deserve it."

"I don't want anything," she protested.

"Not even me?" The smile on his face was teasing, but his eyes showed his insecurity.

She shook her head at him. "Of course, you. But I don't want to rush into anything."

He nodded, his smile a ghost of what it was a few moments ago.

"How about we say we're serious?"

"Serious, as in I stand a chance?"

She smiled, reached across the table and took his hand. "You stand a very good chance. I just want to be sure. And I need time. I owe that to my family. I owe that to you."

"Okay," he said. "Meanwhile, to prove I'm not making all this up, I'll take you in to Canlis for dinner tomorrow."

"Canlis," she echoed in shock. "That's the most expensive restaurant in Seattle."

"I'm going to prove to you that I am willing and able to spoil you," he said. "Or if you want we can run up to Victoria for the weekend. You'll have Memorial Day off, right?"

She just stared at him. "I don't know what to say."

"Say, great ideas, Reggie,"

"You're pulling my leg," she scoffed.

"I'm not, and I'll prove to you that I really have a boat. How about I take you and the girls out on it for the Bremerton Bridge Blast the end of the month to watch the fireworks off the Manette Bridge?"

"We have our Christmas-in-June party that day."

Even the ghost of the smile vanished. "Oh." But he rallied. "Well, we can't miss that. I hope I'm invited?"

"Of course, you are. It's going to be a picnic."

"A picnic, you say. So, it's during the day?"

She saw where he was going. "Which means we would be free in the evening. And Paisley would love going out on a boat."

Actually, so would Molly. Ava would probably keel over in shock.

They finished their burgers, then went back to her house to watch a TV series they'd gotten hooked on. Reggie didn't leave without continuing his marriage sales pitch with some amazing kisses that left her practically panting.

"Just to remind you that we're now officially serious," he said with that big grin of his right before he headed home.

"We are officially serious," she agreed. "But that's all."

Her heart had already committed, but her brain was demanding she go slowly. She wasn't ready to quit her job. There'd be time for them down the road.

Time for them. The idea of spending the rest of her life with Reggie made her feel so lighthearted she wasn't sure if even her toes were touching the floor as she made her way to bed. Christmas all year, that was what it would feel like to be with him.

She could picture them making a good life together, maybe even spending winter in Playa del Carmen after she retired. Ava and Paisley could come down and visit.

Ava. When and how was she ever going to tell Ava?

19

"When we have our Christmas-in-June party at my place you'll all have to hold down the fort come evening," Molly announced to her friends as they met at Horse and Cow to talk Christmas.

"Why is that?" asked Sunny. It wasn't like Molly to duck out on a party.

"Because I am going to be out on Reggie's boat that night, along with Ava and Paisley, watching the Bridge Blast on the Manette Bridge."

"Boat?" Sunny repeated. "What kind of boat does he have, a rowboat?"

"I think it's more than that," Molly said.

"Don't tell me he's got money." Somehow Sunny couldn't picture Reggie being rich. Where were the brand name britches and fancy shirts? He looked like he shopped at Goodwill and not at Nordstrom.

"Actually, he does," Molly said.

"No way!" Sunny exclaimed. "That kind of thing happens in real life?"

"I mean, I don't know how much, but he has enough to live comfortably."

"If you can call the car he drives comfortable," Sunny said.

"Have you seen his house yet?" Arianna asked.

A little red showed on Molly's cheeks. "Well, no, actually he always comes to my place."

"Wait a minute. Maybe he's a scammer. Maybe he doesn't even own a house," Sunny said.

Molly frowned at her. "He's got a condo."

"Is this getting serious between you two?" Arianna asked.

"It is."

"Like, how serious?" Sunny demanded. "Moving in together? And does Ava know?"

"No, and no. Although he has asked me to marry him."

"Oh, my gosh!" cried Arianna. "It's almost like a fairy tale."

"Only without the frog," Molly said with a smile.

"But you don't want to rush into anything," Sunny cautioned.

"Now you sound like my daughter," Molly said. "And I'm not. Although at my age I don't plan on waiting forever, either."

"I'm happy for you," Arianna said. "After all this time you deserve true love."

"As long as he's not lying about the money thing. When are you going to tell Ava?" Sunny asked.

"When we actually get engaged. I don't want to freak her out. You know, she thinks he's too old for me."

Sunny snorted and shook her head. "I wouldn't worry about that. Age is just a number. Look at Travis and me. We're great. Well, except for the situation with Bella," she added with a frown.

"That will work out," Arianna assured her. "Look at you guys—you've found Reggie, Sunny passed her pregnancy test. I'm so happy for both of you."

Romance survivor guilt sledded across Sunny's heart. She had a great man, Molly had, hopefully, found her prince and Arianna was...coping with her mother's disease. It didn't seem right.

"Things are going to work out for you, too," she assured Arianna. As if she knew. Mia still couldn't eat. And that couldn't be good.

"I guess time will tell," Arianna said, and her smile looked forced, like her eyes and her lips hadn't quite connected. "I am bringing someone to the party, though," she added.

"Yeah?" Molly prompted. "Who?"

"My neighbor. He read the newspaper article and now he wants to check out what we're doing."

"Or check you out," Sunny told her. "Oh, that's right. He already has. Nothing like a little Santa mud wrestling to get a man interested," she teased.

Arianna blushed and took a drink of her iced tea.

Well, well, maybe something good was waiting in Arianna's future, after all. Sunny sure hoped so.

"We need to look this man over," Molly said.

"He's just curious," Arianna insisted.

"I think everyone's curious about what we're doing. I've sure had a lot of interest, and nice comments at work," Molly said. "In between the cranky customers. Mrs. Bigman informed me that she's not doing Christmas more than once a year. It would only be more times for her cookies to get lost."

"Maybe nobody wants to eat them and they're getting lost on purpose," Sunny said. "I've had a few fails nobody wanted to eat. Speaking of, once your mom's feeling better, do you think she'll give me some cooking lessons?" she asked Arianna.

That made Arianna's eyes light up. "She'd love that."

"Meanwhile, I've found a dip recipe I think I can handle," Sunny said.

"I saw a cute recipe online for cupcakes baked in ice-cream cones," Arianna said.

"That sounds darling. I'll bring the chocolate mint ice cream to go with them. And strawberry. That way we have red and green for Christmas," Molly said.

"Punch with lime sherbet?" suggested Sunny. She could handle that.

"Absolutely," Molly said.

And so it was decided. There would be some Fourth of July–style games like a water balloon toss, and Travis would be assigned the job of adapting the popular cornhole game to Christmas, making them a game that involved getting bean bags inside Santa's mouth.

The day of the party was sunny and in the mid-seventies, perfect picnic weather. Rae and her man were present, along with Sunny's parents, and a cheer went up when Travis put an arm around Sunny's waist and announced, "We're pregnant."

Except for Bella, of course. If looks could kill, Sunny and the baby would be goners.

Watching Bella, Arianna vowed she would never let her daughter act like that if the day came when Wyatt remarried. It would come, of course. He wasn't wired to be single.

Neither was she. Who knew? Maybe someday she wouldn't be. Having Alden present made her nearly giddy, and she realized she was laughing like a kid with her first crush at everything he said. But how could she not. He was funny.

"No one should be feeding Santa beans," he said as he aimed his beanbag at the plywood Santa's mouth. "He's gonna leave behind more than presents."

"That whole feeding Santa thing, where'd that come from?" Travis wondered as he stepped up to make his throw.

"From some poor dad who was tired of everyone eating the cookies before he could get to them. My mom was always taking the cookie tin away from dad, telling him they were for the company," Alden said.

I'd let you have all the cookies you wanted, thought Arianna.

"Then by the time the whole family came over and swarmed

the dessert table, there was nothing left but crumbs," Alden continued.

"That's rough, dude," said Travis.

"Yeah, but she always baked him his own batch of sugar cookies for New Year's," Alden said.

Alden's family life sounded so idyllic. Siblings and aunts and uncles and cousins. It had always been just her and Mia after her dad died. They'd spent time with Wyatt's parents when they were married, but he was an only child, too. What would it be like to have so many people to celebrate with?

Never mind having a lot of people, she prayed, *I just want my mom.*

The game ended and Travis and Alden were ready for a rematch, but Arianna called in Paisley to take her place. She went to join her mother up on Molly's deck, where she sat next to Bella, who was eating ice cream.

"Do you like my tattoo?" Mia was asking. She put out her foot to show off the tattoo on her ankle and smiled. It was of a cupcake and had the number twenty-five inside it.

"It's cute," Bella said, managing a polite moment.

"Want to know why I got it?"

Bella shrugged. "Okay."

"My husband and I got matching tattoos on our twenty-fifth wedding anniversary. I was a baker and we liked the idea of the cupcake."

Arianna knew what was coming next. It was a heartbreaking story.

"We didn't get any more after that," Mia said. "There was no time."

"No time?" Bella asked, her curiosity piqued.

"He was a fisherman. Every year he'd go up and fish in Alaska."

Bella wrinkled her nose. "Working with smelly fish all day sounds gross."

"Gross I could handle, but it was also dangerous work," Mia

said. "I'd just convinced him to quit. It was going to be his last season."

Bella's eyes began to widen. "What happened?"

"He was lost overboard in those awful frigid waters."

Horrified, Bella swore.

Mia took advantage of the moment to drive home her point. "You know what I learned?"

"Don't marry a fisherman?" Bella guessed.

"That, too. But the big lesson I learned is that life can be short and bad things can happen."

"That was bad," Bella conceded.

"There've been other bad things, too, but I'll stop with this one. It's important to appreciate the people God puts in our lives because they might not be there for long."

Bella was having none of it. She set her jaw and her eyes narrowed. "What if you don't like the people God put in your life?"

Mia shrugged. "Then maybe you need to stop and ask yourself why that is." She turned to Arianna. "I'm feeling tired, hon. How about you run me home and then come back and enjoy the party. You'll have a great view of the fireworks off the bridge from Molly's deck."

"No, I'm done. I'll come back with you," Arianna said.

Bella slipped away to hide from the unpleasant truths Mia had shared, and Arianna went in search of Alden, who'd met them there.

"Mom needs to go home. We've worn her out."

"Let's get her home," he said.

She went to say goodbye to Molly and was intercepted by Sunny. "Why don't you let Sophie hang out here? I can bring her back when the fireworks are over."

It sounded like a good idea. She wanted to keep Sophie's life as carefree as possible and as far away from the shadow of her mother's disease.

"Okay," she said.

Alden was the picture of chivalry, letting Mia lean on him as they made their way back to Arianna's car. It was a short walk to Molly's house, but when chemo sapped your strength, even the shortest walk could feel like miles. Mia sank onto the seat with a sigh.

"I'll go back with you," he said once he'd buckled Mia in, and climbed into the back.

"We overdid it," Arianna fretted.

"No, I'll be fine," Mia insisted. "I'd rather be tired and happy than well-rested and missing out. It was a lovely afternoon. I just wish I could convince you to go back and watch the fireworks."

"I've seen fireworks, Mom."

"You can never see enough. Remember that."

Arianna reached over and laid her hand over her mother's. "I will."

Back at the house, Alden helped Mia out of the car and escorted her up the porch steps and into the living room. "Don't let me end the fun," she said to him. "Stay and keep my daughter company."

"Glad to," he said, smiling at Arianna.

That smile of his was enough to set off fireworks in her chest.

"Is there anything I can get you? Anything you need?" Arianna asked, once she saw her mother settled in bed.

Mia shook her head. "No, I'll be fine. Go on downstairs and enjoy some you time."

It seemed almost wrong to enjoy anything when her mother was so exhausted, continuing to struggle with her treatments. Arianna went back downstairs, dragging her deflated party mood behind her.

Alden stood by the door in guest limbo. "I'm sorry you're going through all this," he said simply.

She nodded. "Me, too. She doesn't deserve this."

"Nobody does," he said. Then, "Do you want me to leave?"

So she could feel achingly, terrifyingly alone? "No. Please. Don't. Want a beer?"

"Sure," he said.

She fetched them beers and they wound up sitting on the front porch swing.

"Wish I had something brilliant to say," he said.

She gave a sad chuckle. "Me, too."

"I mean, I could say something half-ass like, it'll be okay, but I don't know that and I've never been able to lie to people."

"A good quality. More than I can say for my ex," Arianna added bitterly, and took a guzzle of her beer.

"He sounds like a shit."

"He is," she agreed. "I didn't think he was when I married him."

"I hope not," Alden said in mock horror. "I never took you for a masochist."

"I never took myself for a fool, either. I guess I was."

He waved that away. "We're all fools once in a while."

She smiled at him. "Thanks for that. It makes me feel better."

But only for a moment. She packed away her smile.

"You're doing everything you can for your mom and she's happy. That counts for a lot."

Arianna bit her lip and nodded. "She's always been there for me, always been my rock. I don't know how I'll go on if...." Her throat closed over the last words, refusing to let them out.

"I get it," he said. "But I bet you're stronger than you think you are."

"I don't want to find out." She took a long draw on her beer. "Sometimes I wish I could go back in time."

"Yeah," he said slowly. "That show only plays forward. You got a lot of forward left."

Without her mom? The tears spilled out and down her cheeks. He scooted closer and put an arm around her. "You'll get through all this."

"If something happens how am I going to tell my daughter?" she wailed. There it was, the other awful fear. How could she make life okay for Sophie if they lost her mom?

"You'll get through that, too," he said.

And that was all he said. They sat in silence, waiting for the night to fall.

Molly was stowing the leftover potato salad in the fridge when Reggie sauntered into the kitchen. "I'm thinking we should get out on the water pretty soon," he said. "Get our ringside seat."

He looked so cute in his new jeans and red polo shirt and Santa hat. Her heart fluttered with appreciation.

"I'm ready," she said. "Sunny will take care of the rest of the cleanup later."

Back out on the deck, she called to Paisley, who came running, followed by her mother, who was moving at a more reluctant pace.

"I can hardly wait to see this boat," Ava said under her breath as they made their way to Reggie's car.

He'd gotten the windshield and the fender fixed, but it wasn't exactly the car of a rich man. Maybe the boat wouldn't be, either.

But Molly was pleasantly surprised when they went to the Bremerton Marina and he stopped them in front of a well-maintained, good-sized fishing boat, complete with a cabin.

"She's no speed boat, but she gets me where I want to go," he said.

Just like his car, only this boat looked newer. It was easy to see where Reggie put his priorities. He climbed onboard, set down his mini cooler of drinks, then held out a hand to help Molly and her crew on board.

"As long as it has a bathroom," Molly said.

"That's called a head, Mom," Ava corrected her.

"It does," Reggie assured her. "We got to untie her so we can get underway. Want to help me, Paisley?"

"Yes!" Paisley replied, looking like a kid who'd won a trip to Disneyland.

"Okay, I'll show you how it's done."

"I don't think you have to worry about Reggie being broke," Molly said to Ava as he and Paisley got busy untying the moorings.

Ava shrugged. "I guess you're right. But, Mom, he's still too old for you. You know what they say about men over a certain age—they're either looking for a nurse or a purse."

Molly frowned at her. "You really think that applies to Reggie?"

"It could," Ava said stubbornly.

"Well, we know he doesn't need a purse, and he's in pretty darn good shape so I'm probably safe on both counts."

He and Paisley were back on the boat, so that ended the conversation. As far as Molly was concerned, the subject of Reggie's suitability was permanently closed. Ava was going to have to come to grips with the fact that Reggie was going to be part of their lives because Molly and Reggie were serious. And then some.

They slowly made their way out of the marina, and then joined the growing population of bobbing boats, all anchored within sight of the Manette Bridge, which would be the site of the fireworks display. Reggie produced soda for Paisley and wine coolers for Molly and Ava.

"This is my idea of the perfect night—out on my boat with three lovely ladies," he said, and raised his can of Coke to them all.

"It's really sweet of you to take us out on it," Molly said.

"I hope we'll get to do a lot of that this summer. You know, going to Blake Island makes a great day trip. We could go over there and have lunch on a Sunday afternoon. Would that suit you, Ava?" he asked with a smile.

"If I can work it into my schedule," Ava said.

She did have a full social schedule, and her words came across as condescending. It was all Molly could do not to give her a motherly kick in the shins.

Still, the fireworks show was enjoyable, and Paisley was beaming when they left the boat at the end of the evening. "What do you say to Mr. Washington?" Ava prompted when they got back to the house.

"Thank you!" Paisley cried, and gave him a hug.

"You're welcome, and it's Reggie."

"Thanks for including us," Ava said to him, the picture of politeness.

Of course, she was. Molly had raised her right. She just wished her daughter's proper reply could have held a little more warmth.

If Reggie noticed, he didn't let on. "That's what I call a perfect day," he said.

Yes, it was, and Molly wasn't going to let her daughter's disapproval ruin it.

The next day she decided they needed to have another talk, so she called Ava. "There's something you need to know."

"Oh, no. Mother, what have you done?" Ava asked, her voice filled with apprehension.

"Nothing yet. But Reggie's asked me to marry him."

"What! Mom, you hardly know this man."

"Don't go into panic mode. I told him it was too soon."

"Good. You shouldn't be rushing into anything."

It was all Molly could do not to laugh. She'd said those same words to her daughter…right before she learned Ava was pregnant. Rushing appeared to be a family trait.

"I'm not, but we are getting serious, so you'd better start getting used to it."

"Fine, it's your life," Ava snapped.

"Yes, it is, and you'd do well to remember that."

Molly had gotten so accustomed to living in a romantic dead zone that she'd failed to notice how lackluster her life had become over the years. But the luster was back, and she wasn't about to give it up.

CHRISTMAS
IN JULY

20

Pregnancy added a level of sweetness to Sunny's life that no sour teenager or chilly mother-in-law could steal. Which was a good thing, since she was going to be stuck camping at Steamboat Rock in Eastern Washington with them for the Fourth of July.

Riding over the mountains in the truck with the kids made for cozy family time with Bella her usual sullen self and Dylan all bouncy and full of predictions of rattlesnake sightings.

"Rattlesnakes?" Sunny said weakly.

"Don't worry. They're more afraid of you than you are of them," Travis said. "They're easy prey for predators like hawks, so they try to stay out of sight."

"Yeah, but they still bite," Dylan said. "Remember that movie, Dad, where the girl got bit by the snake and almost died? She had to have her arm cut off. What would you do if you had to have your arm cut off, Sunny?"

"She'd beat you over the head with it," Travis said irritably. "Enough already. No one's gonna get bitten and people don't die from a snakebite."

Sunny was already researching on her phone. If they didn't

die, it looked like they'd want to, judging from some of the pictures she saw. *There will be no snakes. This will be fun.*

A new definition of fun. Her family's idea of camping had been road trips and motels. With pools. But Travis loved hiking and the great outdoors so now Sunny did, too. Or would, once they graduated from tents to campers.

Ah, there was nothing like sitting around the old campfire at night trying not to barf at the smell of roasting hot dogs, she thought on day two while her father-in-law told ghost stories and her mother-in-law ignored her. The nausea part of pregnancy wasn't as sweet as the rest of it. At least the kids seemed to be having fun. They'd kept busy all day and now were happily stuffing themselves.

Jeanette stopped ignoring Sunny when, after the marshmallows came out and the fire was dying down, Travis told her they were expecting a little marshmallow of their own. She suddenly looked at Sunny as if seeing her for the first time. Of course, she was only seeing Sunny as a baby barge, soon to deliver a grandchild, but it was a beginning.

"How lovely," Jeannette cooed. "Are you going to want to know the sex of the baby or wait to be surprised? I always think it's nice to wait and be surprised," she continued without waiting for an answer. "And those gender-reveal parties are silly, if you ask me." Not that anyone had. "Of course, we'll have to have a shower."

"Congrats, you two," said Harry, following his wife's lead.

"Thanks, Dad. We're excited," Travis said, and put an arm around Sunny's shoulders.

Yes, they were, and it was as close to a happy-movie moment as a woman could get, sitting there by the fire with her husband's arm around her, looking forward to the birth of their first child. Love, love, love.

And then it was on to scene two, a romantic end to the

night…in a tent, sleeping on the ground. Not really Sunny's idea of romance. Though Travis had agreed to at least bring an air mattress for them.

"It's been a good day," he said as they left the rest of the family around the campfire and made their way back to their tent.

"It has," she agreed.

Dylan had spent the day pranking her at every turn, first by using paper clips to seal their tent flap in the morning, locking them in—when she had to pee!—and then jumping out from behind a tree and scaring the tar out of her when they were hiking that morning. That, after pretending to see snakes, had been the final straw and Travis had told him in no uncertain terms to knock it off.

"I was just having fun," he'd protested, and Sunny had believed him.

Dylan had been warming to her and was only trying to make her feel like one of the gang, she decided. Boys were famous for doing goofy and socially inept things to get a girl's attention. The same method probably applied to making points with stepmoms who were doing their best.

"You've been a damn good sport," Travis continued. "I hope you've been having some fun."

"I have," she said. The state park was a lovely one, Banks Lake providing a blue oasis in the middle of the summer barrenness of rock and desert, and although she'd have preferred to shower in an en suite bathroom, taking advantage of a rainforest showerhead, she really couldn't complain about the facilities. "Tomorrow I intend to catch a fish. But you're cleaning it," she added. The very thought of cleaning a fish made her stomach queasy.

"You catch it, I'll clean it," he promised, and opened the tent flap for her.

She ducked under it. "Home sweet home."

"Any place you are is sweet," he said.

"You're only saying that 'cause it's true," she joked.

"You know it. Are you having fun? Really?"

"I am," she said. *For the most part. Sort of.*

"You scored points with Mom."

She smiled. "That I did. For a minute there I thought she was going to rush over and lay a Gene Juarez gift card at my feet."

He chuckled. "If that's what you want, I will. Come here, you."

Of course, she came.

Much later, it was time to crawl into the sleeping bag. Ready for a night of blissful dreams, she pulled it open. That was when the bliss ended.

"Snake!" Sunny gasped, falling back and crab-walking as far away from the thing as she could.

Fast as she was going, her heart was racing even faster. She was going to have a heart attack right there in the tent. All she could think was snakebite. Dylan's words rang in her head. *Remember that movie, Dad, where the girl got bit by the snake and almost died?*

Travis jumped between her and the snake, shining his flashlight on the reptile. "What the...?" Then he swore. "It's okay, babe."

"Don't touch it," she cried as he reached to pick it up. It would bite him. He'd make her a widow before he even got to see his baby.

"It won't bite." He held up the thing and it hung there like...

"A rubber snake," she said in disgust. "Boy, Dylan got me good."

"Dylan's going to get it good," Travis growled.

"He was just joking around," she said, defending the boy. "Kids go overboard."

Travis shook his head. "He can't be doing stuff like this anymore. He about scared the shit out of you. That can't be good for the baby."

"I'm barely pregnant. I'm sure the worst that will happen to the baby is that she'll grow up to hate snakes."

She. Listen to her, betraying her secret hope that they'd have a girl. A wicked stepdaughter replacement.

"I'm having a talk with him tomorrow, anyway," Travis said.

True to his word, Travis escorted his son from the kid tent to theirs first thing the next morning to apologize to Sunny. Even as they approached, she could hear Dylan protesting, "But I didn't do it, Dad."

The flap flew open and father and son entered, son's face red with humiliation and father's red with anger. The tent lost its cozy feeling and turned claustrophobic.

"I didn't do it, Sunny," Dylan said, and dashed away a tear sneaking out of one eye. "Honest."

"Oh, come on, give it up, Dylan," Travis growled. "You were priming her all day."

"I was just teasing her," Dylan said. "Bella said it would be funny to scare her on the trail. I didn't even know she had that snake."

Bella. Of course.

Sunny reached up and took his hand. "It's okay, Dylan. I believe you."

He bit his lower lip, nodded, blinked back tears.

"And if we do see any snakes today, your job is to throw rocks and scare them away," she continued.

Her words helped dry the tears and he nodded eagerly.

Travis was still frowning. "She's letting you off light."

Dylan hung his head. "I'm sorry, Sunny. I wouldn't have let a snake bite you."

Good news, indeed. "I know," she said. She gave his hand a final squeeze and let go. "How about you do some snake patrol around our campsite before I come out? I don't want to get all freaked out again."

"Sure," he said, nodding eagerly, and made his escape.

"You let him off too lightly," Travis said in disgust.

"He wasn't the mastermind in this. We both know it. He was simply being a prankster, and the potential fall guy."

Travis sighed. "You're right. I need to have a talk with Bella."

"Oh, no," Sunny groaned. Yet another brick in the stepdaughter hate wall because, of course, Bella would lay the blame for her punishment at Sunny's feet.

"Oh, yes. This is going to stop."

"You can't make her love me, Travis."

"You're right, but I will make her show you respect."

He ducked out of the tent, and she could hear him calling in his angry dad voice, "Bella!"

Ten minutes later he was back in the tent, this time with his daughter. Sunny took one look at Bella's face and her morning queasy stomach got queasier. Bella was a veritable fashion show of teen-girl emotions. *And here comes Bella, showing off the latest in our angry stepdaughter line. Notice how well the angle of her chin suits her mood and how the red on her face goes with that summer suntan.*

"Say it," Travis barked.

He may have been the big dog, but his daughter could bark, too. "I'm sorry," she spat at Sunny. She turned back to her father. "There. Are you happy?"

"No, as a matter of fact, I'm not. I'm sick of your shit, Bel, and it's going to end."

"Well, I'm sick of your shit, too, Dad! You left us!"

The muscles in his jaw were working as if he were chewing on something that wouldn't break down. "I didn't leave you. You know that. Your mom and I decided what was best and I moved out so she could have the house, but I've always been there for you," he replied. After the many times he'd lost his temper, his calm under fire was impressive.

"Until her!"

There it was, the green-eyed monster. Sunny wished she could think of something brilliant to say or do but she couldn't. She sat there with her brain dead and her mouth frozen in place, the only thing moving being her roiling stomach.

"Enough." Travis held out his hand. "Phone."

Bella looked at him in shock. "What?"

"Hand it over."

"You can't take my phone," she protested.

"If you want to get technical, it's my phone. I pay for it. You and your brother and even your mother are all on my plan. I allow you to use it. But you're not going to be using it for the rest of the weekend because you need some think time."

Bella made no move to pull it from her shorts pocket. The battle of the wills had begun in earnest. Sunny's tummy was getting more and more unhappy with her.

"Every minute you delay adds another day you'll be without it," Travis said. "So, what's it going to be?"

That ended the battle. Bella glared at him as she pulled the phone from her pocket and slapped it into his hand. "I hate you!"

"Of course, you do. Lucky for you, though, I love you and I'm not going to let you turn into a brat. No matter how much your mother tries to screw you up," he added under his breath as she vacated the tent.

"I hate her, too!" The angry words crashed through the tent canvas. "I hope she does get bit by a snake and dies."

Travis swore and whipped up the flap, ready to go after his daughter.

"Don't. Please," Sunny begged. "It won't help."

He collapsed on the sleeping bag and raked a hand through his hair. "She's driving me right around the bend."

"I know," Sunny said. Now she was going to cry and be sick at the same time.

He studied her. "You okay?"

She shook her head.

"What do you need?"

"Crackers," she managed before she flew out of the tent and upchucked. Yep, there was nothing like a camping trip to bring about family unity.

21

Sophie's dad had wanted to have her for the day on the Fourth of July so she could be with his family for a backyard barbecue. He'd picked her up the day before, and promised to get her back by the afternoon so she could watch fireworks with Arianna and Mia. Alden had invited them all to a party that evening at his parents' house on Kitsap Lake. Arianna worried that it might tire her mother out, but Mia had insisted she'd be fine.

"I don't want to miss a minute of fun if I can help it. Besides, I'd like to meet Alden's mother."

"You gonna do a sales pitch for me?" Arianna teased.

"Maybe," Mia teased back.

She *was* teasing, wasn't she? "But not really," Arianna said, to be sure.

"Give me some credit here," Mia said.

It was the best answer Arianna was going to get. Anyway, her mom had class. She'd never do anything to embarrass her daughter. Arianna was more in danger of embarrassing herself by getting caught looking at Alden all googly-eyed and drooly. *No drooling*, she lectured herself.

Still, when he came over, looking so darned cute in board

shorts and a black T-shirt that showed off a lovely set of pecs, it was hard not to drool.

"I've got the truck all cleaned and Buster's sedated and ready to hide in the folks' basement. You ladies ready to go?"

"We are," Arianna said. But… "Sophie's not back yet."

Darn that Wyatt. He was supposed have brought her back at four o'clock. Arianna had called at three thirty to see if he was on his way and he'd told her he would be in a couple of minutes. Wyatt-speak for when he was good and ready.

It was so inconsiderate to be late. And so… Wyatt. Was it any wonder she was always losing her temper with him?

"Maybe you should call him again," Mia suggested.

She hated to call him again and make a scene in front of Alden. There would be one, of course, because Wyatt would be bound to say something to push her buttons, like accusing her of nagging him.

Arianna rubbed her forehead, frowned. *Just do it. And try to stay calm and sound rational in front of Alden. Better yet, don't let him hear you at all.*

She took her phone out onto the front porch to make her call.

He answered on the first ring. "What is your problem?"

"You," she snapped. "Where are you?"

"I'll be there in a few. We're right in the middle of something here and I'm not dragging Sophie away."

"Alden, you promised you'd have her back."

"I will. Stop nagging."

"I wouldn't have to nag if you'd just do what you promised."

She only got out half the sentence before he hung up. She got her phone in a strangle hold and shook it. "I hate you!"

Okay, get a grip. This isn't helping. She took a calming breath and went back inside.

Her mother and Alden both looked at her expectantly.

She shook her head. "They haven't even left yet. I'm sorry, Alden. This is so typical of my ex. He…"

"Walks all over her," Mia finished. "He always has."

"If you give me your parents' address, I'll put it in my phone and we'll join you a little later," Arianna said. Sometime before the end of the month.

"I have a better idea. Let's pick Sophie up on our way."

"Oh, I don't know," Arianna said. Wyatt's mother wasn't all that fond of her anymore. He'd somehow convinced her what went wrong between them was her fault. And Wyatt would be bound to cause a scene, making her look like a bitch in front of his whole family.

"I think that's an excellent idea," said Mia. "Let's go."

"Maybe I should text that we're coming," Arianna said. Except then, out of perversity, Wyatt would probably take it into his head to bring Sophie home and they'd miss each other.

"Let's go for the element of surprise," said Alden.

"Good idea," Mia concurred.

When it came to dealing with Wyatt, there were no good ideas.

Alden fetched Buster, then they strapped him into his doggie harness in the back of the cab, got Mia settled next to him and then set off for Wyatt's parents' house in Port Orchard.

As they pulled up in front of the house, Arianna could see a croquet set up on the front lawn and several people playing. One of them was Wyatt. There was no sign of Sophie, which meant she was in the backyard, probably playing with some of the cousins. So the only *we* who were in the middle of something was him. The rat.

Wyatt lifted his head as the truck pulled up to the curb, an easy smile on his face. Seeing Arianna in there, next to Alden, the smile became less easy. He said something to the others playing with him—a couple of uncles and a distant cousin Arianna barely remembered—then set down his mallet and started toward where Alden had parked.

"Oh, boy," Arianna muttered.

"It'll be okay," Alden assured her.

He got out of the truck, ignoring the approaching Wyatt, came around and opened the door for Arianna.

Wyatt reached the truck, ignoring Mia, who remained in the back of the cab, acting as if Alden was invisible, and said to Arianna, "What is your problem? I told you I'd be there."

Arianna could feel her cheeks heating with embarrassment. "At four. You were supposed to be there at four. We're expected somewhere."

"So you'll be late."

"Looks that way," Alden said. He stepped in between Arianna and Wyatt. "Shit happens, I get that," he continued calmly, keeping his voice low and even. "But now it's time for Sophie to come to a party with us."

He wasn't much taller than Wyatt but his muscles were sure bigger. Plus, there was something about his stance that said, "Don't mess with me."

Wyatt pulled back his head and frowned at Arianna. "Who the hell is this guy?"

"I'm Alden, a new friend of Arianna and Sophie's." Alden held out a hand toward Wyatt, clearly taking him off guard. *I come in peace...so far.*

Instead of shaking hands, Wyatt took a step back and glared at Arianna. "You didn't tell me you were seeing someone."

"You've never told me when you were seeing someone, either. Which would have been really helpful when we were married." Oh, that was a good one. Seeing the red flood his cheeks felt so rewarding, and she was delighted to find that having Alden for backup kept her from losing her own temper.

"Fine. There's no need to make a big deal out of it," Wyatt said, backing down. "I'll go get her."

"I'll go with you," Alden said easily, and swept out a hand, inviting Wyatt to lead the way.

Wyatt clenched his jaw and strode off toward the house as a fast as he could. Alden kept up easily.

Arianna smiled, climbed back in the truck. "That was a thing of beauty," she said.

Mia chuckled. "Yes, it was. I think Wyatt has finally met someone who won't put up with his nonsense."

"It should have been me."

"It will be from now on," Mia predicted.

A moment later the men were back, Sophie running ahead of them. She scrambled into the back of the truck to join Mia and Buster. "Hi, Grammy! Hi, Buster! Hi, Mommy!" Her forehead was sweaty and her cheeks pink and she had a chocolate smear on her chin, probably from ice cream.

"Did you have fun?" Arianna asked.

"Yeah, I did, but Mommy, I thought you forgot about me."

"Why was that?" Arianna asked.

"Daddy said you'd come get me, but that was forever ago."

"Oh, he did, did he?" *That skunk turd.*

"A little misunderstanding, but it's been cleared up. I don't think there will be many more in the future," said Mia.

"There certainly won't," said Arianna, still steaming.

Wyatt had broken away from Alden without a word and marched back to his game. Alden ambled back to the truck, an easy smile on his face. He climbed back in and put on his seat belt.

"We all ready for fun?" he asked.

"I am!" Sophie crowed.

"Me, too," said Mia.

"Me, three," said Arianna, tossing off her irritation.

"Then let's go," said Alden.

"That was pretty amazing," Arianna said to him as they got underway.

"Sometimes you have to let people know who the big dog is," he said.

"And you're the big dog?"

He grinned. "Arf."

Big dog with a big happy family. Who all seemed delighted to meet her.

"So I finally get to check out my son's neighbor who brings him all those wonderful treats," Mrs. Brightman said, taking Arianna's hand in both of hers. "And Mia, Alden told me about you. I've been watching all the things you've done with your daughter on her YouTube channel. You are positively inspiring. Both of you."

Inspiring. How much warmth that one word packed. "Thank you," Arianna said, right along with her mother.

"Arianna does all the work. I don't know what I'd do without her."

"I can tell she's a treasure," Mrs. Brightman said. She turned to Sophie, who'd grown springs on her feet and was bouncing up and down in anticipation. "And this is Sophie."

"I am," Sophie said with an eager nod.

"It's nice to meet you, Sophie. Do you like trampolines?"

"I don't know," Sophie said.

"Well, we have one set up around the side of the house. Would you like to try it?"

"Yes!" Sophie cried.

"Then, come with me and I'll introduce you to some kids who will show you all kinds of tricks you can do," Mrs. Brightman said. "I'll look forward to getting to know you ladies better as the night goes on," she said to Arianna and Mia, before taking Sophie's hand and leading her off.

"By getting to know you she means telling you how wonderful I am and how much she wants grandchildren," Alden joked. The minute the words were out of his mouth he looked like a man who had stepped into something he'd been avoiding.

"Don't panic," Arianna teased. "I'm not worried you're about to propose." Although, she had to admit, she didn't hate the sound of it.

He retrieved Buster and they started toward the front door.

"And thank you for putting my ex in his place. That was positively heroic."

He smiled. "Yeah?"

"Yeah. Kind of like… Christmas in July."

"Well, then, Merry Christmas early," he said.

Yes, indeed.

The party was in full swing with kids racing back and forth across the lawn or jumping off the dock into the lake, vying with teenagers for a turn in the three-person tow tube behind an uncle's ski boat. As Alden walked across the lawn, he saw Mia was ensconced in a lounge chair, visiting with his Aunt Jane. Sophie and one of his nieces and his two nephews were jumping on the trampoline. His sister, Autumn, had Arianna cornered by the dessert table and was probably grilling her like one of the bratwursts on Dad's grill. He had just dug a wine cooler out of the ice chest and was about to go rescue her when his mom intercepted him.

"She's a lovely girl," Mom said.

"Yeah, she's pretty awesome," he agreed.

"Is this getting serious?"

"We're just neighbors. We're not even dating."

His mother frowned at him. "You don't bring *just neighbors* to a family party. I hope you've at least kissed the girl."

"Now you're wanting a play-by-play on my sex life?"

"Don't be smart. You need to stake a claim on her heart before someone else snaps her up."

"She's going through a lot. The timing's not right. She doesn't need some guy hitting on her while her mother is sick. She needs a friend."

Mom picked up a wine cooler of her own. "You don't know what she needs. Don't you be letting those cold feet of yours keep you from moving forward. You could miss out on something really special."

"If it's meant to be, it'll be," he said.

"That is such a ridiculous saying," Mom scoffed as she took the top off her bottle. "Things don't happen when people stay inert. And maybe this is exactly the right time. For both of you."

He looked to where Arianna and his sister stood. Arianna was sampling Mom's brownies. Autumn said something and Arianna laughed. Her laughter drifted over to him and tickled his ears and made him smile.

"Don't stand there. Go make the girl fall in love with you," Mom commanded. "She's already halfway there."

Was she? He knew what he felt when he was around her. He felt like a kid, itching to get his hands on those presents under the tree on Christmas morning. When she and Sophie had brought over deviled eggs, seeing her sitting in his living room, his house had suddenly come to life, felt full and happy the way it had when he'd gone over as a kid to build birdhouses with his grandpa or fight with his sister over who got to lick the bowl when Grandma was baking a cake. There'd been a lot of Thanksgiving dinners eaten in that house, a lot of family gatherings. Other than the housewarming bash when he first moved in, there hadn't been any since Gram died. What would it be like to have family gatherings in there again? What would it be like to have Sophie running around, chasing Buster, to have Arianna sitting across the kitchen table from him? In bed next to him? In his arms?

No, no, he needed to stop that movie. She was dealing with a shitty ex and a sick mom and he was still leery of getting involved with anyone. The timing really was off. Better to be friends. He could help her, watch out for her, but there'd be no complications for either of them.

He walked over to where she and Autumn stood and handed Arianna a wine cooler. "Is my sister bragging about me?"

"Not till you pay me," Autumn joked. "Seriously," she said to Arianna, "he's a good guy, and I'm glad to see his taste in women has improved."

"Thanks," Arianna said with a smile.

"Yep, the girlfriend from hell about scarred him for life, about scarred us all for life."

He wasn't scarred for life. He was just scarred for... Well, he wasn't scarred for life.

"She used and abused him like you wouldn't believe."

TMI. "Autumn," he said between gritted teeth.

His sister ignored him. "Every time they came over, she managed to do something to create a scene. You're not a scene creator, are you?"

"Better. She's a content creator," Alden supplied, anxious to move the subject away from his last love fail. "Tell her about your website and your YouTube channel and stuff."

Being under the spotlight turned Arianna's cheeks pink. "They're both dedicated to health issues. I'm doing a lot with my mom right now, who's battling cancer. I think we're helping a lot of women."

"That is amazing," Autumn gushed. "You know, I thought it would be so cool to go into medicine like Alden, but then I realized I'm grossed out by the sight of blood and I could never poke someone with a needle. I'm so impressed by people who do what you do."

"You finally admit it. You're impressed by your bro," Alden teased.

"I said people," she retorted with a teasing grin. "And this isn't about you, so shut up." To Arianna she said, "Tell me more about your website. And are you on Instagram?"

Alden watched as Arianna warmed to her topic, talking about some of the great sponsors she'd found and her hopes for becoming a positive force for women's health. "If I can inspire women, and men, too," she added, smiling at Alden, "to make lifestyle changes and get healthy, I'll feel like I'm really doing something with my life."

He looked to where Mia sat, talking to his aunt. It seemed to him like Arianna was already doing something with her life watching over her mom.

"You guys and all your sexy nobility," Autumn said in mock disgust. "All I have is a shoe shop."

That lit up Arianna's eyes. "Shoes?"

"And purses."

"Purses?"

"Okay, I can see where this conversation is heading," he said. "I'm going to go hang with someone who wants to talk to me."

"There's someone who wants to talk to you?" his sister asked in mock surprise.

He gave her the finger and moved over to where Mia was seated, plunking onto the empty patio chair on her other side. "You having a good time, Mrs. W?" he asked.

"Oh, yes," she said. "Your aunt Jane was telling me that they own the house next door."

"Our own family compound," said Aunt Jane. "I hope we can keep the properties in the family for years to come. Gathering here keeps us all connected."

Someone called to his aunt, and she excused herself and moved on.

"You're very lucky to have such a close family," Mia said to Alden. "Not everyone has that."

"I guess not," he said.

"I hope you don't take it for granted."

Maybe he did.

Arianna joined them. The lighthearted smile she'd worn earlier did a fade at the sight of her mother. "How are you doing, Mom?"

Mia waved away her concern. "I'm fine. Are you having fun?"

"I am," Arianna said. "I like your family," she told Alden.

"And I like your laugh. I don't think I've ever heard you laugh before," he said.

She gave a one-shouldered shrug. "Haven't had too much to laugh about in the last year or so."

"You don't want to forget how," said her mother. "It's so nice of you to include us in your family's party, Alden."

"Hey, the more the merrier, that's the Brightman family motto." But shadows were spreading under Mia's eyes and she looked ready to drop. The party probably needed to end for her. "How about we get you home, Mrs. W?"

"I was so looking forward to watching the fireworks," she protested.

"Mom, you really look tired," Arianna said.

Alden was suddenly inspired. "I tell you what. Let's have a preshow." He strode off across the lawn, calling to everyone. "Hey guys, time for sparklers."

Within minutes he had both kids and adults assembled in a line a safe distance apart from each other and in front of the patio where Mia sat on her lounge chair. "And now it's time for our preshow. Uncle Jack, start the music."

His uncle obliged, and "The Star-Spangled Banner" began to play. He and his dad lit the sparklers and stepped aside to let the performers wave them in circles in front of them. It was kind of boring with them all just standing there, he thought, but Mia's face was lit almost as brightly as the sparklers so he'd count it a success.

"Big ending," he called, and they all finished, singing along, "O'er the land of the free and the home of the brave."

"Play ball!" hollered Dad, and everyone laughed.

Mia clapped appreciatively. "You are all very talented."

"See?" Uncle Jack said to Aunt Jane. "I told you we should have gone on *American's Got Talent*."

"You all have a talent for making people feel welcome," Mia said to Alden as the performers scattered in various directions.

"Didn't know that was a talent," he said.

"It is," Mia assured him.

"I think you're a flatterer, Mrs. W. Let me grab Buster and we'll get you to the truck."

"I'll get Sophie," Arianna said.

A few minutes later they were on their way back to Arianna's place, a tired Sophie whining, "I wanted to see the fireworks."

"Be happy you got to play with a sparkler," Arianna said in a tone of voice that didn't invite discussion.

"Humph," Sophie said.

From his rearview mirror Alden could see her crossing her arms over her chest and pouting. It reminded him of his former girlfriend. Sophie was only six. At least she had an excuse for acting like a child.

Once they were back and out of the truck, Mia said, "Don't let me spoil the evening, you two. Stay up and watch the fireworks."

Arianna looked hot in her red top and those white shorts that showed off those perfect legs. His hands itched to take a little road trip along all her great curves and start some fireworks of their own. He stuffed them in his back pockets in an effort to smother the urge.

"We won't get the view we would at Molly's house but I bet we can see something," Arianna said.

"I want to watch," put in Sophie.

"From bed. You'll be able to see out your window," Arianna told her. "Go on in and brush your teeth. I'll be there in a minute."

"No fair," Sophie said, and trudged off.

"I remember those days," Alden said. "It seemed like all the fun stuff happened after us kids went to bed."

"She got to stay up for the fireworks at the Christmas-in-June party, and she's had plenty of fun today. Thanks for including us."

"Glad to," he said.

She pointed to the house. "I'll just go in and get her settled and see if I can find something for us to drink."

"I'll take Buster home and be back," he said.

"Great."

Thanks to doggie drugs Buster was feeling laid-back and happy to get settled on his doggie bed. "I know, I shouldn't go over there," Alden said as he laid Buster down. "But what could I do? She invited me. Anyway, we're just gonna keep things cool. We don't need to get serious. Of course, I like her a lot," he continued. "But, like I told Mom, the timing's not right."

Buster gave a combination sigh-snort.

"You think I should go for it?"

Buster yawned.

Alden took that as a yes. "I'll come back if it gets too loud," he promised, then hurried next door even though he knew Arianna would still be busy getting her daughter tucked in and her mom settled. He plunked down on the top porch step and leaned against the post and thought about the first time he'd seen Arianna out on this porch. She'd been screaming into her phone. Not a good first impression.

After meeting her ex, he could see why she'd screamed. The guy was an asshat.

How had she wound up with him, anyway?

The door opened and she came out, bearing two bottles of beer. She handed him one and sat down on the other side of the step, facing him. "It was a great night. Thanks."

"What do you mean was?" he joked. "I'm still here."

She giggled. "That you are." She looked away, bit her lip.

"What?" he prompted.

"I'm kind of wondering why."

"Why? What do you mean?"

"I mean, are you here as my neighbor? My friend?"

"Both," he said earnestly.

She nodded, took a draw on her beer bottle.

"Uh, is that okay?" he ventured.

"Oh, yes, yes, of course. I just…wanted to be clear. I mean." She sighed. "I suck at relationships."

"If you're thinking about that loser I met earlier…"

"I didn't think he was a loser when I met him. He was cute and fun and full of energy. Everybody liked him."

"Seriously?"

"Wyatt can be charming when he chooses." She took another drink. "And then there was me."

"Whoa, wait a minute. Why did you just say that like that?"

"Like what?"

"Like you're no big deal."

"Because I'm not. I never had big ambitions, never was the top of my class, never—"

"Stop already," Alden said. "Where were you when they were handing out self-esteem."

"Napping?"

"Must have been. You've got a lot going for you. You've got nursing skills, a good heart, a good kid. The guts to climb up on a rooftop in a Santa suit in the rain. What more could you want?"

She wiggled a foot back and forth. She was wearing flip-flops and her toenails were painted red. She had such cute, little feet. He didn't know how they got her through a whole twelve-hour shift at the hospital.

"To be…enough."

"For him?"

She bit her lip and nodded.

Alden shook his head in disgust. "Exes, they really mess with your head."

"Yours, too?"

He snorted. "Oh, yeah. I guess I wasn't enough. Never could do anything right for her. She always wanted more."

"So, what happened?"

"We broke up," he said and took a deep swig of his beer.

"Who broke it off?"

"I guess you could say it was mutual. She wasn't good for me and I wasn't enough for her. She wanted…a doctor."

Getting those words out felt like coughing up phlegm during the worst chest cold on the planet. Damn painful. But maybe it was time he'd gotten them up.

Arianna nodded. "A doctor."

"Yeah," he said slowly. "That's the top of the mountain."

"There are all kinds of other great places on the mountain besides the top," she said. "Do you want to be a doctor?"

"Not particularly. Thought I might go back to school and become a PA. Better money."

"That's a good reason. Better than going back to school to impress someone."

He took in a deep breath, nodded. "I think I spent a lot of time trying to impress her. Maybe that's why I spent a lot of time not being happy. I think people should want to be with you for who are."

She nodded. "I agree."

"So you're not looking for a doctor?" he asked. Out of simple curiosity, of course.

"I just want to be loved," she said. "I didn't think that was asking too much," she added softly.

"It's not," he said. She was so easy to love.

And it was a hot night, turning to dusk. Soon it would be dark and people would be setting off fireworks and all he could think of was setting off fireworks with this woman, who gave so much and seemed to ask so little.

He set down his bottle, moved closer, took hers and set it down, too. "Arianna, be honest. If I kissed you, how would you feel?"

She blinked. Then her face lit up. "Like the Fourth of July," she said and grabbed for him.

22

They came together like two bullet trains. Her lips were like rose petals and her perfume invaded his senses. She felt soft and perfect in his arms and he was on fire. He could go on kissing her forever. In fact it felt…eternal, and like they were the only two people in the universe, like in those movies where the couple kissed and everything around them faded to background blur.

"Oh, man," he managed when she pulled away and looked at him, probably to see if he was still breathing. A good idea, since she'd almost killed him with that kiss.

"I couldn't help myself," she said.

"I'm glad," he said, and grinned.

"Your ex must have been out of her mind."

He grinned. "Yeah?"

"Oh, yeah. It sounds like those wounds are still pretty fresh, though. You're probably not ready for a relationship."

Who said? "Are you?"

"I don't know," she admitted. "But having you in my life, in our lives, feels so right. I don't want you to feel pressured, though. If you're not ready to start something."

"Oh, no, I'm ready. I wasn't sure before, but I think I've

been ready for a while," he said, studying that lovely mouth of hers. He ran a hand up her back, tracing her spine. "You are so beautiful."

She made a face.

"No, I mean it. You are. Inside and out."

"Funny, I could say the same thing about you," she said. "You know, I was so unhappy this last Christmas. Kind of a stinker," she added, not looking at him.

"You were an adorable stinker."

She raised an eyebrow.

"Okay, you were just a stinker, but it didn't take me long to realize that you were adorable," he amended and ran a finger along her jaw. Such soft skin. He moved it to her lips and she kissed it.

"You were so nice, and kind. And you've been so good to us, so…heroic," she said.

Heroic? Him?

"You're like a belated Christmas present."

He laughed at that. "Hey, no such thing since you're celebrating Christmas all year long."

"I am," she said.

The sky was getting darker. In the distance he heard a boom. The fireworks were starting. He ran a hand through her hair, brought her lips back to his, and kissed her again. His mom was right. What was he waiting for?

"You're looking happy," Sunny observed when she came over to Mia's house the next week to shoot some videos.

"I am! We were at the doctor's and Mom's tumor is shrinking. She can actually swallow food again. Not big stuff, like meat or bread. But soft food. We celebrated this morning with yogurt."

"That's great!" Sunny said and hugged her. "Does that mean she gets to have the feeding tube taken out?"

"Not quite yet. The doctor wants to leave it in for a few more months, just to be on the safe side. But I'm sure by the end of the year that thing will be history. So Mom and I want to make a video to share that good news. Maybe toast with one of the healthful summer drinks we're featuring."

"Great idea."

"Let's do the photo shoot first and then we can end with the video."

Arianna nodded agreement and they got busy assembling the drinks to put out on her back patio table.

"Also, since she's feeling so well, she thought as part of our Christmas-in-July celebrations she'd teach us all how to make croquembouche," Arianna said as they worked.

"Croakin' what?"

"It's French—a tower of cream puffs coated and held in place with caramelized sugar."

"I'm all over that," Sunny said. "We could film that getting made as well. People are enjoying following the Christmas-all-year reports."

With everything assembled, Arianna led the way to the patio. She'd cleaned their glass-topped table and scattered silk daisy petals all around.

"Nice," Sunny approved.

"I figure we can put the pitcher here," Arianna said, pointing, "and then arrange glasses on the tray in front of it."

"Perfect," Sunny said, and began shooting pictures as soon as everything was in place.

"How was your Fourth?" Arianna asked.

Sunny shook her head, kept her focus on their display. "Just a barrel of fun."

"Uh-oh."

"Yeah, uh-oh. But hey, life goes on and so do I."

"I've got to admire your determination," Arianna said. She wasn't sure how she'd cope if she were in her friend's flip-flops.

They switched to a different set of glasses, featuring a drink

made with grapefruit, orange juice and tonic water, with festive ice cubes containing rosemary and tiny slices of lemon and
Sunny took more shots from different angles. Arianna would
have stopped with one picture. Which was why Sunny was in
charge of their photo shoots.

Sunny showed her the pictures on her digital camera. A
blurred background of honeysuckle with the drinks in the fore-
ground looked magazine-worthy. Another picture showed the
pitcher, with just a beginning of moisture on it and two glasses
in front of it. As if on cue, a butterfly had swooped past, and
Sunny had captured its visit.

"Perfect," Arianna approved. "You have got a real gift!"

"I'm not the one coming up with this stuff. Let's sample one
of these."

They each picked up a glass and took a sip.

"Oh, yes," Sunny said. "You need to make these for our
Christmas-in-July party."

"They're not Christmassy. I have something better in mind."

"Better than this? Hard to imagine."

"Trust me," Arianna said with a smile.

How she was loving helping to plan their monthly celebrations. With each new party they planned, it buried the unhappiness of Christmas further in the past.

"So, how was your Fourth?" Sunny wanted to know.

"The fireworks were great." Especially the ones she'd made
with Alden. Remembering the feel of his lips on her neck
brought a fresh heat to her face. She realized Sunny was studying her.

"What kind of fireworks are we talkin' about here?" Sunny
asked.

"We went over to Alden's parents'."

"I know that. And then what happened? Tell me you're not
just talking about sparklers."

"There were sparklers," Arianna said, then giggled.

"Oh, my gosh. Tell all."

"He's amazing and I'm in love."

"I'm so happy for you!"

"He's everything Wyatt never was—selfless and humble."

"Then a perfect match for you." Sunny raised her glass. "Here's to perfect matches and happy endings."

"I'll drink to that." Alden was amazing, her mother was beating back cancer. Did it get any better than that?

Unsummoned, a shiver washed over her. Had she tempted fate with that thought?

At that moment Mia came out on the patio, looking refreshed and rested. She'd accented her wig with a scarf and had put on lipstick and blush, which gave her extra color.

"You look great," Sunny greeted her.

"I feel great," said Mia.

"I hear you got good news from the doctor."

"We did. It was very encouraging," Mia said. She picked up a glass "I hope the reel we're going to make involves swallowing."

"That it does," Arianna said and pulled out a chair for her.

She poured a drink for Mia while Sunny checked the light, got her angle figured out and her phone ready.

"Okay, let's do this," Sunny said.

Arianna smiled at all the people she knew would be watching. "Hello, everyone. Mom and I have some good news to share." She turned to Mia. "Mom?"

"My doctor tells me that this nasty tumor is shrinking. And, actually, I knew it even before he told me. I could feel the improvement. I know I still have a ways to go, but when you're battling something like cancer you celebrate every small victory."

"Which is exactly what we're doing with one of the special summer drinks I've come up with for you all to enjoy," said Arianna. "My friend Sunny wants me to make these for our Christmas-in-July party, but I'm going to do something wintrier for that. Stay tuned. I'll share. Meanwhile, here's to you, Mom, to how brave you've been during all of this."

"And here's to you for how supportive you've been," Mia said. She turned to face whoever would be watching. "Whatever you might be fighting, don't fight alone. Find someone who will help you, someone who will have your back. I'm blessed that my daughter has mine and I'm looking forward to enjoying more treats as we get my health back."

Arianna raised her glass to her invisible viewers. "Here's to your good health."

"To good health," Mia repeated, and raised her glass as well. Then they clinked glasses and drank.

Sunny caught Mia's closed eyes and satisfied smile right before ending the reel. "That was the picture of bliss," she said to Mia. "Good job, ladies. You did it in one take."

"Yay us," said Arianna.

"Yes, yay us," said Mia, and Arianna knew she wasn't simply talking about the video they'd shot.

They were comrades in arms, fighting hard against cancer. This victory was exactly what they'd both needed to strengthen their resolve. Arianna shoved away the earlier dark shadow that had passed over her. They would beat this.

She went through the rest of the day, humming as she wrote a new article for the website, humming as she decided what winter drinks she could adapt to their upcoming Christmas-in-July party, and still humming when she went to pick up Sophie from a playdate with a friend later. Alden was working all week, but they'd be hanging out on the weekend and later in the month he was going with her and her family to the Christmas-in-July party at Sunny's house. It was going to be her best Christmas yet.

The morning of the party the women all converged in Mia's kitchen to create a masterpiece. Sophie and Paisley, future baking geniuses, had been included. (Bella had passed on the opportunity. No loss as far as Arianna was concerned. The kid was a regular party skunk, always stinking things up.) Mia had gone through her second to last chemo a couple of days earlier, which meant it was about time for her to start feeling the effects. Arianna had suggested forgetting the idea, knowing how the treatments sapped her mother's strength, but Mia had been insistent.

The day before she had premade the filling and had it chilling so all the women had to do was make the puffs and fill and decorate them. She supervised Paisley and Sophie as they made some small cream puffs of their own so they could each build a mini tower.

"This is a huge project," Sunny said as the girls colored in the living room while the women sat around the table drinking lavender lemonade and waiting for the cream puffs to bake. "I would never tackle this on my own."

"I'll never tackle it again," Molly said. "This is too much work."

"Not even if Reggie asks you to?" teased Sunny, and the others laughed.

All except Ava, who managed a polite smile.

"I see Ava is still Reggie's number one non-fan," Sunny said to Molly later as everyone was packing up and getting ready to move the party to her place.

"She's having a hard time getting past the age difference."

"What is it, exactly?"

"Thirteen years."

"Lucky thirteen. Maybe it wouldn't bother her if he was younger."

"Guess I should have taken up with a millennial. She'll come around. Sixty-eight is young by today's standards."

Sunny sure hoped so. Love wasn't easy when you had people in your life who didn't want you together.

She did her best with the one who didn't want her with Travis as everyone ate their Christmas-in-July turkey sandwiches and played games. After what Bella had said on their ill-fated family camping trip and the wall-of-ice ride home after, it had been a challenge to even manage a smile for her, but Sunny had pretended she had amnesia.

Later in the afternoon it was time to go caroling, and they wandered the neighborhood, dressed in their shorts and flip-flops and Santa hats, serenading the neighbors with Christmas carols and passing out plates of whipped shortbread with sprinkles. Travis sang like a bullfrog and Sunny wasn't much better. But both Molly and Reggie could sing, and Paisley was in her element, belting out "We Wish You a Merry Christmas." Arianna's new love fell right in with the fun, and watched over Mia as if she were his own mother. Oh, yes, he was, indeed, perfect for Arianna.

The only one missing from the caroling party was Bella, who had refused to tarnish her teen reputation with such foolishness, but Dylan had been easily bribed with the promise of frozen hot chocolate when they got back to the house, and he was enjoying teasing Paisley by snatching off her Santa hat every time he got the chance. The neighbors laughed at the group's shenanigans and wished them Merry Christmas in July, and everyone was smiling as they made their way back to the house.

"You are brilliant," said Travis, hugging Sunny as they went up the front walk.

"I am. How will I ever top this?" she joked.

Her happy mood deflated once they were in the house and found no Bella. Travis picked up the note on the counter, scrawled over the menu Sunny had printed. *Went shopping with Mom.*

"What the…? I'm calling Tansy," Travis growled.

Sunny laid a hand on his arm. "Don't."

He scowled. "Bella doesn't get to just up and leave, and Tansy doesn't need to be letting her."

"She wants us to beg. I don't want to give her that power."

"She's supposed to be here. It's our weekend to have her."

"So she'll be back after her retail therapy." *And won't that be fun?*

Travis heaved a sigh and set down his cell phone.

Yep, another successful party.

Was there a patron saint for stepmothers? If so, she and Sunny needed a conference.

Molly's feet hurt. And she was tired. And, for some reason, everyone in Bremerton had decided to come into the post office on their lunch break. But oh, well. She had a plate of cookies leftover from the party to share and she was ready.

Only the night before, sitting on the balcony of Reggie's waterfront condo, watching the ferry come in (she could get used to condo living), she'd told him she was going to make more of an effort at work.

"I still think you should marry me and retire," he'd said.

"There were a lot of times I thought about quitting last year but I'm no quitter and I'm not leaving without my retirement. It's the principal of the thing," she'd hurried on before he could argue that if she was with him, she wouldn't need it. "I like helping people and I think, for a while there, I lost track of that. But when we were walking around the neighborhood, delivering cookies, I remembered one of the reasons I went along with this Christmas-all-year thing. It's not about a monthly party, even though those are fun. It's about my attitude. I should be celebrating Christmas every day, doing my best to keep that joy going, trying to spread a little cheer to people who are having a hard day. Or a hard life."

"Molly, you have got the biggest heart of any woman I ever met," he'd said.

"It could be bigger, but I'm working on growing it."

Which was exactly what she was doing this day. Mrs. Bigman came in, looking sad. Uh-oh. Here was her first challenge.

"Mrs. Bigman, you look like you could use a cookie," Molly said, holding out her plate.

Cookies were obviously not the answer. Mrs. Bigman burst into tears.

"Oh, no. What's wrong?" Molly asked.

"Don't tell me you're gonna have a shrink session," protested the next person in line, a young man whose mama hadn't taught him any manners.

"Just a minute," Molly said to him. She went back to where Helen was trying to get the last of the letters put in the post office boxes. "I need you to come open your window," Molly said to her.

"These should have been out half an hour ago," Helen protested. As if Molly didn't know that.

"Just for a few minutes. I'll help you finish once we have a lull."

"Somebody's complaining about the line," Helen surmised with a frown.

"Nobody will be complaining if we hurry up and help them. Come on."

Helen opened the window next to Molly's and Molly returned her attention to Mrs. Bigman. "Now, tell me what's wrong."

"The cookies," Mrs. Bigman said, her lower lip trembling.

"The cookies," Molly repeated, not following.

"It's my son's birthday."

"Oh, and you want to send him cookies."

Oh, boy, here we go again. Except Mrs. Bigman only had a card.

"He doesn't like my cookies."

"Oh, now I'm sure that's not true," Molly said.

Mrs. Bigman set down the card. "I'll take one stamp. A flag." There were tears in her eyes.

Molly dug out a stamp from her drawer. "What makes you think he doesn't like your cookies?"

"My granddaughter told me. He threw them out. Then he told me he'd never gotten them."

Trying to spare her feelings. Molly suddenly felt very sorry for Mrs. Bigman.

"I know I don't bake as well as I used to. I…forget things sometimes and end up mixing up the ingredients. I guess lately my cookies aren't very good. He used to love my cookies," she finished, and a tear spilled onto her cheek.

"I really am sorry," Molly said. "That has to be hard. But there is good news."

Mrs. Bigman scowled. "What's that?"

"It's only your cookies he doesn't like. He still loves you. In fact, he loves you so much he didn't want to hurt your feelings."

The scowl downgraded to a frown. "Well."

On impulse, Molly grabbed the plate of cookies. "Wait here."

"Where am I going to go? You haven't given me my stamp," Mrs. Bigman groused.

Molly took her plate back to the break room. She dug out her lunch bag and pulled out the quart bag of pretzels she'd brought. She dumped them into the sack, then stuffed as many cookies as she could manage into the bag. They'd surround them with packing peanuts and send them overnight. On Molly.

She handed it to Mrs. Bigman. "Get one of those priority boxes and address it to your son. We're going to send him some cookies he'll like."

Mrs. Bigman blinked in surprise. "Really?"

"Really. And when you get home, call and tell him not to toss these. You had help and they taste fine."

Mrs. Bigman grinned and hobbled off to get a box.

The next woman in line stepped up to the counter. "That was really sweet of you."

"We're here to serve," Molly said. *Christmas all year.*

CHRISTMAS
IN AUGUST

23

Sunny and Travis joined the rest of the clan for Sunny's sister, Rae, and Will's wedding at Lairmont Manor, up north in Bellingham, Washington, not far from Birch Bay, where Will's family lived. The area for the outdoor ceremony was a lovely lawn shaded with trees and accented with hydrangeas and hanging flower baskets. At the end of a brick walk stood a fountain, which served as the backdrop for the bride and groom as they took their vows.

Sunny stood as matron of honor, the beginnings of a baby bump pushing against the gray chiffon of her dress, her hair threaded with pink rosebuds. Rae was elegant in her off-the-shoulder gown. Sunny noted the happy tears in her mom's eyes as she watched her younger daughter make her way to the man she'd chosen to spend her life with.

It brought back memories of Sunny's own wedding, when she and Travis had said their I do's a year earlier at the Kiana Lodge, located in Poulsbo. It had been a gorgeous venue, too, located on the shore of the Agate Passage, giving them a backdrop of sparkling water. How simple life had seemed when they'd first gotten together and how sure they'd been that everything would work out smoothly for them.

Oh, well, no couple's path was ever completely smooth. She hoped it would be a long, long time before Rae made that discovery.

The ceremony ended and it was time to congratulate the bride and groom. Sunny experienced a wistful moment as she watched how happily Rae's new mother-in-law introduced her to her friends. Jeanette had frowned through Sunny and Travis's rehearsal dinner, cried during the ceremony and managed the wan smile of a mourner when she'd introduced Sunny to her friends. Bella had refused to be a flower girl, and come the day of the wedding, it had only been Dylan in the ceremony, standing next to his father, holding the ring.

None of that mattered. Sunny would choose Travis all over again. It was just too bad you couldn't choose the family your groom came with.

The guests settled down under canopies to eat. Catering, done by East-West Catering, offered them bourbon-glazed northwest salmon, chicken poached in white wine and all manner of salads and appetizers, and Sunny was happy her stomach had settled down and she could enjoy it all.

The time came for toasts and, as matron of honor, Sunny was ready to do her duty. "Who doesn't dream of finding that perfect person to share her life with? Some of us don't get it right, and that's sad. But then, there are those of us who do and it gives everyone hope, makes us all believers in love. Rae has found that perfect someone. She and Will are going to be one of love's success stories. I'm so happy for you, sis. I know I don't need to wish you a happy life because you're already living it. But I do. I love you. And I love you, too, Will. Welcome to the family."

"Hear, hear," called out their father and Will's, and the guests echoed the sentiment with applause.

The best man had a sentimental speech, too, but he mostly

remembered lots of fun beer parties and goofy practical jokes in the groom's bachelor days that had Will shading his eyes and shaking his head. "I never thought you'd find any woman crazy enough to want you, dude, but you did. Rae, you're the best. Congrats, you two," he finished.

"Yep, gotta love those best men," Travis whispered to Sunny as she raised her glass of sparkling cider.

The mother-in-law had a speech prepared also. "It's a funny thing about mothers and sons," she observed. "We mothers fall in love the minute we hold our sons in our arms. We kiss their owies, drive the carpools and bake their favorite cookies. We're the one our son looks for in the audience when he's up on stage in that school play. We're the one he tells his troubles to. But a son grows up and falls in love and suddenly there's a new woman his world revolves around, a new woman he's given his heart to. It can be hard to share, hard to let go. And yet, in sharing, we open our lives and a new person comes in. If we're lucky, our loss turns to gain and we inherit someone who will also become precious to us. I'm one of those lucky women. RaeAnn, I'm thankful my son found you, and even though it's still a little hard to share, there's no one I'd rather share with."

Sunny saw her sister tearing up. So was she. Will's mom had it right. Love meant you shared. Even at Christmas, which meant she was going to have to get used to Christmas Future no longer looking like Christmas Past. The last Christmas had felt like a fail. In some ways it had been. But it had also been a reminder that life was about change. Plans shifted, and newcomers needed to be accommodated. Family members moved out and moved in new directions, but the connection was always there and there would always be ways to celebrate it. She'd been so caught up in her frustration she'd failed to see that.

There was something else she'd failed to see. How hard it was to give up the number one spot in someone's heart. And suddenly the pieces began falling into place. She should have seen it from the start.

"You know, I've been thinking," she said to Travis the next night as they shared a Seabeck pizza.

"Uh-oh. Is this gonna cost me money?" he teased.

"Not much. How about you take Bella to dinner tomorrow night while I'm out planning our next party."

His eyebrow shot up. "Take her out?"

"Yeah. To someplace nice, like Anthony's."

"Anthony's! Wait a minute. I'm going to take my bratty daughter out to dinner at a pricey seafood restaurant."

Sunny grinned. "Yep."

"Okay, I'll bite. Why? Tell me why I'm rewarding her for being a brat."

"Because I think she needs it."

"Wait a minute. Is this the same woman that was telling me only a couple of weeks ago not to give Bella power over us? This looks like sucking up to me."

"I think it's more like healing a hurt."

"You're the one who's been hurt in all of this," he said.

"So has she. Remember Will's mom's speech at the wedding?"

"Vaguely."

"Well, listening to her, I realized it's not so much that Bella hates me. It's that she's worried she'll lose you. And I think all this time we've been feeding that worry."

He made a face. "Oh, come on."

"No, really. We keep doing all these things as a family."

"Which is what we're supposed to be."

"And she keeps seeing you happy with me."

"Which I am."

"And where does that leave her?"

Travis rubbed his eyes. "I'm lost here."

"She's jealous. You're the number one man in her life and she thinks she's losing you. I don't know why I didn't see it earlier.

Here I've been trying to make her like me instead of seeing myself through her eyes."

"She should like you. You've been nothing but good to her."

"Maybe she will like me once she knows how much you still love her."

"Of course, I love her, even if I want to throttle her." He scrubbed his face. "Girls. Who can figure them out?"

"Fathers who care," Sunny said. "Call her."

He did, and Sunny could hear his end of the conversation as he paced around the living room. "Hey, cupcake, it's Dad. How about you and me going out to dinner tomorrow?... Yeah, just us. Thought I'd take you to Anthony's. Tell your mom I'll have you back in plenty of time to get your homework done. Okay?... Okay." He was smiling when he ended the call. "You'd think I'd asked her if she wanted to go to Disney World."

"Getting her dad all to herself? It's even better. Pick up a wrist corsage at Flowers D'Amour before you go."

"What is this, prom night?"

"Sort of," Sunny said with a smile. Who knew whether or not her idea would work but it was sure worth a try.

"Very insightful," Molly approved when the women met to finalize the plans for their Christmas-in-August celebration.

"I sure admire how hard you're trying," Arianna said.

"What else can I do?" Sunny said. "Anyway, what's the point of celebrating Christmas if I'm not going to honor the spirit of it. I mean, isn't the whole message of it to love each other?"

"As God loved us," said Molly. "Doesn't do us much good to party if there's no love."

"I just don't think I could do it," Arianna said.

"You do whatever you have to when you have to," Molly said. "I bet this will pay off eventually," she said to Sunny.

Eventually. How long did eventually take?

Maybe not as long as she feared. Travis came home to report that he and Bella had had a good time. She'd called him Daddy, something she hadn't done in a long time, and gave him a kiss when he dropped her off.

"She loved the corsage, by the way," he added. "I didn't think girls liked stuff like that anymore."

"I think when they're young and want to feel grown-up and special, they do."

"And how about big girls? Do they like stuff like that?"

"Sometimes," she said.

Which was the right answer, because the next morning she had a delivery from Flowers D'Amour—a beautiful arrangement of yellow roses, white lilies, peach-colored carnations and yellow snapdragons. The card said *you never cease to amaze me*, and was signed *love, Travis*.

"Oh, babe," she murmured as she carried it to the kitchen counter. "I hope you never stop feeling that way."

One thing she knew for sure. She'd amaze herself if she ever reached a point where she and Bella could finally call a truce.

At least Bella wasn't glaring at her when family and friends assembled at her house for their Christmas-in-August party. The twenty-fifth fell on a Saturday, which made it easy to plan to party all afternoon and into the evening. They were going to string Christmas lights on every tree and shrub in the backyard and by the time night fell, it would look gorgeous. She'd hidden Starbucks gift cards for small amounts around the yard as well as a twenty-dollar gift card for both Liberty Bay Books and Ballast Book Company, two popular local independent bookstores. Molly had contributed money for a grand prize—a fifty-dollar Visa gift card. Sunny had bought candy canes online, and for the kids there would be a competition to see who could find the most. The winner would get a free pizza from Seabeck Pizza. Oh, yes, this was going to be a fun day. Plus, she'd come up with a fabulous ice-cream dessert involving chocolate chip mint ice cream and hot fudge spread over a chocolate cookie crust and topped with whipped cream. It would never appear on Arianna's health-wise website, but everyone would enjoy it all the same.

The day was complete when Jeanette and Harry joined them. "Well, why wouldn't we?" Jeanette responded when Sunny enthusiastically thanked her for coming. "It is a standing invitation, isn't it?"

"Of course," said Sunny.

"This is such a cute idea," she added as Sunny gave her the rundown for the day's activities.

Would wonders never cease?

"I'm glad our grandchildren have such a good example of how to live right in their lives," Jeanette said as Sunny settled her on the balcony with an iced coffee.

Sunny wasn't sure what to say to that.

"She's the same as she's always been, Mom," Travis pointed out as he sat down next to her. "About time you realized it."

"I've always known," Jeanette huffed. "Isn't it time for you to go pick up my grandchildren?"

"I'm on my way," he said, taking the hint.

"The less time they spend with their mother and that…man, the better," Jeanette muttered as he left.

"That man?" Sunny prompted.

"That loser boyfriend of hers. He still hasn't found a job."

Neither had Tansy, who'd been talking about getting one for the last two years. A fact that hadn't bothered Jeanette.

"And now she's moved him in with her. A terrible example to set for the children."

Ah, there it was. Tansy had finally done something of which her former mother-in-law disapproved. Would wonders never cease?

Molly and Reggie were the next ones to arrive. "We're here," she announced, beaming.

"Let the fun begin," he added.

Rae and Will showed up, beaming like newlyweds should,

followed by Sunny's parents, then Ava and Paisley. Arianna came with her gang just as Travis showed up with the kids. Dylan smiling, Bella...not pouting. Progress. Let the fun begin.

The treasure hunt was a success, with almost everyone who participated finding something.

"This sucks, we didn't find anything," Rae complained, plopping onto a patio chair next to their mom.

"You found true love and just got a truckload of presents," Mom informed her. "No whining."

Which prompted Rae to teasingly stick out her tongue at Mom.

Everyone pitched in to string the lights, even Bella, when Travis said he needed her to advise him on how to arrange the ones on the rhododendrons he'd been assigned to decorate.

She wasn't so inclined to help set out food on the picnic table on the lawn, and Sunny was shocked to see Jeannette actually scold her. "Your stepmother went to a lot of trouble. The least you can do is help her."

Bella knew better than to argue with her grandmother, but she shot Sunny a sullen look before going into the kitchen to grab a bowl of chips.

Baby steps, Sunny told herself. Were they even stepping yet?

She decided she wasn't going to let the teen sullens ruin her mood and fetched the bowl of three-bean salad from the fridge.

The table was laden with goodies, including a salad that Molly had brought featuring raspberries, Jell-O and whipping cream. It looked more like dessert if you asked Sunny, but hey, you could never have enough dessert at a party.

And, speaking of... "Okay, guys, wait till you taste my amazing Christmas-in-August dessert. Don't anybody take another bite," Sunny commanded. "You need to save room for this."

It would be a hit with everyone, especially the kids. You couldn't go wrong with ice cream. She hurried up the stairs, fetched her fabulous achievement from the freezer and then hurried back out and down the steps to the lawn.

"Hey, babe, let me get that," Travis called, coming her way.

"I've got it," she assured him.

Right before her foot missed the step. The dessert went flying and so did she.

24

Sunny was in a kaleidoscope of confusion. Her right ankle was on fire and she had stars in her eyes. Or maybe they were circling around her head like in some kind of cartoon. Like in a cartoon. Ha ha. Except she didn't feel like laughing.

She was vaguely aware of Alden and Travis laying her gently on the pavement of the patio under the deck. "Careful of her neck," Alden cautioned.

"Neck?" she repeated weakly.

"It's okay, babe. We gotcha," Travis said.

"I don't know what happened." One minute she was upright and now she was…down. And in agony.

Mom was on her phone. "Yes, that's the address. Get someone here right away. She's pregnant!"

"My head," Sunny groaned.

"Good thing it's hard," said Travis. "You're gonna be okay. The ambulance is on its way. What's taking them so long?" he demanded.

How long had it been? An eternity. Everything was spinning.

"My ankle," she groaned, then let out a screech as Alden examined it.

"Probably got a fracture," he said. "Not to worry. You'll look great in a boot."

"The baby," fretted Jeanette.

"Oh, my God, am I going to lose the baby?" Sunny shrieked. Shrieking was a bad idea. Some nasty demon got mad and drove the hatchet in her head deeper. Arianna was by her side, telling her not to panic.

More players arrived. EMTs. "Hey, Alden," said one. "What's the story?"

"She fell. Hit her head on the railing. Fractured ankle, I'm guessing, and a possible concussion."

"My dessert," she moaned. She'd been so proud of that dessert, sure everyone was going to love it. Even Bella.

"It's okay, babe," Travis said.

"Okay," she repeated.

Arianna and Alden followed Travis and the ambulance, and both sets of parents got in their cars and followed them. Rae and Will left for the hospital also. The remaining partiers stayed behind to clean up the mess. The kids were subdued, especially Bella, Molly noted. She looked as white as a ghost.

"Honey, why don't you run and get me a broom and dustpan," Molly said to her, figuring the child needed something to do.

Bella bit her lip, nodded and raced up the stairs.

"Is the doctor going to make Sunny all better?" Sophie asked.

"Yes, he is," Molly said.

"Like he's making my Grammy better," Sophie said, with an enthusiastic nod.

Like they hoped that the doctor was. It was great to see Mia eating again.

"Kids, how about you take up the dirty plates and bowls?"

The other three nodded and got busy.

Ava fetched paper towels and a waste can. She knelt down and began mopping up the ice cream.

"Careful, there's broken glass," Molly cautioned.

Ava nodded and kept mopping. "Poor Sunny," she said as Reggie and Mia passed them, taking serving dishes back up into the house. "Of all the people for this to happen to. She's been working so hard on all these parties, trying to make everyone happy." Bella had returned with the broom and dustpan, and Ava gave her a disapproving look.

Bella bit her lip and dropped them, then turned and ran up the stairs.

"Ava, doll, your timing is perfect," Molly scolded.

"I think it is, as a matter of fact. It's about time that kid thought about someone other than herself."

"She will, once she grows up a little bit," Molly said, and hoped she was right.

Twenty minutes later everyone was waiting to hear how Sunny was doing. Ava was still puttering in the kitchen, wiping down counters. Out the kitchen window Molly could see Paisley and Sophie, subdued and sitting on a blanket under the apple tree in the corner of the yard, watching while Dylan kept himself occupied tossing a softball up in the air and catching it.

She and Reggie went out on the deck to sit down and discovered Bella sitting on the top step, crying softly. Mia sat next to her, an arm around her shoulder.

"Uh, maybe I'll go make some coffee," Reggie said, and disappeared back in the house.

Molly settled in a chair, ready to pitch in and help Mia with the girl if she needed it.

"It's my fault," Bella was sobbing. "I said I hoped she'd die."

"She's not going to die," Mia said firmly.

"I didn't mean it."

"Of course, you didn't."

"She hates me!"

"She doesn't hate you. In fact, she wants very much to be your friend. But then you already know that, don't you?"

Bella wasn't confirming or denying.

"I'm sure you always hoped your mom and dad would get back together." Bella was still silent, so Mia continued. "Even though they both moved on, they didn't move on from you, and they never will."

"How do I know they won't?" Bella asked in a small voice.

"Grown-ups are funny that way. Sometimes they fall out of love with each other, but they never fall out of love with their children. Sometimes they even meet someone really nice who falls in love with their children, too."

This brought on fresh stormy tears.

Mia hugged the girl against her. "Everything will be all right, and you have a chance to help with that."

"How?" Bella stammered.

"By being kind. That's all it takes."

Bella nodded and rubbed her forehead.

Molly smiled. Mia hadn't needed any backup. She had this.

As it turned out, Sunny had a chip fracture on her ankle and a mild concussion. The baby was fine, thank God. "It could have been so much worse," she said to Travis as he drove her back to the house.

"It could," he agreed. "No more carrying stuff up and down stairs for you, Mama."

"Don't worry. I have no intention of ever falling again. I just got in a hurry."

"How about now you get in a hurry to take it easy until the baby comes?" He reached over and took her hand. "You scared the shit out of me."

"I'm glad I didn't scare it out of myself. That would have been so embarrassing," she joked.

Back at the house everyone fussed over her, settling her on the couch, propping her foot up with pillows.

"I'm glad you had the grace to wait to bang yourself up until after the wedding," Rae teased her. "That stupid boot would have really wrecked the pictures."

"I'm so glad it wasn't worse," Mom said, kissing her forehead. "I'll stay overnight, and help you make sure she's all right," she said to Travis.

"I'm fine," Sunny insisted. Now that she had a Tylenol in her.

"We should go and let you rest," Jeanette said. To Travis, "Your father and I will take the kids home."

"If you need anything or have any questions, call," Alden said to Travis.

Sunny was wrung out like a sponge but she managed a good-bye smile for everyone. Dylan actually kissed her cheek before following his grandpa out of the house. Bella didn't even look her way as she rushed out the door past her grandmother.

What did you expect? Sunny asked herself. This wasn't the movies where the bad thing turned out to be just what everyone needed to get to something good and messy relationships got tied up in a neat little bow. Start the happy music with the ending credits. Show some bloopers.

The only blooper had been her fall and she sure had no desire to replay that.

The next day was Sunday and she and Travis lazed around the house, watching movies, him feeding her leftovers from the party, along with Tylenol at regular intervals. Molly and Ava called to check on her and Arianna stopped by to see how she was feeling.

"Foolish," Sunny confessed. "But I'll recover from that."

They were still visiting when Travis's phone went off. It was Tansy's ringtone.

"She's probably hoping to hear I croaked in the night," Sunny muttered.

"What?" he snapped into the phone. "No, she didn't lose the baby. She's doing fine." His eyebrows went up. "Yeah?... Okay, sure. Yeah, I'll be over."

Sunny frowned. "What does she want?"

"The kids got get-well cards for you."

"Get-well cards," Sunny repeated.

"Yeah. Tansy wants me to come over and get them. Want me to pick up anything while I'm out?"

"No, I'm good. Although I sure wish I didn't have to wear this darn boot," she told Arianna as Travis went to fetch his car key. "I feel like Frankenstein's monster."

"It's what all well-dressed klutzes are wearing this year," Arianna teased. She sobered. "You gave us all a scare."

"I gave myself a scare." Sunny bit her lip. "If I'd have lost the baby…"

"But you didn't. And you're getting get-well cards from the kids. That's huge progress."

"I'm sure Jeanette made them. She's determined they're going to learn manners," said Sunny.

"It's a start," Arianna said.

Sunny had to smile. "When did you turn into such a positive person?"

"Am I?" Arianna sounded surprised.

"Maybe that's not the right word. I don't know what the right word is, other than you're not so somber, not so unsure of yourself. Remember how tentative you were when we first did your website?"

"I guess I was. I was so sure I'd fail, I was afraid to get my hopes up. Sometimes I still can't believe how well my little business is doing."

"That's because you're doing something important. I'm glad I get to be part of it."

"Funny what a difference a few months make," Arianna mused. "This time last year I thought my life was over."

"It just goes to show, you never know," Sunny said.

Boy, you sure didn't. Travis returned with two card-sized envelopes, one pink and one white. She started with the white one. It featured a dog on the front, drinking from a toilet. *Be sure to drink plenty of fluids,* the card advised.

"I can guess who this is from," she said, and opened it. Sure enough, it was signed *Dylan.*

She moved on to the next card. It had a woman in a dress and heels. She was holding a bunch of balloons and getting lifted into a blue sky. "It's hard to keep a good woman down," she read aloud. She looked at Travis in surprise. "A card saying something nice?"

He shrugged.

She opened it, and under the printed *I Know You'll Get Well Soon,* Bella had written *I'm sorry,* and drawn a heart next to the words.

It was the movie moment Sunny had thought would never happen. She burst into tears.

CHRISTMAS
IN SEPTEMBER

25

It was turning out to be a beautiful Pacific Northwest September. "I always say our summers run from July through September," Molly said as the friends met at Horse and Cow to discuss their plans for Christmas in September. Another Saturday was chosen, this one falling close enough to the twenty-fifth to count.

"But by the end of the month we may want to move the party indoors," suggested Sunny, who was accessorizing her high fashion jeans, top and jacket with a bright blue walking boot.

"We can do it at my house," Arianna offered. "I think Mom would like that." Even though her chemo was done, her mother was still dealing with its aftereffects, trying to get back her energy.

"How's she feeling?" asked Molly.

"Glad to be done with chemo. We're still doing soft foods but maybe by Thanksgiving she'll be able to eat some turkey."

"As long as she can eat stuffing," said Sunny. "That's the best part of Thanksgiving. Speaking of food, what do we want to have for our party?"

"Apples," said Arianna.

Molly made a face. "Just plain apples?"

"Baked apples," Arianna elaborated.

"Apple crisp," Molly argued, "with sugar and butter. You can bake those apples for your website."

"It doesn't hurt to eat healthy once in a while," Arianna said with a frown.

"It hurts me," said Molly. "But all right, go ahead and bake your apples. I'm bringing apple crisp, though. And whipped cream."

"What should I bring?" Sunny asked.

"Yourself," Arianna told her. "You get a pass until the boot comes off."

"Which should be by Halloween," Sunny said. "I'll be down to a walking brace, thank heaven. Meanwhile I can at least bring chips for this. And I can organize the games."

"That goes without saying," said Arianna. "Maybe we should play back-to-school-type games."

"Hangman!" said Sunny. "Holiday hangman."

"That sounds so…creepy," Molly said in disgust.

"But it's a good word game," said Sunny. "My sister and I played it when we were kids."

"Who didn't?" Molly said.

"Me?" ventured Arianna.

"Your life has been deprived," Sunny told her.

"I don't want to play games about hanging people," Molly said firmly and that settled that. "What else can we do?" she mused, tapping her chin thoughtfully.

"Story problems!" Sunny crowed.

"Eew," said the other two.

"No, I mean funny ones," Sunny said. "Like, if I left a dozen cookies out for Santa and the elves ate half of them and he only ate two because he was pacing himself, how many cookies would be left on the plate?"

"I say don't leave him any. Eat 'em all," said Molly, and Arianna giggled. "But that's a cute idea," Molly continued, dredging a French fry through her ketchup. "Fits with the back-to-school theme. I think we should give all the kids school-type prizes—pens, fancy notebooks, funny erasers."

"They do almost everything on computers nowadays," said Arianna. "But Sophie still loves her arts and crafts."

"Okay, then. I'll pick up a bunch of things—glitter, glue, colored paper, stickers."

"Oh, yeah, you can't go wrong with stickers," Arianna approved.

Their waiter appeared. "What else can I get you, ladies?"

"I'll have another glass of white wine," Molly told him. She sent a smirk Sunny's way. "I'm drinkin' for two."

"Good thing you're not driving," Arianna said.

"That's why I live down the street from you, designated driver," Molly said.

"Anything else?" he asked.

"Yes. Dessert," Sunny said. "You drink for two and I'll eat for two," she told Molly.

Arianna shook her head. "You guys."

They made her smile, and were good medicine for her. It seemed like lately she had little more energy than her mother, and the girlfriend moments worked like a tonic.

"You know you love us," joked Sunny.

"I do," Arianna said, suddenly serious. "You've helped me stay sane. I really don't know what I'd have done without you these past few months."

"You'd have managed," Molly said. "You're stronger than you think, girl, and you're doing great."

"I'm managing, but there are times when I feel almost as tired as Mom is." Keeping worry at bay was hard work and worry had a way of sneaking up on her like a vampire and draining her dry. "Between the business and taking care of Mom and

Sophie, every once in a while I have to check to see if I've still got a grip on my life."

"You do," Molly assured her.

"Thanks to my friends," she said, and smiled at both of them.

"You really are doing fine, and you'll continue to, no matter what," Molly said to her later as Arianna drove her home.

"No matter what," Arianna repeated. Three words that should be stricken from the English language.

"Your mom was telling me only the other day how proud she is of you. You pulled yourself out of the pit of despair and you haven't looked back."

Arianna gave a snort. "Nothing to look back at. You know, when Wyatt said he wanted out I thought it was the end of the world."

"Funny how there are always new worlds waiting to be explored," said Molly.

Yes, there were.

Christmas in September was a smash hit and Sunny's heart was full to overflowing to see her entire family present. In addition to the games she'd planned, they played teacher, allowing each kid to assign the grown-ups funny tasks. The best was Bella's assignment for her dad.

"Not the chicken dance!" he protested.

"Extra credit," said Bella.

"I don't want extra credit," he said.

"It's either that or miss lunch," Bella said sternly.

"I'll dance," he decided, and Sunny filmed it, already envisioning that up on TikTok.

She got another even more important video, one of Mia talking about life lessons she'd learned, her daughter seated next to her. "You should always give people the benefit of the doubt because you never know what they might be going through," she said. "Always forgive because if you don't the person who will suffer the most is you. And, finally, be grateful for each moment you have here because each one is a gift."

She reached out and took Arianna's hand and squeezed it, and Arianna managed a watery smile.

"Your followers will love this," said Sunny. "And now, how about doing that latest dance craze that's on TikTok, show 'em how to live every moment to the max."

Mia looked horrified. "Oh, I couldn't."

"Sure you could," said Sunny.

"How about we do a group dance," Mia proposed.

"Not the chicken dance," put in Travis.

Everyone agreed. The coffee table was moved and the kids donned their Santa hats. Mia didn't last long and sat down on the sofa, but Travis and Will made a chair and picked her up and started dancing with her.

When you're too tired, let your friends carry you, Sunny thought. Another good life lesson.

The day wrapped up with the kids opening presents. To Sunny's delight, Bella actually smiled and thanked her for the retro boho embroidered shoulder bag.

"Do you like it?" Sunny asked. Good grief, she sounded like an eager loser, hoping to win points.

"I do," Bella said. "And Dylan and I have a gift for you." She hurried to her backpack and dug out a small package.

"For me?"

"Well, for the baby," Bella clarified.

Sunny opened it to find a colorful play rattle designed to look like some sort of bug.

Now it was Bella asking, "Do you like it?"

"I do, and so will the baby."

"I'm not gonna have to change diapers, am I?" Dylan wanted to know.

"Real men change diapers," Travis said, and Dylan made a face.

"I'm sure we can find something for you to do to help that

doesn't involve poop," Sunny told him. "Thanks for this, you two."

With that, it was time for more food. To Sunny's surprise and Arianna's delight, the baked apples were a hit. Which was just as well since they'd lost Molly, who was down for the count with a nasty cold. Poor Molly. It was too bad she had to miss out.

Theraflu instead of apple crisp. What a lousy substitution. Molly gave the pillow she'd dragged out to the couch a punch and pretended it was the unknown germ spreader. Why didn't people stay home when they were sick, anyway? She sneezed and her cat, Marlow, who'd been on her lap, gave a start. It was probably loud enough to be heard all the way down the street at Arianna's where everyone was partying without her.

She sighed and selected a fresh movie to watch on TV. A rom-com? Hmm. No, that would rub it in that she wasn't with Reggie and make her grumpy.

"You go to the party without me and have fun," she'd said.

"It won't be any fun without you," he'd argued.

"Sure it will. Anyway, one of us ought to be able to enjoy the festivities."

"There'll be more."

There would. Colds didn't last forever. A week and she'd be up and running again. Okay, not exactly running. Running wasn't something she did anymore. But trotting. Darn, she hated to miss the fun, though. What a party animal she'd turned into!

Her doorbell rang and she frowned. Everyone knew she was sick, so it couldn't be anyone she wanted to see standing on her front porch. She'd ignore whoever it was.

The doorbell rang again. And then again.

No, not coming to the door in fleece jammy bottoms with smiley faces on them and my hair sticking out every which way and no makeup. She was no fashion model like Sunny, but she wasn't a total slob, either. Even though being sick made slobs of everyone, she didn't want to show that face to the world.

Her cell phone rang. Reggie.

"Answer the door," he said. "There's a delivery for you."

"A delivery?" she repeated.

"Come on, open up."

"Oh, all right," she said.

She threw off her blanket and sent Marlow jumping, then shuffled to the door, opened it and...eeek! "Reggie!" She slammed the door shut.

"Hey," he said on the other side. "Open up."

"Not looking like this," she said.

"I don't care what you look like."

"Well, I do."

"Come on, Molly. I got something for you."

"I got something for you, too. Germs. You don't want them."

"I never get sick. Let me in. Come on, I came all this way." From downtown Bremerton, a big ten-minute trek.

"Please."

"Okay, wait there."

She left him on the front porch and hurried to the bathroom where she brushed her teeth and her hair and put on her eye makeup and some lipstick. Yep, now she looked...like a vampire made up for the undead ball. When you were sick, it was hopeless. Nothing made you look good. Hopefully that old saying that love was blind was true. And if not blind, maybe at least it was nearsighted.

She went back and opened the door and he stepped in, bearing a large can of chicken soup in one hand and a bottle of champagne in the other. "I brought medicine."

"Aww, Reggie, you are so sweet. I'll save it for us both to drink when I'm well."

"You might feel better later, after you eat my secret recipe chicken soup."

She laughed. "I might at that. Thank you."

"I think I should stay and heat it up for you."

"No, you shouldn't. I'll make you sick."

"You could never make me sick. Come on, don't you want some company?"

Actually, she did, but she hated the idea of passing her germs on to him.

"You can't be having fun all by yourself here."

"You can't have fun when you're sick."

"You can try," he said.

"Okay, then, social distancing, and open the window so we get some fresh air in here."

He obliged, then put the champagne in the fridge. He returned and joined her on the couch where she'd flopped once more.

"This is not social distancing," she informed him.

"All you got is a cold. I'm not worried." He put an arm around her. "Let's watch a movie. What have you got on the menu?"

"A romantic comedy," she said. Funny how she was in the mood for one now that Reggie was with her.

He nodded approval. "Good. I like a happy ending. Maybe I'll pick up some romance tips."

"You're already a pro," she assured him.

"Yeah?" He smiled.

"Oh, yeah."

"Then lay your head on my shoulder and I'll see if the young buck in this movie is doing things right."

He wasn't at first.

"What a turkey," Reggie said.

"If he got it right at the beginning, there'd be no story," Molly pointed out. "Every relationship has to have a challenge."

"There's challenges and there's clueless, and if you ask me, that man is just plain clueless."

She paused the movie and looked up at him. "Reggie, were you ever clueless?"

"Probably. But I never found a woman I really wanted to stay with. Not until you."

She smiled at him. "I feel the same. There's been no one since my husband. I honestly didn't think I'd ever find another man I could love. And then you came along."

"So we've each found our someone."

"We have," she said with a smile.

"Then how long are we gonna wait to make it official? Life's short, Molly. I want us to be together while we still got some good years ahead of us. How about I give you a ring for Christmas?"

"Which one?" she quipped, and he laughed.

"Let's go shopping once you're well. What do you say to that?"

He was right. They loved each other, enjoyed each other's company. She knew she wanted to be with him for the rest of her life. It was silly to wait.

"I say, let's go shopping," she said.

"All right!" he said. "This calls for champagne. Where do you keep the champagne glasses?"

"In the cupboard above the fridge."

She'd never bothered to store them any place more accessible. She hadn't exactly been living a champagne kind of life so what had been the point? Except now it looked like she'd be using those glasses more. Christmas, New Year's Eve, Valentine's Day, all with Reggie. Yes, it was time to move them to a lower cupboard.

"There's a step ladder in the pantry," she said.

"I don't need no stinkin' step ladder," he joked, and proved it by reaching up and pulling down two glasses. "You think Ava will be happy for us?" he asked. "I think she's starting to like me."

She should, Molly thought. She would. She'd come around.

He poured champagne for them, then returned to the couch. "Here's to you, Molly. You've made me the happiest man in the world."

"Here's to us," she said.

They clinked glasses just as her door opened. There stood Ava, staring at them with a disapproving look on her face. "I brought you some leftovers from the party. I thought you were sick," she added accusingly.

"I am," Molly said. A sneeze emerged in time to prove it, making her jiggle her glass and spill champagne in her lap. "Oh, good grief," she muttered.

"You probably shouldn't have company if you're sick," Ava said, looking disapprovingly at Reggie.

"Reggie's not company. He's my fiancé."

Ava gaped at them. The bag of goodies she'd brought dropped to the floor. "Your what?"

26

"You heard me," Molly said.

Ava looked like an elephant had just stepped on her foot. "I thought you were going to take things slow."

"We have been," Molly said.

"Ava, I promise I'm gonna be good to your mom," Reggie said.

Ava made no reply to that. Instead she said, "I have to go. Paisley's waiting in the car." Then she was gone.

"That went well," Reggie muttered as the door shut behind her. He picked up the dropped bag and stuck it in the refrigerator. "What's your girl got against me, anyway?"

Molly hated to tell him. It was bound to hurt his feelings. She hesitated.

"There's got to be a reason, but I can't figure out what it is," he said as he rejoined her on the couch. "Help me."

"She thinks you're too old."

Instead of looking hurt or insulted, his eyes opened wide in surprise. Then he began to laugh. "That's it?"

Molly shrugged and nodded. "According to Ava, men your age want either a nurse or a purse."

The laugh got bigger. "I don't need a purse. And do I look like I need a nurse?"

"No, you don't. You're probably in better shape than me."

"If I did need a nurse, I could afford to hire one." He downed the rest of his champagne. "I guess this doesn't match up with a romantic movie ending."

"Our story's not over yet," Molly said. "Ava will come around."

"I hope so, 'cause I sure don't want to give you up."

"You won't have to because I'm not giving you up," Molly said firmly. She downed what was left of her champagne, then snuggled up against him. "Let's finish this movie and see if the man in it can get in touch with his inner Reggie and wow the woman."

They did finish the movie, but for Molly their happy time had lost some of its luster. *Thank you, Ava, for ruining what should have been a perfect evening.*

After Reggie left, Molly put in a call to her daughter.

"What?" Ava answered.

"Don't you dare get like that with me, young woman," Molly scolded. "You and your sour face managed to ruin what was a perfect moment, and I'm telling you right now I'm not going to have you ruining all the moments to come."

"Mom, you said you'd take it slow."

"I changed my mind. I love Reggie and I want to be with him."

"And how long do you think that will be?" Ava retorted.

"You are unbelievable," Molly said in disgust.

"I don't want you to get hurt. He's old, Mom."

"He's hardly ancient. And, anyway, since when is it a crime to be old?"

"It's not."

"Good. Then you can give it a rest."

"He's a bad risk. He probably can't even get it up."

"Now that is enough," Molly snapped. "You should be ashamed."

"*I* should be ashamed. I'm not the old man trolling for someone to push his wheelchair."

"I never thought I'd see the day when my daughter was prejudiced."

"Oh, come on, Mom," Ava said in disgust.

"You are. Aging happens to us all. It's happening to me."

"You're not that old," Ava protested. "Mom, you already buried one husband. Do you want to bury another?"

"Oh, honey, he could as easily outlive me. Don't you get it? This is a golden time. I've found romance again after all these years on my own. I'm with a good man and I'm having a good time. Do you honestly want me to give that up?"

Her daughter's, "No," sounded reluctant.

"No one knows how long they'll live. No one has any guarantees that life will be perfect. You know that. You've had your share of disappointments, relationships that didn't work out. You are well aware of how hard it is to find someone worth giving your heart to. I have, and right now my life is darn close to perfect. I don't want you messing that up with all your disapproval and dire predictions."

Ava sighed heavily. "I'm not trying to make you miserable."

"I know. You are, though, and I need you to stop raining on my parade. Okay?"

There was silence on Ava's end.

"Okay?" Molly prompted again.

"Okay."

"Please make an effort to be nice to him."

"I will," Ava promised. "Anyway, it's your life."

The same thing Molly had said more than once to her. "You're right. It is. And I intend to enjoy it."

And if Ava would truly give Reggie a chance, they could all enjoy it together.

★ ★ ★

Alden was at work when his past came into the emergency room. It was all he could do not to squeak, "Cynthia?" when he saw the admission papers. Oh, no, of all the emergency rooms in all the world.

"Oh, Alden, thank God," she said as she entered the screening room.

Thanking God for him? There was a new one.

"I think I'm having a heart attack," she said.

There was no history of heart problems in her family, and she didn't look like a woman in the middle of a heart attack. No sweating and her coloring was good. She didn't look like she was dizzy.

But it wasn't his job to diagnose her. His job was to take her vitals, get her hooked up to an EKG monitor and get a reading.

Her oxygen looked good, but her pulse was slightly elevated. "Are you dizzy?" he asked.

"No. Should I be?" she asked, her voice rising.

"I just need to find out how you're feeling."

"My chest hurts, that's how I'm feeling!"

"Okay, we're gonna get you all checked out," he said, keeping his own voice level.

Check her out. He remembered doing that when he first saw her at the Whaling Days festival in Silverdale a couple of summers earlier. She'd looked hotter than a solar flare in shorts that almost covered her butt and a low-cut red top, long blond hair swept up into a ponytail. He'd gotten pretty hot himself, just gawking at her.

She'd caught him staring and given him a smile that said, "Come on over and try your luck."

He had, and boy, had he felt lucky when, after some flirting and a hot dog and beer, she gave him her phone number. And boy, had he been a fool.

Yet now here she was looking at him like he was the hero of

the hospital, as if he held her fate in his hands. He'd been sure he was in love with this woman, been close to her. How was he supposed to hook her up to the electrodes and stay detached? Somebody else was going to have to do the electrocardiogram.

Except they were slammed and there was no one else. "Get a grip," said Felicia, one of the other ER nurses. "You're a professional."

He swore under his breath and marched off to get the machine. There was a reason doctors were encouraged never to treat their own families. Too emotionally involved.

You're not involved with her anymore, he reminded himself. *This is no big deal.*

"Thank God it's you. I'd be embarrassed to have anyone else treating me," she said when he came back with the machine. "It would be so awkward."

Would be? It already was.

It was even more awkward hooking her up to the machine, sticking the sensors on her chest, under her boobs. Aack!

They're just boobs, they're just boobs.

You knew these boobs. He was going to have a heart attack.

"This is so scary," she whimpered.

"No need to be scared," he said. *Be professional, be professional.*

He was glad when he was done and could step over to the machine. Physical distance.

Except what about emotional distance? It was as if his memory had swung a lasso and was pulling him back to her against his will. It hadn't been all bad. *Here, put on these rose-colored glasses and take a look.*

Was this fate?

No, it was torture.

The reading came out fine and he got to, once again, get personal as he unhooked her.

"What does it mean? Am I dying?" she asked.

"You're gonna be okay," he said. But was he? His head was a mess.

"You're lying to me," she accused. "You can't bring yourself to tell me the truth. Oh, my God, I'm dying."

"Cynthia, you're not dying. You'll be fine," Alden said.

"Oh, what do you know?" she snapped, the same old Cynthia he'd once been crazy about.

The memories fell away and landed on the floor. It was fate all right, confirming that he was well rid of her.

The doctor read the printout, asked her what she'd been eating and the problem was quickly solved. Jalapeño poppers combined with tequila had brought on a good case of heartburn—nothing a strong dose of antacid wouldn't cure. She would be released back into the wild.

She managed to find Alden before that, though. "Alden, do you miss me?"

Maybe he would have deceived himself into thinking he had if he weren't with someone so superior, someone who didn't manufacture drama simply to get attention. Someone who was really going through serious shit and doing her best to do it with a brave face.

"I'm with someone," he said simply.

"So am I," said Cynthia in her well-used snotty voice. Oh, yeah, he should have read the script. He was supposed to be a broken man, barely coping without her.

"Well, good luck to him," Alden said. The poor guy would need it.

As he moved on to the next patient, he couldn't help marveling over how miserable he'd been after they'd broken up, how often he'd thought about her, how often he'd questioned his own worth and veered away from relationships, not wanting to get hurt again. He'd let a reality TV caricature do that to him.

He'd almost let her get inside his head and mess him up again.

Stroking his ego (for a second), looking at him with those big blue eyes filled with terror.

A pair of hazel eyes came to mind, set in a round face with sweet kissable lips. Yep, fate had sent Cynthia to the emergency room all right—to remind Alden how lucky he was to have found Arianna and what a fool he'd be not to make what they had permanent.

Except, with everything she had on her plate, would she be ready?

CHRISTMAS
IN OCTOBER

27

The neighborhood was decorating for Halloween, and it seemed everywhere Arianna looked, she saw skeletons or sheet ghosts hanging from trees or tombstones on lawns. When she was a kid, she'd loved all that stuff. Even as a grown-up, but this Halloween all those grisly symbols of death depressed her. She and her mother had danced on the edge of the River Styx and it hadn't been pleasant.

She forced herself to concentrate on the less gruesome aspects of fall—autumn leaves and pumpkins, yummy fall foods. She spent a lot of time coming up with healthful recipes and fall fitness tips for the website. She'd picked up a new sponsor, a fresh meal delivery company, and she had done a couple of videos making dinner from their boxed offering as well as posting pictures. It all helped her turn her focus away from what she saw every time she drove down her street.

"When are we going to carve pumpkins, Mommy?" Sophie wanted to know as they passed the pile of pumpkins on their way into the supermarket.

Jack-O-Lanterns. More Halloween ghoulishness. Ugh.

"Soon," Arianna promised.

"Can Alden come over and carve them with us?"

"We can ask him."

Alden seemed to be game for just about anything. It was one of the many things she loved about him.

Love, what a funny word it was. One minute you could be talking about loving pizza or chocolate cake and the next using it to describe how you felt about a person. Arianna smiled. Alden was not only pizza and chocolate cake, he was also starry nights, rainbows and a perfect sunny day all rolled into one. She was sure he had feelings for her, but were they strong enough to move their relationship forward?

She'd been tempted to ask on more than one occasion but had always chickened out. What if he said he wasn't sure? Maybe he didn't want to commit for the long haul. Wyatt had already said no to forever. She didn't think she could risk that kind of rejection again, not on top of the year she'd had. Better to walk around with her eyes wide shut, in happy ignorance. Enjoy what she had with Alden—whatever that was—and not expect it to last.

"I'm an expert pumpkin carver," he bragged when he stopped by the house the next day and Sophie offered her invitation.

Sophie let out a whoop. "Can we get our pumpkin now, Mommy?"

Mia wasn't feeling well and was in bed and Mommy was in the middle of making chicken soup for her. "A little later," she said, which pulled out Sophie's lower lip. "No pouting," Arianna said.

"Yeah, pouting's not good," Alden said, backing her up, and tousled Sophie's hair. To Arianna, he said, "If you're okay with it, I could take her. I need to get some stuff from Safeway, anyway."

This was a first and felt somehow very important, a step toward a new level of trust. Arianna hesitated.

"Let's go, Alden," Sophie said, racing to get her coat.

"I'll drive carefully," he promised.

"Okay," she said. "Thanks."

"No problem," he said and sauntered out the door after Sophie.

Arianna letting him take her girl to pick out a pumpkin—it was as if they'd crossed a threshold of sorts. Definitely a sign that they were getting closer. How close would she let him get?

At the store Sophie had a hard time picking the perfect pumpkin.

"How about we take home more than one," he said. "Let's get three. One for you, one for your mom and one for your Grammy. Then you can have a whole pumpkin family on the front porch."

"Yes!" Sophie said enthusiastically.

Yes! thought Alden. Carving three pumpkins should take some time, which pretty much guaranteed an invitation to stay and sample that chicken soup.

"You're ambitious," Arianna observed when they set their pumpkins on the dining table.

"Sophie couldn't choose so we decided to make a family," he said.

"This one is you, this one is Grammy and this one is me," Sophie said, pointing to each.

"That's a lot of carving," Arianna said.

"Alden and me are good at it," Sophie said confidently. "Huh, Alden?"

"You bet," he said.

"I'll carve another one with Daddy for his house," Sophie said as Alden helped Arianna spread newspaper over the kitchen table to catch the pumpkin mess.

Daddy was lucky he even rated a pumpkin, considering how little time the tool spent with his kid. He'd only taken her a few times since the Fourth—never when it was helpful to Arianna, of course. It seemed to Alden that she let the guy walk all over her, never sticking to their schedule, usually bringing Sophie back later than he'd said he would. Arianna really needed someone in her corner. And Sophie needed a man in her life she could depend on. That man should be Alden.

Arianna produced a giant bowl for the pumpkin innards. "Be sure to save the seeds so we can toast them," she said.

Pumpkin carving was high art as far as Sophie was concerned. Many faces had to be tried out on paper before they could draw them on the pumpkin. Arianna looked over their shoulders several times as Alden helped Sophie bring her ideas to life. "Nothing scary," she'd say. Or, "That looks just like Grammy."

"How about this one for you?" he asked, showing her his design. The pumpkin would have glowing eyelashes, and full lips like hers.

"Is that what I look like?" she joked.

"You look way prettier," he assured her, and she laughed.

Once the pumpkins were done, it was time to put flicker candles in them and set them out on the porch. Arianna took pictures to post on Instagram—of the pumpkins, of Sophie with the pumpkins and then one with Alden and Sophie, the artists and their handiwork. It all felt so natural, like they'd been together for years, like they belonged together. He hoped he wasn't imagining it because he was really loving being involved with this family. Especially Arianna.

"I'd better take Buster for a walk," he said when they were done.

"Can I come?" asked Sophie.

Alden looked at Arianna.

"Sure," she said. "After you're done, come on back for soup and bring Buster over with you."

Like a family, he thought. Like what he'd been wanting. How easy it all felt when you were with the right woman.

Alden was weaving himself so into the fabric of their lives Arianna couldn't imagine him not being with them. It felt too good to be true. Later, after Sophie was in bed and Mia had gone to her room to read and it was the two of them and Buster on the couch, watching a movie, she wanted desperately to ask, "Does this feel as right to you as it does to me?"

She didn't. She couldn't take the risk of scaring him away, even though everything seemed so perfect, and she was so happy. Everything had seemed so perfect when she was with Wyatt. And then it hadn't been. In the end she hadn't been enough. In the end maybe she wouldn't be enough for Alden, either.

And yet Alden kept coming back. On his next night over, he came bearing the game Candy Land to play with Sophie.

"We have that game," she said. "That's for little kids."

"My bad," he said.

"But I'll play it with you, Alden," she offered.

Mia, who was sitting on the couch, crocheting, chuckled. "Very noble of her."

"And very thoughtful of you," Arianna said to him. Alden, she was beginning to realize, was a big kid himself.

"You know who thought up this game?" he asked Sophie as they set it up. She shook her head and he continued. "It was made up by a lady who had polio."

"What's that?"

"It's a disease people used to get before we came up with a vaccine. Grown-ups got it and so did kids. A lot of times it hurt them so bad they couldn't walk."

"Couldn't walk?" Sophie echoed, horrified.

"Yep. This lady had it, and she had to be in the hospital. She felt sorry for the kids who were there who had it and couldn't walk, so she made up this game for them. That was a long time ago, and people are still playing the game."

"Which just goes to show that good things can come out of bad," Mia said from her post on the couch.

Arianna knew the purpose behind that statement. Her mother was trying to send her a message.

It was one she didn't want to receive. Mia was having trouble swallowing food again and they had tests scheduled at the hospital for the following day. She half wished they didn't have to go.

"It'll be okay," Alden assured her later when the two of them were walking Buster.

"You know it won't."

He was silent a moment. "Let me rephrase that. You'll be okay. I've got your back."

He took her hand and they walked on, past the ghosts and skeletons and yards filled with fake tombstones.

The news was, indeed, bad, and Arianna and Mia's friends came over to try to cheer them up, bearing chocolate. Sunny had also brought a couple of bottles of chocolate wine.

"It goes down easy," she said to Mia.

Which was more than Arianna could say about the knowledge that the tumor was growing again. It wasn't right. They'd fought so hard. Her mother had been making such great progress. And now this.

"Movie night. What are we going to watch?" Sunny asked Mia.

"*The Ghost and Mrs. Muir,*" Mia said, and Arianna's heart gave a painful squeeze.

"Oh, no, Mom. Not that one," she protested.

"I've never seen it," said Ava.

"It's an old movie," Mia said.

"About death," Arianna added with a scowl.

"No, about hope," Mia corrected her.

"Crud in the mud," Arianna muttered, and went to fetch wine glasses.

Molly joined her in the kitchen and put an arm around her shoulders. "You'll have to suck it up. It was her choice."

"I can't do this," Arianna said in a low voice, and took a couple of angry swipes at the tears cascading down her cheeks.

"So many things we say we can't do that we have to do anyway," Molly said sadly. "I'm sorry."

So was Arianna. She was crying uncontrollably at the end of the movie when an old Mrs. Muir died, releasing her young and beautiful spirit, who then walked off into the heavens with her beloved captain who had haunted her way back when.

"I hate this movie," she grumbled.

"I love it," said Mia. "Mrs. Muir gets united with her true love in the end. It makes me happy. Your father was the love of my life and I'm looking forward to being reunited with him."

There was nothing Arianna could say to that. Her loss would be her mother's gain. Still, she barely slept that night, turning her pillow into a marsh of tears. How on earth was she going to be able to let go when the time came?

28

The Christmas-in-October party was bittersweet. Molly was showing off her new bling and she and Reggie were taking suggestions for the best month to get married. "Christmas," he insisted.

"Valentine's Day," said Sunny. "It's such a romantic time to get married."

"Yes, but who would come. You'll all be out celebrating," said Molly.

"November," Reggie said. "The month to be thankful, and that says it all because I'm thankful I found this woman."

"I want to be flower girl," Paisley said.

"That goes without saying," Molly assured her.

With that settled, Paisley was ready to play with the kids and leave the grown-ups to the boring activity of sitting around and talking.

There was plenty of activity for the kids, including a pumpkin-carving contest, and even Bella had fun doing that. She also got into going from house to house, wearing Santa hats and delivering net bags filled with candy corn and caramels. Reverse trick or treat.

Arianna and Sunny escorted them while Molly and Ava helped ready the treats and games back at Mia's house. Mia wouldn't be able to eat any of the cookies Arianna had baked, but she'd left her mother sipping on hot cider and chatting with Alden and Reggie, who had come dressed like a giant pumpkin and dubbing himself the Great Pumpkin. How much longer would her mother be with them? She bit into a thumbnail and gave it a vicious rip.

"Great idea," called one of the neighbors, waving at them.

"We're full of great ideas," Sunny said as they walked on.

"That we are," Arianna said. "Although I've got to admit, I'm not sure how thankful I'm going to be feeling next month. Somehow, this all feels so…inconsequential in light of what's going on with Mom."

"I can sure understand that," Sunny told her. "In some ways I guess it is. But when you stop and think how throwing these parties has lifted our spirits, brought us and our families closer together, I think it's been worth it." She rubbed her growing belly. "If we don't celebrate the good things in life all that's left is sorrow."

Arianna nodded. Of course, what Sunny said made sense, but she wasn't the one about to lose her mom.

"Sophie needs this. She needs these good memories to hang on to when Mia isn't here anymore," Sunny continued.

Arianna bit her lip and nodded.

Sunny slung an arm around her shoulder. "We'll get you through this, girlfriend."

They would certainly try, but in the end Arianna knew the only person who would be able to get her through what lay ahead was herself. She tore into another fingernail.

The kids came storming back into the house, pumped over how many neighbors had raved over the simple treats they'd shared.

"Mrs. Cho even gave us all a cookie," Sophie reported.

"It was awesome," Dylan added.

"Well, I hope you saved room for pumpkin casserole and cookies," Molly said to him.

"Cookies, yeah," he replied, obviously not ready to commit on a cooked stuffed pumpkin.

But when it came time to eat dinner, he was the first of the kids to ask for seconds, and that had Molly smiling, since the pumpkin casserole had been her idea.

They didn't make a late night of it, mainly because Mia was looking so tired.

"You look tired yourself, and I bet you're ready for some Halloween partying with just you and Alden," Molly said to Arianna.

Arianna looked to where Alden was lounging on the couch, Sophie snuggled up next to him. "You don't have to rush off," she said, insisting on being polite.

"No rushing, but I am going to start moving the troops," said Molly.

"Those two kids sure are a perfect match," she said to Reggie a few minutes later as they walked back down the street to her house.

"Just like us," he said. "You want to hang out at your place or come over to mine?"

"I'm in the mood to watch the ferries come and go," she said.

"All right. That way I can get out of this costume. The Great Pumpkin can only last for so long."

She followed him to his condo, parking in his extra space, and then up to his unit that overlooked the historic Turner Joy, a leftover ship from the Vietnam era. Next to it was the marina where his boat was moored.

He went to change and she walked over to the window to enjoy the view. A lit ferryboat was coming in from Seattle, gliding over the water as if by magic.

"It's a great view, isn't it?" he said, joining her. He'd changed into his favorite well-worn jeans and an equally worn Seahawks sweatshirt. "Do we want to live here after we're married?"

"Oh, yes," she said. "I can walk to the post office from here, plus it's smaller than my place, easier to clean."

She would want to put her own touches on it, though. Like the rest of his lifestyle, Reggie's decorating tastes were simple. He had a leather sectional in the living area, arranged to enjoy the fireplace and the flat-screen TV that hung over it. The table in the dining area was small and one picture hung on the wall— that of a sailboat cutting through a choppy sea. His bedroom held a bed and a chest of drawers and that was it, and the guest bedroom had a sofa bed and a desk. No pictures in either of them.

"Do what you want with the place," he'd said. "Make it homey."

She intended to.

"So, what'll we do? Cards? A movie?"

"I'm ready to sit and not think," she said.

"You got it," he said with a smile.

The smile suddenly changed, and he blinked and shook his head. Staggered.

"Reggie! What's wrong?" she said, reaching for him.

His words game out a garbled foreign language she couldn't understand. *Oh, no. Oh, no, oh, no, oh, no!*

She guided him to the couch. "Reggie, can you hear me? Can you understand what I'm saying?"

She wasn't sure whether he could or not. He looked at her, confusion plain on his face.

She raced to the hall table where she'd dropped her purse and fished out her phone and dialed 911. "I think my man is having a stroke!" She quickly gave the dispatcher the information, then raced down the stairs to the lobby to let the medics into the building, not wanting to wait for the elevator. There she paced and prayed and paced some more.

It took forever for the EMTs to come. What was taking so long? Were they in the middle of a hot poker game?

At last they arrived with a gurney and all manner of equipment. "Please save him," Molly pleaded as she followed them across the lobby. As if they weren't going to do their best to do exactly that.

All the way to the hospital she prayed and cried, tried to imagine her world without Reggie in it. For one despairing moment, her daughter's words descended on her. *He's too old.*

No, he wasn't. He was too young for this, too fit. "You are not going to leave me, Reggie Washington," she vowed.

From the Saint Michael's waiting room, she called Sunny and told her what had happened.

"I'll be right there," Sunny said, and ended the call before Molly could tell her she didn't need to come. She didn't need to, but Molly was glad that she was.

Her next call was to Ava and she made it with a certain amount of dread, sure that Ava would say, "I knew this would happen."

Instead her daughter said, "I'll be there as soon as I can drop off Paisley somewhere."

Neither her friend nor her daughter could change the outcome of this awful situation, but their comforting presence would be the medicine Molly needed to keep her going. She debated calling Arianna and decided against it. Arianna had enough on her plate. She didn't need a helping of Molly's misery added to it.

Ten minutes later, though, Arianna called her. "How are you doing?"

"I'm...a wreck," Molly confessed. "Who told you?"

"Ava. She's bringing Paisley over to spend the night. I figured that would be a better help to you than adding to the crowd at the hospital."

"I'm sorry Ava called you. You're already dealing with so much."

"Not a problem," Arianna assured her. "Sophie adores Paisley, and this will be a treat for her. Just keep me posted, okay?"

"I will," Molly promised, although she had no idea when she'd have any news to share.

Ava was the first to find her. "You must have broken the sound barrier getting here," Molly said, hugging her.

"Just about," Ava admitted. "How are you doing, Mom?"

"Lousy," Molly admitted. "I still don't know anything. I don't even know if..." She couldn't finish the sentence.

Ava grabbed her and hugged her fiercely, and that was when she broke down and sobbed. Her daughter led her to a seat, pulled out tissues and simply sat there, an arm around Molly's shoulders. Funny how many times it had been Molly hugging her distraught daughter. Failed sports team tryouts, subtle discriminations that had hurt, breakups, career setbacks—Molly had been there for all of them, walking her daughter through life's challenges the best she could. Now their roles were reversed. Only they weren't mother and daughter, they were two women facing a typhoon-sized life storm together.

"There isn't even anyone I can call," Molly opined. "The only family he has is that cousin of his and I have no idea how to contact him."

"He has us," said Ava.

Us. What a great word that was!

Molly called in sick the next day. The rest of the crew could worry about the supply of flower stamps and whose package had gotten lost. For the moment nothing mattered but Reggie. It was the same with her daughter and her friends, who were all with her in his room when the doctor arrived to check on him.

"Well, now, young man, it looks like you've got quite a fan club," he said to Reggie, who didn't have anything to say in return. "The good news is that your stroke was a mild one and you received medical help right away. The not so good news is that it's going to take you a while to recover."

"How long?" Molly asked.

"A lot of that will depend on Reggie here and how hard he works."

"He's a hard worker," Molly said, and squeezed Reggie's hand.

"That's good. A positive attitude and determination are key."

The stroke had occurred on the right side of Reggie's brain and would affect movement on the left side of his body.

"It's going to be a long road," Arianna warned Molly. "Once they discharge him, he'll have to go to rehab and start physiotherapy and occupational therapy right away."

"I'll be with him every step of it," Molly said. "Just so we get to the end of it," said Molly.

"You will, and even if he doesn't make a full recovery, he'll still be able to function."

"You are going to recover, Reggie Washington," Molly said to him when it was finally the two of them alone. "Completely, do you hear? You aren't getting away from me that easily." She heard a weak chuckle as she bent to kiss his forehead. The Reggie she knew and loved was inside that injured body and he would find a way to break free.

But when she visited him a couple nights later, she found it hard to keep a positive attitude.

"My arm don't feel like it even belongs to me," he complained. "I'm half a man."

"Only for the moment," Molly said.

He shook his head. "Walk away, Molly. Keep the ring and walk away."

"Walk away? What kind of lightweight do you think I am?" she protested in disgust.

"I'm no good to you. I'm not gonna get better. You don't need to be stuck with me."

"I am not stuck and I choose to be with you."

He looked down at his affected arm and then began to cry, sobs that shook his big body.

She stooped and hugged him fiercely. "Reggie, we'll get through this. Don't give up."

"I'm not a man. I'm just a shell."

"You're more of a man, even in that hospital bed, than most men will ever be. Now, don't you go giving up. This is not the end of our story."

It only felt like it.

"We are a sad bunch," Sunny said as Arianna, Molly and Ava all sat around her kitchen table on the first Saturday in November.

No one said anything to that.

"We need to do something in November to celebrate."

"No, we don't," snapped Arianna. "I'm done celebrating."

"Me, too," Molly said. "Reggie's turning into the stinker of the rehab center and yelling at everyone from the nurse's aide to his physical therapist. He told me to go away yesterday."

"That's not our Reggie. What did you do?" Sunny asked.

"I went away. Then I went home and cried."

"This is all normal," Arianna told her. "Coping with the aftermath of a stroke is an emotional roller coaster."

"I hate roller coasters," Molly grumbled.

"Listen to us. We're all miserable and complaining and it's almost Thanksgiving," Sunny said.

"You don't have anything to be miserable about," Arianna said irritably. "It's easy to celebrate when your life is perfect."

Whoa, how about a nice verbal slap for the holidays? thought Sunny. Okay, so she did sound like Little Miss Clueless. But why pick on her? Was it her fault that her life happened to be good at the moment?

"Sunny's right," Ava said.

"Not you, too," Arianna said in disgust.

Uh-oh. That look on Ava's face meant trouble.

Sure enough. "You're suffering, but that doesn't mean everyone else's life is perfect. Do you think you're the first woman to have something go wrong in her life? Do you think you're the first woman to have a shitty ex?" Ava demanded of Arianna. "What do you know about absentee fathers and trying so hard to find someone worth bringing home to your kid just to find out you picked wrong again? What do you know about having to explain to your daughter why she has no daddy in her life like her friends all have?"

"What do you know about your mother dying?" Arianna came back in a heated retort.

Ugly silence reigned.

Finally Ava broke it. "I don't know anything about that, and I hope I don't have to for a long time. But my mom just almost lost the second love of her life and she's fighting hard to keep his spirits up. Sunny had the stepdaughter from hell and it took falling and almost breaking her head to get the kid's attention. We all go through stuff, but we're supposed to be helping each other get through it. And, darn it all, we all still have something to be thankful for."

Arianna scowled and bit off the nail on her index finger.

"You've got a great guy in your life," Ava continued. "Reggie didn't die. Sunny's been the kind of friend to you that people make up and put in books. She's been a good friend to all of us," Ava added. "Our kids are doing well and are healthy. We still have things to be grateful for and we need to remember that. And we need Christmas in November!"

"Well, I don't," Arianna growled, and pushed away from the table. "I'm going home...to my wonderful life."

A moment later the door was slamming behind her. Sunny took a sip of her latte and Molly studied her mug.

"That went well," Ava said.

"Uh, yeah," said Molly.

"So what are we going to do for Christmas in November?" Ava asked.

Molly gave the table a thump. "We are going to count our blessings. Let's get planning."

29

It wasn't right. First divorce, now losing her mom. And all her friends could do was sit around and spout platitudes about being thankful. They were welcome to a nice giant-sized helping of her life.

She returned home to find her mother and Sophie cuddled on the couch, Mia supervising Sophie as she worked on crocheting a Granny square.

"Look at my square, Mommy," she said, holding it up.

Arianna fell onto a chair and tried to smile. "It looks great."

"You're back sooner than I thought you'd be," Mom said.

"We were done," Arianna lied. She'd been done.

And now her friends were probably done with her. Why had she been such a snot? She sighed inwardly. Once upon a time she'd been…nicer.

She wasn't the only woman in the world to go through hard times. She wasn't the first woman in the world to be facing losing someone she loved, and she wouldn't be the last. This was life. And what made her so special that she couldn't share space at the pity party with her friends? Honestly, had she really had the nerve to minimize everything they'd gone through? She was out of control.

Sunny was right. They needed to concentrate on things they could be thankful for. She needed to concentrate on things she could be thankful for. She'd survived divorce and moved on and was doing good things with her life. She was seeing the best man since God created Adam. Her mother had given her a great life growing up and she had a darling daughter.

And good friends she didn't deserve.

She jumped up. "I'll be right back."

"Where are you going, Mommy?" Sophie asked.

"I need to do something."

Ten minutes later she was ringing Sunny's doorbell. Sunny opened the door and her eyes flew open.

"I'm sorry," Arianna said. Sorry and pathetic. "You should all hate me. I hate me."

"We don't and you shouldn't. Come on in."

She followed Sunny back to the table where Molly and Ava were seated. "I'm sorry," she wailed. "I'm a horrible person."

"Oh, you are not," Molly said, waving away her self-loathing.

"It's okay," Sunny told her. "We all have our moments, and we know you're under a lot of pressure."

"That's no excuse for the way I acted. One of the biggest blessings in my life is all of you and I feel terrible for insulting you. I'm sorry for what I said." She fell onto the nearest chair, grabbed a napkin and blew her nose.

"We all say things we shouldn't once in a while," Ava said, looking at Molly.

"I want to be thankful, I really do. I don't want to focus on how empty the glass is. I want to focus on what's left in it. Help me get through this, you guys. Please."

Sunny laid a hand on her arm. "You know we will."

The twenty-fifth of November was the day after Thanksgiving. The women decided to make a day of it, starting with lunch.

After a quick game for the kids, the party would be moved to the rehab center so Reggie could be a part of their celebration.

But first there was Thanksgiving. Molly, Ava and Paisley celebrated it at the rehab center with Reggie. He burst into tears at the sight of them.

"My girls," he said happily.

"Look at you, all dressed up with that bow tie," Ava said.

"Your mama gave it to me. She's gonna make sure I look like a successful man of the world."

"I made you a card," Paisley said, handing over her creation, which boasted a turkey traced from her hand, colored in brown and tan.

"Very artistic," he approved.

"How are you doing?" Ava asked as they made their way to the dining room.

"Better every day," he told her, leaning on his walker. Ava looked skeptical but he continued, "I'm going to get out of here in time for Christmas."

If he did, it would be the best Christmas present Molly ever got.

"Mom, I don't know if he's ever going to make a full recovery," Ava said in a low voice later as they drove home, Paisley in the back seat, singing to a Christmas song playing in her headphones.

"I'm sure he will," Molly insisted. "He's working so hard. But even if he doesn't, it doesn't matter."

"It should. This won't be easy."

"Love doesn't stop at hard," Molly said, "and I'll take as much and whatever kind of time I get with him. He's worth it."

Ava nodded. "I have to admit, he is."

"I only hope you find a Reggie of your own someday."

"I'm not holding my breath."

"Don't give up. You never know," Molly said. "Love has a way of surprising you."

"And tipping your life upside down," Ava pointed out.

"I think maybe I needed to get tipped."

She certainly had, and not just in her love life. In getting proactive and making the most of every day, in keeping the holiday joy going, she'd found a new zest for life. A year of Christmas was turning out to be the best year she'd had in a very long time—even with all the challenges they were facing. She had no idea what her upcoming Christmas would hold, but whatever was waiting, a new and improved Molly was ready for it.

Sunny was celebrating Thanksgiving with her in-laws. Not her first choice, but she was determined to be a good sport. The kids were with the Weed for the day, but Sunny and Travis would have them the following day for their Christmas-in-November party, which worked fine for Sunny.

Not so much for Jeanette. "They should be here, with us," she said as everyone sat down at the table. Divorce is a terrible thing. "When Harry and I got married, it was for life."

A life sentence, thought Sunny.

"All this swapping out spouses," put in Grandma Hollowell shaking her head.

Oh, boy, was this how the day was going to go?

"In some cases it's called trading up, Gram," said Travis, and laid a hand on Sunny's thigh.

"You certainly did better than Tansy," said his mother.

Was that a compliment? Sunny wasn't sure.

Jeanette tsk-tsked. "That new man she's with is horrible."

"So, Uncle Joe, how's the car business going?" Travis asked his uncle, steering the conversation into more neutral waters.

Jeanette frowned at having her commentary on the family marriages interrupted, but took the hint and started the peas going around the table.

Grandma Hollowell took the casserole dish of Kahlúa yams

Sunny had brought and spooned out a large helping. "These look wonderful, Jeanette."

"I didn't make them. Sunny did," Jeanette said.

Grandma took a bite. "My, they are delicious. And so unique tasting. I don't think I've ever eaten anything like this. What's your secret, dear?"

"Kahlúa," Sunny said.

Grandma looked confused. "Kahlúa?"

"You've heard of Kahlúa, Grandma. It's a liquor," Travis explained.

Grandma dropped her fork like it was on fire. "Liquor! Someone should have told me." She scowled at Sunny.

Sunny could feel her face catching fire. Was it too late to bolt and go to her parents' house?

"Lips that touch liquor will never touch hers," Harry murmured, and Grandma shot him a look that said, "You are in trouble, young man."

"There's no alcohol in there, Grandma," Travis explained.

"You just said there was," his grandmother huffed. "What a thing to bring to Thanksgiving when there are children present."

The only children present were in college.

Oh, good grief, enough of this…bullying. "The alcohol bakes out," Sunny told her. "I got this recipe from my mother and I love it, but please don't feel you need to eat it just to be polite."

Grandma Hollowell blinked in surprise at Sunny's stern tone of voice, then harrumphed. "Pass the potatoes, please, Jeanette."

"And pass me your yams," Grandpa Hollowell said to his wife. "I'll eat 'em."

"You'll do no such thing," Grandma snapped.

"So, the Seahawks are doing pretty good this year," said Uncle Joe, taking his turn calming troubled waters.

Thank God the family had a couple of diplomats in it. Conversation lightened up and the stuffing and potatoes disappeared from their serving bowls. So did the yams, and Sunny bit back a smile when she saw Grandma Hollowell sneak another bite of hers. Travis squeezed her hand under the table and winked at her.

"You handled Grandma just right," he said when they drove home.

"You could have warned me what she's like," she said. Thank God the old bat hadn't been at their wedding.

"Didn't think to. Anyway, it's good for people like my grandma to get hauled out of their comfort zone once in a while."

"I guess. I don't like being the one to do the hauling, though."

"Yeah, but you did it so well."

"I'm tired of trying to make everybody like me." She'd jumped more relationship hurdles in the past few months than an Olympic runner.

"You don't have to try, babe. You're great just the way you are."

She smiled. "Thank you. And now you don't have to get me anything for Christmas because what you just said was the best gift ever."

It had been a year of gifts in spite of the relationship challenges. Thinking about the good changes she'd seen in her relationship with her step-kids, thinking about the new member of the family that would be arriving in the new year, of the good friends she'd made, she couldn't help but be thankful.

Thankful…hmm. Now there was an idea for a perfect activity for the next day's Christmas-in-November celebration.

It had been a quiet Thanksgiving for Mia, Arianna and Sophie. Mia couldn't swallow more than butternut bisque and Arianna hadn't felt like cooking. She'd done a turkey breast and made Stove Top Stuffing and gravy, along with a small fruit salad for Sophie and herself and had called it good with that. Sophie had been up for trying the bisque, which her mom had made earlier and posted on the website, but one spoonful had been enough to convince her that she preferred stuffing.

"And fruit salad," she said, helping herself to more.

After that it was time to build a fire in the fireplace—making sure to pull out the damper—and watch the Grinch steal Christmas, with mother, daughter and granddaughter all curled up on the couch.

For a moment Ariana found herself wishing Alden was with them. He'd become such an integral part of their lives the picture seemed incomplete with him missing. But he had a family of his own. He couldn't be with them all the time.

He'd offered to take them to his parents' for the day, but Mia was so exhausted Arianna knew that wouldn't have worked. She didn't want to do anything to make her mother weaker. And the idea of putting on a happy face and socializing felt overwhelming.

She looked over to where Mia sat, her eyes drifting shut, Sophie cuddled against her. Mia was getting worse. God only knew how many more moments like this one they had left. Arianna found herself clenching her fists as if she could somehow hang on to it.

The doorbell jarred her out of her reverie.

"I'll get it," Sophie said, jumping up, and startling Mia awake.

"Look out the window and make sure it's someone we know," Arianna said, even as she set aside her throw.

"Alden!" Sophie cried, and threw the door open wide.

"Gobble, gobble," he said, ruffling her hair. Buster, who was with him, raced into the room and began jumping on Sophie's leg, begging for attention.

"You were at your parents'," Arianna said, confused.

"We finished dinner and Mom said to get out of her hair." He held up a half gallon of ice cream. "Who wants pumpkin ice cream?"

"Me!" cried Sophie, her attention diverted from the dog.

"I didn't think you'd have time," Arianna said as he slipped off his coat.

"I'll always have time for you," he said. The look in his eyes warmed her better than any cozy fireplace fire ever could.

They settled in with their ice cream and went back to watching the Grinch do his best to ruin Christmas. It felt so greeting-card perfect. Arianna tightened her hold again, this time on Alden's hand.

Between work and spending as much time with Reggie as possible, Molly was pooped, but she still gathered up her leftover pumpkin rolls from the day before and went with her daughter and granddaughter to Arianna's house to celebrate Christmas in November.

The celebrating started with lunch, which featured a turkey casserole Arianna had concocted and her butternut bisque, along with everyone else's leftovers and was followed by baking pumpkin cookies to distribute at the rehab center while the kids all designed Merry-Christmas-in-November cards for Reggie. Next came white elephant gift stealing, with the prizes piled under Arianna's tree, which Sophie had decorated with cutout turkeys. Dylan was thrilled with his Whoopee cushion, which nobody wanted, and Molly and Sunny fought hard over the Frango mints.

They'd just finished when Alden arrived, freshly showered after getting in some sleep after working his shift and ready to spend the rest of the day partying. "Did I miss all the fun?" he asked Sunny.

"Not quite. We have one more game," she said.

"Yay!" chorused Sophie and Paisley.

"I want everyone to write something you're thankful for on a slip of paper and then put it in this Santa hat," she instructed, holding up her favorite hat with *I've Been Good* embroidered on it. "I'll read them and we'll see if we can guess who wrote what."

Dylan's was easy enough to guess. His slip merely said *pizza*.

My kids and my wife was Travis. *Grammy* was Sophie. Paisley had written *my grandma and mom*.

Getting to be part of all this took a couple of guesses.

"Alden?" Arianna ventured and he grinned.

"I thought this sounded kind of out there when you all started it, but it's been great. This whole getting together and finding a reason to celebrate every month—that needs to catch on," he said.

"I'm happy we've been able to focus on appreciating each other," Sunny told him, and smiled at Bella, who smiled back.

The list of things everyone was thankful for continued. Sunny pulled out a slip of paper that was not limited to one thing. "My mother," she began. "My daughter, the amazing man in my life."

"Oh, that's Arianna," Rae said with a grin.

"Yep," Arianna said, and blushed.

"There's more," Sunny said, and read, "My friends."

"We're thankful for you, too," Molly told her. "And you, Mia. Watching how you've dealt with your health challenges has been inspiring."

"It's not like I had much choice in the matter," Mia replied.

"You did. There's always a choice," Molly said. "You can complain and be bitter or you can get on with it. We've all seen how you've used what you're going through to help other women. That's what I call turning a negative into a positive."

Sunny grabbed her nearby glass of sparkling cider. "Here's to turning negatives to positives. And here's to Mia."

Everyone grabbed their glass and toasted their friend.

And later, as they gathered around Reggie in the dining room of the rehab center, they made another toast led by Molly. "To Reggie, getting better every day."

Arianna wished she could say the same thing about her mother. "I have this awful feeling she's not going to make it to

Christmas," she said to Sunny as the gang passed out pumpkin cookies to the residents.

"I'm so sorry," Sunny said. "What can we do to help?"

"What can anyone do? I am working on being thankful that she's survived this long, but it's hard. You know, Christmas is her favorite time of year and I'm worried she's going to miss it."

"What if Christmas came early?" Sunny suggested. "What if we all came over and decorated the house tomorrow?"

Gratitude swelled Arianna's heart. "Would you?"

"Of course. I'll talk to Molly and Ava. Rae and Mom will want to come, too. We're on it. Don't you worry."

"That will be great. We're missing a few decorations. I never could de-stink the Christmas stockings we'd hung by the fireplace last year."

"There will be stockings," Sunny assured her.

The next afternoon a crowd of friends invaded Mia's house. "What's this?" Mia asked from her spot on the couch as they came in bearing bulging bags and boxes.

"Christmas decorating," Sunny told her, giving her a hug.

Arianna's heart squeezed as she saw her mother's eyes light up. They would have Christmas, after all.

"We are going to turn this place into a Hallmark movie set," Molly said, pulling out a ribbon garland.

"We heard you needed some new stockings," said Sunny's mom, and pulled out three red felt stockings, bearing appliques of mittens and trees. Arianna's and Sophie's names were embroidered on two. The third read *Grammy*.

"Those are charming!" Mia exclaimed.

Even Bella had come along. "I found a recipe for stovetop potpourri," she said, holding up a grocery bag of ingredients for Mia to see.

"That's really sweet of you. Thank you," Mia said to her, and Bella's face flushed with pleasure.

"Come on out to the kitchen and I'll get you set up," Arianna said to her.

"I'm sorry about your mom. She's so nice," Bella said as Arianna pulled a pot from the stove drawer.

Arianna sighed. "It's hard. You assume people are going to be in your life forever and then, suddenly, they're gone. It sure is important to appreciate them while they're here."

Bella nodded. "I know."

Did she? Did anyone really get it? It was so easy to take loved ones for granted.

"We should make a video," Arianna said to Sunny.

"Sure, if you want. How about when we're done?"

Arianna shook her head. "No, let's do it now, when we're in the middle of it. I want people to see my friends in action, helping us."

"Okay," Sunny said, and fetched her phone. "We're going to shoot a quick video. Is everyone okay with being on camera?" she asked the others.

"We're going to be famous? Great," joked Molly.

Everyone else was fine with the idea, so Arianna positioned herself front and center in the living room, while they moved around her, setting out candles and greenery, along with Mia's beloved nativity set. The turkeys were gone from the tree and the vintage gold beads were getting strung on it. Christmas music played softly in the background, accompanying the chit-chat and laughter.

"Merry Christmas, everyone," Arianna said. "As you can see, we are busy decorating for the holidays. Normally, at my house, we wait until December first to do this, but Mom's not feeling well…" She could feel her throat closing up. She cleared it and forced herself to continue. "Her tumor is back. Not the news we'd been hoping for, obviously. But we're not going to let that stop us from celebrating the joys of the season, just like we've been doing all year long. If you're facing similar health challenges with a member of your family, I urge you not to put off anything. Celebrate that birthday early. Have your Christmas now. Make the most of every moment because, as we're learning, none of us knows how many we'll have." She motioned to the beautiful scene emerging around her. "How lovely is this? And how blessed am I to have such good friends who've all come over to help my family get a jump start on the holidays. I hope yours are merry and bright, but if you're struggling through dark times, fight the darkness and light those candles right now."

As if on cue, Ava was helping Sophie light a candle in the middle of an arrangement on the coffee table.

"Perfect," said Sunny, ending the video.

"When we're all done I'll get a picture of all of you in front of the tree," Arianna said.

Which she did. She also had Sunny take one of her and Mia and Sophie together on the couch. And then she got Ava to take one of her and Sunny, who was going to get special acknowledgment on the website. She'd caption it *everyone needs a sister of the heart*. It was so true.

"Wow, Christmas central," said Alden when he came over later, carrying a canvas grocery bag filled with who knew what, Buster at his side.

"You like it?" Arianna asked.

"Yeah. It's seriously impressive. Did you do all this?" he asked Sophie, who was hanging on his arm.

"I helped," she said.

"Everyone came over yesterday," Arianna elaborated.

"They should go into business."

A side hustle for Sunny and Molly? Maybe.

"And the tree looks like a Christmas tree again," he observed.

"Yes, it does. We're going to do Christmas early this year," Arianna said, and her smile faltered.

He got her meaning and he, too, sobered. He nodded. "Good idea."

"Want to have Christmas with us next weekend?" she asked.
"Sure."

Funny, last December she'd been snapping at Alden. This December he was joining her family to celebrate Christmas. This December he was like...family.

She reined in her thoughts before they could drag her further down the yellow brick road. They were in a relationship, but he'd given no indication he wanted to make it permanent, and she wasn't about to push. *Enjoy what you've got right now*, she told herself. Just like she was doing with her mother. Every moment was worth savoring.

"Are we going to have presents?" asked Sophie.

"Of course," Arianna said just as her phone rang.

It was Wyatt. Oh, joy. He was supposed to be picking up Sophie for an overnight. If he was calling, it was probably to cancel. Actually that would be fine with her, and she suspected Sophie wouldn't mind staying put.

She moved into the kitchen to take the call. *Don't lose it. Don't yell.* Things had been somewhat better since the incident on the Fourth of July, but this man tried her patience like no one else.

"What is it, Wyatt?" she said, keeping her voice calm.

"I'm having car trouble. You need to bring Sophie over to my parents'."

"Why don't you use their car?" Honestly, it was so... Wyatt of him not to think out the details.

"Because I'm not there."

"Then why is Sophie going there?"

"Because that's easiest. I've got someone picking me up and I'll pick her up at my parents'."

Someone picking him up. Arianna knew what that meant. The someone was a girlfriend.

"Am I going to be picking her up tomorrow, too?"

"No. I'm gonna borrow my mom's car. Look, just do this, okay? It's not that much out of your way."

Actually it was. It was forty minutes from her place to theirs, and Alden had only just arrived. She sighed. "Okay. Fine."

"Wow, just like that? No ragging on me?"

"Goodbye, Wyatt," she said. Calmly. Yay for her.

"Okay, sweetie, it's time to go see Daddy," she said to Sophie. "Get your things. I'm going to take you to Grandma and Grandpa's."

"Okay," Sophie said happily and ran upstairs to fetch her backpack.

"You're taking her?" Mia asked.

Arianna made a face. "Wyatt's having car problems." Then she smiled. "But I think I handled that rather well. No yelling. Frustration, but no yelling."

"I'm proud of you," Mia said.

Arianna shrugged. "Just keeping the Christmas spirit going."

"Mrs. W and I will do that while you're gone," Alden said.

He wasn't going anywhere. Was it a sign or a wish?

"So, Mia, I bought a little something for us to kick off the season with," Alden said after Sophie and Arianna had left. "You up for a holiday drink?"

"I am," she said.

"Okay, be prepared to be amazed. I got this recipe from my sister and she guarantees it will make you merry if not bright."

Mia chuckled and he went to the kitchen and got to work pulling the drink makings out of his bag. He filled two glasses with the vodka, cranberry juice and sparkling soda he'd had chilling in his refrigerator. He added the requisite dash of lime and garnished it with mint, then took a moment to admire his handiwork. Just like in a magazine. He took a picture with his phone in case Arianna would want to post it somewhere.

"Fa-la-la," he said as he walked back into the living room. He handed a glass to Mia.

"That is so pretty," she said.

"It should go down easy," he said, and hoped he was right.

She took a sip and smiled. "Ah, a lovely drink. One of life's many pleasures."

"You gotta live it up," he said.

"While I still can," she added. Then, seeing his uncomfortable expression, said, "I know my time here is ending. But I'm glad God let me stay around long enough to see my daughter find her feet again. You've been a big part of that."

Not really. "She's got her friends."

"Of which you are one," Mia pointed out. "Don't worry. I'm not saying that to pressure you in any way. I just want you to know how grateful I am that you've been part of our lives." She saluted him with her glass and took another sip of her drink.

So did he. He usually preferred beer to fancy drinks but this one was going down pretty darned easy.

They talked some more, her reminiscing about past Christmases and encouraging him to do the same. And soon their glasses were empty.

"I think we need a refill," he said, and went back to the kitchen for seconds.

Music had been playing the whole time they'd been visiting and partway through their second drink helping "The Twelve Days of Christmas" began to play.

"I always liked that song," Mia said.

"Lots of versions of it," he said. Then, inspired, suggested. "Want to make up one of our own?"

She giggled. "Why not? You start."

He turned off the music, saying, "We don't want competition."

"No, of course not," she agreed.

He downed a good-sized swallow of his drink, thought a moment, then announced, "Okay, I got it," and sang, "On the first day of Christmas my true love gave to me some socks that were super stinky."

She laughed. "Oh, that is an excellent beginning."

"Your turn. See if you can top that," he said.

She took a thoughtful sip of her drink, then sang, "On the second day of Christmas my true love gave to me two candy canes."

"And some socks that were super stinky," they sang together.

"On the third day of Christmas my true love gave to me, three onion rings," he sang, and together they sang the next two lines.

The song went on—four shots of whiskey, which called for another drink, then, "Five pounds of fudge," they chorused as the door opened and Arianna walked in.

"What on earth are you two doing?" she asked.

"Drinking song," he said. "I made my new specialty. Want one?"

"After seeing my ex? Yes," she said.

Alden made her a drink and she settled on the couch next to her mother to hear what they'd come up with so far, giggling as they sang.

"Okay, your turn," he said to her.

"On the sixth day of Christmas my true love gave to me six pairs of sexy panties," she warbled. Then her face turned red.

"I like it," he said and saluted her with his glass. He hoped he'd inspired that line of thought.

She quickly downed half her drink. "No more R-rated lyrics."

"Well, that's no fun," he cracked. "Your turn, Mrs. W."

Mia was smiling at her daughter. "On the seventh day of Christmas my daughter gave to me…"

"What happened to true love?" Arianna interrupted.

"It's the same thing," Mia said, and continued, "Seven days of lovely memories. Although it's been more like thirty-five years. Thirty-six next weekend."

Alden looked at Arianna. "So, you got a birthday coming up?"

She sighed. "I'm getting old."

"No, you're hitting your prime," Mia corrected.

"Looks like we'll have more than just Christmas to celebrate next weekend," Alden said.

"Christmas is enough," Arianna told him.

"Yeah? We'll see."

The singing continued, and the true love items ranged from eight baby monkeys to twelve cans of beer. By the end of the song, both Mia and Arianna were tipsy. And laughing.

"Oh, my gosh, I just realized something," Arianna said. "I'm not sitting around hating on Wyatt. And there's a fire burning in the fireplace and no smoke," she added with a giggle and a hiccup.

"You've come a long way, daughter," Mia said, smiling at her.

"I'll drink to that," Alden said, raising his near-empty glass. "To getting past the bad stuff."

"To getting past the bad stuff," Arianna agreed.

There was more bad to come but at least her Wyatt misery was behind her. The rest she'd face when the time came.

Meanwhile, "On the first day of Christmas," she sang, beginning their song all over again. Ho, ho, ho...hic!

CHRISTMAS
IN DECEMBER

30

Molly had added another bobblehead to her collection and had mini candy canes on hand to give to all good little postal customers. Even the naughty ones.

"It's the season to be jolly," she told Mrs. Mason, who rubbed her hip and frowned.

Molly frowned back. "Have you stopped getting your massages?"

Mrs. Mason shrugged. "They get a little expensive."

Molly grabbed a piece of paper and scribbled down her address. "You come over to my house tonight. I'll have someone there who can help you."

Mrs. Mason looked at her in surprise. "Really?"

"Really."

"Oh, Molly, bless you," said the woman.

"I have been blessed," Molly said, thinking of Reggie.

On her lunch break she called her friend Rachel, the massage genius. "Can you do a house call tonight?"

"For you, I can do some juggling," said Rachel. "How does seven work?"

"Great."

"Your hip bothering you?"

"Not mine, one of my customers."

"You're paying for your customer to have a massage?"

Postal regulations were strict regarding what kind of gifts postal workers could receive from customers, but as far as Molly knew, there was nothing that said she couldn't do a kindness for a friend. Still... "You don't need to go blabbing this all over town."

"And you don't need to be paying me. I'll do it for free. After all, it is the season of giving."

"Yes, it is," Molly said, and thanked her.

She returned to her window, full of Christmas spirit.

Until she saw the long line that had grown. Helen was doing her best to keep up, but...'twas the season.

Molly took down the closed sign and smiled at the next customer in line, a woman with a bag full of packages to go out.

She was aware of a man a few people down the line, checking his cell phone, looking from her window to Helen's and frowning. Oh, boy, the Grinch had hit town. Molly suspected no candy cane would sweeten his mood.

She was right. When he stepped up to her window, he greeted her with, "You should put more people on this time of year."

She could almost hear Helen over at her window, thanking Santa for sparing her from having to deal with this holiday turkey.

"It is a busy time of year," Molly said. "How may I help you?"

"Stamps," he said shortly.

"Angels? Madonna and child?"

"Anything."

She nodded and pulled out a sheet of angels. This guy could probably use some angels to watch over him.

He paid for his stamps, snatched them and started off.

"Sir, wait," Molly called.

He turned, the frown still on his face.

"I have something for you."

"What is it?" he demanded, marching back to the window.

She pulled out a handful of wrapped miniature candy canes and held them out. "To thank you for your business."

He stared at them, nonplussed.

"I bet you have some kids in your family who will enjoy these," she said.

He looked sheepish as he took them, his cheeks a little rosy, and muttered a thank-you.

"Merry Christmas," she called as he hurried away.

Oh, no, and here came Mrs. Bigman, with a small shopping bag, which Molly was sure would contain a cookie redo.

"Giving away treats, that's very nice of you," she greeted Molly.

"Trying to keep the holiday spirit alive," Molly replied.

Mrs. Bigman surprised her by saying, "You've done a good job of that all year, and I know people don't always make it easy for you."

One of the culprits was standing in front of her, but that had changed after the great cookie rescue. Mrs. Bigman had mellowed.

She reached into her bag and pulled out a round tin of butter cookies with a bow on it. "These are for you. I didn't bake them," she added with a smile in case Molly thought she was trying to pull a fast one.

The Christmas spirit flew past Molly and blew her a kiss. *Thanks for doing your part to spread the joy.*

"Aww, that is so sweet of you," Molly said. "Thank you. It means a lot."

"You deserve it, dear. And now, I need a stamp." Mrs. Bigman dug in her bag and produced a greeting card–sized envelope. "No Christmas cookies this year. My son's getting a gift card."

"I'm sure he'll appreciate it," Molly said.

Their transaction was quickly done, and Mrs. Bigman left with a merry wave and a candy cane in her coat pocket.

And Molly was left with a smile. This job wasn't so bad. You simply had to have the right attitude.

Molly and Sunny showed up at Arianna's house early Friday evening to celebrate her birthday, bearing gifts and pink champagne cake from McGavin's bakery in Bremerton.

"This is going to be your best year yet," Molly predicted, handing over an envelope.

Arianna opened it to find a gift card for Massage Envy in nearby Silverdale. "A massage. That sounds like such a luxury," she said.

"We all deserve a little luxury once in a while," Molly said.

"I have something for you, too," Mia told Arianna, and presented her with a box wrapped in white paper and tied with a blue ribbon.

She opened it to find a leather-bound photo album. "So that was the mysterious Amazon delivery you wouldn't let me see the other day," Arianna said, smiling at her.

"I think you have some photos on your phone that you might enjoy putting in it, and I'm sure you'll have more to add in the coming year. To capture all those new adventures," Mia said.

And replace the photos she'd burned a year ago. Arianna hugged her mother and kissed her cheek. "Thank you."

As if on cue, the doorbell rang.

Molly opened it and there stood Alden. "Here's the next part of your birthday celebration," she announced.

"You ready to go out to dinner?" he asked Arianna.

"We're all going to stay here and party while you're gone," Molly said.

And make sure Mia was okay. She had the best friends.

She and Alden wound up at Anthony's, enjoying a window table that gave them a view of the ferry traffic. "This is really sweet of you," she said.

"That's me. Sweet," he said, brushing off her compliment.

"Actually, I wanted to make this night special. You've had a bumpy year and I figured it was time you made up for it." He started making up by ordering champagne. "Appetizers?" he suggested.

"And champagne?"

"Why not? It's your birthday. And how do the prawns look?"

"Expensive," she said.

"But good?"

"Well…"

"Or filet mignon?"

That was even pricier. "Prawns are great," she said.

And they were. So was the chocolate mousse he ordered for their dessert.

"This has really been special. I don't know how to thank you," she said.

"You just did. Happy birthday." He looked out the window at the ferry gliding toward the dock. "We gotta go. We have a ferry to catch."

"A ferry?" she repeated.

"Nothing like a birthday ferry ride," he said, and signaled for the check.

Twenty minutes later they were standing outside on the ferry, watching as it slid away from the dock, which was festively lit for the holidays.

"I love riding the ferry at night," she said happily.

"I love riding the ferry at night with a beautiful woman," he said.

"That was sweet. Kind of a movie moment," she said.

"I hope so. I've got another one coming up. Let's get out of the cold," he said, motioning toward the covered outside area. "I have something for you, but I don't want it to drop overboard." He led her to a seat, then put an arm around her, snuggling her close. "It's kind of cold here, but I want privacy."

Ooh, that promised something good.

Instead of kissing her, he kept talking. "I know we've both struck out with relationships and maybe my timing's all wrong, maybe it hasn't been long enough, but I realized a while back that I didn't want to lose you." He fumbled in his pocket, pulled out a ring box and she let out a little gasp. "I guess you know what's coming next. Arianna, I can't imagine life without you. I am crazy in love with you and every day I love you more. I want to be a permanent part of your family." He opened it and a solitaire diamond winked at her. "I guessed at the size. I hope you like it. Most of all, I hope you'll say yes. I want to spend the rest of my life with you. I want us to celebrate Christmas together all year long for the rest of our lives."

All those emotions she never thought she'd feel again—joy, excitement, hope—were dancing in her chest, moving up into her throat, making it hard to speak. She bit her lip.

"Crap, I'm blowing this."

"No, you're not. Oh, my gosh, I can't believe something so good is happening to me. Someone so good."

"So is that a yes?"

"Yes!" To prove she meant it, she grabbed his face and kissed him for all she was worth.

"Wow," he said after a very long kiss. "I thought I knew what love was, but I didn't have a clue till I met you. Arianna White, you are the best thing that ever moved in next door to me."

"I bet you weren't so sure at first," she teased.

"Well, once I figured out you weren't lethal," he teased back. "Although you are a killer kisser."

A killer kisser. Wyatt had never said anything like that to her.

"I like that," she said.

"Give me another. Let me die and go to heaven."

Of course, she obliged. Many times. The round-trip ferry ride from Bremerton to Seattle and back took two hours. It felt like two minutes.

"Are you okay to wait and put your ring on after I give your mom a present tomorrow?" he asked. "I have something for her, too. In fact, I was going to give you both your presents at the same time but decided that was lame."

"There's been nothing lame about you," she said, and they strolled off the ferry and back to his truck, hand in hand.

"Did you have a nice time?" Mia asked when she came in.

"I did. It was perfect," Arianna said.

"Good," said Molly with a nod.

"I made more Granny squares," Sophie announced, holding up three for Arianna to see.

"Very nice," she said. Every one of those squares would be precious to Sophie because of who had helped her make them.

The blanket Mia had been working on was almost done and equally special. It would be a family heirloom.

Her mother was making such thoughtful gifts. Arianna wished she'd been more creative with hers. Perfume, even though it was Calvin Klein's Eternity, Mia's favorite fragrance, didn't seem like much. The very name seemed a mockery. How much of that would Mia even use? But then what could Arianna get her that she'd be around to use?

Sadness suddenly floated a black cloud over her earlier happy mood and she gnawed off the nail on her pinky finger.

"Where did you go to eat?" Sunny asked.

"Anthony's. He splurged. The whole nine yards—appetizers, dessert, champagne."

"I'm glad you had a good time," said Mia. "Promise me you'll continue to celebrate."

After she was gone. Mia didn't say the words in front of Sophie but they both knew what she meant.

"I'll do my best, Mom," Arianna said. At least, with having Alden by her side, she'd have a better chance of celebrating in a way that honored her mother.

He was over the next night, Buster with him, and bringing presents for Mia and Sophie, as well as red velvet cupcakes and eggnog. Sophie was delighted with the heart-shaped necklace he gave her.

"To my girl," she read on the card. She smiled at Alden. "I like being your girl, Alden."

"Good," he said. "And now, here's something special for your Grammy." He leaned over and handed Mia a small, wrapped box.

"Oh, Alden, you shouldn't have," she protested.

"Hey, you can't invite yourself over for a Christmas celebration and not bring presents, right?"

There was no card with the box. In light of Sophie's, it seemed odd that he hadn't bothered.

Mia opened her present and took out a gold chain necklace bearing the infinity symbol. "Oh, my, it's lovely," she said reverently.

He reached in his shirt pocket and pulled out a small gift card. "Oh, I forgot to give you this," he said, and handed it over.

Mia took it and read it, and her eyes got big. So did her smile.

"What does it say, Grammy?" asked Sophie.

"It says, to my future mother-in-law," Mia replied, her eyes filling with tears. "Really?"

"I hope that's okay," Alden said. "Because I am in love with your daughter. I want to spend the rest of my life making her happy."

"You have no idea how happy this makes me," Mia told him.

"I want to be there for Sophie, too," Alden continued. "Sophie, is it okay with you if I marry your mom and we all live together?"

"Buster, too?" Sophie asked.

"Buster, too," he said.

Sophie nodded enthusiastically. "Oh, yes. Let's do that."

"I guess you can show them your present now," he said to Arianna, and she pulled the ring box out of her sweater pocket and slipped it on her finger.

"Now it's official," she said.

"A perfect Christmas present," Mia murmured as Sophie examined the new bit of sparkle on her mother's hand.

Yes, it was, thought Arianna, looking at the best thing she'd ever moved in next to.

"Baby, baby, that's some bling," Molly said. Arianna was showing her ring off as the friends gathered at her house for a quiet celebration before Christmas.

It was just the women, no children—Bella was back at Sunny's house with Travis, keeping the younger ones entertained—and there was plenty of eggnog with rum and Christmas cookies and chocolates. Mia had been too tired to party and was in her bedroom, resting, and her absence was felt.

"I'm glad he proposed while Mom was still around to see it. I know she's been worried about how I'll cope when she's gone," Arianna said. Alden would, of course, be a great comfort, and he was the love of her life. But no one and nothing replaced a mother. "I already can't cope. I can't even bear to think about it."

"Then don't. Not yet," said Ava. "Your mom's still here. Don't let the shadow of what's coming ruin right now."

"She's right," Molly agreed, "but that's easier said than done."

"We're back on the feeding tube," Arianna said. "It's too hard for her to get down anything but tea and juice. If she makes it through Christmas, I'll be grateful."

"Why is it so many people seem to die at the holidays?" Sunny said with a sigh. "There should be a moratorium on death until after New Year's."

"That's no way to start the year," Ava protested.

"There's no good time to lose the ones you love, trust me. My husband died right before Father's Day," said Molly.

"All right, guys, we need to lighten the mood," Sunny said. "How about sharing the best Christmas present we ever got?"

"That's easy. Alden," Arianna said.

"Spill the beans. How'd he propose? All we know was that he was taking you out for your birthday," Sunny said.

Arianna happily related his ferryboat proposal and then the way he'd brought Mia and Sophie in on everything. As she talked, happiness rushed in and blew away the dark cloud she'd been sitting under. With Mia so sick and Wyatt planning to steal Sophie for the day again, it wasn't going to be an ideal greeting card–style Christmas, but that was okay. For her, Christmas had come early.

31

Christmas Day was special for Molly. Reggie was out of rehab and she was staying at his condo, making the day as perfect as she could. He was still working on his mobility and strengthening his arm, but he was making progress, walking with a cane, and his doctor was pleased.

She and Ava had bought him a tree and decorated it with colored lights, silver ribbons and blue balls. Very manly. They'd bought some glass ornaments shaped like vintage cars as well, wrapped them and put them under the tree for him to open. They'd ordered a complete dinner from the local Safeway—no muss, no fuss—and Ava and Paisley had baked cupcakes and decorated them with sprinkles. Lots of sprinkles, Paisley had insisted, and on most of the cupcakes Molly could hardly see the frosting for those sprinkles.

Reggie insisted that he loved sprinkles. The more, the better.

With the help of the occupational therapist, he'd managed to get ahold of a gift bag, and he looked on with a big grin as the three women opened it and pulled out printed tickets to Disneyland. Paisley jumped up and down and whooped, then rushed to hug Reggie. Ava gaped in amazement and Molly said, "Reggie, what on earth?"

"I want my girls to enjoy the happiest place on earth," he said, "and I hope by the time school's out I'll be ready to go with you all and go on those rides with Paisley."

"Thank you, Grandpa Reggie," Paisley said. "I always wanted to go to Disneyland."

"Me, too," Ava said with a laugh.

"Me, three," put in Molly.

"Now, Molly girl, open that other one."

"You already gave me a lovely ring. There's nothing else I need," she said, but she picked up the white shirt box wrapped in silver paper and tied with a blue ribbon. Had Reggie ordered an article of clothing online for her? That would be interesting, considering his own taste in clothes.

But when she pulled aside the tissue paper, she got the shock of her life. "What's this?" she demanded, frowning at him.

"It's me making sure you'll be okay no matter what."

"What is it?" Paisley asked.

"A will," Molly said, still giving Reggie the stink eye. "You already scared us half to death. I don't think this is funny."

He sobered. "It's not meant to be funny. I want you to know that, no matter what happens to me, you will be okay. You're my beneficiary, and I've left something for Ava and Paisley, too. I don't want any of you to have to worry about money ever again."

"Oh, Reggie," Molly said, her eyes filling with tears.

"It's awfully sweet of you," said Ava.

"You girls have taken care of me. I'm only returning the favor," he said. "Anyway, I have to do something with my money. I can't take it with me."

"And you can't go, not for a long time," Molly informed him.

"Sure not planning on it. I want to spend a whole lot of Christmases with all of you."

"Let's drink to that," Molly said, and went to fetch the eggnog.

★ ★ ★

Sunny's Christmas was looking very different from the one the year before. Her whole family was together, both the one she'd grown up with and the one she'd married into.

"This candy cane pastry is so cute," Jeannette said, and pulled out her phone to take a picture of it.

"Never mind the pictures, Mom. Let's eat," Travis said.

Her father seconded it. "And I'll take some of that wassail you made, Rae."

Once everyone had their food, it was time to open presents. Jeanette was thrilled with the air fryer Sunny and Travis had given her and Sunny's mom was delighted with her Keurig. The kids enjoyed their present treasure hunt and there were whoops and squeals of delight with each gift card they found. Travis had splurged on perfume for Sunny, her mother had made sure she'd have enough Starbucks to last her through Valentine's Day and Jeanette had given her a cookbook, Ina Garten's *Cook Like a Pro*. Had Travis blabbed about her beef Wellington disaster?

No matter. "I'll get a lot of use out of this," she told her mother-in-law.

"Good. Man doesn't live by take-out alone," said Jeanette.

Okay, so Sunny still hadn't earned the perfect-wife award. But at least her mother-in-law was accepting the fact that she was there to stay.

The gifting went on, accompanied by smiles and thank-yous. At last there was nothing left under the tree. Soon it would be time to eat the ham and garlic mashed potatoes (which Sunny knew would be as good as anything Ina Garten could come up with). Everyone was happy. Sunny was happy.

But the tiniest bit disappointed. The kids had come to accept her, even like her a little, and she'd hoped to find some small thing under the tree from them. There'd been nothing.

Oh, well. Better luck next year.

She was about to get up and start working on pulling dinner

together when Bella said. "Sunny, me and Dylan have something for you." She pulled a shiny red gift bag from behind the overstuffed chair she and Jeanette had been sharing and handed it over.

"For me?" From the kids! Sunny dug into the tissue paper and pulled out a mug that dubbed her the world's best stepmom. "Oh, my gosh," she said, teary-eyed. "Thank you."

"Very sweet," Jeanette approved as Sunny gave both kids a hug.

"The good guys always win," Travis whispered when nobody was listening, and kissed Sunny.

The kids left to go spend the rest of the day with their mom, and it was hard to let them go, but Sunny made sure they saw her drinking wassail out of her mug before they left. The rest of the family hung out, ate dinner and stayed to play Heads Up. By the time they all left, she was ready to kick back and watch a Christmas movie with Travis—*Christmas on Candy Cane Lane* on the Great American Family channel.

"Happy endings all 'round," he joked when the ending credits rolled.

"There's nothing wrong with happy endings," she informed him.

Nothing at all, and this was going to go down as her best Christmas yet.

Mia made it to Christmas, but Arianna knew it would be their last one together. Alden had wanted to take her and Mia and Sophie to his parents' house for their Christmas celebration, but Mia had been too tired. So he'd promised to come over later.

Meanwhile Arianna and her mother and daughter opened presents and had a holiday brunch—breakfast casserole for Arianna and Sophie. Prepared tube food for Mia.

Mia had finished the blanket she'd been crocheting for Sophie, who was thrilled and wrapped in it right away. Mia had ordered books online for Arianna, all on various health-related topics.

"I thought you might find some good information for the website in them," she said.

Arianna had come up with one final present for her mother—a picture Sunny had taken at the Christmas-in-July party and Arianna had framed it. It showed all three of them in their Fourth of July tops and shorts and sporting their Santa hats. Mia was wearing her wig and smiling, and Sunny had caught Sophie mid-laugh.

"This is a treasure. I'll keep it on my bedside table," Mia said, and held out her arms for a hug.

She'd lost weight and there was hardly any of her to hug. Arianna bit back the tears.

By late afternoon Mia was fading. "I think I'll go up to bed," she said.

"I'll help you," said Arianna.

They left Sophie enthralled with the adventures of *Shaun the Sheep* and made their way upstairs, Mia holding her mother's arm.

While Mia used the bathroom and brushed her teeth, Arianna put the treasured picture on the nightstand.

What was this? She picked up the pink envelope sitting there. It had her name on it.

"What's this?" she asked as Mia came out of the bathroom.

"That's something for you to open later."

"Later? Later when?"

"You'll know," Mia said.

She didn't need to say anymore. Arianna dropped it like a burning coal.

Mia was at her side now, looking adorable in the Christmas jammies Arianna and Sophie had given her earlier in the month. But frail. So frail.

"Oh, Mom," Arianna said, tears filling her eyes.

"No crying. It's Christmas Day, and this day is a good day. We don't want to mar it with tears."

Arianna swallowed hard, trying to be brave.

"You go on down and enjoy the rest of your day with your daughter and the evening with your darling when he gets here." Mia put a hand to Arianna's cheek. "Thank you for a lovely day. I know you have many more ahead of you."

"She's right, you know," Alden said later when it was the two them alone on the couch, enjoying the glowing lights on the Christmas tree.

"I wish people didn't have to die," she said, wiping at a tear.

"I know," he said. "But you wouldn't want you mom to keep going, feeling more miserable all the time." He kissed the side of her head. "The Christmas story makes everyone's story better."

They'd had music streaming in the background. "O Holy Night" began to play. Like a message.

"Kiss me," she said, and he did, and there with his arms around her, she felt comforted.

The Weed had the kids for Christmas, but offered to give them up on New Year's Eve and Day because she had plans to go into Seattle and party.

"Super Mom until they get in the way of her fun," Sunny said in disgust.

"Hey, it works for me," Travis said. He studied her. "You okay with not going out?"

"I'm fine," she assured him. "Baby and I are perfectly happy to stay in. I can make that baked brie cheese in puff pastry I've been wanting to make."

"That'll be great for us. I'll pick up chips and pop and hot dogs for the kids."

"I'll teach them how to play Pig," she said.

"Dylan already knows how to be a pig," cracked Travis.

"The card game," she clarified.

"Oh, my gosh, that goofy thing your family plays? I had the world's sorest nose after that game."

"Yeah, but wasn't it worth it? You didn't end up being a pig."

He rolled his eyes.

"We can play Spoons, too," she said.

"No, I've seen how violent that game gets. I don't need you getting hurt. Pig will be fine."

"Okay. Pig and Wii bowling."

He chuckled. "You are such a party girl."

"What's life without a party?" she retorted.

Indeed, and the kids were perfectly happy to play games on New Year's Eve, and Travis and Sunny made it into a real party by letting them each invite a friend.

Food, laughter, happy kids. Oh, yes, happy New Year, Sunny thought as she cheered Bella on when it was her turn to try to bowl a strike.

Bella had knocked down eight pins when Sunny's phone rang. She saw the name on the screen and her heart felt like a bowling ball had crashed into it. Arianna and Alden had planned a quiet evening with Mia and Sophie and should have been happily watching TV or playing a game. There was no reason Arianna would be calling her, except...

She took the call. "What's happening?"

"It's Mom."

THE NEW YEAR

32

"She couldn't breathe," Arianna explained. "We're at the hospital and she's on oxygen."

"I'll be right there," Sunny said.

"No, don't come. There's nothing you can do. Just please let Molly and Ava know and...pray."

She wasn't sure what she wanted her friends to pray. The inevitable had come. Mia would soon be gone.

This couldn't be happening. Not her mother. Not yet.

She sat in a chair next to the bed, wishing Alden was with her, but thankful he was watching over Sophie, and doubly thankful that Sophie had already been in bed by the time they decided Mia was going to the hospital.

She heard footsteps and turned. Alden! "Where's Sophie?" she demanded sharply.

"I took her over to Ava's to spend the night. Molly and Reggie are there and they're all partying. She doesn't know your mom's here. I just told her going to Ava's was a New Year's surprise." He came and stood behind Arianna, put his hands on her shoulders. "I couldn't let you be here alone."

She nodded gratefully, returned her attention to the frail figure on the bed. She could almost feel her mother straining to be free, to move on. She was the only thing holding Mia there.

"Oh, Mom, how do I let go?" she whimpered, and Alden squeezed her shoulders. "You've always been there for me. I can't imagine this world without you in it." *I'm not letting go!*

But by morning she knew she had to.

It was a peaceful departure. The nurse on duty unplugged the life support system, and Arianna held her mother's hand. "Go find Daddy, and be happy," she said.

The monitor told her when her mother had left, and she threw herself over her body and wept, Alden holding on to her the whole time. New Year's Day. Her mother had left her to start the New Year alone.

But not alone. Alden was with her. She had her daughter, her friends.

And a big mother-sized hole in her heart.

It was a struggle over the next few days. The first challenge came the afternoon of New Year's Day, trying to help Sophie understand that now that Grammy was with the angels, she wouldn't be with them anymore.

"But I want her here," Sophie protested tearfully.

You and me both.

"We didn't finish my blanket."

"I know, and I'm sorry. I'll help you finish it." *After a few YouTube tutorials.* "Meanwhile, you can curl up in the blanket Grammy made you." Arianna wrapped the blanket around her daughter's shoulders. "Can you feel her?"

Sophie sniffed, nodded and smiled. "I can."

Thank God for a child's imagination.

Ava showed up with Paisley, bringing the distraction of a playmate, and helped Arianna make her to-do list. The business of death was a long and complicated one, that demanded forms be filled out and plans be made.

Mia would be buried next to her husband in the nearby cemetery. There would be a memorial service…later, when Arianna could deal with it.

During the week her friends circled around her, notifying Mia's small circle of friends, taking care of meals, helping her write Mia's obituary. Sunny set up a memorial page online and helped Arianna post pictures. Alden went with her to the funeral home to pick out a coffin, then, later, to the bank to get Mia's will out of her safety deposit box.

She'd left the house to Arianna and also made her the beneficiary of a small insurance policy. Thankfully, her mother had no debts to settle, but credit card companies had to be notified and utilities taken out of her name and changed over. Social Security had to be notified. The list of things seemed never-ending.

"This won't be finished in a week," Ava warned. "It takes an average of 570 hours to wrap things up."

Arianna stared at her, horrified.

"Possibly less in your mother's case. But there are tax forms to fill out and… Hey, it's okay. We'll get through this," she said as Arianna began to hyperventilate. "One step at a time."

Arianna took a deep breath. "One step at a time."

"And you've got Alden and all of us to help you."

Yes, she did, thank God. He and Buster moved from his house into hers, and he took some time off work to make sure he was never more than a wish away, holding her at night and letting her cry.

After posting a picture and announcement about Mia's passing, she let her website lay fallow, letting Sunny take care of responding to the condolences for her. There would be time to jump in and start the New Year later.

February brought a celebration of life, and friends and neighbors gathered in the large meeting room at the Marvin Williams Center, all wearing valentine colors of pink and red. Molly and

Sunny and Ava and the girls had made enough frosted heart-shaped cookies to serve a multitude. Alden's mom and sister had ordered appetizers from Safeway and provided sparkling cider and punch. Donations had been made in Mia's name to World Vision and the local Goodwill, but Alden and Reggie decided flowers were needed and made sure that several vases of red and white roses sat around the room.

That night, while Alden was at work, she stayed up late and watched *The Ghost and Mrs. Muir* in honor of her mother. Cried so hard she got a headache.

But later, in bed, in the arms of sleep, she dreamed her mother and father were standing by her bed, hand in hand.

"We're so happy now, darling," Mia said. "Please be happy for us."

"I will," Arianna promised.

That morning she woke up with a shaky sigh and an equally shaky smile, and went to her mother's bedroom. She hadn't been in it since she'd picked out the burial clothes for Mia and being there felt strange and wrong.

She forced herself to sit on the bed, looked at the framed picture of Mia, Sophie and herself, caught in a moment of bliss.

We're so happy now, darling.

She sobbed, picked up the pink envelope and opened it. She wiped away her tears, slipped out the pink stationery and read.

Dear darling daughter,
I'm sorry you had to see me grow weaker this past year, but I'm grateful I've been able to see you grow stronger.

Arianna let out a wail. She didn't feel strong, didn't even know how she was managing to keep going.

Sophie and Alden, that was how. Her daughter needed her. Her man loved her. To not keep going would be unfair to both of them.

She got her sobbing under control and returned to the letter.

I know you'll continue to get stronger. Remember, not all endings are happy, but some turn out to be beginnings, and they can lead somewhere good. Live each day as if it were your last, never let anyone steal your joy, thank God for your blessings and continue to celebrate Christmas all year long. Make this New Year a new beginning and be happy. I'll see you someday in Heaven.

Love, Mother

Mia read the letter again, let the tears flow, and then put the letter back in the envelope and dried her tears and blew her nose. She moved the picture from her mother's bedside table to hers and tucked the letter in the drawer. She knew she'd read it many more times throughout the year.

On Valentine's Day Sophie came home from school, full of news of how her day had gone at school. Arianna dutifully looked at every valentine she'd received, then the two of them crafted a valentine card for Alden.

Late that night she was waiting up for him with champagne on ice, Buster keeping her company on the couch.

Make this New Year a new beginning and be happy, her mother had said. She could do that. She would do that. She was smiling when he came in the door. It was something she hadn't done much of in a while, and it felt good. It made him smile, too, and if Mia happened to be taking a moment to watch from Heaven, Arianna was sure she was smiling as well.

The next morning, with Sophie off to school and Alden still sleeping, she made herself a latte, ordered a fancy planner online and then called Sunny. "So, what are we going to do for Christmas in March?"

33

That same month there was another celebration—a baby shower for Sunny and the little girl who was about to make her appearance. Molly's house was full to overflowing with couples crammed into the living room and overflowing into the kitchen, drinking beer and pop and eating the crab cakes and mini sausage rolls Molly and Ava had made. Molly's cat was hiding in her bedroom and even the aroma of crab couldn't lure him out.

Molly was putting a fresh batch of crab cakes on a platter when Sunny joined her in the kitchen. "This is the best party ever."

"That's quite the compliment, coming from the queen of parties," Molly said, handing her one. She studied Sunny's bulging belly. "Looks like the baby has dropped."

"Yep. I feel like I've a basketball in me and it's gonna fall out any minute. I can't find my feet." She held one out. "How does it look?"

"Very nice. That pedicure Travis got for you has turned your fat little foot into a work of art."

"Ha, ha," Sunny said, right before she shut her eyes and pressed her lips together and groaned.

"What?" Molly prompted.

"Just felt kind of yucky for a moment." She rubbed her belly.

Kind of yucky. That could mean anything. It seemed a little early for her to go into labor, but what did Molly know? Her labor adventures were lost in the mists of time.

Travis joined them in the kitchen. "Hey, when are we gonna open the loot?" He looked at Sunny, caught the expression on her face. "Babe, are you okay?"

"I..."

"Oh, no. You're going into labor." He checked the floor. "Has your water broke?"

"No, I'm fine," Sunny said, taking a breath and smiling. "It was nothing."

"You sure?" he asked.

She nodded. "I'm sure. Come on, let's open presents."

Back they went to the living room, to settle in together next to Reggie on Molly's couch.

Molly sidled up to Arianna. "I think Sunny just had a contraction. I don't think she's due for another couple of weeks, though."

"Could be Braxton Hicks," Arianna said, looking to where Sunny sat. "Or she could be going into labor early. With first babies, you never know."

Alden was shoveling the presents in front of them and Sunny was smiling at him.

And then she wasn't.

"Hmm," Arianna said.

"Babe?" Travis said in panic.

"I think I'm having contractions," Sunny said.

"Okay, let's time this," Alden said calmly.

Everyone sat in silence, staring either at Sunny or their cell phones and watches.

Six minutes went by. "Owwww," she said, her features scrunched up.

"Oh, my gosh, are you going to have it here?" Bella worried.

"We need to get her to the hospital," said Sunny's father.

"Let's see when the next contraction starts," Alden said, but he was drowned out by a panicked father and father-to-be.

Not to mention a mother-in-law, who was determined to take control of the situation. "Help her up!" Jeanette commanded.

Both Harry and Sunny's dad rushed to help. Her father caught his foot on a wrapped box and fell into the pile of presents. Harry tripped over him.

Travis turned into a soccer player, kicking gift bags out of the way. "Don't panic. We gotcha."

"Let's just give this a moment," Alden said, but Molly knew that wouldn't be happening.

"I can't have the baby here in the middle of the presents," Sunny protested.

"Gross," said Dylan, making a face.

Suny grabbed her belly. "Aaaah."

"Breathe, babe," Travis said, and demonstrated what they'd learned in their childbirth class. "Where are my car keys?"

"They're in your pocket," Sunny told him. "Will you get me out of here?"

"We're going. Right now," he said, and took her arm and escorted her through the crowd.

Ten minutes later a parade of cars was racing to the hospital.

An hour later the same cars were sedately making their way back to Molly's house. False alarm.

But two days later it was the real thing, and after ten hours of labor, Sunny and Travis welcomed baby Linette into the world.

"They named her after me," Jeanette told Molly as they stood in front of the nursery window.

Linette... Jeanette. Right. Molly nodded politely.

Of course, Linette was the most beautiful baby ever, and Bella was busy taking babysitting classes at the Y so she could be ready the second she was needed.

Come April, baby Linette had enough Easter dresses—gifts from family members as well as friends who all had been dubbed honorary aunties—to keep her fashionable the entire week before Easter Sunday. Santa Bunny made another appearance for the Christmas-in-Easter celebration, which delighted Paisley and Sophie. Sunny was delighted to see her stepdaughter actually posing for a picture this time around. Looking disgusted and embarrassed but at least she posed, and that was good enough for Sunny.

Arianna watched it all, smiled and wished her mother were present. "Resurrection," she repeated often to herself. New life. And once in a while she could almost hear her mother whispering, "I'll see you in Heaven."

Mother's Day was hard, but Arianna forced herself to concentrate on the fact that she had a wonderful future mother-in-law in her life. Alden's family pulled her into their circle, and on Mother's Day she and Sophie were at Red Robin with the rest of the crowd, whooping it up.

"How am I doing, Mom?" she whispered that night before going to sleep.

She got no answer. Mom was probably happily busy, enjoying good health in her new and better life.

Arianna didn't really need an answer, anyway. She knew she was doing pretty darn good. She still had her teary times, and knew she would for a long while to come, but she also had happy memories to comfort her, and plenty to keep her busy as her online business continued to grow.

There was no Christmas-in-June party because it was time for the next big event—Molly and Reggie's wedding. He walked slower than he once had, but he was more than able to walk down the aisle with his bride after they said, "I do."

The guests were made up of Molly's family and all her friends, but Reggie did have one person present—the cousin he hadn't seen in years.

"We need to stay in touch," Lionel told him. "We're all we got."

"We got a lot more than just us now," Reggie told him as he

stood with his good arm around Molly, Paisley hanging on to his other arm.

It was going to be a family-style honeymoon, with everyone off to Reggie's place in Mexico to enjoy the beaches and maybe even some fishing.

"I'm so happy," Molly told Arianna. "It's true what they say. Love does make the world go 'round."

Molly made sure that Arianna caught the bouquet. "Set the date already," she said, and hugged her before they left.

Yes, set the date. Arianna had sorted through the last of the details of death. Alden was getting ready to sell his house...to his sister. Perfect. What were they waiting for?

That night she dreamed she and Alden got married. It was snowing and she wore a red velvet gown with a fur-trimmed hood and they left the church in a sleigh. And her mother was there, along with her father, waving them off.

"A Christmas wedding," she said to Alden when he finally woke up and came downstairs for coffee.

"Yeah?"

She nodded. "I saw Mom last night." He looked at her in concern and she held up a hand. "It's all good."

CHRISTMASTIME AGAIN

Come the first Saturday in December there was a wedding in the charming Bavarian village of Leavenworth.

"Look, Mom," Arianna said as all her bridesmaids gathered around her. She held up her hands with perfectly manicured nails that hadn't been bitten in three months, and the women applauded.

"Your mom would be so proud," Molly said and hugged her.

Ten minutes later Molly walked her down the aisle at the Mountain Springs Lodge, and Sunny and Ava, Bella and Alden's sister were her bridesmaids, with Rae serving as matron of honor. Sophie and Paisley took their job as flowers girls seriously and were meticulous in scattering white and red silk rose petals before the bride. Alden's brother was his best man, and Travis and two of Alden's buddies from work and one of his basketball pals all acted as groomsmen. His friends had already been invited to some of the monthly Christmas parties and were becoming an integral part of a growing circle of celebrants.

Even though the newlyweds would be staying at the lodge, a

sleigh was waiting to tour them around town before the party started, making Arianna's dream come true. Paisley and Sophie were disappointed that they hadn't been invited to go along on the ride, but Ava promised them one the following day. She would be keeping Sophie while the newlyweds enjoyed a week in Hawaii.

Later, as everyone danced and partied, the four girlfriends posed for a photo op.

"We love you, and we're so happy for you," Molly said as she hugged Arianna.

"Yes, we are," agreed Sunny. "Just remember one thing."

"What's that?" Arianna asked.

"As soon as you get back from your honeymoon, it's time to start planning what we're going to do for Christmas in January. Got to keep sharing the Christmas spirit," she added with a wink.

Yes, they did.

And yes, they would.

★ ★ ★ ★ ★

RECIPES
FROM *THE TWELVE MONTHS OF CHRISTMAS*

GREEN JELL-O SALAD

Ingredients:

16 oz (1 tub) cottage cheese
8 oz (1 can) crushed pineapple, drained
3 oz (1 package) lime Jell-O
12 oz (1 tub) whipped topping (e.g., Cool Whip)

Directions:

In a large bowl, combine cottage cheese and pineapple. Sprinkle lime Jell-O over it and mix, then fold in whipped topping.

Note: If you prefer not to use Cool Whip, you can substitute lightly sweetened, stiffly whipped cream (3 cups' worth)

DIRT CAKE

Ingredients:

2 packages (28 oz) Double Stuf OREO, crushed into crumbs
¼ cup butter, softened and room temperature
8 oz cream cheese (1 package), softened and room temperature
1 cup powdered sugar
3 ½ cups milk (whole or 2%)
2 (3.4 oz) packages instant vanilla pudding
12 oz (1 tub) frozen whipped topping, thawed
1 new 8-inch plastic flower pot or bucket (or, if you prefer, a 9x13 pan)
Gummy worms and small plastic flowers for decoration

Directions:

Cream together butter, cream cheese and powdered sugar, and set aside. In a separate bowl, mix together the milk and pudding, then set in the fridge to set up for about two hours. After it's set, fold in cream cheese mixture and whipped topping, until well-combined. Line the bottom of your pot with foil and then layer with 1 ½ inches of cookie crumbs. Place pudding mixture over that and then continue to layer, topping it off with the last of the cookie crumbs. Refrigerate for 2 ½ hours or overnight. Decorate before serving.

PUMPKIN COOKIES

Ingredients:

¾ cup butter, softened
1 cup light brown sugar, packed
2 eggs
2 cups flour
½ cup canned pumpkin puree
½ tsp baking powder
½ tsp baking soda
½ tsp salt
½ tsp cinnamon
½ tsp nutmeg
¼ tsp ginger
¼ tsp cloves
1 tsp vanilla
½ cup golden raisins
½ cup white chocolate chips

Directions:

Cream together the butter, sugar and eggs. Press out the water from pumpkin puree with a paper towel, then add to creamed mixture. Mix together the dry ingredients and stir in. Fold in white chocolate chips and raisins. Roll dough into 1-inch balls, then roll in more sugar and place on lightly greased baking sheets. If dough is sticky (if you didn't drain the pumpkin enough, it might be), then refrigerate for a few minutes to make it easier to work with. Bake 12–14 minutes at 350 F.

ACKNOWLEDGMENTS

I am so grateful to the many people who helped me write this book. First of all, a big thank you to my friend, retired nurse, Roger Spiese, who took a painful journey down memory lane, reliving his wife's brave battle with cancer and allowing me to chronicle it in this story. This book is dedicated to her.

Thank you, also, to my wonderful street team member Shari Drehs Bartholomew, charge nurse extraordinaire, who gave me a glimpse into the world of nursing. I could not do what you nurses do! I'm also grateful for the continuing input from my fabulous agent, Paige Wheeler, and brilliant editor, April Osborn, for helping me bring this story to life. And thank you to everyone at MIRA for turning this story into a book. I love the cover!